VICTORIAN ROGUES COMPILATION

VANESSA BROOKS

Published by Blushing Books
An Imprint of
ABCD Graphics and Design, Inc.
A Virginia Corporation
977 Seminole Trail #233
Charlottesville, VA 22901

Vanessa Brooks
Victorian Rogues Compilation

EBook ISBN: 978-1-61258-942-8
Print ISBN: 978-1-64563-151-4

v1

Cover Art by ABCD Graphics & Design

ELSPETH

VICTORIAN ROGUES, BOOK ONE

Published by Blushing Books®,
a subsidiary of
ABCD Graphics and Design
977 Seminole Trail #233
Charlottesville, VA 22901
The trademark Blushing Books®
is registered in the US Patent and Trademark Office.

Vanessa Brooks
Elspeth

EBook ISBN: 978-1-61258-370-9
Cover Art by ABCD Graphics & Design

CHAPTER 1

She stood on the second-class deck of the steamer ship leaning upon a side rail as she waved her white lace handkerchief to her husband Henry. He lifted his hat to her, gave a mocking bow, inclined his head, spun on his heel and stalked away without giving her or the ship, a backward glance. Elspeth watched until she lost sight of him amongst the press of people milling about the dockside. Her face had healed quickly after that terrible night. Thankfully, her cheekbone remained intact. Henry had been conciliatory on their final night together. He had begged to be allowed into her bed one last time, explaining that he wished to try and get her with child, giving her something positive to take home to England, a gift to his parents.

Since he'd been sober and had asked so politely, she'd reluctantly acquiesced. He tried at first to arouse her but eventually seemed to realise that her cringing form would never trust him again, and he'd taken her perfunctorily.

They'd barely spoken above the necessary that morning, and now he was gone. She knew it was probable that she would never see her husband again. A dart of intense hurt and loneliness lanced her. It hadn't taken Elspeth long to realize that Henry never really wanted a wife. He'd taken her virginity without a moment's pause as to her naivety about the act, much less considering her comfort or desire. Once he was bored with her… he'd found others to warm his bed. A niggling doubt that she was somehow at fault for their failed marriage continued to plague her. If only she had been more worldly. She closed her eyes, struggling against her painful memories. Squaring her shoulders and straightening her back, she took a restorative breath, stepped bravely away from the ship's side, her place immediately filled by another waving passenger as she pushed through the crowds of spectators to make her way inside second class.

Her cabin was small but adequate, having everything she required, including a porthole window. She shared a water closet down the corridor with four other cabins. Her fare had cost Henry a substantial thirty-five pounds for a single second-class passage. Elspeth noticed her small trunk had been brought up by a steward and sat at the foot of her bed. She set about unpacking. Emptying everything she owned, she tidied away her clothing into the single wardrobe and chest of drawers, which doubled as her bedside cupboard. Once the task was completed, Elspeth acknowledged her rumbling tummy and headed out to find somewhere she could get a restorative cup of tea and perhaps something to eat.

Henry had explained the voyage to England would be easier now that the Suez Canal had opened up the previous year. The White Star RMS *Oceanic* would be able to cut their voyage by weeks now that the need to travel so far out of the way had been eradicated. Elspeth was excited about travelling through Egypt. She hoped that she would be able to spot a pyramid or two. She was managing to keep her painful memories at bay by dealing with practical concerns. She was leaving the land of her birth where her parents were buried, possibly forever. Everything she knew about living thus far had been gleaned here on the sub-continent. India was her home. She was leaving Bombay probably forever since she'd no plans to return. The act of saying farewell to this continent was profoundly wretched for her, and she knew that she needed to keep focused upon the here and now if she were to remain stalwart.

As she made her way along the outside deck, she passed a metal staircase leading directly to first class. Elspeth glanced right and left but there was no member of the crew about, the linked chain that held the sign, "private," hung upside down, leaving the ascending stairs invitingly open. She looked about her, and since she saw nobody in the vicinity, hurried up the steps. Most passengers were either on the shore side of the ship waving goodbye to family and friends, or in their cabin waiting to set sail. The crew were busily engaged, preparing the ship for cast-off.

Curious, but meaning no harm, Elspeth wandered the first class deck, peering in through open doors, admiring the salubrious surroundings given to the more affluent passengers. She came to a large salon with double doors opening outward onto the deck. Peeking inside, she looked about the sumptuously appointed room, which was set out with circular tables surrounded by comfortable looking tub chairs. The nearest table was set for tea, fully laid out with a silver tiered tea canopy and laid upon each tier were sandwiches and cakes of all varieties. On the highest section sat three small crystal dishes, each filled with exotic fruit salad and topped with whipped cream.

Elspeth edged forward, hungrily tempted by the delicious looking food. A man's voice startled her. "Good afternoon," he called. She turned and fled but forgot that the ship's doorway had a raised doorframe. She tripped and sprawled headlong to the floor. Her bag contents flew everywhere; she hurriedly crawled after them, chasing her personal belongings.

"I'm so sorry; I had no intention of startling you. Here, let me help you up. Steward! Steward, some help over here, if you please?" Strong arms lifted her, setting her back onto her feet. A steward arrived; he ran hither and thither collecting the spilled detritus from her bag. Elspeth apologised and protested it was her own fault as she frantically collected up the final items from the deck before thanking the steward profusely for his help.

She walked over to her rescuer and thanked him shyly. He was a youngish man, perhaps in his early thirties. Warm brown eyes regarded her kindly from below a curling mop of light brown hair that had a tendency to flop forward over onto his forehead. His friendly face was singularly attractive, although his even features were at first glance nothing special. He looked… nice.

"Sit, join me, how'd you like your tea?" he asked jovially.

"Um, I really shouldn't be here. I'm trespassing from second class," Elspeth confessed quietly.

He regarded her with amusement. "Naughty girl, who is your travelling companion, your husband?" His gaze fell to her ring hand; he noted her gold wedding band.

She shook her head blushing. "No, I travel alone. My husband is a captain in the Queen's Lancashire Regiment. I am travelling back to England to live with his parents."

"You are travelling alone, without even a maid for company?" he queried with a frown.

"Yes," she replied. He so obviously disapproved. She tried to appear nonchalant. What else could she do? Elspeth lowered her eyes as she felt her cheeks heat crimson with embarrassment.

"Hm, well I think it might be prudent that you and I join forces as I too am travelling alone. Professor Adam Beresford, at your service, Mrs.?"

She lifted her head and gaped at him, he had more than surprised her by his kind offer. Giving herself a mental shake, she stretched out her hand.

"Wooten, Elspeth Wooten," she said as he took her hand. His grip was firm. He grinned affably at her.

"Right, well now that we are properly introduced, please take a seat. Do you take both milk and sugar in your tea?" She nodded and sat, unable to repress the smile that tugged at her lips. His eager warmth was reassuring, his nature seemed boyish; he was so friendly and amenable. He handed her a china cup and saucer then passed her the sandwich plate. She selected the nearest sandwich, which turned out to be filled with cucumber. She nibbled delicately at the crust free bread and studied him. Meanwhile, the young professor gulped down at least two cheese sandwiches. He happily expounded upon his work for the London Antiquities Museum, enthusiastically describing some of the artefacts that he'd found on his recent travels.

"I have to say that I am surprised at your husband allowing his beautiful wife to travel so far away and all alone. If you were mine, I'd not let you out of my sight! I am excessively possessive about my treasures."

Elspeth had no idea how to respond to his double entendre, so she remained silent. It seemed to dawn upon the professor that he had completely monopolised the entire conversation. He glanced at the sandwich platter and saw too that it was empty. "I say, Mrs. Wooten, please forgive me. I appear to have devoured all the sandwiches! Here, have some cake instead." He thrust the cake plate under her nose and she chose a small chocolate éclair.

"Your turn. I fear that I have bored you enough with my obsessions. Tell me where are you heading once we arrive in England? I think you mentioned having a home in Lancashire?" He leaned forward in his chair, showing genuine interest. Elspeth set down her plate.

"In actual fact, I am not returning home. My home is, was, India, I was born there. My in-laws live in Lancashire; my husband wishes me to live with his parents from now onward. I shall possibly never return to India again." Her green eyes sheened over with unexpected tears, and she fell silent, unable to continue as a wave of homesickness swept over her, leaving her feeling shaken and extremely emotional. A white handkerchief appeared in her line of vision, and a large hand squeezed her shoulder.

"I did not mean to upset you, Mrs. Wooten. Come, chin up, deep breaths in and out, that's the way of it, good girl!" She did as he suggested, breathing deeply.

"Your husband's a damn fool. If you were mine, I'd not let you out of my sight for a single moment!" Elspeth gave him a watery smile.

"Yes, so you said earlier on."

He grinned. "I did, didn't I? And I am sure I shall say it again."

She giggled.

"Now that's better. You should laugh like that more often. You have a beautiful smile and a very fetching laugh."

"Thank you, as do you, kind sir," she teased gently back, and he winked.

"Is your cabin adequate; is there anything I can get for you or do for you?" he asked her seriously.

Elspeth shook her head. "You have already done so much, thank you, Professor."

"Please, do call me Adam when we are in private conversation." He glanced about him, noticing the stewards clearing away the tea accoutrements. "I think tea time is finished, but I beg that you will join me for tea again tomorrow. Same time, same place, so that I may bore you again with my interest in ancient civilisations." He stood up and held out his palm in order to help her rise. Once she was standing, he held onto her hand longer than necessary, gazing into her eyes. "Your eyes are uncannily like the *Netra-Baagh,*" he muttered to himself.

"What is the Tiger's Eye?" she asked. He was startled.

"You speak Hindi… Obviously. I will show you one day, perhaps. Join me for tea tomorrow, and I shall tell you the tale of the *Netra-Baagh, Shiromani,* in its entirety. Come, I shall walk you back down to your deck and see you into your cabin." Despite her protests, he insisted. They chatted easily together as they sauntered down to second class, where he turned away and left her outside her door, with a touch to the brim of his hat.

Those early days at sea passed pleasantly for Elspeth. Every day she waited in her cabin, and at precisely three o'clock, the steward would knock at her door to collect her and escort her up the forbidden stairs into the first class salon. There a sumptuous tea awaited her, along with the charming professor. Adam regaled her with tales of his wild, exciting adventures, most of which she was certain were wholly embellished for her entertainment. Adam insisted every word was true, but Elspeth took everything he told her with a pinch of salt.

With charming self-deprecation, Adam Beresford told her the tale of the *Netra-Baagh,* the Tiger's Eye, *Shiromani,* "the elevated jewel." A glittering emerald that he claimed was handed to him by the maharaja himself, a gift for saving the life of his precious son, who, he told her, was drowning in the lake that surrounded the palace where he lived. The children that the prince was playing with had underestimated the depths of the crystal clear waters of the massive lake and the danger that depth represented to the small prince. After diving in one day, the child had struggled to stay afloat. Although the bottom of the lake looked close, it was deceptively deep. The prince was out of his depth. Adam, who had been walking nearby admiring the amazing structure of the sumptuous palace, responded immediately to the youngster's cries for help. Quickly stripping his outer clothing, he dived into the waters of the Man Sagae Lake, having no idea that the boy he was rescuing was, in fact, the prince. The following day, servants from the beautiful Jal Mahal Palace sought him out at his lodgings. They invited him to return with them to visit their illustrious master; their polite request was obviously more of a summons. Adam allowed them to escort him to an audience with one of the most powerful maharajas in India. He was also one of the richest. In gratitude for his son's life, Maharaja Sawi Singh II, presented Adam with a gift, a fabulous jewel, the *Shiromani,* the elevated jewel, the *Baagh-Netra*—Tiger's Eye. The egg-sized emerald was cut and polished so that it captured the light, turning it into a flashing iridescent green, just like the glinting eye of a tiger glimpsed within the depths of a dark jungle.

It was said to bring great fortune and good luck to its owner but only so long as the stone was given as a gift for valour. If it were sold or stolen, then the opposite effect would take place, and the jewel would become a curse, heaping disaster upon the new owner.

"Perhaps one day I shall show it to you," he said, finishing his tale. Picking up his teacup, he drained the dregs.

"Do you have many weird or wonderful artefacts to take back to London from your present trip?" Elspeth asked, intrigued.

"I suppose you might think so. I have an embalmed mummy, still packed into its sarcophagus," he sounded smug.

"A mummy?" she queried, never having heard the expression before.

"Yes, a body nearly a thousand years old. One that has had all the soft innards removed to be stored in jars in preparation for the pharaoh to use once he has arrived in the spirit world and can rebuild his body."

"But how did they remove the organs without destroying the body?"

Adam gave her an assessing look. "That is very gruesome information. Are you quite sure you wish me to impart the gory details?" Elspeth nodded enthusiastically.

"Well, at first they used hollow reeds as tubes to suck out the brain through the nose cavity but later on…" He halted as Elspeth clapped her hands over her mouth, her eyes wide with horror.

"They did not!" she exclaimed in horror. He nodded solemnly, his brown eyes twinkling.

"That is utterly disgusting!" she spluttered.

"Isn't it just? I did warn you," he chuckled delightedly.

"Please, no more organ removals, I beg of you!" She wagged her finger at him, and he laughed again. "What of their customs and beliefs?" She was genuinely interested.

"The Egyptians believed the pharaoh would need sustenance on his journey and supplied him with jars of grains, fruits, dried fish and meat, in fact, all manner of foods to sustain him on his celestial way. His favourite pet would be slaughtered or entombed along with him. Often, servants and even his wife or concubines were entombed. They were there to attend to his needs when he reached the other world." Adam caught sight of Elspeth's face as she sucked in a breath with shock.

"That is despicable! What of those poor people's right to life?" She had no idea how adorable she looked in her righteousness.

"That was their ideology. I find historical cultures and customs utterly fascinating; however, they are not always palatable. I want to share the many customs and historical practices I have learned with as many people as possible. We are so inclined in England to think that our way is the only way. Many people close their minds against different principles and to other cultures. I want to open people's minds and show them the fascinating wonders of the ancient world!" Elspeth listened and found his enthusiasm endearing.

"Just don't tell them about the brain and organ removal, etcetera!" She chortled.

Adam watched her as she chuckled with merriment and it occurred to him that he might be falling in love. It had never been a state he had given much thought to before, and he certainly never supposed such a thing would catch him quite so unawares. Yet all at once, without a shadow of a doubt, he knew that he could love this beautiful woman. His heart twisted painfully with the realisation that she was already married to another man.

CHAPTER 2

It was after they'd finished tea a few days later, that Adam raised the subject of her joining him for dinner in the first class dining room. "I should very much like you to join me for an evening meal on Saturday night. Selfishly, I want to show you off to the other passengers as I twirl you around on the dance floor afterward."

Elspeth set her cup down on her saucer with a clatter. "I am sure that would be a bad idea," she told him, looking anxious.

He winked audaciously at her over the rim of his teacup. "What? Nervous that we might set all the old tabbies a-twittering?"

"No, but *you* jolly well ought to be, after all, you are a respected professor, a gentleman of learning. What of your reputation?" she chided.

"Me?" He chuckled. "I have found that being a little eccentric only adds to my appeal as a professor."

She sighed; he always had the smart answer. "Well the subject is moot, for I have no evening wear for such a formal occasion."

He leaned toward her and tapped the end of her nose. "Have no fear, my dear, for I have found you the perfect dress. I even have the shoes to match." Again he winked, insufferably pleased with himself.

"How?" she asked.

He gave the most self-satisfied grin. "There is a shop for ladies to purchase froufrous and such, here on the first class deck. I spotted a few unique readymade gowns for sale as I walked past the window. I observed one *particular* dress hung upon a mannequin. It was made for you, Elspeth. The chartreuse green of the material will enhance your eyes and look gorgeous against that titian hair of yours. I had a powerful yen to see you wear the gown, and so I bought it for you. So there will be no excuses, Cinderella. You shall go to the ball, and I shall masquerade as your prince charming!"

Elspeth couldn't help but laugh, so it was agreed that she would dine with him on the following Saturday, which was only two days hence.

The dress Adam bought for her was the most beautiful gown that Elspeth had ever owned. Swathes of green silk draped from her shoulders, twisting then parting to cup her breasts before knotting and rouching, wrapping her figure. The effect was to hug her curves, thus making her appear more womanly than she had ever seen herself. Silk flowers in muted shades of pink and lavender, trailed over one shoulder and followed the curving line of the material that slanted across her waist and hip to form a pretty bustle behind her. The back of the dress then fell from the bustle in a waterfall of filmy material to the floor. Her shoes matched the pale green of the dress perfectly, and when she slipped the dainty things upon her feet and turned to gaze at herself in the mirror, Elspeth was delighted with her reflection. Never before had she witnessed herself looking so fine. She marvelled at Adam's perception, her dress was perfectly sized. She was unaware that he had asked a cabin steward to check her clothing and shoe sizes before his purchase.

When the waiter ushered her to their table at seven o'clock, Adam was already seated, awaiting her. He stood immediately to greet her, waving the waiter away as he bent to kiss her cheek. He then pulled out her chair, seating her himself.

"You look stunning, so beautiful. I am the luckiest fellow aboard." They chatted easily together as dish after delicious dish was set before them and then, as coffee was served, the band arrived. As they played, a few sedate couples took to the floor. Adam and Elspeth sipped their coffee and watched the couples dance. Then the unmistakeable melody of a waltz brought Adam to his feet. He bowed to Elspeth and held out his palm, entreating her to dance with him. Smiling, she placed her fingers in his, and he led them both onto the floor. They were joined by a number of younger couples who also enjoyed this romantic of all dances.

Elspeth found herself held firmly against Adam's chest as he guided her confidently about the dance floor. She realised as she was twirled, dipped and spun that she was falling for this intelligent, charismatic man. She decided that she needed to be more circumspect. She knew that she should keep her feelings hidden and protect herself from further heartbreak. She was, after all, a married woman and look how well that had turned out.

As soon as the waltz finished, she made her excuses, needing to escape. She turned to a passing steward, requesting that he guide her back down to second class. Adam noted her sudden change of attitude with misgiving. Oh, he understood her mood swing completely, but he had no intention of hurting her or leaving her open to other people's ridicule. His feelings for this lady were strong and protective. He had never felt such fervour for a woman before, and he wanted to see how she continued to affect him. If she was the woman for him, then he would move heaven and high water to make her his. He was a determined man, an academic man to be sure, but a man who made things happen. He had fought his own way through life, and he usually achieved any goals he set himself. He watched as she turned to look back at him. Her eyes met his, and he hoped that she could read correctly the promise that his gaze held.

THEY WERE TRAVERSING the brand new Suez Canal, only opened the previous year. Instead of taking tea immediately, Adam and Elspeth were pressed up against the ship's rail, watching with fascination as they entered this innovative waterway. It was narrower than they expected and due to the flat terrain, they could see for miles in either direction.

Elspeth pointed to a group of men who rode hell for leather along the shore pointing at the ship, shouting at them in another tongue. They were seated upon an ungainly creature's back. They appeared as interested in the ship as they in them. "Bedouin Arabs are a proud people and mighty fierce. Wonderful horsemen but more usually found upon the backs of camels when in this region of Egypt."

"So those strange creatures that they sit astride are camels?" she asked, intrigued, shading her eyes and squinting to see better into the glaring sun.

"Yes, they can survive desert conditions much better than horses. See those humps on their backs?" He pointed. "They are designed to store fluid and nutriments for long periods of travelling through dry, arid conditions."

Elspeth spun about to face him, her face aglow with excitement. "The ship makes a brief stop in Egypt does it not? I can leave the ship when we reach there and explore. Oh, but I have always wanted to see the pyramids, why on earth didn't I think of this before?" she exclaimed excitedly.

Adam glowered down at her. "Absolutely not, I forbid it! Arab men do not respect women. No, it will not do. You would most likely vanish, never to be seen again!"

She scoffed at his fears. "Stuff and nonsense, I shall speak to the purser about it."

His hand caught her elbow and gave her a shake. "Do that, young lady, and I shall be obliged to take you across my knee and spank you soundly. I shall be forced to lock you safe inside my cabin until we reach English shores!" He was incensed with her, but then he saw her blanch, watching as her hand flew to her pale face and unconsciously rubbed her cheekbone. Adam realised something was seriously amiss.

"Mrs. Wooten… Elspeth, whatever's the matter?" he asked, quietly urgent. She shook her head, her hand dropped like a stone to her side. Adam realised something was definitely wrong. A dark thought dawned on him.

"Did your husband hit you?" he asked bluntly. When she failed to reply but simply stared at her feet, he persisted. "Henry Wooten hit you, am I correct, Elspeth?" She nodded, letting out a long drawn breath, her hand drifted up to her fully healed cheek.

~

HER MIND RETURNED to that fateful day. The day her father had died, the pivotal moment her circumstances changed forever… The heat of the sun beating down upon them reminded her of the day her father died. It had been similarly hot as she stared at the corpse, her own flesh and blood, her father, Albert Merryweather. Surely she should weep, feel his loss? Yet she felt… nothing. The ululating wails of the house servants, the polite condolences made by the orderlies who had collected his body, none of it meant a thing to her, she was completely numb. Elspeth lowered her gaze from the cobalt sky. Shading her eyes, she squinted through the glare of the Indian mid-day sun. Her attention centered upon a rising cloud of dust; a figure emerged from the midst of the sandy haze. It was him. She knew his stature when astride a horse; hadn't she watched him play polo often enough? She knew the captain would come as soon as he'd heard that her father had died of a sudden heart attack, but word had spread quicker than she'd anticipated. She turned and fled inside the bungalow. She wasn't ready, not yet. She'd refuse to see him. Their major-domo, Ashok, would turn him away, explaining that she was overwrought and not at home to visitors.

In her room, ear pressed to the thin panelled door, she heard the deep timbre of his voice rise above the constant drone of insects and the soft whoosh of the ceiling fan, kept constantly turning by the punkawallah seated outside on the veranda constantly working the pulleys to agitate the house fans.

Henry Wooten was demanding that tiffin be served. Agitated, her hand flew to her throat; he would not leave then. A sudden knock at her door, followed by his gruff voice startled her.

"You cannot hide from me, Elspeth. Come out!" She leapt back from the door in shock as the handle turned and it swung open. She gasped, "You cannot enter my bedroom, leave now, go!" But he stayed, his gaze held her pinned like a specimen butterfly.

He stretched out his arm, palm up. "Come, take tea with me. We must talk."

Her ayah, Abha, bustled in and shooed him out of the doorway, yapping in Hindi too fast for Elspeth to follow. She urged them both out from the room and into the living area of the house. She gave small pats to Elspeth's person, urging her onward toward the settee where Elspeth reluctantly sat down opposite the captain and allowed Abha to serve them tea.

He watched her as keenly as she watched him, however, she was subtle in her scrutiny, giving him fleeting glances over the rim of her teacup; he stared openly at her. After only a few moments, he placed his cup down with decisive firmness and began to talk. It took her a moment to understand his words. He was offering her marriage, her only alternative other than returning to England, a homeland she'd never visited.

Born in India to low ranking civil servants, she knew no other world than this. She wanted to remain here on the sub-continent where she felt at home. Born of non-military personnel, but not the child of high-ranking civil servants, Elspeth's life was lonely. She was caught sandwiched between the rigid class systems of the British Raj.

Her mother, like so many, had succumbed to the cholera outbreak five years previous. Her death had left Albert and Elspeth leading an awkward and lonely life, sequestered in their small bungalow together. Death was a daily occurrence in India, but instead of cheapening life, the daily reminder of the struggle to survive, for both humans and animals, only strengthened Elspeth's regard for the individuality of every one of God's creatures.

Elspeth longed for family, for friendship. Perhaps if she married this captain from the Queen's Lancashire Regiment she might finally achieve both?

"Yes," she answered quickly, afeared that should she hesitate, he might withdraw his offer.

His face stilled, his almost navy eyes narrowed, holding her green-hazel gaze. "You accept?" He sounded surprised.

"I do," she whispered. Then stiffening her spine, she raised her head and met his gaze squarely. Clearing her throat, she replied firmly, "Yes, I do."

"Why? Oh never mind. Well, I am glad that you are being… sensible." He stood up and she rose too.

"I will arrange everything. I am sorry for your loss." He stepped around the bamboo occasional table scattered with their tea paraphernalia, moving to stand before her. He bent and pressed his mouth firmly to hers. She froze as the tip of his tongue slipped between the seam of her lips, sweeping the length of her softly parted mouth before abruptly withdrawing. Inclining his head to her, he spun away, calling loudly to Ashok for his hat and riding crop as he strode from the room without once looking back.

Elspeth sat with a sudden thump onto the bamboo settee. She trembled as she stared vacantly into space and recalled the first time she had become aware of the handsome Captain. It was while she'd waited outside the civil administrative offices for her father to finish work for the day. Seated upon the warm dusty floor of the open veranda near the ever present punkawallah, she'd failed to notice the cobra slithering towards her over the sun heated wood. A warning shout, a pistol shot and strong arms, which swept her safely out of harm's way—her first introduction to Captain Henry Wooten.

It had been love at first sight, compounded by a hard smack to her buttocks and a growled warning about keeping a vigilant eye out for predators. To him it was an incident soon forgot, but from that day forward, Elspeth deliberately placed herself in his line of sight, and to her delight, he had recently begun to acknowledge her. At first he simply nodded, moved on and ignored her, but as she blossomed into a shy, titian beauty, the captain would stop and bow, occasionally even taking her small hand into his and kissing her palm. His dark blue gaze as mesmerizing as any snake's could be.

To Elspeth he appeared a knight in shining armour, the man who'd rescued her from a serpent. He had literally saved her life. By gazing deeply into her eyes as he reprimanded her with his husky voice, he'd compounded her view of him as her hero. To her young romantic eyes, he was perfection personified.

The bungalow she lived in was the property of the British Raj. They owned the bamboo campaign furniture and the beds. Their servants were paid for by government coin, and so her father's death left her penniless, a woman living alone on the sub-continent without male protection. Not a good position to be in, especially within this poverty stricken, socially rigid territory of the British Empire. Elspeth knew that she was utterly dependent upon the charity of a philandering rake, Captain Henry Wooten. As she watched him over the intervening years, she'd become only too aware of his immoral proclivities. However, nothing she'd heard about him changed her devotion to her devilishly handsome saviour.

Captain Wooten was known to the English community as a man without morals. A gentleman he was not. It was even rumoured that he kept a concubine in his quarters. Elspeth was certain the rumour was true and no well-connected mater would allow her precious girls anywhere near the man. Elspeth knew that she would become a pariah of Anglo-Indian society once it became common knowledge that she was affianced to the rogue. However, army society was a completely different story; she could perhaps make friends with other officer's wives. There was a social way of life inside the military, which was wholly separate to the civil society of Bombay.

As Elspeth watched Henry from afar, placing herself into his path whenever she could, her father was blinded to everything other than work and ambition. He failed to notice his young daughter's growing infatuation with an unsuitable man. The young and impressionable girl put Wooten upon a pedestal, one that even the captain himself, conceited fellow he was, would have conceded was too high an accolade for one such as he.

Elspeth was fully aware that she'd chosen to marry the *"Saphed Daanav"*—"white devil"—labelled as such by his Hindu house servants. Wooten proudly proclaimed their name for him, wearing it among his men as some sort of badge of honour. Notwithstanding, she had made her decision, chosen her destiny, making a choice of her own free will... *but oh, sweet Lord, whatever had she done?*

ARMY LIFE SUITED WOOTEN. He was the only son of a second son, one Sir James Wooten, landed gentry seated in county of Lancashire, England. Henry's cousin Edward had inherited the title "Lord Wooten," on the death of his father, Lord George Wooten, James's elder brother.

When Henry turned twenty-one, his father gave him three choices. One, marry well and wait for his parents' demise to inherit the small manor house, his childhood home. Two, take orders and go into the Church, or three, join the army with a commission bought for him by his parents. Henry chose the third alternative. Having a hankering for adventure, it seemed to him to be far and away the best solution.

He found himself living on a continent, the kind of place he'd always dreamed of. During the day, he followed army strictures to the letter and played the part of an officer and gentleman in the officer's mess. At night, the wilder, darker side of the sub-continent seduced him. Henry quickly became a devotee of the intoxicatingly exotic.

Nowadays he needed more and more of the unusual to slake this thirst for potent diverse sexual conquest. An initiation by a friend, another captain, a man who preferred handsome young men to women, introduced Wooten to sleek, dark-eyed youths. They willingly joined him in his bed at night, their hard cocks clasped in his pumping fist and his tackle buried deep inside their tight young arses. This nonconformist sexuality excited him for a brief spell, but it soon began to pall. As a red blooded, heterosexual male surrounded by sloe-eyed, eastern beauties; Asian women so submissive that he could take one any which way he desired, young men soon lost their novel appeal.

His constant need for diversion meant that, after a while, two or three women in his bed no longer excited him. He cast his jaded eye about for other diversions and found his eye constantly drawn to the feminine curves of Elspeth Merryweather.

Surreptitiously, he watched her blossom. Her purity and innocence fired his imagination, titillating and taunting him. He felt compelled to breach her maidenhead. He wanted to be the man whose cock inspired the look of awed surprise a virginal woman gave to a man the first time she witnessed his erection. He longed to hear her moans as he licked her virginal cunny or forced her to suck his cock. The list of sexual "firsts" was endless. He dreamed of making Elspeth Merryweather carnally aware.

If he bored of her, he would fill her with his seed and pack her off to England to bear him a son. There they could live in his parents' house in Lancashire, leaving him free to continue whatever new debauchery he could conjure, undisturbed by a whining, clingy wife.

THEIR WEDDING WAS a small civil ceremony. Neither bride nor groom had any family to attend; Wooten's regimental adjutant and his wife agreed to act as witnesses for the couple.

Elspeth's meagre belongings were moved into their new married officer quarters which comprised a small bungalow, set amongst similar properties, situated inside the British Army barracks on the outskirts of Bombay. The bungalows were far enough apart to ensure a semblance of privacy but close enough for social contact. They were allocated a cook and two young female house servants. Only higher ranking officers had the luxury of a major-domo, common to most non-military civilians.

On their return home, Henry dismissed the servants, swept her up into his arms and carried her over the threshold into their bedroom, whereupon he kicked the door shut behind them and set about removing every last stitch of her clothing, ignoring her feeble request for modesty. The way he intently watched her face as he roughly handled her shrinking body, unnerved Elspeth, and instead of the romance she expected on her wedding night, the conjugal act had been an uncomfortable experience for her, both physically and emotionally. Henry seemed to delight in degrading her, but the more he taunted her, the more she withdrew into herself.

Henry was bitterly disappointed. Having a virgin was not all it was cracked up to be. Elspeth did not respond to him in bed as he'd expected. When she failed to show him the awe he'd hoped for, he became cruelly demanding, deliberately inflicting pain on her to force some reaction from her. He would force her to her knees and shove his cock into her mouth. He debased her anally, ignoring her scream of pain as he forced his way inside her dry, forbidden entrance. One day he tired of tormenting his wife and turned away from her. Once again the lure of opiates and almond skinned, kohl-eyed sirens called to him, and he was not inclined to resist their lure.

~

ELSPETH WAS UTTERLY MISERABLE. Marriage to Henry was not at all as she'd imagined it to be. She found that once the numbness of her father's death had worn off, she'd missed him. Her grief at his passing began to overwhelm her, probably because her marriage proved to be such a disaster. She took some solace in reading and riding, the latter only when the all-pervading humidity permitted. Elspeth was glad of her husband's return to his previous lustful partialities; at least it kept him from her bed. The unhappy couple existed in an uneasy truce for some six months, until one night, a ferocious thunderstorm brought the tension between them to a cataclysmic head.

Elspeth awoke in the depths of night, disturbed by tropical rain hammering upon the roof. She lay tangled in her sticky bed sheet; humidity causing it to cling to her like a second skin. She listened fearfully to the tempest raging overhead. Thunder rolled and lightning filled her room periodically with luminous flashes of light.

A sharp cry rent the muggy air, a woman wailing in distress. Drowsily, Elspeth forced herself from her bed. She assumed the cries came from Geeti, the younger of her two house servants. She was a shy girl of nervous disposition and the only one who lived in. Elspeth knew her to be afraid of the fierce storms common to their area.

Stepping into the central living space of the bungalow, she heard another screech. It seemed to be coming from Henry's small box room, furnished with a single bed, meant for a major domo they did not have. Henry had moved into the room, choosing to sleep in there after she'd failed to satisfy him in the bedroom. Elspeth crept to the door and pushed it ajar. Something clattered to the floor and painfully caught her bare foot. She bent down, feeling about in the darkness. Grasping what she believed to be a stick, she brought it to her eye level just as dazzling light lit up the room. The object was Henry's riding crop.

Glancing into the room she saw Henry silhouetted by the illumination. He was bending over Geeti, his body half blocking Elspeth's view but she saw that the girl lay face down upon the bed, her golden skin beaded with perspiration and she could hear Geeti whimpering piteously, her distraught voice begging in Hindi for sahib to stop. Elspeth realised immediately that Henry was engaged in something lewd. As she stared, she realised that he was sodomising the helpless little maid. Impaled between Geeti's buttocks, his pistoning hips drove his cock further into the girl's behind.

Sickened, Elspeth turned away, but too late. Henry had seen her. "Come here," he snapped. Taking a tentative step toward him, she halted as the light faded from the room. They were again plunged into inky black. After a moment, another burst of lightning enabled him to see her and he snagged her wrist, drawing her relentlessly to his side. "At least this way I don't need rubbers."

He leered, gesturing downward at his groin as he thrust hard into Geeti. She gave another pain filled wail, but Henry drowned her out with his yell of completion.

Elspeth felt hot tears of anger and despair spill down her cheeks. She fought her husband's grip on her wrist. In his final throes of orgasm, he'd yanked her hard against him; his head came down now and he kissed her mouth roughly, his teeth catching the tender skin of her lower lip. Radiance from the storm lit up his face and Elspeth gasped. It was obvious to her that he was drugged, pupils enlarged so black they filled each iris. She cringed, twisting her head away, managing to break the slobbering, unwanted kiss. He withdrew his flaccid shaft from the still weeping Indian girl.

"See, I have a pretty friend for us to play with," he slurred, gesturing to poor Geeti who was crying piteously, her face buried in the bed clothes. Elspeth gasped as brilliance lit the damage Henry had visited upon the poor servant's buttocks, which were covered in angry looking welts. Henry had beaten her with his crop.

"Turn over," he ordered her sharply in Hindi. The girl gingerly rolled onto her back. It was clear that Henry had whipped her harshly because the girl winced, attempting to avoid contact with the bed. Elspeth found it painful to watch as Geeti's wide almond-shaped eyes fixed fearfully upon her sahib, her mouth constantly moving as she whispered, begging in her native tongue for reprieve.

"Draw up your knees and part your legs," he ordered severely. Geeti obeyed instantly.

"Wider," Henry barked, in English.

Bright light again brought the room into stark relief and Elspeth saw the woman's splayed limbs, her dark haired sex lewdly displayed. Her sleek golden skin contrasted against the white of the bed sheets.

"Lick her," Henry ordered, his voice brusque. Elspeth snapped her head up, staring at her husband. Surely he couldn't mean what she thought he'd meant? Henry yanked her closer to the bed. She noticed his erection starting to jut out of his gaping trousers, he was becoming aroused again. *"Lick her cunt,"* he hissed despotically. She watched his member jerk, clear liquid leaked from the blunt head and shone wetly in the repetitive flare of the overhead storm.

"No-noo!" She shook her head, adamant. His hand swiftly caught her skein of hair hanging loosely down her back. He wrapped the length around his fist and propelled her forwards. Pushing her to her knees, he forced her face down into the apex of Geeti's legs, directly onto her musky sex. Elspeth gave a keen of protest, Geeti wailed, twisting her hips away from Elspeth, her distress finally seemed to register in Henry's drug crazed mind because he let go of Elspeth's hair. She lifted her head and he drew back his arm, punching her with the full force of his clenched fist. She just managed to twist her head aside so that his blow caught her cheek bone and not her nose. The light eclipsed from the room and again they were plunged into darkness. Elspeth took the opportunity to escape. Leaping to her feet, she staggered away; ignoring Henry's bellowed command for her to stay.

"Come back, you bitch!" His angry shout reverberated after her. Reaching the relative safety of her room, she slammed the door. She fell onto the bed listening fearfully for sounds of angry pursuit. None came, but she trembled violently, shaking with fear and reaction at what had occurred.

At some point during the night she must have slept, because she found herself awaking in the calm of morning to the usual sound of parakeets chirruping and monkeys chattering outside. Dragging herself upright, she winced at the pain in her head. Lifting her hand, she gingerly explored her painful cheek. It felt hot and swollen. Reaching for the bedside bell, she rang it, alerting the servants to her wakefulness. Geeti arrived with her breakfast tray, avoiding Elspeth's gaze as she placed it across her mistress's lap. Then she produced a folded note and handed it over before bowing, eyes cast downward; she pressed her hands together in a salaam and left, closing the door softly behind her. Elspeth shook out the letter nervously. Henry's bold black scrawl covered the page. She scanned the contents quickly and sucked in her breath. He apologised for the previous night but told her that he was sending her away. He wanted her to travel to England and live in his parents' house in Lancashire. He wrote that he feared that should she remain with him he might truly harm or maim her. He confessed that he had no control over himself whilst under the influence of the opiates that he craved and feared he could no longer live without.

He couldn't do this to her! She wouldn't go! Elspeth shoved back the bedclothes and set aside the tray. Grabbing her robe, she hurried from the room still dragging on her dressing gown as she flung open the door to Henry's room. The bed was made and there was no sign of her husband. She sped through the bungalow yelling for Geeti. The young Indian appeared nervously in the doorway of the kitchen. "Memsahib?"

"Where is my husband?" Elspeth asked urgently.

"Master gone, he leave note," Geeti replied, unable to meet her mistress's eyes.

"Do you know when he will return, did he not say?" Elspeth pressed her. The girl looked at the floor. It was obvious that Geeti didn't feel comfortable around Elspeth after the previous night. Exasperated, Elspeth returned to her bedroom to retrieve Henry's letter.

Rereading it, but slowly this time, she saw that he'd stated that his detachment had been posted north for a short term. He wouldn't be returning home to Bombay until a day or so before her ship was due to set sail for England. Elspeth tapped the folded letter with her finger, thinking hard. She realised that she could possibly persuade him otherwise, but after last night's performance, perhaps it was for the best that she left Henry and India behind. An adventure overseas, the opportunity to see her homeland, and a readymade home to go to, would that really be such a bad thing? The alternative was to stay here and watch Henry deteriorate as he demanded more and more lewd acts from her, and his sinking so deeply into a total lack of self-control, quite frankly terrified her.

Leaving was the better of two evils. Rather than stay in India tied to a depraved madman, and one who treated her with no consideration or respect, she would leave. Henry was cruel to her. He was a debauched man whose dark morals threatened her very soul.

Resigned, Elspeth accepted that she'd had to leave Henry. Looking back, she accepted he had been right so send her away to England for her own safety

"ELSPETH, Elspeth, where have your thoughts got to? Tell me true now, did Wooten abuse you?" Adam repeated, nudging her gently. "Hmm?" She continued to rub her cheek absently as she came out of her reverie. Adam was silent as he watched the myriad of painful emotions flicker across her face. He attempted to govern his rage toward Henry Wooten. He could see how deeply the man had hurt his wife. Elspeth whispered her answer to Adam's question so softly that he had to strain to hear her.

"Yes… just the once, but I think Henry feared that he would hurt me more severely at some point. He decided it was sensible for me to leave and travel to England and live with his parents. He was hopelessly addicted to the opium drug you see."

"And you married him knowing this?" he was incredulous.

"No, I had no idea he was addicted at the time. I knew that he was different, strange, but he had saved me from a serpent, and I saw him as my saviour after my father died. He was like my knight in shining armour coming to my rescue when my world had fallen apart. It was only afterward that he became… unkind."

Her understatement told him she'd omitted much of her tale. Her darkened, pain-filled gaze moved him deeply, and he trembled with the need to hit something. If Wooten stood before him now, he would pulverize the man. He took a steadying breath, and he reached for her small gloved hand, kissing her palm. "I am so very sorry, Elspeth. You have to know that I would never harm you. A spanking is not about lashing out or hurting. It is a caring way to keep a child or lady from doing something foolish and unsafe. Did your father never spank you as a child?"

"No, never and my Ayah was always so kind and gentle, she would never have struck me."

"Well, I assure you that if you attempt to leave this ship before we reach England, I shall keep my promise and put you over my knee. You will not like it, but it will not harm you, it will only sting enough to remind you that I wish to keep you safe. I shall then lock you in with me until we arrive because I care a great deal for you, Elspeth. Actually, more than a great deal." She lifted her gaze to his. They stood in silent communication for some moments before he broke the spell by gently taking her arm. "Come, we need refreshment. I suggest we go inside for tea."

CHAPTER 3

She allowed him to lead her inside the ship, her thoughts centered upon her acknowledgement that she had most definitely married the wrong man. They usually conversed and laughed their way through the whole tea ceremony, but not today. Today's conversation was subtle, but each understood the other's subliminal message and answered in kind. When they had drained the pot, Adam moved to sit beside her.

"My cabin is 201," he told her in a low voice, "I shall wait awhile and wander the deck. People will assume that you have returned to second class. I shall join you shortly." Glancing about him to ascertain no one watched, he slid the key to his cabin from his pocket into his palm. Elspeth made some inane comment about the weather, they talked blandly for a few moments before she dabbed her mouth and stood, holding out her hand.

"Once again, Professor, thank you for the most delightful tea." She spoke just loud enough for her voice to carry to others seated in the vicinity. He, in turn, took her proffered hand in his and squeezed the key gently into her palm.

"It is my pleasure, Mrs. Wooten. I do so enjoy your scintillating company. Would you care to join me for tea again tomorrow?" he asked, making sure that most of the people seated nearby could overhear him.

"Yes, indeed, you are too kind, Professor. I bid you good afternoon, sir." She turned, leaving Adam alone. He sat for a few moments before getting up and sauntering out onto the deck where he walked about nodding and touching his hat to any passengers whom he encountered.

Elspeth only met two people on her way to Adam's stateroom, a pair of ladies who barely acknowledged her "good afternoon," intent as they were upon their own conversation. When she arrived at 201, she hastily unlocked the door and slipped inside. The stateroom appeared large in comparison to her meagre box-like cabin. It had the luxury of a separate water closet with lavatory.

She stared at the double bed, where she was about to commit a mortal sin and break her marriage vows. Henry had already broken his, and she knew that he intended to continue doing so for the rest of his immoral life. He was not a man to deny his baser needs. As his wife, she had discovered that to her cost. He wanted to send her home to his parents carrying his child but Elspeth knew that she was not pregnant because she'd had her menses soon after boarding the ship. What if she became with child through lying with Adam? Henry's parents would be none the wiser about the babe's conception and, according to their son; they would be thrilled to have a grandchild and heir. A deception perhaps, but now that she had left Henry far behind in India, it was the only way they would ever have a grandchild now that she was on her way to England.

Once she was settled in Lancashire, she would most probably never take a man into her bed again. To die without knowing what it might have been like to lie with Adam, to only have the sullied memories of Henry to take with her to her grave, seemed incredibly cruel. She wanted to be loved by the professor, she felt compelled to be with him. Could something that felt right really be so very wrong?

"I believe that you are overthinking this." The deep voice startled her out of her reverie. It was Adam. He had pushed open the unlocked door and leaned against the door jamb, watching her intently.

"I know that you are right, and I am worrying about my soul. But there is really no need to because I know that I shall be yours, whatever my conscience tells me is the right thing to do." She shrugged her shoulders, resigned to her fate. "There is no other choice for me, you see I-I want you so very much, Professor Beresford," she answered with an honesty that moved him. Aware of her gaze fixed so trustingly on his. Adam felt too emotional to speak. He shut and locked the door, moved to where she stood and pulled the hat pin from her straw bonnet, untying the ribbon beneath her chin. He tossed it aside onto a chair, placing the pin on a chest of drawers. Holding her head in his palms, he slid his hands either side of her temples deep into her simple chignon of soft billowing hair. He loosened the tresses as he tilted her head to study her face. He took a moment to cast his gaze over her delicate features, noting the depth of trust that shone in her beautiful verdant eyes before his mouth crushed hers, his lips claiming her as his own, just as he'd wanted to do ever since he'd first laid eyes on her beauty.

Elspeth melted against him, marvelling at the strength of her feelings for this learned man. Whenever Henry had touched her, she had remained clinically observant throughout his harsh love-making, whereas now, she was a mass of tingling expectation. She was unable to tell where she began and he ended, such was her overwhelming desire. The details of their love making blurred into a blinding, sinuous touch, of give and take, and oh the taking… It was nothing like the marital act she had experienced with Henry. This heated loving that seared her soul and ripped her emotions to shreds, reformed her, lifting her into a paradise, a place of incredible, blissful pleasure that she had not thought existed in this world. She'd found her nirvana.

Afterward, she lay upon his chest and wept. He didn't seem to find her tears odd, and she felt no need or compulsion to explain. When she was calm, they slept awhile and then he loved her again, but slowly, until the same magical reaction claimed them both. But this time after her wild cries of release, she did not weep. Instead, she drifted into a deep restoring sleep, feeling safer than she had ever done before in her entire life, clasped in his protective embrace.

Adam awoke early and marvelled at the beautiful woman slumbering in his arms. He would never let her go. She was his, now and forevermore. He determined to find a way to make things right, so that he could claim her as his wife and his alone. He watched as her eyelids fluttered open and the last vestiges of dreamy sleep drifted from her green eyes as she focused on his face. A sweet smile curved her lips and he leaned in to kiss her good morning. He cupped her rosy tipped breasts and suckled at her taut nipples. She moaned his name as her legs shifted apart in unconscious wantonness. His hand drifted over the soft contours of her stomach down to her mound. He cupped her mons, his thumb dipping into her folds caressing the ridge of her hardened clitty. She was dewily wet for him.

"Hold me," he whispered, not needing to explain his meaning for she understood, taking his aching member into her palm, exploring his thick shaft and heavy sac below. Adam groaned. His mouth covered hers, igniting the flame between them until it burned so hot he slid between her legs mounting her amidst her encouraging sighs, plundering her sweetness until they lay exhausted in a tangle of damp sheets, each panting and replete.

There was a sudden knock at the cabin door. "Quick, into the water closet," he ordered. She dashed at once to hide. She could hear the low murmuring of male voices through the door. Suddenly the door was pulled wide, and she gasped with shock, taking a quick step back. "Don't worry, it's only me," Adam chuckled as he reached for her. She fell into his arms, breathing a sigh of relief and saw that a tea tray had been placed upon the bed.

He gestured for her to climb back in between the sheets and poured them a cup of tea, which they shared. He fed her slices of fruit cake and shortbread biscuits, while he expounded on his plans for them after they arrived in England. She remained silent after he had finished talking. Gazing at him imploringly, willing him to understand what she was about to say.

"Adam, I have to travel on to Lancashire as arranged. I owe Henry's parents that much, surely you can see that?"

"No, no I don't see anything of the sort. For God's sake, Elspeth, you cannot, in truth, be serious?" He spread his hands, appealing to her common sense.

She remained silent, her eyes entreating him to comprehend her choice.

"I shan't let you leave me, not ever. Forget this misplaced loyalty to Wooten's parents. We will get you a divorce and—"

She interrupted, "No Adam, no divorce, at least not yet, I owe Henry that much."

"You. Owe. Him. Nothing. He mistreated you, Elspeth, *he hit you*!" He ground the words out between gritted teeth, then stopped, afraid he might say more and wound her, something he would never willingly do without regret.

"He saved my life once… and in a way, this time too. By sending me away to live with his parents, I believe he was attempting to protect me," she told him softly.

Adam banged his hand violently against the wall making her jump. "Stop it! Stop this nonsense, or I warn you, Elspeth, I will turn you over my lap!"

She shook her head slowly from side to side. "Beating me will not change my mind."

"*Beating you? Beating* you? I would never *beat* you! But so help me God, I will spank your stubborn bottom until you can't sit for a week, if you don't stop this idiocy right now! Elspeth, you know that Henry cared nothing for you, but now that you belong with me, I shall protect and love you until the day I die!" She stretched out her hand to gently stroke his arm as she sensed his tension.

"Yes, I belong to you, Adam. Darling, I give myself to you in body and soul, but you have to accept that I legally belong to Henry as his wife and I have to do right by his family. Be patient, my love and I will eventually become yours as you will be mine." She gave him such a sweet smile, but Adam was filled with a jealousy that was beyond controlling. He shoved the tray to the floor and rolled on top of her kissing her with fierce possession. She recognised his desperate need to brand her as his mate. She yielded, submitting to his demanding body, parting her thighs, making it easy for his weighty cock to claim her with one deep thrust. This was different from their night of loving passion. This was pure dominion; she understood his need to pound her into submission. The way she felt about him meant that she revelled in his turbulent possession. His rough thrusts felt good as he claimed her, and all too soon, the spiral of lust imploded in on her just as violently as his plundering thrusts and she keened her release.

"You're mine, not his, know that you're mine, Elspeth!" he roared as his cock filled her with his seed, marking her as his in the only way that he could whilst she still remained married to another man.

"Yes, Adam, I am yours, I shall always be yours," she whispered, soothing him, her arms tight about his shoulders, holding his weight down upon her as he pinned her to the bed, his cock buried in her body joining them as one. As he lay in her tender embrace, he felt slayed by the gift she gave him, the very gift of herself.

They managed to smuggle Elspeth out of the stateroom in the same way they'd smuggled her in. She made her way downward to second class back to her own small cabin without anyone seeing her but the steward, who unlocked the chain across the gangway for her. He raised an eyebrow, but said not a word as she thanked him. Once inside the cabin, she pulled the curtains, threw herself onto her narrow bed and immediately fell into a deep sleep.

Adam walked into the breakfast room murmuring a few polite "good mornings" to passengers and waiters alike. He did justice to a hearty breakfast of bacon, sausage and eggs and downed two pots of Earl Grey tea before setting off to walk the entire first class deck twice over.

At tea later that day, each of them thought the matter resolved between them. Adam assumed that Elspeth accepted his decree and that she would travel onto London with him, when they docked. Elspeth thought that Adam fully comprehended her need to do right by Henry and his family before they could even think about being together. She was sure that he had accepted the fact she would travel to Lancashire once she was ashore, and so the subject was not raised again between them for the remainder of their voyage.

Their days began to fall into a regular pattern, tea at 3:00 pm in the first class lounge. After they'd eaten, Elspeth would say her farewells, just loud enough for anyone sitting nearby to overhear before discreetly making her way down to Adam's stateroom where she awaited his arrival. Their passion never dwindled, if anything their fervour only deepened their love for one another.

Elspeth questioned his attraction to her only once. It was after a late afternoon of lovemaking that she made her self-deprecating remark. She quickly found herself yanked naked across his thighs. Squealing with alarm, she struggled, but he landed a sharp smack to her backside and ordered her to remain still and hear him out.

"I cannot understand why you hold yourself in such low esteem. You are a beautiful young woman, one of the loveliest I have ever seen. I adore your interest in the world about you and the insightful observations you make. Our conversations have made me think about so many things differently. Elspeth, I want to spend the rest of my life with you, and so I will not have you denigrate yourself. I am going to punish you now but not solely for that reason. I want you to understand the difference between the abuse Henry used toward you, and my form of loving correction. Do you understand?"

"Yes," she replied softly.

"Good. I shall give you thirty smacks, and all shall be forgiven."

She felt his arm lift and then his hand fell with a clap onto her tender bottom cheek. She yelped. Silently he thrust a pillow at her and she cuddled it, burying her face into the soft fullness to smoother her next cry, which came quickly as Adam's hand began to rain down punishment, alternating spanks on either buttock. She squirmed and bucked as the heat built in her nether end. Her gasps were accompanied by a few tears, but Adam silently spanked on, giving her the final five in rapid fire succession.

"All finished," he said as he rubbed the sting from her buttocks. She slumped across his lap and wept for a little while. When he helped her up and cradled her against his chest, she buried her head into his shoulder, feeling shy and embarrassed.

He stroked back her flaming hair. "Your face is almost as red as your hair!" he told her with a chuckle. She huffed. "Don't be cross, I adored spanking you. You'd best be a good wife because I shall certainly want to spank you for the slightest misdemeanour."

His words had the strangest effect on Elspeth. A shaft of desire ran through her body, direct as an arrow straight to her heat filled apex. She moaned and he instantly knew why. "My wanton lady, you liked your spanking didn't you?"

She was mortified. "No, no… I—"

He interrupted her protestation. "Shall I prove it to the both of us?" he asked her, his voice husky with lust. She tried to pull away, but he held her firm upon his lap and slid his palm between her legs, his fingers dipping with ease into her soaking channel. A wet sucking sound belied her denial and she could only sigh as his mouth covered hers. His erection swelled rampant against her leg. Tipping her onto the bed, her legs fell apart by their own volition, and he claimed her.

The feel of his swollen flesh entering her, taking her, branding her as his, only moments after he had spanked her, overwhelmed her. His dominion of her body thrilled and excited, so without needing more than his cock filling her, joining them, she climaxed calling his name, her talisman in the turbulent sea of ecstasy. He gave a shout, and she felt him spasming deep within her flesh as he filled her with his seed. He collapsed onto her bosom. She pulled him close, crooning words of love, and he, in turn, whispered his adoration for her.

ONE AFTERNOON, a rare rainy day, they entered the northern waters of the Atlantic. They were lying on Adam's bed, when he rose and took a tooled leather casket from his wardrobe handing the box to Elspeth. "What is this?" she asked.

"Open it and see." He curled next to her again and watched her face as she lifted the lid. Her mouth dropped open as she gazed at the flash of iridescent green fire that almost blinded her. She turned astonished eyes to him and he gave a slow grin. "I don't tell lies, Elspeth. Everything I have told you about my adventurous life, is true. You are holding the *Shiromani.*"

"It is beautiful; the most stunning object I've ever beheld." She squinted reverently into the shimmering depths of the mystical stone. "It must be worth a fortune!"

"It is, but I cannot sell it because of the legend and its power. I shall keep it for the time being, but one day I shall give it away, as I am meant to do if I wish to keep the magic luck alive, and I do." He retrieved the casket and replaced it inside his wardrobe.

Elspeth watched him and said solemnly, "I hope the jewel will bring us luck."

He came over to her, and kissed her on her lips. "That is why I shall keep it, just for a while, until everything is resolved and you are legally, as well as willingly, mine."

She ran the back of her hand gently down his rough cheek. "I have told you over and again that I am yours."

He took her hand in his and turned it over, pressing his lips against her palm. "Thank you, but I shall not rest easy until you have my name and are legally my wife. My passion is possessive I know, but it is who I am."

"I love who you are, and I love that you love me," she replied seriously.

"I am a man who gives his heart but once and only once. I shall love you and only you for all eternity." He kissed her soundly. After they had drawn apart, she asked him what his future plans were for the *Shiromani.*

"I shall bequeath it to the museum of course."

She frowned. "But don't you run the risk that they will sell it at some point in the future?"

He chuckled. "You cannot legislate for everything in life, my sweet. Each man, or woman, can only do their part. What happens to the gem later on is not my concern."

She shook her head. "I disagree. I think that you should keep it and bequeath it after your death."

He touched the tip of her nose with his finger. "My, how serious you look… I have not fully decided what I'll do with the jewel. Come now, time marches on, and we need to get you back down to second class before anyone notices you're missing."

~

THE DAY they finally docked in London was grey, dull and wet; nothing like the weather she was used to in India. It was also exceeding cold! She quickly realised that none of her clothes were going to be warm enough for a British autumn. She felt chilled to the bone.

They had parted on loving terms the previous night. Elspeth felt bad about deceiving Adam, promising him that she would wait for him on the dockside until first class passengers disembarked. Although she felt guilty, she needed to get to Lancashire and make peace with her in-laws before she could return to his waiting arms. Adam was adamant that they'd travel together in his carriage to his home. Elspeth knew what he thought of her plan, but she decided the only way to achieve her aim was to enact this small measure of independence, although she knew that Adam would more than likely view her actions as pure stubborn defiance. Her lip twitched as she imagined his ire and any subsequent punishment. No doubt he would turn her over his knee, but strangely, the thought of him spanking her simply sent a quiver of delicious excitement tingling down her spine. She trusted him and knew him well enough now to know that he would never abuse her as Henry had. Any punishment Adam deemed necessary would be fairly and lovingly given.

First class passengers would leave the ship via a sturdily roped gangplank onto the centre of the dock. They were not hurried by the ship's crew and breakfasted in their usual leisurely manner before leaving the ship. In contrast, the second class gangplank was set to the aft of the ship where passengers were ushered off before breakfast and along a much steeper and narrower plank. They arrived onto the dock behind stacked crates that awaited loading, ready for the next voyage. Because her small trunk was light, she was able to carry that along with her carpet bag, and this meant that Elspeth was one of the first people off the ship.

She made her way along the dockside, shivering in the dank and cold atmosphere. She pulled her thin shawl tight about her, but nothing prepared her for the English climate. None of her dresses or shawls would be suitable to wear in this chilly weather. She walked away from the ship ever onwards, along the long straight quay toward a distant group of people. She was hoping to spot a carriage for hire.

Eventually, a dilapidated building came into sight. Barrels stood dotted about outside the scruffy looking structure, which turned out to be a tavern. Sailors lounged, sucking on their long clay pipes, their tankards of ale set upon the upended casks. To the side of this building, a number of hackney carriages stood, obviously awaiting trade from the docked ship. Elspeth approached the first and naively asked the cab driver if he was going in the direction of Lancashire. He guffawed, shaking his head. He pointed to a coach at the end of the queue. It was dark green but did not carry the hackney cab insignia. Elspeth toiled over to it, lugging her trunk, which was now beginning to feel rather heavy. She was about to ask the driver the same question when the window of the carriage dropped down and a portly man stuck out his head. "Am I addressing Mrs. Henry Wooten?" he called to her. Elspeth nodded with relief; someone had been dispatched to collect her after all.

"Climb aboard, madam, the driver will stow your luggage. It is a pleasure to make your acquaintance. I am Horace Trubshaw, of Naughton, Trubshaw and Leeves, solicitor to the late Mr. James Henry Wooten senior." Elspeth shivered, *late?*

Shaking with cold, she settled into the seat opposite the lawyer. Mr. Trubshaw sympathetically reached for a tartan blanket folded on the seat beside him and handed it to her. She took it gratefully, tucking it warmly about her knees. "I am taking you to our London office to explain some rather sad family circumstances. I would prefer to wait and answer your questions upon our arrival, Mrs. Wooten." Elspeth nodded her agreement and sat silently for the remainder of the twenty-minute journey.

Once they arrived, Mr. Trubshaw ushered her into a wood panelled office where a cheery fire burned in the grate. He gestured her to a chair, whilst seating himself in another. Elspeth settled her carpet bag on the floor beside her.

"I won't beat about the bush, Mrs. Wooten; both your in-laws are recently deceased."

Elspeth gasped. "How, I mean what happened to them?"

"I am saddened to say there was an almighty fire in the house and neither survived. Your husband is naturally heir to the property, but I am reliably informed that it is ruined beyond repair."

"What of my husband's cousin, Lord Edward Wooten?" she asked.

"Another blow for you to endure. His Lordship resides in the debtor's prison, most of his land is gambled away, leaving huge debts secured against the property, all as yet unpaid. Unfortunately, I have no good news to share with you, dear lady."

Elspeth sat silent, digesting the lawyer's catalogue of woe. Mr. Trubshaw coughed politely. "I can arrange passage back to the subcontinent for you, should you so wish? There was the sum of twenty-five pounds in Mr. James Wooten's bank account, which is now Henry's. I have banked twenty pounds in your husband's name and have taken the liberty of keeping five back for your own immediate use."

Elspeth stretched out her arm, lifting her carpet bag up onto her knee. Rummaging inside, she found her reticule and dug into the side pocket, pulling out Adam's calling card, which she held out to the lawyer. "Professor A. Beresford, Helen House, Crosby Square," he read aloud.

"Yes," Elspeth replied, "would you be so good as to have my trunk forwarded to this address? If there is any need to contact me, I shall be residing there." She stood up and held out her hand, which the lawyer shook while looking somewhat perplexed by her calm acceptance of the situation.

"You are intending to travel to this address now, ma'am?" he asked.

Elspeth smiled. "Indeed I am, sir."

"Then I insist you allow my driver to deliver you and your trunk to your destination, Mrs. Wooten. It is not so far from here, in the parish area of St. Helens. I have to say you have been very calm and brave under the circumstances. I had expected some histrionics or the vapours at the very least!" He looked mightily relieved that he had not had to deal with either.

Elspeth nodded and smiled. "They breed us tough out in the

sub-continent, Mr. Trubshaw. I thank you for your kindness and for the use of your carriage."

"You are most welcome, dear lady. Oh and here is your five pounds, please sign here to say that you have received the sum." He moved over to his desk and pushed a ledger toward Elspeth. She accepted the pen and signed where he indicated. Tucking the notes that he gave her into her dress pocket, she shook Mr. Trubshaw's outstretched hand. They wished one another good day and Elspeth left with a somewhat lighter step.

She was free to go to Adam. She felt as though a huge burden had been lifted from her shoulders. There was nothing to keep her from him now. Yes, she was still married to Henry, but Adam said he would take care of that situation, and she believed him. She couldn't wait to see him again. She hurried over to where the coach awaited her.

Outside, thick fog had rolled in from the river Thames. It was all enveloping and everything was muffled, sound eerily deadened. The coach that Elspeth travelled in came to a halt. She peered through the carriage window, and although she could hear muted shouts, she could see absolutely nothing but drifts of dirty cream mist. The door suddenly opened; the driver tipped his hat to her. "There's been an accident. The road is blocked by spilled marrows where a cart was knocked over in this blessed 'pea soup.' Crosby Square is at a junction up ahead a short way, missus, on your left. I suggest you get out an' walk from here, 'tis only a hundred yards away at best. I'll deliver the trunk when we get moving."

Elspeth drew her thin shawl about her and took up her carpet bag. The driver lifted her off the carriage step, setting her down upon the pavement. He pointed beyond the spilled cart to where a yellow gas light glimmered, casting a dim glow on a road junction. "See how close we are to the Square? Simply walk ahead and turn left, you'll find Helen House soon enough." He tipped his top hat to her before turning away to offer his aid to those intent on clearing marrows from the thoroughfare.

Elspeth shivered as she walked briskly away, her footfalls muffled by the thickening fog. As she rounded the corner of Crosby Square, she was shocked to witness two men attacking another over on the opposite side of the street. They had floored an elderly man. While one thug kicked him cruelly in the stomach, the other quickly set to emptying his pockets. Without a care for her own safety, she launched herself across the road and onto the back of the man who was putting his boot into the old gentleman. Leaping onto his back from behind, Elspeth raked her nails across the assailant's eyes. He grunted and swung back, catching her painfully in the side with his elbow, and she was forced to loosen her grip. He twisted suddenly and grabbed her, flinging her against the iron railings before punching her hard in the stomach, causing Elspeth to stagger backwards, falling hard to the ground, cracking her head on the pavement.

Everything went black.

CHAPTER 4

She could hear male voices murmuring softly somewhere above her but no voice that she particularly recognised. Her eyes fluttered open. She didn't know the room she was in or either of the two darkly dressed men who hovered beside her bed. The younger of the two reached for her hand and took her wrist in his. "How do you feel?" he asked.

She shifted slightly and pain filled her head. "My head aches," she answered reedily.

"I am not at all surprised to hear that; you took quite a blow. Might I ask your name Miss?"

"Yes, of course. I am… er, oh this is ridiculous. I am… oh I know my name but I cannot think of it right now. What happened to me?"

The older gentlemen spoke. "You came to my rescue and quite bravely so, I have to say. I was set upon by brigands, and you frightened them away but not before they robbed the pair of us, I am sad to say. You are presently residing in my lodgings. I am Mr. Arthur Brown, and this other gentleman is a doctor, a good friend of mine, Dr. Andrew Philpot. You have been asleep for the last twelve hours or so, and I was becoming concerned. I asked Dr. Philpot to call in and take a look at you. Now that you are awake, is there someone we can send for on your behalf, dear lady?"

Elspeth lay still, feeling thoroughly confused. She had no recollection of the events that Mr. Brown had described and could not remember anyone or anything, not even her own name. "I cannot remember anything, nothing, not even who I am or where I live!" Agitated, she attempted to sit up, but swooned and dropped back against the pillows.

"Now, now, do not fret, my dear, you are among friends. This is not an unheard of phenomenon when there is a severe blow to the head involved. Come, Mr. Brown, we shall consult in the other room."

The next time Elspeth awoke, a candle was lit, and she supposed that she was alone in an otherwise darkened room. The bed that she lay upon was an old fashioned canopy bed, draped with moth eaten curtains that could be pulled to surround it. The sheets she lay in were thin and grey. The heavy flocked paper on the walls peeled in places from damp and the dusty carpet was so threadbare that she could see through holes to the unvarnished floorboards beneath. A chest of drawers, missing two of its knobs and an old armoire that leaned drunkenly, stood across the room. A trunk stood against one wall, and it was the trunk that drew her eye. Something pulled at the edge of her memory but the meaning of it eluded her. She closed her eyes and tried to sort out her fragmented thoughts, to remember her name, but there was not even a glimmer of knowledge as to who she was. Tears slid unnoticed down her cheeks as she struggled to recall her Christian name. She jumped with surprise when a cold hand touched her face and stroked her forehead. "Hush, child, don't fret. The good doctor came up with a solution, at least for the time being." Elspeth opened her eyes and saw that it was the elderly gentleman; she even recalled his name, Mr. Brown. She felt reassured that she still remembered that. He gazed down at her with pity in his pale rheumy eyes.

"Dr. Philpot is going to put a notice in the newspaper about you, so that any family who misses you might contact him and thus be reunited with you. We shall put it to my neighbours that you are my niece, fallen on hard times and come to visit. I did have a niece once, she was called Bunty, but alas, she died young. However, no one knows that hereabouts and so, with your permission, I shall call you Bunty. Just until you recall your own name. What do you say, m'dear?"

"You are very kind, Mr. Brown, but I cannot depend on your generosity for very long."

"You let me worry about that, m'dear. After all, we do not know that you won't recall your identity tomorrow and be on your way home! Now then, do you think that you might manage a little broth?"

Elspeth nodded and Mr. Brown moved slowly away into another room from where she heard the clink of metal on china.

IT SEEMED that they had been optimistic about Elspeth's memory returning. Day after day passed by, and soon she realised that she had been living at Mr. Brown's lodgings for a whole month. Elspeth learned that Arthur Brown was a cartographer who drew maps, principally for the well-known *Atlas* magazine. Unfortunately, Mr. Brown's eyesight was failing, and Elspeth offered to help him with the smaller detail of his drawings. She kept their humble accommodation as clean as possible and ran errands for the aging gentleman. He enjoyed her company, and it seemed to her that he began to truly believe his own fabrication that she was his niece, Bunty.

Elspeth felt the cold more than most, and she was bemused by her lack of ability to undertake tasks that others took for granted, such as simple tea making. It was as if she had forgotten all the normal life skills she should possess. How could she know that England was an alien culture to her? Or that she had never made a cup of tea or cooked a meal in her life before? She assumed that she was English born and bred, not once did it occur to her or Arthur that she was from India, having had no first-hand knowledge of English culture.

One day, Uncle Arthur, as she now called Arthur Brown, asked her to take a silver jug to Mr. Goldberg, the pawnbroker, whose shop was situated just down the street from their lodgings. Elspeth readily agreed, and wrapping herself in the thick warm knitted shawl that the doctor had kindly procured for her, she set off with the jug, walking briskly to the shop as requested. Once inside, she saw that there was a ragged youth already at the counter. She wandered about, gazing at the amazing selection of curios that were crammed into the small dark space. Old books, china and silver vied for space on the shelves with an odd collection of old coins, jewellery, clocks and even toys. Objects of all description filled this intriguing establishment. Elspeth even spotted an open box full of teeth and another one full of what appeared to be human hair.

The conversation at the counter was clear, and she couldn't help but listen to the discussion between the owner and his young customer. "Ten shillings the lot," Mr. Goldberg stated firmly.

"*What?* These coins are Greek gold, and this ere necklace is Spanish silver!" the boy complained.

"Take it or leave it, lad, that's my price. Make up your mind." Mr. Goldberg shrugged. Elspeth watched as the youth held out a grubby palm and snatched the ten shillings. He left the shop, grumbling under his breath.

"What can I do for you?" the pawnbroker asked her. Elspeth pulled out the silver jug. "I don't happen to deal in stolen goods, my girl," he told her with a frown. Elspeth blushed.

"It is not stolen sir; this belongs to Mr. Brown the cartographer. I am his niece Bunty and he sent me here with the jug to sell." Immediately Mr. Goldberg's face cleared.

"I heard tell his niece was living with him now. So how is your old uncle keeping then?"

"He is well, I thank you, sir, although his eyes do give him some trouble."

Mr. Goldberg nodded sympathetically. "Good thing he has you here to help him then, Miss..."

"Bunty." Elspeth waited as Mr. Goldberg turned the jug upside down and peered underneath at the base.

"Two bob," Mr. Goldberg stated firmly. Elspeth didn't argue but held out her hand and took the two shilling pieces that the pawnbroker dropped in her palm. "Last of his mudlark stock is it?" he asked.

Elspeth frowned. "I'm sorry, but what is mudlark stock?"

Mr. Goldberg grinned, showing a couple of large gold teeth. "Huh! He hasn't told you about his mudlarking days? Well, you just ask him about that when you get home."

Elspeth nodded and turned to leave. "If you want to try your hand at mudlarking, bring me your finds, and I'll give you a better price than others around here might," he called after her. She didn't reply but ran home to ask "Uncle Arthur" about mudlarking.

"YOU MEAN that you dig in the mud of the river bank when the tide is out and you find treasure?" She was amazed at his explanation of mudlarking.

Arthur looked up from his table where he was still at work drawing. "Not as easy as all that, m'dear. Some days there's nothing to be found and others a piece of coal may be your only haul but there is nothing quite like rubbing the dirt from something and realising that you've found treasure! Gold, silver, jewellery all carried to you by the tide to wash up on the edge of the Thames."

"I shall go tomorrow and try my luck." Elspeth felt a glimmer of excitement at the thought of digging for treasure.

"No, Bunty, you will not." Her face fell at Arthur's stern pronouncement. "You are a gentle young woman. It would not be safe for you among the vagabonds who dig along the embankments. Besides, not all that you find on the river bank is wholesome. Suicides from Blackfriars Bridge often lodge along the shoreline, there are packs of wild dogs that live off the flesh of the poor unfortunates, and they are not averse to attacking a vulnerable living human. Had you been a brawny fellow, well things might be different, but you are not. So no, you may not go mudlarking tomorrow. You are my responsibility now, and I will not allow you to put yourself at risk in such a way."

"I have an idea, I shall go to Mr. Goldberg's and buy some boys' clothing first thing tomorrow and dress in disguise." Elspeth stated, completely ignoring Arthur's warning.

He looked thoughtfully at her, merely nodded and gave little notice of her pronouncement. Since she would need money for clothing and she had none of her own, there was no point in continuing the discussion. "Is that stew about ready, m'dear?" he asked, adroitly changing the subject.

Elspeth stirred the contents of the black pot set upon the iron trivet on the fire. "Yes, I will serve if are you ready to eat, Uncle?"

Arthur smiled and nodded. He blessed the day that his sweet niece had come to live with him. What a boon she was to have around. His finances would just about stretch to feed the extra mouth, but since Bunty had arrived and his life had become more comfortable, he certainly didn't begrudge the extra expense. She was a good girl and kept their two roomed, rented lodging as clean and tidy as she possibly could under the imposed conditions of their poverty. She had listened when he imparted his small menu repartee and followed his cooking instructions to the letter. She managed to cook simple meals on Arthur's small weekly budget. She also ran errands for him, but more importantly, Bunty was helping him with his drawings on the days when his eyes became too dull to see his work, an event that seemed to happen with more frequency as time passed. Arthur knew that he was getting old. He'd fretted about what would become of him in his dotage until providence had sent him Elspeth, to become Bunty, his niece. He liked having the girl around, and his concerns for his future had abated with her arrival.

All in all, Arthur was delighted by the turn of events and preferred to forget that Bunty was in no way related to him. It was an innocent deception, one that made him feel more comfortable about the situation. He no longer worried about her memory returning or the fact that if it did, she might leave him to manage his own affairs, which would leave him alone once again. The likelihood of that happening seemed like a remote possibility with every passing day.

THAT NIGHT ELSPETH lay wakeful in her bed. She continued to sleep in the bedroom that Arthur had vacated for her when she had been first carried there by the men who had rescued them from their attackers. Arthur now slept in the main living area on a truckle bed. This room tripled up as a kitchen and office as well as his bedroom. During the day, the small truckle bed slid neatly underneath the huge table where Arthur laid out his large parchments on which he drew his commissioned maps.

That morning, Elspeth had washed out her dress and discovered the enormous sum of five pounds in her pocket. She had immediately hidden the money from Uncle Arthur under the mattress of her bed. It had been an instinctive action at the time but one that left her feeling incredibly guilty. Arthur had shared everything he had with her, and here she was, concealing money from him. She tossed and turned trying to decide what to do for the best. If she kept the money hidden, she could use small amounts to buy coal and food to supplement them both, she could also buy her boy-clothing to dress in so that she could go mudlarking. If her memory returned and she needed to travel somewhere else, at least she would have enough left for her fare. Not happy at her deception and yet not wishing to hand over her funds, Elspeth decided to keep her secret.

The following morning, she threw her shawl around her shoulders and took up her provisions basket. She muttered that she needed to buy dry goods and left, heading for the pawnbroker shop. Uncle Arthur barely acknowledged her as engrossed as he was in plotting the grid for a newly commissioned map.

Arriving at the shop, Elspeth espied the very same lad who had been in the shop on the last occasion that she was there. He appeared to be listening to her request to Mr. Goldberg for boys' clothing, showing open curiosity. When she fingered the fine tweed trousers and cloth cap on top of the pile of clothes that Mr. Goldberg had shoved in front of her, the youth had asked why she wanted to buy boys' clothes. "I wish to take up mudlarking and I am told by my uncle that I should only go dressed as a boy." Elspeth saw no reason why she shouldn't be truthful about her reason for wanting the clothing; after all it was only a small deception to be kept from Arthur.

"These 'ere togs is too good for mudlarkin'. You need to be in rags to blend in with that filthy work. What the devil would a girl like you be up to doing, digging about in the mud?" he asked, suspiciously.

"I need to make some money for my keep that is why, not that it's any of your business!" she answered tartly.

The lad cocked his head, pursing his lips he gave a low whistle. "Well now, you'd best come along 'o me, miss hoity-toity, an' I'll show you where ter get yer rags. You don't wanna be paying old Goldberg's prices jus' to go mudlarkin'!"

"Oi you, hop it! Stop stealin' me customers!" Mr. Goldberg pointed at the door. The scruffy youth grabbed Elspeth by her arm and yanked her outside. Not halting for a second as she complained, he continued pulling her along beside him.

"Where are we going!" she asked indignantly as she was forced to almost run to keep up with the boy.

"Mr. Jones, the rag an' bone man, along Market Street. You'll get your lads' togs there right enough. Come on!"

When they were halfway up Market Street, the boy stopped and shoved open a pair of high wooden gates that had seen better days. Elspeth gazed about her curiously. She espied a solid looking bull dog that leapt to his feet, rushed toward them barking and snarling ferociously, only to lurch to a stop with a yelp, when the rope tied about his neck ran out of length.

There were piles of "stuff" everywhere. A huge pile of bones lay to the left of the gates. "What on earth does anyone want with bones?" Elspeth wondered aloud.

"They're used by the apothecaries to make tablets. They grind them bones down into a powder and mix with the medicine to make pills."

Elspeth shuddered at the sight of the gruesome pile of animal remains. They walked on past a heap of broken carriage and cart wheels stacked up beside a pile of broken doors. A mountain of rusty iron goods took up the entire opposite side of the yard.

Elspeth suddenly realised that she was here in this very odd place with a total stranger whose name she didn't even know. Perhaps she had been too trusting? She caught the boy's arm, pulling him to a stop. "I-I don't know your name, but I am—"

"Bunty, Mr. Brown's niece, yeah, I know." He pulled his arm free from her grip. "I'm Scrounger."

"Scrounger… but what is your real name?"

"Tis' me real name! That's what folks hereabouts call me, an' that's what I answer to, Miss Hoity-Toity."

"I am not hoity-toity! You know my name, so use it!" Elspeth was hurt that he should think that she was stuck up.

"Come on, *Bunty*, this way," he winked, using her correct name and softening his tone, so that Elspeth felt mollified. He knew just where to go, so she followed him, anxiously keeping an eye out for the snapping and snarling dog.

They rounded the end of the yard, and Scrounger led her to a pile of rags. He began to yank out clothing piece by piece. Pairs of trousers, shirts and waistcoats, sorting them from the clothing stack. He cast his practised eye over each garment before flinging back the more unsavoury items. Finally satisfied with his choices, he handed them over to Elspeth and told her to hold them up against her to see if they would fit.

There were two pairs of knee britches, which came well below her knees to her calves and two grubby shirts, each missing their once attached stud collars. A black hat and an old cap in Harris Tweed along with a pair of braces completed her selection. Then she spotted an old black woollen cloak, which would be warm and hopefully keep the worst of the wet weather at bay, and so she snagged that as well.

A thick-set, bald but bewhiskered man appeared beside them. He held out his hand. "A tanner," he stated baldly. Elspeth felt cowed by the man and was disinclined to argue the cost with such a burly fellow. She placed the requested sixpence into his huge grubby hand. They beat a hasty retreat, leaving the dog and his similarly featured owner, behind.

On the walk back to Arthur's, they stopped at a baker's stall to buy a bag of sticky buns. They shared the sweet doughy treats as they walked, weaving between the stalls of the market that gave rise to the name of the street. Elspeth kept a bun back for Uncle Arthur to enjoy with his tea. Scrounger led her along the pavements beside the Thames until they came to the Wapping stairs that led down onto the river bank.

Fewer waterman steps existed now that the new Thames embankment was finished but enough still remained for the purpose of mudlarking. The steps were built against the riverside wall where the dirty brown waters of the Thames lapped up against the stairs. Today, the river's level almost reached the uppermost step. The tide was in and so there would be no mudlarking for the rest of that day. However, as Elspeth listened carefully, she was tutored by one of London's finest and most successful mudlark hunters. She learned about the times and rhythms of the Thames capricious tides, the best places to go for the choicest pickings along the shoreline and the pitfalls of ignoring the weather, all taught to her by her newfound friend and prince among mudlarks, Scrounger.

CHAPTER 5

Adam Beresford missed the evening edition of the newspaper because he was on his way to Paris for an exhibition of ancient Egyptian artefacts. The museum was exhibiting some of their rarer finds, and Adam was to oversee the shipment, transport and protection of the items on loan from his London museum.

At first when he left the ship, he had been simply annoyed that Elspeth had not come to his carriage for their pre-arranged assignation, but when he had finally given up waiting on the dockside and ordered the driver to take him home, he found that her trunk had been delivered to his address. He forgave her for her small deception and waited eagerly for her arrival. He told his housekeeper, Mrs. Carron, to prepare for a mistress to join him, living in the house, and although the woman muttered oaths under her breath, she did as her employer asked and made preparations for her arrival. She emptied drawers then made room for dresses within her master's wardrobes.

Day after day Adam waited expectantly for his love and still she did not come. Finally, hurt and angered by her silence, he wrote to the house in Lancashire asking her what was causing her delay?

Again the unnerving silence through lack of any reply infuriated him and hurt his pride. He chased about in fruitless searches, but as a professor with no deep understanding of ladies and their subtle ways, Adam concluded that, although he had thought his deep affection reciprocated, he had been duped. He felt that he had been used by Elspeth for her own amusement to counteract her boredom on the long voyage to England.

As heartbroken as he was, Adam threw himself into his work and pushed her to the back of his mind. He wanted to throw out her trunk, the sight of it only served to confuse and wound him further, but he found he could not bring himself to give the order for it to be simply discarded. He set off to Paris where he would remain until the end of the month-long exhibition.

So no one replied to any of the adverts placed in the newspapers by Doctor Philpot. He and Arthur Brown concluded that Elspeth was most probably a high end servant, mayhap a governess. Possibly she had no family to care for her whereabouts, so they insisted she remain with Arthur, living as his niece Bunty, until such time as her memory returned to her.

ELSPETH BECAME a familiar sight to the other ragged mudlarks working the Thames' shore. Thanks to Scrounger, she now knew when to expect low tide and learned from him how to dig carefully in the sticky mud of the river bank. Gradually, she recognised "finds" for herself within the silt. Other regular mudlarks began to call greetings to her upon her arrival.

Before long, she was going down to the river alone, no longer requiring Scrounger's informing presence. At first she was only able to supplement their meagre coal supply but then she found coins, pottery and jewellery to sell to Mr. Goldberg, putting the money he paid her toward the purchase of pies and other foods that would not test her culinary inexperience, since they required her to simply heat them through.

She would wear her boy clothing and wash her feet in a pail of cold water at the day's end. By wrapping her voluminous cloak about herself, Arthur did not realise her deception. Once clear of the house in the mornings, she would don her tatty bowler to cover her bright hair, which she plaited and wound about her head each day. She would leave her cloak with Mr. Goldberg to run down to the river bank, often one of the first mudlarks to arrive at low tide. It never ceased to amaze her how the currents brought such treasure to her, items displaced from a ship's cargo, or from people discarding odd items into the river where they were carried by the strong current to end up deposited in the silt for her to find. Elspeth started to know instinctively the way that the tides worked and which steps might yield up the best treasure at low tide. Sometimes the Wapping Old Stairs or the Aldermen steps, but if the tides had been high and rough, then she would head further afield to the Queens Stairs, situated beyond the Tower of London where she would explore the shoreline in front of the Traitor's Gate. Of course, there were terrible sights to behold, bloated carcasses; the remains of both animals and humans, but possibly her unconscious memories of what she'd witnessed of Indian poverty inured her against the harsh penury she was now witnessing on a daily basis.

It was a day when she knew the tide would soon be returning fast. Time was of the essence if she were to find anything of value that day. After an hour or so of fruitless searching, her eye was caught by movement above the steps. A man stood there. Drawing his arm back, he threw something into the fast returning river water. He repeated his action twice more before turning and leaving.

Elspeth looked over to where the objects landed in the river and spotted faint movements upon the surface of the water. Concerned, she made her way over to the river's edge as quickly as the mud would allow. Squinting against the glinting reflections of light, she shaded her eyes and saw to her horror, two small kittens struggling in the water. One of the three must have sunk soon after it had landed in the river. Quickly rolling up her trouser legs, she waded into the brown water and managed to grasp the two tiny drowning creatures, thrusting them into her waistcoat to keep them both warm whilst she searched for their sibling. Despite plunging her hand repeatedly into the cold water, feeling along the silt of the river bed, she failed to locate the third kitten.

With the bedraggled cats tucked inside her ragged waistcoat, she hurried back to Mr. Goldberg's shop to change her clothes. While she changed, the pawnbroker offered to rub both kittens dry with a rag, and despite complaining loudly about the futility of saving them; he went off and located an empty eyedropper which he gave to Elspeth suggesting she use it to feed them milk.

Arthur instantly stopped his drawing when she showed him her rescued kittens, and between them, they managed to feed the pair then settle them into a basket of bundled rags, which they set cosily beside the fire. For a few days both the ginger kittens thrived, but then one of them lost interest in feeding, and despite Elspeth and Arthur's diligent attentions, it died. Elspeth found the stiff little body early one morning. She cradled it upon her knee and wept bitterly over its sad fate. Arthur gently removed it from her, replacing it with the remaining kitten for her to cuddle while he took away the small body for burial.

The remaining kitten thrived; very soon it was sleeping with Elspeth on her bed each and every night. The warmth and comfort of his loving purrs were a huge solace to her and she adored him, naming him Lucky Chance although he was soon answering to Lucky. He rarely went out and enjoyed spending his day watching Arthur's pen as it scratched wriggling lines across paper, marking the lines of roads and rivers. At first they worried the cat would attempt to catch the pen, but so far, Lucky had been content simply to watch the movement of the drawing. Arthur surmised that the kittens had been too young to learn hunting from their mother and so Lucky was never trained to pounce.

~

ONE EVENING, when the tide was starting to rise and the gloaming had given way to darkness rather more quickly than she had anticipated, a loud whistle blast startled her. She had found nothing at all that day, staying longer than she'd intended in the hope that she might at least find some coal for the fire.

She waded slowly across the glue-like mud until she stood beside the wall hidden below the lip of brick that screened her from any person standing above. Shivering with cold, she huddled against the slimy green stones and waited for the loud blasts from police whistles to pass by, the shouts and pounding feet growing closer. Then suddenly an object flew through the air and landed in the mud nearby whilst above she heard the rattle of metal. She discerned a sack but remained hidden and did not attempt to retrieve it until she was certain the rumpus from the road above had moved on.

When all was quiet, she pulled her bare feet out of the goo and slowly squelched over to the sack. The water was returning and walking becoming difficult. She grabbed the bag by the rope tied at the neck; the rope was secured up above tied to a large rusting iron ring used to moor boats at high tide. Elspeth realised that someone securing the rope in this way was the cause of the grating metallic noise she'd heard. The person who had thrown the sack over the wall had obviously intended returning for it at some point. She undid the rope about the neck of the sack, leaving the empty rope line hanging down. Clasping the hessian bag, she took it with her, making her way back to the Alderman Stairs. She sat down on a step, settled it into her lap. Unknotting it, she peered inside. Immediately she was dazed by iridescent green light that filled her vision. Strange images swirled about in her mind; she was clasped in the arms of a naked man. Elspeth shuddered with disquiet, and putting a hand to her head, she trembled. A chill ran through her that had nothing to do with the bitter cold surrounding her. Quickly she tied up the bag, shaken by her strange reaction to whatever gleamed inside the sack.

After quiet contemplation, she decided to take the bag back with her. She moved in the shadows of the dark, misty streets, arriving at the pawnbroker's as he was about to shut up shop. She sluiced the mud from her legs with a pail of cold water provided by Mr. Goldberg. Then she collected her cloak and covered her boy clothes, making her way back to Arthur's, where she hurried to her room, to change into a dress before preparing their meagre supper.

After the meal, Elspeth fetched the sack to show the contents to Arthur. The jewel's brightness was magnified by flames from the fire and green reflective light shimmered and danced upon the dingy walls of the living area, giving the dank room an eerie underwater feel.

"I do believe it to be an emerald of some enormous proportion. Wherever did you come by it, Bunty?" Arthur asked, gazing with awe into the depths of the gleaming gem stone.

"I was walking beside the river today, when a man ran past me on the road, he threw it to the shore and scurried away. I was concerned that the bag might contain more kittens, and so I made my way down onto the mud and retrieved it," she guiltily improvised, not wishing to upset the old man by mentioning her mudlarking activities.

"Did you not shout to him once you realised what the sack contained?" Arthur asked bemused, still staring mesmerized at the gem stone.

"Yes, of course, but he carried on running, then policemen arrived and gave him chase."

Well, at least that part was true enough. She felt a headache begin to pound at her temples as the green light projected by the emerald pierced her eyes and seared her brain. Fleeting images of a man's face once again flashed across her mind, a clearly defined image of a man with soulful brown eyes and wavy hair, which flopped endearingly over one eye. He seemed familiar, yet she had no recollection of him and no name for him.

"We must make enquires and return this beautiful emerald to its rightful owner," Arthur said as he reluctantly pushed the gem back inside the hessian sack.

"Perhaps I should take it to the police, tomorrow morning." Elspeth suggested.

"I am not certain that we can trust any man's honesty with a prize such as this. It must be worth a fortune, especially a stone of this size. There will no doubt be a reward for its return and I think that you should claim it, Bunty, for you have nothing in this world to call your own."

She shook her head. "I would share it with you, Uncle."

"Well, well, we shall see; you are a good girl. I only wish you were truly my niece but either way, reward or no reward, we must do what's right and return it to the legal owner." He patted the sack and held it out to Elspeth. "Place it under your mattress, m'dear, and say nothing about this to anyone. Men and women have had their throats cut for a lesser prize than this."

Elspeth nodded, then hugged him and kissed his wizened cheek before going to do as he advised.

That night her sleep was disturbed by dreams of the same brown haired man whom she'd seen in her vision. He was holding her naked within his arms whilst making love with her. She awoke in the morning sweaty and restless, deeply disturbed by her night of erotic fancies.

It was a full three days before the newspaper billboards carried headlines that screamed of the theft of items stolen from the office of one Professor Beresford, of the London Museum of Antiquities.

Elspeth cleaned herself up as much as she could, but her dress was ragged now and her boots permanently scratched. Her hands were chapped and sore; her nails short and chipped, encrusted with mud from the Thames around and under her cuticles. No amount of washing and scrubbing removed the tell-tale signs of mudlark dirt.

Arthur drew her directions to the museum, and she set off after her meagre breakfast, of the crust taken from what little bread they had left. It was a misty morn, but thankfully, not the all pervasive yellow fog that caused her to cough. Once she arrived at the museum, Elspeth stood outside and admired the stone pillared edifice of the splendid building. She stared in wonder at the impressive architecture before plucking up her courage to enter by the main entrance into a round atrium entrance hall. She walked hesitantly over to the imposing reception where she stood and waited for the uniformed clerk manning the solid mahogany desk to notice her. After waiting for a couple of minutes, she coughed politely. The florid faced man glanced her way, giving an audible huff of distaste as he did so. He drew himself up and peered down his nose at her. "Well, what is it?" he asked her impatiently.

"I should like to see Professor Beresford if you please," she murmured politely.

"Professor Beresford is a very busy man. What is it that you want, woman?" he barked.

Elspeth coloured up and shifted her feet, feeling embarrassed. A group of well-dressed ladies and gentlemen entering the museum glanced her way as the man's voice carried easily across the stone atrium. "I am here because I might have information about the recent robbery."

"Why have you not been to speak with the police on the matter?" the clerk asked suspiciously.

Elspeth hesitated before asking, "Would you prefer that I did so?"

"Yes! Now go on, be off with you!" The man waved his hand under her nose, dismissing her. Disappointed but refusing to be cowed, she turned and walked over to one of the stone benches dotted around the edges of the entrance area. She sat down for a moment to think. A younger non-uniformed man approached her, smiling kindly. "You are allowed inside the museum you know. This is for all manner of personage to visit and see the wonders collected from around the world." Elspeth tilted her head up and gave him a grateful smile. "Thank you, I should particularly like to see the sarcophagus." Where had that come from she wondered? Did she even know what a sarcophagus was? She thought about it and realised that yes, in fact, she did. She knew somehow that it was the coffin of an Egyptian pharaoh. How she knew this, she had no idea, but the fact that she did know, pleased her.

"Sarcophagi, we are lucky to have more than one!" The young man looked pleased by her interest. "Come along with me, and I shall take you to the section of the museum you require." Bemused but too shy to argue, Elspeth followed him meekly. She couldn't resist casting a triumphant look over at the burly fellow who had been so unhelpful to her.

"I am Mr. Harris by the way," the young gentleman told her as he held open yet another of the numerous, heavily polished, dark wooden doors. These were set every few yards or so, thus splitting up the museum collections into various sections of interest.

Elspeth introduced herself. "Miss Brown."

Mr. Harris nodded his acknowledgement of her name as he continued to lead her further into the museum, only speaking when he wished to point out various exhibits as they walked through the building. Elspeth found herself fascinated by the various displays and stopped to gaze inside a glass case of ancient Greek and Roman items of jewellery. They finally arrived at the Egyptian section and Elspeth gasped at the sight of the three large sarcophagi. One lay flat upon the floor open with the bandaged mummy resting inside the coffin. The other two stood upright. One remained closed, while the other stood open but empty.

As she gazed in awe at the ancient burial items, a powerful vision flashed across her mind, an image of a man's face, the same brown haired man from her erotic dream. Then a kaleidoscope formed with that of another man. A tanned, black haired man, his face contorted with rage as rough words and spittle sprayed from his furiously, twisted mouth. Elspeth stumbled. A bright green film washed over the men's faces causing them to distort and waver. Elspeth pressed her hand to her temple, swaying, her mind trying to dispel the frightening imagery that swamped her senses. Her body reacted to the overload of emotion by shutting down. Silently, she crumpled to the floor.

She opened her eyes and closed them again. Where was she? She tried to regain her wits. Images fluttered and hovered at the edge of her consciousness, confusing any rational thought. The museum, that was it, she was in the museum. She reopened her eyes. The face of the man from last night's dream swam before her, hurriedly she closed her eyes again. This was making no sense, no sense at all.

"Elspeth… darling? Come now, wake up, open your eyes," a soft male voice coaxed. Her eyes fluttered open and she stared into a pair of anxious brown eyes.

"Who is Elspeth?" she croaked, confused. The man's forehead furrowed with concern. "You don't know?" he asked, bewildered.

"No. Should I? This seems to me to be a very odd conversation," she replied woozily, shutting her eyes again. Then realising that she lay upon the floor, she attempted to sit and slumped sideways, dizzy. The brown eyed man cast a glance to his side and Mr. Harris appeared in her line of vision. The two men lifted her to her feet but kept their arms about her waist as they guided her forward. "Come, we will take you into the bursars' office where we can talk. Harris, would you be so kind as to fetch this lady a glass of water?"

Mr. Harris cleared his throat. "Professor, she said that her name was Miss Brown."

"Did she indeed? Thank you, Harris, I can take things from here. Would you be a good chap and fetch that water for… er, Miss Brown?"

"Yes, sir." Mr. Harris turned away, and Elspeth found herself led inside a masculine looking, wood panelled office. A high backed gentlemen's chair stood centered in front of a desk. Her host seated her there and stood back to gaze at her with a most peculiar expression on his face, one that Elspeth found difficult to fathom.

"So now that we are alone, would you care to explain where the hell you have been for the past couple of months and why you are calling yourself Miss Brown?"

He leaned toward her and placed his hands on the arm rests either side of her, pushing his face into hers.

Elspeth drew as far back into the chair as she could and her jaw dropped in surprise. He continued, "I have been out of my mind with worry! *How could you do that to me...* Why did you not wait for me when the ship docked?" he chided crossly.

She closed her mouth and swallowed nervously. It was obvious that this angry man recognised her, but she had no idea who he was. Mr. Harris appeared with a glass of water and the professor swung away from Elspeth, presenting his back to her. She drank thirstily and handed the empty glass back to Mr. Harris. He took the glass, glanced at the professor, and gave Elspeth a weak smile before leaving the room, pulling the door shut behind him.

Adam knew he needed to remain calm. Keeping his back to her, he took in several steadying breaths before turning around to face her again. "Perhaps you would explain in your own words what happened?" he asked, this time in a more conciliatory voice. He leant back and rested his haunches on the mahogany wooden desk, crossing his feet at his ankles, his hands gripping the desk edge either side of him. He waited, watching her. She was so thin, dirty and bedraggled. What on earth had happened to her to reduce her to this pitiable state?

She lifted her eyes to his imploringly. "I-I assure you that I do not know you, sir, and yet, you seem to know me?"

Adam frowned. "You do not recognise me, but I am told that you asked to see me at the clerk's desk?" He watched her face for signs of subterfuge, but she exhibited none. If anything, she looked eagerly at him and rummaged in her scruffy reticule for the hessian sack which she held out to him.

"I am a mudlark and the other evening at twilight I was on the shoreline close to the steps when a man ran past being chased by the police. He threw this down onto the river bed almost at my feet. I picked it up and after looking inside I took it home to my uncle and we discussed what the right thing to do would be. We decided that such a theft would soon be reported and when it was, why then, we would be able to return the jewel to its rightful owner. I believe this belongs to your museum, Professor?"

Intrigued, Adam took the hessian bag, pulled it open at the neck and tipped the contents into his hand. As the *Shiromani* stone fell into his palm, it flashed iridescent green, gleaming brightly. It was obviously undamaged and unharmed. He gasped in surprise. "My God, the stone has returned you to me," he whispered with awe.

"I beg your pardon, Professor, but I have returned *it to you*."

Elspeth sounded more like her old self, and Adam lifted his eyes and winked at her. "So you did, my darling!" She looked startled by his endearment.

"You said that you knew me. Perhaps you would tell me where from?" she asked.

He shook his head. "No, not just yet, for I want to hear where you have been all this time. Please, just tell me your story, Elspeth."

"You keep calling me that but I assure you that you are mistaken. My name is Bunty." Hesitant at first, she told him all that she knew of her simple, short tale, staring up at him hopefully when she had finished her woeful saga. Adam was astounded. She had absolutely no recollection of him or her past life, none whatsoever? What to do? He thought rapidly. If he told her the truth, would she stay with him? She couldn't recall her feelings for him, they had been lovers but they were unwed, and so she would feel no obligation to him. Indeed, she might even feel it an imposition to remain with him and think herself a burden to him. She was, in fact, still married to another man. If he explained that to her, would she, having no memory of Henry's cruelty toward her perhaps decide to return to India, back to that bastard who was still her lawful husband? Adam knew with unwavering certainty Elspeth would not stay with him unless she thought them married. The result of her leaving now would be that he would be unable to protect her in her present vulnerable state. Telling an untruth went against Adam's honest nature and ingrained integrity, but in this unprecedented situation, he found himself lying to her for her own good.

"I hope that what I tell you now is a relief to you and not a shock, for I am your husband, and you are my beloved wife, Elspeth. I have been out of my mind with worry ever since you went missing. These past few months have been utter hell for me, and then suddenly, out of the blue, you appear here at the museum, unkempt and dishevelled with no memory of our time together. I am astounded but, Elspeth, darling, I am so very relieved to see you alive and well."

He knelt before her and took her grubby hand in his. Turning it over, he drew her hand to his mouth and pressed his lips against her grimy palm.

"You're my husband, truly?" she whispered, shocked. He smiled reassuringly. "I am indeed. Very shortly I shall take you home; there I will see to it that you get a hot bath and that you are well fed before I tuck you up into a warm bed. Tomorrow, a physician will attend you to give you a thorough medical examination."

Adam's heart ached as he watched as tears slid down her pale cheeks. She nodded her assent silently, giving a small tremulous quirk of her lip; it seemed to Adam she no longer recalled how to make her mouth work to achieve a proper smile. He felt at peace with his decision to deceive her about their marital state. She needed him to care and rescue her, something he would gladly continue doing for the rest of his life. A practical thought occurred to him. His housekeeper, Mrs. Carron, might not think they were married. However, she was fully aware that he'd been looking for

Elspeth. He could easily convince her that they'd been wed aboard ship; after all, a man was unlikely to share every detail of his life with his housekeeper. Adam relaxed; everything would be fine.

"Come, darling, my brougham awaits you, let me take you home and introduce you to our small household." He held out his hand to her. She hesitated, turning wide uncertain eyes upon him.

"I-I have to go home first, to explain what has occurred to Uncle Arthur, because he will worry if I don't return back soon," she protested weakly.

"I will pen him a note and have it delivered," he reassured her. Moving to the desk, he pulled a sheet of paper towards himself and did just that, blotting the letter, folding and sealing it.

"But who will prepare his supper tonight? No, I fear I must go back to settle him. I will come to you tomorrow." She felt strongly that Arthur deserved better than her abandoning him quite so abruptly. Adam blew on the seal to cool his note, pocketed it, and went to her. Slipping his arms under hers, he hauled her slight form easily to her feet. Wrapping his arms about her, he cradled her against his chest. She felt so small and vulnerable. Her frail condition brought his protective nature to the fore.

"You are my wife, Elspeth, and what you need is nourishment, rest, loving and care. You will do as I say and come with me now. This man Arthur managed his life well enough without you, and he will manage again now that you are back in your rightful place. Do not argue with me over this. I will have my way because your welfare is my first concern. I'll have you know that I take my responsibilities extremely seriously. We are leaving now. Come along, my dear."

Elspeth found herself propelled toward the door. She had no choice but to capitulate; she was simply too weak to resist his forcefulness, and besides, the thought of a warm bath, food and clean sheets, was quite irresistible. It was a relief to lean on this man, apparently her husband, and allow him to take care of her. The men who robbed Arthur on that fateful day, must have taken her wedding ring, along with every other valuable item she'd owned except, she recalled, the five pounds she'd stuffed into her skirt pocket; they had missed that.

Mr. Harris was anxiously hovering outside the door and hurried over to them as soon as they appeared. "You have ascertained the lady is well?" he asked.

"Yes, and, in actual fact, I have to explain that this lady is, in fact, my wife. She has been missing for a couple of months, ever since we docked ship. It appears that she has been suffering from some sort of amnesia. I am taking her home with me directly. Do not expect me in tomorrow." Mr. Harris looked amazed, but he promised fervently to deliver the entrusted note to Arthur Brown. He watched as Adam helped Elspeth toward the exit, shaking his head with astonishment.

CHAPTER 6

When the carriage arrived at Helen House, Adam insisted on carrying her to the door. He did, however, agree to set her down on her feet at the door step. Adam unlocked the door and ushered her inside. Elspeth looked about her curiously.

Since her amnesia, she had only seen the interiors of poorer houses, mostly divided up into small rooms for tenants. She was not to know that, having never before set foot on English soil, this was the first full-sized house that she'd ever been inside. Helen House was built of a reddish-brown brick; two square bay windows were set either side of the front door. The hall floor was paved with diamond shaped tiles and the walls half panelled with oak. A tall hat stand for both hats and coats with a base designed to hold umbrellas, stood against one wall.

Adam divested himself of his coat and shouted out for his housekeeper, Mrs. Carron. There was a rapid tattoo of footsteps on the tiled floor and a thin, severe looking woman, with her dark hair fixed into a tight bun atop her head, came scurrying through from the back of the house.

"Lawd bless us, 'tis yourself, sir. I wondered who it could be, coming in at this time of the day!" She addressed Adam, but her sharp-eyed glance took in Elspeth's ragged state. She pursed her lips into a thin line as she awaited an explanation.

"Now, now Mrs. C—calm yourself! I have wonderful news. I have found my wife, Elspeth. It seems that she suffered an attack of amnesia and we need to nurse her back to health. I should like a hot bath drawn for her and some broth prepared, tea, some sandwiches and cake would be much appreciated. I think tea in the parlour, and as soon as possible if you please!"

"*Found your wife,* sir? Why, I didn't know that you had a wife, or that you'd gone and lost her!"

"Now then, Mrs. Carron, I'll have none of that. You know that I have been searching high and low for Elspeth. I am certain that I mentioned that we were married while aboard ship, on our way back from the sub-continent." Adam smiled reassuringly at Elspeth who was looking increasingly pale and anxious.

"No sir, you neglected to mention that you'd wed the girl," Mrs. Carron sounded so hostile that Elspeth turned toward the front door as if wishing to leave. Adam felt his temper rise at his obstreperous housekeeper. He had never known her to be quite so rude before. He reached for Elspeth and drew her to his side, his arm firmly circling her shoulders.

"Sandwiches and tea now, then a bath, and ask Mrs. Donald to make some broth. Put a bed warmer into our bed and see to it immediately, or you may leave my house today and find yourself another position, Mrs. Carron."

The woman flushed unbecomingly at his rebuke. "No need to talk that way, sir. I was surprised that's all." She turned a simpering face to Elspeth. "Welcome home, Mrs. Beresford. Do go into the parlour where the fire is lit. It should be nice and warm in there. I'll get Cook to ready the food while I go and run a bath for you, ma'am." She turned away as Elspeth whispered a soft thank you.

"She doesn't like me," she muttered.

Adam opened a door and stood back so that she could enter the room. “She was surprised, that’s all. She has always been a dour woman, but she’s efficient. If you dislike her, we can find another housekeeper.”

Elspeth looked curiously about the well-appointed parlour; it was warm in the room. A coal fire glowed in the black grate. The walls were covered in dark blue and grey flocked wallpaper while a blue floral Axminster carpet covered the floor. An oak mantel fire surround was dressed with a pair of candle sticks and two Staffordshire flat backs, one modelled as a shepherd and two sheep and the other a shepherdess holding a lamb. A heavily carved, bevelled mirror hung above the fireplace, and in the centre of the mantel, sat a cushioned topped humidor box for cigars.

Two upholstered navy blue fireside chairs were set either side of the hearth and a brown leather Chesterfield sofa was pushed up against the opposite wall. Two mahogany bookcases with cupboards at the base, stood set either side of the chimney breast. Long swathes of navy blue velvet dressed the bay windows and were held back by ornate swag tiebacks. A piano stood in one corner of the bay window at one end of the Chesterfield. To the right of the door was a large jardinière, in which lived an enormous aspidistra. It was a masculine yet cosy room, and to Elspeth’s eye, luxurious. She sank into one of the fireside chairs and laid her head back with a sigh. Her eye lids dropped as she relished the warmth.

“You must feel the cold,” Adam said, watching her relax into the chair’s embrace.

Her eyes flew open, and she stared at him. “What do you mean… does the cold not bother you?”

“You were born and lived in India, Elspeth. The weather here must be a shock to your system. I am used to the chilly weather conditions.”

“I was born in India? How do you know that?”

“Darling, we met aboard the ship when you were travelling to England, you explained everything about your life on the subcontinent.”

"Goodness! Tell me everything I told you. I had no idea where I was from! This explains why everything I do and see seems so utterly alien to me, and here I thought it was all due to my memory loss."

Adam crossed his legs and pondered on how much to tell her. He was anxious about his deception regarding their marriage and worried that her memory might return too quickly, and he would lose her again. Luckily a knock sounded at the door and Mrs. Carron appeared with a tray of tea things. She fussed about, pulling out an occasional table tucked behind the piano to place the tray on. Adam welcomed the interruption, but Elspeth chaffed at the delay in conversation. Finally, with everything arranged to her satisfaction, tea poured and sandwiches offered, Mrs. Carron left the room and closed the door. "So tell me about myself," Elspeth pressed as soon as the housekeeper had gone. Adam took a bite out of his Gentleman's Relish sandwich. Elspeth gritted her teeth in frustration. "Professor, *now* please!" Her plea sounded more like a command to Adam who quirked his eyebrow at her.

"All in good time, you must eat something first," he demanded. She folded her arms and slumped into her chair, a sullen look crossing her face. She had gone for so long with a blank wall of nothingness for a memory. Her start in this world began the day she'd met Arthur. She had no childhood or parental memories, simply a large vacuum in her mind. This seemed to her an unfair ruse of Adam's, and so she sulked, glowering at him from the depths of her arm chair. He watched her with some amusement. "All right then, I shall tell you something that happened aboard the ship and then you must promise to eat while I talk, yes?" She sat up, nodding eagerly, waiting to hear what he had to say.

"I put you over my knee one day and I spanked you, and I assure you that I would have no hesitation in doing so again. So I suggest, dearest, that you hurry up and eat something and rather quickly if I were you!" She gasped, and he chuckled at the look of indignation that spread across her mulish face; however, she did immediately lean across to pick up a triangle of sandwich, biting into it.

A moment later, a look of utter bliss crossed her face. "Mmm, what is this sandwich, it is utterly delicious!" Adam picked up a triangle of the same type and took a bite.

"Roast beef and grated radish, hmm, I detect a sprinkling of salt, very tasty I agree. So while you eat, I shall tell you what I know about you. If at any point your memory returns, please interrupt me." Elspeth nodded her assent and carried on chewing, now that she was eating, she realised just how hungry she actually was.

"So, your name is Elspeth Wooten, and you were the widow of one Captain Henry Wooten of the Royal Lancashire Regiment. I understand that you were based in Bombay. By all accounts, your marriage was not a happy one. However, you were widowed and sailing to England. We met aboard the ship, fell in love, married and then arrived in England. For some reason you disembarked first and took a carriage to visit your deceased husband's solicitor. I know that he organised for his carriage to drop you home here when you left but you never arrived, your trunk was delivered and is still in our bedroom, but you vanished until today."

Elspeth took all this in and asked, "Do I have parents and siblings?"

Adam shook his head. "You told me that your mother died of cholera five years ago and your father of a heart attack more recently. You also told me that you were an only child with no relatives in either India or England."

Elspeth sipped her tea before asking, "And what of my deceased husband's family?"

"I understand your lawyer explained that they had perished in a fire? There was a letter that arrived here for you from him shortly after you went missing. I opened it in your absence. I hope you don't mind? I thought it might help me to find you. I have it here somewhere if you would like to read it sometime. I am sorry it is not a happy tale."

She nodded thoughtfully. "That is fine, I understand. You said we met aboard the ship but not before then?"

"You took my breath away when I first saw you, Elspeth. You quite literally fell into the tea lounge! Truthfully, we were unable to resist one another. The captain married us and we decided to have a church wedding on our return to England."

"I wish I could remember you and our wedding," she said mournfully.

Adam set aside his plate and hunkered down before her, taking her hand in his. "Look upon this as an opportunity. You had a desolate, sad life before I met you, and as I got to know you on our journey aboard ship, I watched you became easier. You became much lighter and more confident. Now all you have is a blank memory, but this could be an opportunity for you to develop your own personality, be the person you want to be and not that woman shaped by her previously wretched experiences." He lifted her hand to his lips and then grazed her cheek with his finger. She found herself moved by his words and nodded agreement, too overcome to speak. He seemed to understand and changed the subject as he returned to his chair.

"After you are settled in bed and asleep, I shall visit the police and notify them of your safe return and that of the emerald. Then I need to see your solicitor and advise him you are returned safely. If there is still time, I shall also visit the Vicar of Saint Helen's to set in motion a day for our wedding, but perhaps I should leave that until tomorrow, after the doctor has visited."

Elspeth covered her mouth, stifling a yawn. Adam stood, holding out his hand. "Come, sleepy-head; let's get you into a warm bath and abed. You look exhausted. Can you walk or shall I carry you?"

"I can walk, thank you," she took a step forward then staggered. Adam immediately swept her up into his embrace and carried her up the stairway, ignoring her feeble protests. He dismissed Mrs. Carron and took Elspeth into his bedroom to undress. He set her on her feet and steadied her until he was certain she could stand without aid.

"Thank you, I shall call for you after I am bathed," she told him.

He shook his head. "There is not an inch of your body that I have not kissed, and I will not leave you as weak as you are to bathe alone."

She stepped back. "I don't remember, and I am embarrassed. Let me see to my needs by myself, please."

He cupped her cheeks with his palms and kissed her forehead. "I am your husband, and I will undress you. I really would rather not spank you while you are so frail, but I will if I must." She flushed and attempted to twist out of his grasp. There was a sudden stinging slap to her buttock and she gasped, frozen with shocked surprise.

"That was just a warning smack, so unless you want a thorough spanking, I suggest that you lift your arms and let me undress you without any fuss." Elspeth shut her eyes, hiding from her own embarrassment and allowed him to remove her clothing. He left her thin shift on and led her to the bathroom where steam rose from the claw footed bath tub. He picked up a glass bottle and poured lavender bath salts into the water. Then he bent and lifted her foot and she placed her hand on his shoulder to balance as he removed each of her black stockings in turn. He noted with pity, the darns and rips in her hosiery. Then he quickly pulled off her shift and lifted her into the heated water. She had no time to complain but simply sighed as she slid into the warmth of the tub. Glancing about, she saw the latest Thomas Crapper fully flushing lavatory. A wash stand stood beside the W.C. one with taps that indicated running water, just as on the bathtub. She had become used to using an outhouse, shared by the occupants of the tenement building. Elspeth happily decided that she could very quickly become accustomed to this form of luxury.

Adam gathered up her clothing and left her to soak. He ran downstairs with her tattered garments and instructed Mrs. Carron to burn the lot. When he returned to the water closet, Elspeth was attempting to wash her hair. Gently he removed the lavender soap from her hand, then massaged the sweet smelling foam into her tresses. She sighed, relaxing against the bath end, moaning with pleasure as his fingers slid over her scalp. Finally, he fetched the water pitcher from the bedroom and filled the jug with fresh water. He rinsed her hair fully three times in order to wash away the suds. He asked her to stand then wrapped her in a large warm towel. Lifting her from the bath, he carried her through to their bedroom where the fire was crackling cheerfully. He dried her, noting that she was far too thin. He could count almost every one of her ribs if he so wished; it cut him to the quick to see her looking so frail. He towel-dried her hair until it was as dry as he could make it. He then handed her a comb. She proficiently untangled the damp mass, divided it, plaited it, tying the ends with pink ribbons that Mrs. Carron had retrieved while unpacking Elspeth's trunk. All of her thin summery clothing hung in the armoire, her lingerie in the chest of drawers. Adam's clothes were packed tighter now that he had to make room for his new wife's clothing.

Adam pulled a warm flannel nightdress over her head, kindly donated by Mrs. Donald. He removed the warming pan from the bed, before lifting her into the pre-warmed sheets and tucking her in cosily. Elspeth sighed. She was clean and warm, snuggled comfortably against plump feather pillows, settled between the crisp white sheets of Adam's large double bed. For the first time since she woke up at Arthur's she felt safe, even loved. Tears of gratitude filled her eyes, and she reached for his hand. "Thank you, Professor."

He bent and kissed her forehead. "I know that you feel I am a stranger to you, but I love you, Elspeth, and I know that you will come to love me once more." She smiled up at him, wanting to tell him all about her strange dreams but felt too tired to talk anymore, her eyes fluttered closed and she slept.

Adam sat beside her on the bed for a few moments, simply

thanking God and his angels that she had been found safe and relatively well. He decided that he would leave his visit to St. Helen's Church until the following day. He wanted to be there when Elspeth awoke. He would explain his deception regarding their marriage to the vicar tomorrow and request him to ask God's forgiveness for his white lie. Sighing, he rose and left the room with one last backward glance at his love, reassuring himself that she was really there, asleep in his bed, safe under his protection at last.

~

ELSPETH AWOKE as Mrs. Carron set a tray down and lit the oil lamp beside the bed. "The professor ordered Cook to make chicken broth to be brought up at six. She said to say that she will coddle you an egg if you would like that after your broth is finished. There is also milk junket here for you."

Elspeth stretched her arms and yawned before answering. "Thank her for me but the broth will suffice." Mrs. Carron stoked the fire and left the room, giving no acknowledgement to Elspeth's, softly called, "thank you."

Lying in bed for a few luxurious moments without moving, simply relishing the comfort of the soft, fresh linen that cradled her, she watched the flames from the rejuvenated fire as the flickering light played across the ceiling. She lay and thought about what Adam had told her earlier on, about her memory loss being an advantage, pointing out that she could become whomsoever she wanted to be. She had no recollection of the troubled life she'd lived before. She was married to a man who purported to love her and his actions, so far, mirrored his words of affection. She was now the mistress of a substantial home. She was cared for and safe at last. There was nothing to stop her exploring her character; she could become any sort of person she wished to be, and Elspeth found that thought exhilarating. She pictured the professor. He was a nice looking man with a kindly face and manner. She liked him, but could she love him? She concluded that she probably could, given some time. She mused on being a wife, and that despite the loss of her memory, she knew in detail what transpired between a man and a woman. She flushed as she recollected her erotic dreams featuring the professor; oh yes she knew fully what to expect.

CHAPTER 7

Adam returned to find Elspeth awake but still lying down, a tray of broth set beside the bed, as yet untouched. He chivvied her to sit up and placed the tray upon her lap, urging her to eat. He was feeling euphoric after his visit to Elspeth's solicitor. When Adam had first visited him after Elspeth's disappearance, Mr. Trubshaw had been shocked to hear that his client had not made it to the professor's house that day she'd first arrived from India. Today, he was extremely relieved to hear of her reappearance, and the two men marvelled about the coincidence of her turning up at Adam's place of work. Indeed, the lawyer had been most concerned about the attack and Elspeth's subsequent memory loss.

It transpired that a letter had arrived only the previous week from Henry Wooten's Commanding Officer and Mr. Trubshaw had been intending to call around to Helen House to discuss it with Adam. He persuaded Mr. Trubshaw to open the letter himself to ascertain the contents before they approached Elspeth. The news it imparted lifted Adam's spirits considerably, and he felt no guilt at his relief when Trubshaw announced Captain Henry Wooten's demise, his death having occurred during a bloody skirmish outside the Khyber Pass.

Adam now watched Elspeth carefully as he spooned broth into her mouth. He felt a strong sense of peace that she should be sitting there in his bed, fully under his protection. At least now with Henry Wooten gone, he could make her his wife in honesty. They could marry legally and she would be his wife in truth, with no shadowed past standing between them. It was up to Adam to care for Elspeth, and he would do so to the very best of his ability. He loved her deeply. He pushed the dilemma of sharing his knowledge of when and where Henry died to the back of his mind. That was a problem to be resolved at a later date. Luckily, Mr. Trubshaw had entrusted him with the letter for Elspeth, and had promised to keep the contents to himself, until such time as Elspeth needed his verification of events.

Elspeth finished her soup. Adam took up the glass that contained the milk dessert and began to feed her that too, spoonful by spoonful. She ate each mouthful obediently, and as he fed her, he stared into her wide green eyes. She didn't break the gaze and studied him back. Each felt a rising desire for the other, but each felt that to acknowledge it would be brazen under the circumstances.

"I shall sleep in another room tonight. I feel it would be for the best, just until the doctor has examined you tomorrow and pronounced you well."

Elspeth nodded her understanding. "Does Mrs. Carron live in?" she asked.

Adam nodded. "Yes, so does Cook and Martha. Mrs. Carron and Mrs. Donald have rooms up in the attic and Martha has a pallet in the scullery."

"Oh, poor Martha, she ought to have a room at the very least!" Elspeth chided him.

Adam looked somewhat abashed at her criticism for he hadn't given the matter much thought before. "Well, as mistress of the house you can attend to that problem when you have your strength back, but for now, I want you to rest, eat and regain your health."

He ran his hand over her hair and fingered a lock that trailed over her shoulder. It gleamed like burnished copper in the lamp light.

"Professor?"

"Hmm?"

"Do you have any family?" she asked curiously.

"I do; an older brother, James and a younger sister Amanda. She is still under age and lives with James and his wife, Felicity. James has two children, George and Madeline, known as Maddie to family. They are nine and six. My brother inherited my father's estate as the eldest son."

"Your parents are deceased then?" Elspeth watched as Adam's face clouded over.

He nodded an affirmative. "Sadly yes, they were killed in a train derailment in 1865 near Staplehurst, in Kent."

Elspeth sucked in her breath and placed her hand over his, giving a squeeze. He held onto her, brushing his thumb backward and forward over the top of her hand. "That is dreadful, whatever happened?"

He gave a grim smile. "They'd been to Paris for a few days, in order to celebrate their pearl wedding anniversary and were journeying home when disaster struck. Workmen were replacing new track and they misunderstood the time-table for the Folkestone train. The train times varied with the arrival of the passenger ferry from France. The train's departure time was dependent upon the tides for the ferry landings and they varied from day to day. The workmen had removed the old track from the bridge that crossed the river at Staplehurst, just beyond Headcorn Station. The train derailed, plunging the carriages into the river below. Ten people died, including both my parents, and forty-three people were seriously injured that day."

He stopped and Elspeth held out her arms. He leaned forward into her embrace, and they sat quietly that way for some moments. "Charles Dickens, the famous author was aboard the same train, but he was travelling in one of the only coaches not derailed.

Unfortunately, it was due to that disaster that the public discovered he had a mistress, Ellen Ternan. She and her mother Frances were travelling in the carriage with Dickens. By all accounts after the accident, the great man was quite the hero of the day. He ran to help the injured, pulling many to safety before help arrived. When the injured passengers had all been rescued, he ran back to collect his manuscript, *Our Mutual Friend,* which he had left behind inside the train carriage. The railway workers shouted warnings for him to leave it because the carriage was so precariously balanced, but he wouldn't heed them and fetched it regardless."

There was complete silence as Elspeth digested the horror of Adam's tale, and he brooded on the memory of the loss of his parents. There was a tap at the door and Mrs. Carron entered. "Oh, I didn't realise that you had returned, sir. Shall you be a wanting your supper now?" she asked as she collected Elspeth's supper tray.

"Yes, I shall be down shortly, thank you," he replied. "Oh, and, Mrs. Carron, can you ensure that there are sheets on the spare bed, I shall sleep in there tonight."

"Very good, Professor."

Elspeth waited until the woman had left the room before turning to Adam. "You can sleep in here with me, I really don't mind."

His gaze riveted on her. "I thought you might prefer me to sleep separately, especially since you cannot remember what we had and were to one another."

Elspeth plucked at the sheet and began pleating the edges between her fingers. "I've had some very… um… personal dreams about you, even before I recognised you at the museum."

"Dreams?" he repeated. She blushed and nodded, not quite meeting his eye.

"I see… so what are you saying—"

"That you don't have to sleep elsewhere. I realise because of my dreams that we had a-a, passionate marriage."

"Would you prefer me to stay here with you tonight?" he asked as he lifted her chin with his finger so that she had no choice but to look him in the eye.

She stared back at him, wide-eyed but not knowing how to answer him. If she answered "yes," would he see her as wanton? If she answered "no," would his feelings be injured?

Adam had no control over his manhood's lustful reaction to her soft compliant words. He found himself embarrassingly and uncomfortably hard. He shifted his seat to accommodate his swelling groin. "Darling, believe me, there is no right or wrong answer here. I will stay or go, just as you wish and make no judgment either way. Decide what it is that *you* want me to do." He waited patiently, his eyes held hers. Her softly murmured, "stay," had his cock rampant. He leant forward, kissed her forehead then leapt to his feet and crossed the room. Elspeth watched with surprise as he yanked open the door and yelled to Mrs. Carron, telling her there had been a change of plan, and he was sleeping in his own room with his wife. She heard the housekeeper's acknowledgement float back before Adam shut the door.

"Just so you understand, I shall not be claiming any conjugal rights from you tonight, Elspeth. I wouldn't expect that of you until a doctor has given you a thorough medical examination, and besides, you need your rest." Her gaze lowered to his groin where the strain of material stretched over his quite obvious arousal.

"If you say so," she answered, her voice sounding throatily knowing.

His eyebrow lifted. "Why, you little hussy, your memory cannot be that impaired! She had the grace to blush and lowered her head, Adam chuckled delightedly. "Have no fear, for as soon as the doctor pronounces you fit for purpose, you will be reliving your erotic dreams in the flesh. Right now though, I intend to eat my supper downstairs, but I want you to stay put in bed, nice and warm and relaxed. Would you like anything sent up, something to eat or drink perhaps?"

Elspeth cocked her head and considered. "Some more tea would be nice, and mayhap I could borrow a book to read?"

Adam placed a perfunctory kiss on her forehead. "I will have tea sent up. Have you read the book, *Jane Eyre?*"

Elspeth shook her head. "I have no recollection of it if I have."

"It's written by a woman called Charlotte Bronte; originally she used the pseudonym name, Currer Bell, which is on the title copy of my mother's book. I think you will enjoy the tale and empathise with the heroine, especially after your experiences to date. Although, I warn you that *Jane Eyre's* considered quite a controversial tale." Adam was as good as his word and left the bedroom, returning with the novel. Elspeth reached for it gratefully. It would be a treat to simply lie abed and read.

When he entered his bed chamber later on that evening, he was surprised to find Elspeth still awake. She looked up as he entered the room. "I have to tell you, Professor, that I absolutely adore this story, even though it is so very sad when Helen dies."

"Was I right to think that you might empathise with Jane and Helen, after your own dreadful experiences?"

She nodded. "Yes, you were right, Professor, I do."

"Elspeth, please try to stop calling me Professor. My name is Adam."

She smiled ruefully. "I'm sorry, Prof… I mean, Adam."

He pulled off his cravat and unbuttoned his cufflinks. "It's late, put the book away and lie down."

"I just want to finish this chapter, and then I shall sleep."

Adam walked over to her bedside and plucked the book from her hands. Closing it, he set it down beside the bed. "Do you need the lavatory?" he asked.

She glared at him mulishly. "I said that I wanted to read to the end of the chapter," she huffed belligerently, crossing her arms.

He tapped the end of her nose. "I am your husband, and since I am responsible for your welfare, I say it is way past your bed time. Now, I shall ask you once more, do you need the water closet?"

Elspeth stuck out her tongue. Adam stared at her with some consternation. He was surprised by her little act of defiance but also amused by her childish behaviour. It showed a measure of returning confidence, and he was pleased that she felt able to behave in such a relaxed informal way around him. He chuckled and moved to sit beside her on the bed.

"Come now, sweetheart, you need a good night's sleep if the doctor is to pronounce you free from bed rest tomorrow." Elspeth sighed resignedly, but slipped obediently down against the pillows. He kissed her lips and turned back into the room, continuing to disrobe. It did not escape his notice that Elspeth watched him, although whenever he glanced her way, she quickly pretended to be dozing and snapped her eyes shut, but he knew the little minx was spying upon him as he undressed. Every time he turned to look at her, she hurriedly closed her eyes again. Adam found her action rather arousing and his shaft eagerly responded by leaping to its fully extended length. He went into the privacy of the water closet and dealt quickly with his aching member, a few hard pumps of his fist, and it was all over. He cleaned himself up, washed and used tooth powder to clean his teeth, before joining Elspeth in their bed.

However, his ministrations failed to curb his body's reaction when holding her as she snuggled close against his side. She lay her head into the crook of his shoulder with a tired sigh then promptly fell asleep. She slept peacefully through the night. Meanwhile, Adam lay on his back with his darling clutched tenderly to him, marvelling that he had her back with him again. He remained wide awake, plagued by an aching cockstand that refused to deflate.

CHAPTER 8

The following day, Elspeth awoke alone in the bed. She swept her palm over where Adam had slept, and finding the sheets were cold, surmised that he had been gone for some time. There was a tap at the door, and a young rosy cheeked maid appeared carrying a breakfast tray. “Morning, ma’am. Mrs. Donald asked me to assure you that you only have to ask if there is anything you would especially like to eat. The master told me to tell you that he’d be back fairly soon with the doctor but to stay put in bed until after the doctor has visited. Shall I stir up the fire a bit?”

Elspeth picked up her tea and took a sip before answering. “Yes, please, and what is your name?”

“Martha, ma’am, I’m the maid.” She bobbed her head and smiled at Elspeth.

“Do you live in the house, Martha?” Elspeth asked as she opened up her coddled egg.

“Aye, ma’am, I have a pallet in the kitchen scullery. When the doctor’s been and gone, I’ll come back and help you dress.” She threw coal on the fire and turned toward the door.

“Wait!” Elspeth called. So this was the maid with no room of her own.

"Yes'm?"

"I shall be looking at the servant's quarters later today. Please be so good as to inform Mrs. Carron to prepare for my inspection. I intend that you shall have a bedroom of your own, Martha. I will not have a maid sleeping in the scullery."

Martha looked awe struck. "Lawd bless you, ma'am, I'm used to it, and it be perfectly natural for the maid to sleep on a pull down pallet. Don't you fret none about me, missus."

"No, Martha, no maid of mine shall live in, without a room to call her own. I have been shown kindness in my own hour of need, and I intend nothing less toward you."

Martha straightened up, still clutching the poker from the fire. She stared at Elspeth, as if seeing her for the first time. "I-I don't know what to say to you, ma'am, other than to give you my thanks and to say that you shall have my undivided loyalty, whether or not Mrs. Carron allows this idea." She replaced the poker and fled, leaving Elspeth even more determined that Mrs. Sourpuss Carron should have no say in the matter at all. She was determined to be the person whom she wanted to be, just as Adam had suggested. Her appetite seemed to have returned and she ate a hearty breakfast before darting into the water closet to wash, before the doctor arrived.

The doctor pronounced Elspeth both slightly undernourished and underweight, but otherwise he said she seemed to be remarkably well. Adam saw the man out and then made his way over to the vicarage, where he was ushered into the vicar's study. By the time he left, he had confessed all to the vicar who strongly counselled him to tell Elspeth the whole truth about Henry before their wedding day.

Meanwhile, Martha helped Elspeth to dress. They selected the warmest gown that she owned. Although the dress was made of the thickest taffeta, this would be no match against the chill of an English winter. They decided to leave off her crinolette since Elspeth had no plans to leave the house that day. It was smaller, this fashionable replacement for the crinoline yet it still hampered movement through doorways and was a hazard around furniture. Unfortunately, Elspeth only owned two very thin silk petticoats and she wore both for warmth.

Martha offered to go and shop for the warmest shawl that she could find, and Elspeth gratefully agreed. Elspeth then wrapped herself in two of her thin silky shawls. Obviously, they had been brought over when she travelled from India, where she supposed the weather was very much warmer. She quickly descended to the warmth of the parlour and summoned Mrs. Carron.

WHEN ADAM RETURNED HOME, he was astounded by the caterwauling coming from inside the parlour. The door of the room suddenly flew open, and Mrs. Carron barrelled into the passage. Her face was puce and her mouth set in angry lines. She came to a halt when she saw him and cried, "Oh, Professor, I am pleased to see you. Your wife seems to be coming completely unhinged! Please inform her that it is not her role to usurp my position as housekeeper and I…"

"Yes, thank you, Mrs. Carron, you are free to carry on with your duties. I shall speak with my wife." He deliberately interrupted her flow of complaint.

Unfortunately, Elspeth chose that moment to appear in the hallway behind the housekeeper and took umbrage with him. "Don't you dare take that horrible woman's part, I am your wife and the mistress of this house! I will *not* be told how to manage servants living under our protection!" She stamped her foot to emphasise her point, obviously incensed by his conciliatory manner toward Mrs. Carron. Adam understood her ire but was utterly flummoxed by her tone of voice. This was not his gentle Elspeth's usual intonation. As much as he abhorred her stridency,

Adam refused to discuss Elspeth's shortcomings in front of his housekeeper.

Brusquely dismissing Mrs. Carron, he grasped Elspeth's elbow and guided her firmly inside the parlour where he shut the door and spun Elspeth about to face him. "Now what is all this about?" he asked in a reasonable yet firm voice.

Elspeth stalked over to the fire and stood with her back to it, soaking up the heat. "You pointed out to me yesterday that the one benefit of losing my memory was that I could develop my own character and become whomsoever I wanted. I have given your advice a great deal of thought and decided that you are right."

Adam wandered over to the nearest fireside chair and sat down. He crossed his legs and watched her, feeling somewhat bemused. "I am glad you have made that decision, but what has that to do with this rumpus with Mrs. Carron?"

"I want Martha to have her own bedroom, and I want to use one of the sitting rooms in the attic for her. The housekeeper and cook each have their own bedroom and a sitting room each. My suggestion is that they all share a parlour and each woman would have a bedroom. Mrs. Carron told me it wasn't to be borne, and I disagreed with her and gave her notice. She had the temerity to tell me that you hired her, so only you could fire her. It was at that point in the conversation that you arrived. I expect you to back me up. You must tell her to pack her things and go!" She tapped her foot again with agitation.

"Hmm, well, I think it is a little early for you to be making such drastic changes to our household. After all, you only arrived yesterday! I suggest that we let things settle down a little and allow Mrs. Carron to get used to having a mistress about the house before you go about rocking the boat."

Elspeth spun around furiously. "What? You would undermine my authority as your wife?" Adam groaned inwardly. How could he now tell her that they were unmarried? He felt it would be a huge mistake to tell her while she was so obviously enjoying having a home to run and organise. Besides, he only had to wait until Saturday and then she would be his wife in truth. He looked up into her angry face and decided that at the very least she needed to calm down.

"Sit down and listen to me!" he ordered, pointing at the other fireside chair. She flung herself down into the chair opposite him with an audible huff. "I tell you now that I shall not tolerate temper tantrums, Elspeth, or a lack of respect toward me. I understand that you do not recall our wedding service aboard ship, and that is why I have arranged for another in church on Saturday, when we will make our promises to one another and you, my dear, will promise to obey your husband. I assure you that disobedience and outbursts of childish temper will rapidly result in a trip across my knee resulting in a very sore posterior for you. Are we clear so far?"

Elspeth scowled. "Nothing you say is making any sense! You told me yourself to make the best of my situation and to develop my own personality, yet here you are threatening me for doing that very thing!"

Adam pondered for a moment. "Look, my dear, all I ask is that you consult with me first before attempting to make any drastic changes to our household." He saw her mouth open ready to give debate and held up his hand to forestall her. "We will find space for Martha in due course, and you may inform her of that fact, but let us deal with one issue at a time. The most important objective for me at the moment is to provide you with warm clothing. I can see the goose bumps standing out on your arms from over here." She appeared mollified by his concern and nodded her acquiescence. He smiled at her.

"Believe me, becoming strident and bold will not lead to marital harmony between us, Elspeth. I don't propose to be a hen-pecked husband. I will be head of my household and the arbiter of my wife's behaviour." Before Elspeth could reply, there was a knock at the door and Mrs. Carron was back. "There's a gentleman to see you, Professor, he says he knows the mistress, a Mr. Brown?"

"Uncle Arthur!" Elspeth exclaimed, jumping to her feet, delighted.

"Show him in, Mrs. Carron and fetch a pot of coffee and chocolate, also some of Cook's delicious seed cake," Adam instructed.

"I will see what Cook has made, sir." The housekeeper disappeared, returning a moment later with Arthur Brown. She ushered him into the parlour. Elspeth went straight to him, throwing her arms about the frail old gentleman.

Arthur patted her back then stepped aside, holding her at arm's length to gaze at her. "How beautiful you look returned to your proper setting." He turned to the professor and held out his hand. "Arthur Brown, at your service, sir, I am sorry for the distress your wife's disappearance must have caused you. I assure you that I tried to find out where your wife rightly belonged. A friend, Doctor Philpot, kindly paid for a two week advert to be placed in a local and a national newspaper about the disappearance of Bunty, but nobody responded. It was most kind of you to send the note last evening, I should have been extremely anxious about her otherwise."

Adam shook the elderly gentleman's proffered hand and gestured him to one of the fire side chairs. "I am indebted to you, Mr. Brown, for taking such good care of my wife."

Arthur seated himself opposite Elspeth. "I tried my best, but in all truth, she mostly took care of me, Professor Beresford. I shall miss her dreadfully, even though I am, of course, delighted that she is reunited with her husband." He smiled at Elspeth and she smiled back.

"How is Lucky, does he miss me?"

"He slept with me last night but kept wandering into the bedroom to look for you. Would you like me to carry him around here for you one day next week?"

"Lucky?" Adam queried.

Elspeth turned to him brightly. "We rescued a kitten; he is my devoted friend. I named him Lucky Chance, for obvious reasons."

She spun back to speak again with Arthur. "No, please don't carry him here, he might break free and become lost. I shall collect him when I have found a box for him to travel in."

Adam frowned at this exchange. "No, I will collect him. You are not to wander the streets alone." There was an interruption at this point as Mrs. Carron brought in the tray and set it down, pouring out coffee for both gentleman and a cup of chocolate for Elspeth. The seed cake was cut and distributed and then Mrs. Carron left them.

"We are to re-enact our vows on Saturday at eleven o'clock, please join us, I am quite sure Elspeth would like you to walk her down the aisle." Adam sent Elspeth a questioning glance and she nodded enthusiastically.

"Oh yes, please, would you do that for me, Uncle Arthur?"

Arthur looked delighted but bashful at the suggestion. "I should be delighted by the honour, but do you think you should still be calling me uncle now that you are restored as Elspeth?"

She looked crestfallen by his suggestion. "I am sorry. If you would rather I didn't, then, of course—"

"No, no!" Arthur interrupted, "I truly adore that you call me uncle."

Elspeth scrambled to her feet and crossed over to the old gentleman, planting a kiss on his wizened cheek. "I have no family except you and the professor so I really want to remain as your niece and keep you as my uncle. Please, would you be so kind as to give me away when I marry the professor on Saturday?"

"I have said that I would be honoured to do so, and I should also be delighted to remain as your Uncle Arthur. Thank you, child."

Adam watched indulgently. He was determined that Elspeth stop calling him "the professor." Each and every time she did so, it reminded him that, to her, he was virtually a stranger. He wanted to reunite with her, to remind her of their love for one another. It was obvious to him that she felt more at ease with this elderly man, this *Uncle Arthur,* a man who was, in actual fact, a stranger to her.

The only way Adam could see them reconnecting again as a couple was to find that physical attraction that they had for one another whilst aboard ship. He determined that he would make love to her that night to awaken her passions, and hopefully, her heart.

After Arthur had left, they discussed how best they might help him. Elspeth suggested finding Scrounger and offering the lad payment to help Arthur, but Adam was loath to do that, more than loathe, in fact. He was alarmed by Elspeth's tales of mudlarking and roaming the rougher areas of London with nought but a street lad. His own ideas for helping Arthur were far more practical. He would give him the reward money for the *Shiromani* stone's recovery. He thought to offer the cartographer a position at the museum. He explained to Elspeth that they held hundreds of ancient maps, some in a dreadful state of repair, some simply faded, all in need of restoration and cataloguing. Adam thought that Arthur might be the perfect man to manage the two-person team put in charge of the precious charts. The two young men working on restoration were skilled at document repair but not particularly knowledgeable about ancient maps, they'd proved disorganised and slow. Adam thought perhaps Arthur might manage the department since he understood and respected cartography.

Elspeth clapped her hands excitedly. "You should have told him of your plans while he was here. Why did you wait until he'd gone before suggesting this?"

Adam frowned. "Because I wanted to discuss the idea with my wife first, that is why."

"Oh, I see. Well, I think perhaps you were being pompous and rather mean in not mentioning this until now. He seemed so frail and despondent when he left here, and you could have given him some hope for the future and allayed his fears!" Her voice had grown more strident as she spoke, and Adam stared at her. She lifted her chin mulishly and glared back at him.

He wondered what had happened to turn his sweet girl into this rather churlish woman. "I want you to go upstairs to our bedroom and await me there. I shall be up directly." He pointed at the door. Elspeth looked puzzled.

"Why?" she queried.

"Because, my dear, that is the third time today that you have spoken to me in such a rude and disrespectful manner, and I will not tolerate it." His voice dropped an octave. "We shall continue our *discussion* in the privacy of our room. Now go before I forget propriety and deal with you right here and now in the parlour!"

Elspeth harrumphed, but made her way out of the room and up the stairs as he'd ordered. She was livid, stomping hard on each and every step as she ascended. She also objected to Adam's commanding tone. He was the one who had encouraged her to become whomsoever she wished, and now that she was trying to be the strong and capable woman whom she had chosen to be, he objected! When she reached their bedroom, she slammed the door shut behind her so hard that even the front door below vibrated with the impact.

Adam left her alone upstairs to stew for a while. He was not impressed with the obvious signs of temper she'd portrayed. He calmed himself before going to join her in the bedchamber. When he entered, she was standing by the window, staring down into the street.

"Would you care to explain your current mood?" he asked.

She turned to face him, her arms wrapped tight around herself. She was feeling the chill air despite the fire and watched the street, anxious for Martha's return with a warm shawl in which to wrap herself. "You told me to become whomsoever I wished, and so I am trying to be a strong and capable woman."

Adam sighed and went to her, drawing her into his arms. "My dear girl, you *are* a strong and capable woman! Look at what you have endured so far, even removing that part of your life that you have forgotten. You have survived poverty and mudlarking, cared for Arthur and yourself really quite admirably since this English way of life was utterly new to you. Elspeth, you are now restored to *me,* and as your husband, it is *my responsibility* to take care of *you.* Because of his kindness to you, I shall extend my consideration to Arthur. However, I will not tolerate your rudeness and lack of manners toward me. I intend to make certain that such behaviour is not readily repeated. Wait here and do not attempt to leave this room," he cautioned. Then he disappeared out of the room altogether leaving Elspeth with a worrying sense of foreboding.

She decided that it would be in her best interests to exit the room and so, without any second thought, she did. As she scuttled speedily down the stairs, she heard Adam utter a loud oath. Then with horror, she realised that he too was thundering down the staircase in hot pursuit. She flung herself into the dining room opposite the parlour and slammed the door. Frantically spinning about, she looked for something, anything, with which to bar the door. She focused quickly upon a china cabinet. Putting her shoulder to one end of the heavy piece of furniture, she attempted to shift it across the floor to the doorway, but it was too heavy and wouldn't budge. Giving the cupboard one last frantic heave, she felt it shift slightly. She pushed again and this time, it shuddered violently.

The sound of tinkling glass inside the cupboard escalated into the noise of china falling and smashing. The continual clatter and clinking of breakages filled the room as the domino effect of broken porcelain echoed ominously. Elspeth covered her mouth with both hands in horror. She was alerted by the creaking of the door to Adam's arrival. She turned and watched round eyed as the dining room door swung inward and Adam stepped into the room. He didn't look very happy. In fact, his face was extremely drawn; he looked rather vexed, his mouth set into a thin line of disapproval. His eyes were what scared Elspeth the most, because the only way she could describe them was boiling; he was quite obviously angry.

He closed the door behind him with a click. Elspeth edged back and away from him, burbling apologies for the damaged china as she felt her way along the edge of the oval dining table. She watched as he pulled out one of the heavy, velvet covered chairs and set it in the open area at his end of the room. "Come here," he growled. Elspeth remembered that Adam had stated he'd spanked her once aboard ship, but she had no recollection of the event and was fearful of his obvious intention do so now. Elspeth had witnessed many women in the poorer areas of the city being beaten by their men folk, and she had no desire to be treated as barbarically as they, so she shook her head at him negatively and continued to move backward until she stood at the opposite end of the table to him.

Adam stood deceptively still for so long that she was thrown off guard. When he lunged, charging toward her, there was a silly but desperate chase around and around the table. Elspeth's skirts hampered her stride, and as she stumbled, she felt her upper arm grasped firmly from behind in a relentless grip.

Having caught her, he marched her to the chair and seated himself, pulling her unceremoniously down across his lap. She wished she had a bustle to hamper his actions, but alas, she didn't own one. She felt him attempt to lift her thin gown and petticoats and tried to prevent him by grabbing onto her skirts. He was much too determined and ripped the material from her palm, keeping her hand and the cloth grasped securely in his.

"No, Professor, I shall be even colder than I am now!" she wailed.

"Then allow me to warm you up, you defiant little waif!" She felt his hand undo her drawers with one tug; her bottom felt the chill of the unheated room.

"No please!" she entreated. Then she gasped, and her breath caught in her throat as the first slap landed on her shrinking flesh, another and another until she lost count of his smacks and a furnace built in her nether regions; the cold room was soon forgotten.

He had her hands and skirt with her petticoats all wrapped up and pinned in his large hand. She wriggled and flapped about like a newly landed fish unable to make any headway or evade his punishing palm. Gasping, she tried to make sense of the stinging pain, but he was not spanking in any form of rhythm or pattern that might have helped her to cope with the searing punishment.

No, it was obvious to her that he was totally intent on her chastisement. Elspeth felt something building inside her as the scalding pain rained down upon her tender buttocks and upper thighs. She opened her mouth and a loud and incoherent wail echoed about the room. "Oh good, I am glad to hear that I am making some impression on you! You deserve this and more, but a spanking will suffice for now, just to show you that I will not tolerate the level of disrespect, disobedience and defiance that you have displayed this day. I shall deal with the destruction of the china later on." His spanks increased, and Elspeth squealed with the pain and frustration of being entrapped and spanked like a wilful child. She kicked her legs and shifted to and fro in an attempt to free herself, and then she lunged for his calf and bit him.

"Ouch, *Bandar*, still defiant I see... Well, I can soon put an end to that!" Adam snarled, furious now. He tipped her up higher, lifted his knee then began to spank her much harder, levelling spanks up and down thighs and legs. Elspeth registered that he'd called her a monkey in Hindi, and then all she could focus on was the fact that her thighs and legs felt as though they were being whipped with a red hot coal shovel. At first she yelled blue murder, but then she found that she could no longer keep up her howling due to her nose running and her tears choking her throat, so she simply sobbed. Her weeping developed into garbled apologies, and then the gradual realisation that perhaps Adam was justified in chastising her had the salient effect of quieting her, and she lay passively across his lap accepting his physical rebuke.

Elspeth now wept with genuine remorse, so it took her a moment or two to realise that the spanking had finished and Adam was, in fact, making soothing, shushing noises and rubbing her bottom in what she supposed he thought was a kindly manner, but she'd really rather he didn't because the stinging was almost unbearable. However, she refrained from telling him so, just in case he continued to spank her for being disrespectful. Finally, he upended her into his arms and, highly embarrassed, she hid her face in his shoulder. She wasn't sure that she would ever be able to look him in the eye again.

"Up with you, my little mudlark waif!" Adam shifted her off his knee. He kissed her forehead and led her to the edge of the room where the two walls joined. "Put your nose in that corner. I want you to think about how you might have achieved your aims today without such rude defiance toward me, and while you are ruminating, I shall check on the damage you've wrought in the china cabinet." Elspeth stood docilely in place where Adam positioned her. She actually did feel very ashamed by her volatile behaviour and fully intended to make him a pretty apology.

"Bloody hell!" she heard Adam gasp. Elspeth spun around at the sound of more splintering glass and china. Adam had pulled the doors open and broken porcelain spilled out in shards onto the floor.

"I'm so sorry, was anything very precious?" she asked anxiously. There was a small silence.

"My mother's tea service, my brother let me take it since he inherited everything else," he answered dolefully.

"I feel terrible; how can I repay you, Professor?" Elspeth did indeed feel awful and full of guilt.

He glanced over at her. "Make no mistake, Elspeth, I shall exact recompense later today, and any guilt you are currently feeling will be exonerated by the time I have finished with you. Now put your nose back into that corner and think on that!"

There was a sudden slam of a door and shrill voices raised in anger; they seemed to be just outside in the hallway. Adam cast an eye over his wife to check her skirts were down and that she was decently covered before he opened the door into the hall. "Stay precisely where you are," he instructed, leaving the room, pulling the door tightly shut behind him.

Elspeth sighed and relaxed, some of the tension left her body as she took the opportunity to cup her sore behind, rubbing and massaging her stinging rump. She felt contrite but strangely calm now that Adam had left her alone to ponder on her behaviour. She flushed with shame over the way she had treated the kind professor. He had been nothing but considerate toward her and she had repaid him by breaking his dead parents' mementos. She groaned and decided that she had deserved every smack he had given her, but what had he told her before departing? The spanking hadn't been given for the smashed china; he'd then promised to take her to task for that poor choice of action later in the day. Elspeth groaned, did he mean another spanking perhaps? She thought about the man whom she now called husband. He was an attractive fellow to be sure, strong and athletic despite his dusty archaic profession. Elspeth squirmed as she ran her hands over her own heated flesh. A much unexpected and newfound sensation was awakening between her thighs, it felt rather... pleasant. The more she thought about being spanked by the man she was to call husband, the more exquisite this sensation became. Elspeth rubbed her thighs together, recalling how he had tugged her across his lap and felt the strangest urge to touch herself. She glanced over her shoulder, the door was still shut and she could hear loud arguing. She edged her fingers toward the joining of her legs and thighs, a sudden loud howl of outrage from outside caused her to jump guiltily. Immediately, she dropped her arms back down to her side.

CHAPTER 9

"Give me that!"

Out in the hall, Mrs. Carron and Martha appeared to be engaged in a tug of war with what Adam perceived to be a woman's shawl. "Ladies, stop this at once and explain to me the meaning of this rumpus?" Adam boomed. Really, this female propensity for arguing was becoming intolerable. In the years he had moved into Helen House, his household had been a peaceful retreat. One where the daily rhythms of life ran serenely day in day out without change, but ever since Elspeth had been restored to him, his household had been fraught with angst, and he was damned if he would tolerate it for one moment longer.

Mrs. Carron turned to him indignantly. "The maid has returned with madam's shawl but she won't relinquish it to me so that I can take it to your wife, Professor, sir!"

"The mistress asked me to buy a warm shawl and bring it directly to her, and that's what I intend to do, an' anyways, I has a message for madam, from the dressmakers!" Martha screeched indignantly.

Adam plucked the shawl from Martha's grasp. "I shall present this to my wife myself, thank you, Martha." He smiled at the maid and turned again to address the housekeeper. "Mrs. Carron, I have decided that Martha is to be promoted to my wife's personal maid. You will need to relinquish your parlour upstairs, and both of you will share her parlour with Cook from this point forward. I shall speak with Cook myself about the new arrangement. I favour the hiring of a maid of all work, one who will preferably live out. Please see to that hiring as soon as possible, Mrs. Carron. Martha, I assume this new arrangement is agreeable to you?"

Martha beamed at him. "Oh yes, sir, very agreeable!" She cast the housekeeper a triumphant smirk.

"Very good, then you may begin to serve lunch after you clear up some broken china in the dining room. My wife has had an accident in there and there are breakages. I beg that you will both be careful not to cut yourselves. Martha, I wish you to continue with your usual chores until such time as a new maid is appointed."

Martha bobbed a curtsy. "Of course, sir, Oh, and, sir? *Thank you*, sir!"

Adam liked the girl and agreed with Elspeth that she deserved better treatment. He just objected to the aggressive way Elspeth had gone about attempting to persuade him. "You can move into your new room as soon as possible. Mrs. Carron, you will assist Martha in this task." The housekeeper appeared to be grinding her teeth; she only just managed to give Adam an affirmative nod. He dismissed the pair, calling after Martha, "One moment, you mentioned that the dressmaker sent a message for my wife?"

She turned back to speak with him. "Yes sir, Mrs. Heally said that she could call after luncheon today to take madam's measurements. She also said that she has a couple of warm day dresses made up from a previously cancelled order. They can be adjusted to fit madam, just as a temporary measure, until her own clothing is made." Adam made an approving sound in his throat and waved the maid away back to the kitchen.

Adam returned to the dining room stealthily and caught the movement of Elspeth removing her hands from her backside. She had quite obviously been soothing her chastened flesh. He smiled, shaking his head. He was amused rather than annoyed with her. Adam moved to stand behind her and draped the warm, woollen shawl about her shoulders. "From Martha. Apparently, the dress-maker is attending us after lunch to take your measurements. She will make you a complete new wardrobe, and she has some all ready made up dresses from a cancelled order, which may suffice in the meantime."

"Thank you, Professor," Elspeth whispered.

"The vicar is coming over for tea later this afternoon. He wishes to speak with you before we take our wedding vows on Saturday. Martha is to become your personal maid, and I have ordered Mrs. Carron to make the arrangements up in the servant quarters so that Martha has her own room. You may inspect the changes when they have sorted the bedrooms to their satisfaction. In future, my dear, I insist that you discuss these things rationally with me before going off at half-cock like you did today. Am I quite clear?"

"Yes, sir," she mumbled, ashamed. Adam turned her to face him, but she kept her eyes fixed on his waistcoat.

"Look at me." He tilted her chin up to meet his gaze. "Do you have something you wish to say?"

Elspeth met his warm brown eyes; he no longer looked annoyed. In fact, she was surprised to see he looked slightly amused. "I am very sorry for my appalling behaviour. I am mortified that I broke your parents' precious china. I feel just terrible about that, although it wasn't a deliberate act. I do humbly apologise. I feel awfully guilty."

He gave a wry grin. "Apology readily accepted, but there is no need to be concerned over guilt. I fully intend to take care of that later on. Follow me into the parlour for we need to let the servants in here to clear up the mess and light the fire, so that the room is warmed before luncheon."

The rest of that day passed in a haze of endeavour, and by evening, Elspeth was absolutely drained. At least she felt warmer now she was garbed in a fashionable winter dress of bombazine. Another couple of gowns made from the same material of silk and wool, plus a sumptuous green velvet ensemble, all hung in her wardrobe. Her chest of drawers brimmed with new underclothes, and she was now the proud owner of the latest bustle, two new cloaks, one fur trimmed and the other plain. The vicar had seemed happy with her answers to his interview with her and had patted her hand before departing, praying over them both and asking God to bless their upcoming union. At last they were alone, and Elspeth gave a huge sigh of relief as she sank into her fireside chair. How quickly one had become her chair and the other, the professor's.

"There is still a matter between us," Adam remarked heavily. She frowned, unsure to what he was referring.

"After we finish dinner, I wish you to retire upstairs and change into your nightgown, lay face down on our bed, and await me," he instructed firmly.

"I'm afraid I don't quite understand?"

He saw genuine confusion cross her face. "Do you recall me explaining this morning that I would deal with your guilt for the episode of broken china later on in the day?"

Her pretty face suffused with colour. "Oh er, yes, um, now I understand."

He was touched by her remorseful acceptance. She was behaving in a much more biddable fashion since her spanking that morning; it had obviously had the desired effect.

Elspeth paced their bedroom nervously awaiting the professor's arrival. The curtains were closed, and the fire burned cheerily in the grate, but the warm cosiness of the room did nothing to bolster her spirits. She was certain that the professor meant to spank her again. She wasn't so concerned about the painful aspect of the punishment to come, no, rather her reaction to the *thought* of said punishment, or, if she was honest with herself, the position that she would be placed in for said spanking, laid across her professor's knee. She moaned softly.

Elspeth was titillated by the thought of a repeat spanking, one just like she had received that morning. Her bottom had felt slightly achy afterward, but as the day had progressed, that discomfort had abated, but her ardent feelings toward Adam had not. Elspeth froze, listening. She plainly heard his step upon the stairs. Oh Lord, he was coming.

Adam entered the bedroom then stopped short at the sight of Elspeth dressed head to toe in a diaphanous white nightgown, transparent where the candle light reflected through the fine material. His manhood awoke and stretched. As they stared across the room at one another, each became carnally aware of the other. Adam collected himself and asked her to sit upon the bed. "The prerequisite of a wife is to obey her husband," he told her, while pacing back and forth. "I have taken into account your lack of knowledge regarding both marriage and English custom due to your memory loss, but I am of the strong opinion that you earnestly require a lesson in obedience. I intend to teach you that your actions and modes of poor behaviour will have certain consequences. I spanked you this morning because of your deplorable manners. I intend to spank you now for your actions, firstly in running away after I asked you to wait here for my return and then again later you ran about the table attempting to evade me."

He stopped pacing and glared at her. "If you had listened to me when you disembarked from the ship, you would not have fallen foul of thieves and your memory would still be intact. I warn you now that I intend to be harsh with you tonight, Elspeth. I instinctively feel that this is a lesson you need to remember and learn. A lesson, as I explained in obedience, one to keep you from repeating the same mistakes over and over. I shall waste no more time in lecturing. Turn about, lift your nightgown and bend over the side of the bed."

Elspeth, wrung her hands. "Surely my apology and the punishment you gave me this morning was retribution enough?" she beseeched.

"Obviously not, since you are still arguing and disobeying me right now," he reprimanded sternly.

Elspeth swallowed nervously at the tone of his voice. She stood up turned to face the bed, hesitated momentarily then reached for the hem of her nightdress and pulled it up about her waist. She leant forward and positioned herself as he requested, bent over the side of the bed.

Adam's shaft stood to full attention at the sight of her shapely, naked bottom presented so compliantly meek as she awaited his punishment. Firmly reprimanding his cock for thinking so lustfully, Adam moved to Elspeth's side and slid his hand over her proffered cheeks. He marvelled at the sight of her unblemished skin and the silky feel of her curved orbs and shapely thighs. "Move your legs a little further apart," he instructed. Unable to resist the tempting sight, his hand slipped between the peachy divide of her bottom and cupped her female mound. If he were surprised by her ragged indrawn breath, he gave no sign, probably because he was reeling in surprise at the discovery of her juicy female nectar leaking profusely from her Venus mount. She was sexually excited.

"Professor?"

Her repetitive use of his professional title instead of using his Christian name, again irked him. "*Adam,*" he insisted, following that up with a correctional swat, smacking down hard on her delectable backside. She squealed in surprise and reacted by dipping her hips. Adam had broken the carnal spell between them. He brought his hand down again, this time marking her pale flesh with a large red hand print. He spanked rhythmically, enjoying the sight of her quivering flesh and moans of discomfort. Then he halted, walked over to his dresser drawer and retrieved a strap that he had slipped out to purchase from the tanners, while she was otherwise engaged with her dressmaker.

It was fourteen inches long and two inches wide, made of high quality, oiled supple leather, absolutely ideal for the chastisement of wilful, naughty wives.

Elspeth, thinking her punishment at an end, began to straighten and rise from the bed. With surprise, she felt the professor's hand on the small of her back urging her downward again. She complied with a disappointed sigh, one that morphed into a shriek of pain as a line of heat singed across her poor buttocks causing her to leap from the bed in shock.

"Back into position," he ordered tersely. Elspeth reluctantly lowered herself back down onto the bed, all the while babbling apologies in the vain hope that he would not strike again. He did, of course, not once but many times, leaving her nether regions sizzling and feeling as though they were the same size as her brand new bustle and as scalded as a cat on a hot tin roof. She was incoherent in her distress, wailing and sobbing, begging forgiveness and apologising. Adam stepped back and admired his handiwork. He felt pleased that he had not injured her, nor broken her skin. For a novice husband, he congratulated himself on correctly chastising his wife-to-be. Hopefully, he would not have to repeat such a harsh lesson again. In fact, from the sound of her weeping, Elspeth would remember this strapping for some time to come. Adam felt confident the deterrent would be enough to avoid a repeat of her past behaviour.

He laid the strap aside and sat beside Elspeth. He ran his hand over her enflamed, swollen nates. He couldn't resist dipping down betwixt her thighs just to see whether the pain of her chastisement had halted the flow of nectar from her inner core. However, she was just as slippery as before. His fingers deftly parted her plump labia lips and swirled happily in the silken channel of her womanhood. Adam was in utter thrall of his manhood and could not have stopped his action had he tried. It didn't escape his notice that she lay passive under his questing fingers. Indeed, her tone had soon changed from one of despair to one of panting encouragement.

Then quite suddenly she rolled away from him and jumped from the bed. "The bump to my head has done me more harm than I imagined," she exclaimed.

"What?" he asked flummoxed.

"Instead of dreading my punishment tonight, I-I was excited by it... I waited up here for you and anticipated being over your knee again... oh goodness, I must be very sick. I-I need to see a doctor!" She covered her face with her hands and began to weep.

Adam reached for her, and she allowed him to pull her between his parted knees. He swept the curling mass of copper hair away from her tear stained face. "Darling girl, there is absolutely nothing wrong with you, I promise. I have heard that sometimes a woman has this type of bodily response to chastisement. The spanking you received tonight hurt you very much, did it not?" She took a shuddering breath and nodded vigorously. "You would prefer not to be strapped in future?" he questioned. She shook her head as fresh tears tracked down her face.

Adam chuckled. She glared at him. "You find my distress amusing," she accused crossly.

"No... endearing. I shall share a secret with you; however, you have to promise never to reveal that I told you this." Elspeth nodded, intrigued. "My brother James once confessed to me that his wife Felicity had the same reaction as you when he spanked her. Apparently, he spoke to a physician about it. The doctor explained that heating a lady's rear end brought blood to the region of her womanhood, which, in turn, caused her body to prepare her for the conjugal act. In short, a woman becoming wet is a normal physical response to being spanked."

"Ooo..." Elspeth flamed with embarrassment at this frank disclosure.

"Indeed it was rumoured that Prince Albert, God rest his soul, spanked Queen Victoria quite often in the early days of their marriage. Apparently, she was prone to fits of ill humour and the prince found spanking his wife to be an excellent cure for her tantrums and doldrums." Adam took advantage of the fact that Elspeth was astounded by this titbit of dubious information and took a moment or two to process what he had just told her. He stood up, reached for the hem of her nightgown and whipped it up and over her head. She immediately objected, attempting to hold onto the flimsy gown, but it was gone before she knew it.

He swept her naked into his embrace and lowered his mouth to hers. She mewed but made no other protest or attempt to pull away. His hands explored her soft flanks and smooth limbs as he plundered her mouth. His member sought the heat of her sweet belly; her breasts pressed up against his brocade waistcoat, the material chaffed her nipples causing them to burgeon. His hand swept up to cup one rounded, buoyant dumpling and his thumb worried the delicious nub at the summit. He growled, awash with primal desire. Aware that he was close to throwing her onto the bed and ravishing her in a completely selfish way, he stepped back and reached for the bed covers. "Slide into bed, keep warm, while I disrobe."

She obeyed, wincing as her chastened rear came in contact with the sheet covered mattress. Twisting onto her side, she watched him with bright eyed interest as he began to remove his clothing. Adam winked at her but made no attempt to conceal any part of his body from her avid gaze. He was amused by her blatant voyeurism. It pleased him to see that her sensuality had returned, perhaps it had never left her?

He took his time hanging up his frock coat and placing his trousers into the wooden trouser press. He unbuttoned his stud collar, placing it, along with his woollen underwear, into the laundry basket out in the water closet. Then he strode purposely to the bed, as naked as the day he was born. He was curious when Elspeth slid sinuously out from the bed and slipped onto her knees before him. When she leaned in to kiss his rampant cock, he was astonished. It appeared that his manhood was shock proof and simply leapt up with delight when Elspeth opened her mouth to accept him. Adam simply thrust his hips toward her and his shaft slid effortlessly inside her succulent ingress. Her lips closed about him, and her cheeks hollowed as she sucked him further into the hot, wet cave of her mouth.

He groaned. Watching her at her lascivious deed was as arousing as the seductive action. Adam gathered the skein of her titian hair, wrapping it around into a pony tail behind her head. He used his hand to control her silky mane, guiding her head back and forth as he wished, causing her moist lips to slide deliciously up and down the entire length of him. His sac tightened and he knew he was close to spending. "I am very near to filling your mouth, pull off me," he warned gruffly, but she ignored him, choosing instead to suck harder, Adam relaxed and gave himself up to the moment.

He had warned her he was near, and this then, was her choice. Truth be told, he wanted to spill in her sweetly succulent mouth. He felt that the act would mark her as his, her very willingness to accept his sap in such a way told him in more than words that she gave herself to him. The deep prolonged growl he uttered as the pleasure pulsed from deep within his balls, shifting to speed along his shaft, warned her of the impending flood just as he jettisoned his essence. Elspeth managed to swallow most of his emission, but she became overwhelmed by the sheer quantity of fluid ejaculated. He muttered sweet praises after he'd come, calling her amongst other things, "his good little waif." Elspeth thrilled at his rapturous response and with her own part in giving him that gratification.

When he had disrobed, she had admired the gradual reveal of his male physique. The hard planes of his body and those parts of him so unconsciously disclosed excited her. The coiling of carnal tension that built somewhere deep within her felt familiar. The hair that covered his chest, the way it tapered down in an arrow to his well endowed groin, the tumescent rise of his engorged manhood, the strength of his hard thighs and long legs, all culminated in an overwhelming need to pay homage to him as a man, hence her desire to take his member into her mouth and worship with her tongue. She revelled in the grunts and groans he gave as she suckled him, filling her with a sense of atonement but also giving her a sense of power over him.

He lifted her to her feet; scooping an arm under her he carried her effortlessly, placing her on the bed. He lay beside her, kissing her ardently. His hands toyed with her breasts, sending delightful waves of pleasure coursing down to her very core. His mouth trailed after his hands to the peak of her breast where he suckled the puckered tips causing her to toss about with wild abandonment.

SHE WAS unable to focus on anything other than Adam. His fingers slid down her flanks into the soft secret nest that guarded the pearl between her legs. She wantonly threw her knee aside, granting him access to her precious core. His mouth trailed kisses from her breasts, following the path his hand had previously taken. He parted the fur at her apex and lapped at her dew coated quim, Elspeth bucked, moaning, she whimpered his name.

Adam smiled. It was music to his ears hearing his Christian name at last upon her lips. Hands grasped his hair while her fingers curled tight against his scalp. His tongue swirled over her womanhood finally latching onto her hidden nub. Instantly she bowed, arching her hips, offering herself up to his mouth, he knew then that she gave herself over to him body and soul.

As Elspeth spiralled ever upward toward the inevitable zenith, Adam rose above her, clasped her flanks and drove himself deep inside. He kept his eyes trained upon hers. The mirrored connection between them heightened their pleasure to an almost spiritual level of completeness.

The sensation of heat from her spanked bottom, combined with the delicious pounding of his hardened maleness, completely overwhelmed her senses; she began to keen long and low. His gravelled shout as his own satisfying release flooded her channel, blended with her ragged song of rapture.

They lay spent, he still firm inside her, their breathing erratic. "You said *Banda,* earlier on today and I knew that you'd said monkey but I don't know how I knew that. The other thing is that, I… well… I, recognised you," she whispered.

"How so?" he shifted sideways, removing his weight from her body, she had certainly captured his attention.

"I dreamed of-of, what we have between us… of our passion."

He raised himself up on one elbow and looked down into her face. "You mentioned something of this earlier on today. When exactly did these dreams begin?"

She gazed at him thoughtfully. "It was after I found the *Shiromani,* I became plagued by a certain type of dream, you and I… well… I think you can guess."

He kissed her gently. "We were making love?" he suggested, leaning in to kiss her even more fervently. "We made love aboard the ship quite often. You remembered our love because of the jewel —I told you it was magical."

She shook her head. "I don't remember how you came by the emerald." He rolled onto his back taking her with him, and tucking her securely under his arm, he retold her the tale.

CHAPTER 10

Saturday was dull and cold but at least the all pervading fog was held at bay by the chill breeze. Elspeth dressed for her wedding in one of the two dresses Mrs. Heally had brought for her. She chose an elegant green velvet ensemble, a dress of high fashion that made full use of the new modern bustle. The colour and style suited her to perfection. It was trimmed with white lace at cuff and neck, topped off with a sweet white bonnet, cunningly designed with matching veil and netting front and back which pulled down to completely cover her face. A saucy little *chapeau,* decorated with silk roses and foliage of orange and green ostrich feathers, complemented her outfit perfectly.

Ruminating, while Martha dressed her hair, Elspeth replayed the conversation of the previous night. Adam had completely shocked her. He'd finished the tale of being presented with the Shiromani jewel and then he'd taken her hand in his and confessed to deceiving her about their marital state. Remaining silent throughout his explanation, she'd listened with growing confusion to his justification for his action and his declaration of love for her. He'd kissed her and asked her pardon, which she'd automatically granted, with the proviso that he take her to see Mr. Trubshaw, the

Wootens' lawyer, on Monday, to hear what he had to tell her about everything. Adam had readily agreed. They'd settled down for the night, he had tucked her against his chest, his arms snug about her. Adam fell asleep, but she had lain awake until the wee small hours, her sense of security completely shattered by his disclosure. He had told her that the vicar had insisted that he share the fact that they were unwed before he would marry them. Elspeth pondered; did this mean that if the vicar had not made that a condition of the marriage, Adam would never have told her the whole truth?

At first she debated whether to marry him at all, but then she realised that she wanted, nay, *needed* to wed him, if only for the security of being married. Deciding that she couldn't live with the awful bleakness of having no past, no family *and* no future, at least, married to the professor, she would have a husband, home and security. Elspeth listened to the small voice in her head that added, *and love…* Yes, she finally admitted to herself, she wanted Adam's loving, but did her feelings go any deeper than that? She conjectured the matter but finally, too bewildered and exhausted to come to any conclusion, she'd slept.

By the time she was completely ready to leave for the church, she knew that she was going to marry Adam. He had set off for the rectory early to meet with the vicar and his brother James, who was coming to stand for him in the church. Uncle Arthur was speechless when Elspeth entered the parlour. With tears in his eyes, he kissed her on both cheeks, held her at arm's length and gazed at her admiringly. "You are a wondrous sight for an old man to behold!" he told her and then, tucking her arm through his, they walked the short distance to the church.

Standing inside the knave, she heard the murmur of many voices. She leaned forward to peek and saw a number of people sat in the pews. Who were they, where had all these people come from? Uncle Arthur patted her hand reassuringly. The bridal processional had begun to play; their cue to walk down the aisle.

At the altar stood Adam and another man she took to be James, his brother. A taller, thinner version of Adam, bewhiskered, yet thinning on top.

"Who giveth this woman unto this man?" the vicar asked sonorously. The service passed her by in a haze, until suddenly the vicar pronounced, "You may kiss your bride," and Elspeth found herself Adam's wife in truth.

Dazed by the introductions to Adam's friends and work colleagues, she stood outside the church accepting what appeared to be a never ending line of folk congratulating Adam then kissing her. She was relieved when a kindly female face appeared before her and she was pulled in for an affectionate hug. "My dear, it is so nice to meet you. I am your new sister-in-law, Felicity, I am James's wife and I should like to introduce Amanda, she is Adam and James's younger sister, also your sister-in-law." She stepped away to allow a younger woman to take her place.

This girl had rich golden hair artfully arranged on top of her head, blue eyes sparkled with merry delight; she was a beauty. She clasped Elspeth in a warm embrace. "I am so glad to make your acquaintance," her softly spoken voice melodious.

"It will be wonderful having sisters, I am so pleased to meet you both." Elspeth beamed at them both, and the three ladies stood smiling at one another. Before any of them could begin a conversation, James appeared by his brother's side. He reached for Elspeth's hand and raised it to his lips.

"Enchanted, madam," he exclaimed gallantly.

"Are we ready to depart?" Adam asked, glancing around his family and Uncle Arthur questioningly. "Cook will have our wedding celebration prepared, so shall we?" He waved his arm in the direction of Helen House and everyone slowly walked together making polite conversation.

Cook did them proud; she produced a home baked wedding cake as her wedding gift. James, a keen photographer took photographs of them both cutting the cake with his newly acquired box Kinnar camera.

All too soon Elspeth found herself alone in the bedroom with her new husband.

Adam quickly surmised that something was amiss with his wife. She had been cool toward him all day, and she had barely smiled at him. He was certain she was annoyed with him about his deception over their wedded state, and frankly, he didn't blame her. She was putting her hat away into a hat box, when he called her over to him. She finished stowing the pretty piece of nonsense amongst the tissue paper, while he waited patiently. Finally, she turned to face him, casting him a rather aloof glance.

"I humbly apologise for deceiving you, Elspeth. It was very wrong of me I know, but I was terrified you might disappear again if there was no legal tie to me. If your memory had been intact, I would never have dreamt of using such deception, but as it was, you didn't know me, or have any feelings for me. I was afraid that you wouldn't stay if I asked you to. Can you honestly say that you would have agreed to stay here alone in this house with me, if you had known we were unwed?"

Touched by his simple honesty, she mulled his words over.

"I have been asking myself that very same question ever since you told me the truth last night, and I still don't know the answer," she sounded so melancholy.

He moved across to her and wrapped his arms about her. "Have I told you the moment I fell in love with you?" She shook her head. "You tripped and sprawled onto the deck, your bag contents scattered everywhere. The thing I loved about you was the fact that you got straight back up and began to gather up your things, not simply leaving it to the steward but getting on with the task yourself and with a self deprecation that many women of today have lost. You have an inner strength, Elspeth that I admired in you from the start, and that fortitude has shown time and again with every difficulty you've encountered. If you feel brave enough, I suggest that we move forward together and leave this chicanery in the past. We are man and wife at last, you no longer have to face life alone. This is a new beginning for us both, and I promise I shall never lie to you again. I love and adore you, Mrs. Beresford, I promise to protect you and keep you safe with the best of my ability, and from this day forward, I shall do everything in my power to make you the happiest woman alive!" He kissed her then. At first she held herself stiff in his arms but as his kiss grew more insistent, she relaxed onto his chest and enjoyed his plundering of her mouth.

~

He undressed them both, removing each piece of clothing slowly, revealing her gradually, taking his time, showing her due reverence. This was her wedding night, and he wanted it to be as different from the bullying night spent with Henry as he could make it, even though she had no recollection of her first time.

Adam pressed his lips gently against every bare part of her as he removed her clothes, thus exposing her body. Standing finally in her shift and stockings, he rolled those downward, his lips trailing a path along every inch of her exposed flesh, until finally he lifted each of her feet to his lips. Then he knelt at her feet and lifted her knee length shift, bunching it around her hips. She rested her hands lightly upon his head while her fingers played with his springy waves of hair. He wrapped both arms about her and pulled her mons to his mouth. Immediately, her hands twisted his hair in a painful grasp. He lifted his hand and covered hers until she slowly released her fingers and relaxed.

His tongue swiped up her cleft catching her tiny jutting clitoris in a long slow swipe that ended with him sucking the small protuberance so hard that he felt her knees give way. He scooped her into his arms and carried her to the bed where he carefully placed her against the pillows and removed her shift. Now that he had her naked, he took his time in arousing her. Teasing her, until she no longer felt human but became instead a writhing mass of primitive sensation. She didn't recognise herself in the sounds that she made. Surely those animalistic grunts and groans did not belong to her?

After he paid homage to her breasts, he kissed and licked his way down to her core, her dew flowed freely, and he thrust his palms under her bottom and lifted her to his mouth. At first, he plunged his tongue into her channel until she twisted to and fro, far too much for him to continue his ministrations, so he plunged his thumb inside her and used his index finger to slide through the divide of her bottom cheeks until he came to her anus. His fingers slippery with her fluids, he circled her rosebud and pressed inside, thus anchoring her. Pumping his thumb and finger in and out of her channels, he returned his lips to her swollen clitty. Almost at once, Elspeth bowed against his mouth, and her keening wail rent the air, a small grin of smug achievement split his face.

Adam could wait no longer, his cock weighty with leaking sap, a sure sign he needed to claim his woman. Sliding up her body, he nudged his way into her moist entrance and plunged home. He rode her roughly. She matched him thrust for thrust, cry for cry, until his own roar of completion drowned out her melodious wail of satisfaction. They fell asleep in one another's arms, and throughout the night, Elspeth found herself awakened by his sorcerer's call. They slept late the following morn but no one disturbed them. When Adam finally left the matrimonial bed due to a call of nature, he found a breakfast tray set ready outside their door. It was well after noon when Elspeth finally rang for Martha. The following day was spent in much the same way and all too soon it was Monday.

Elspeth had hoped that meeting Mr. Trubshaw would trigger the release of her memory, but she had no recollection of ever having met the lawyer. He confirmed everything that Adam had told her and could shed no more light upon her first husband's death, than the communication originally received from his Commanding Officer. Mr. Trubshaw gave Elspeth details of a bank account he had opened in her name that held twenty pounds, which had been all that remained of her in-laws' money. No funds had been received from Henry's demise, and Elspeth had no wish to follow up on either the details of his death, or his financial situation at the time. She had no recollection of Henry Wooten, and she preferred to let sleeping dogs lie.

Adam was a little concerned by how subdued his wife seemed after their meeting with her lawyer. He directed the coachman to take them directly to Farmer and Rogers on Regent Street. When Elspeth questioned him, he told her that as a wedding gift to her, he wanted to replace the broken tea service with a new one of her choosing. Elspeth immediately brightened up and considerably so, when Adam graciously accepted her offer to buy the china as her wedding gift to him, stressing that it was she who had broken the plates. Farmer and Rogers, a popular warehouse store that imported desirable objects d'art, from the Far East and India, had become a Mecca for fashionable people of means. Society had become obsessed with everything oriental and the store boomed with success.

Elspeth stared about her in absolute awe. She had never seen somewhere so full of beautiful things. Bolts of expensive cloth vied for space with Japanese fans, parasols, scent bottles and all manner of chinaware. She stopped spell bound before a lacquered, handmade parquetry box. When she lifted the lid she was delighted that it tinkled with a sweet tune. Adam thought his sister Amanda might like it for a Christmas gift and made a mental note. They left the lovely thing behind and continued on their way until they reached the china department. There were so many different patterns to choose from, many with gold rims and ostentatious birds and flowers but Elspeth's eye was caught by a pretty blue and white design, labelled The Willow Pattern. She called Adam to her side and asked him if he liked the set. He confirmed that he did and signalled to the shop manager that they wanted the tea service wrapped and sent on to Helen House.

After their shopping spree, Adam insisted that they go on to the

Cafe Royal for some lunch. Elspeth thoroughly enjoyed her turtle soup, and while they both tucked into cutlets, Adam proposed they go from there to the museum for the afternoon. While they travelled in the coach, Adam produced a key. "This is a spare key to the staff entrance at the museum. Keep it somewhere safe because, as my wife, I think you should have your own key so that you can always come and find me if you should ever have need of me." Elspeth was touched and kissed him, before tucking the key safely into her reticule.

Mr. Harris seemed delighted to see her and make her acquaintance properly this time. Elspeth recalled him being amongst the guests at her wedding. He explained that he had urgent business to discuss with Adam. Adam suggested Elspeth take a look around the museum alone for while, just until he and Mr. Harris had discussed museum business.

Elspeth shrank from wandering the public areas alone, so Adam took her up the many flights of stairs to the third floor where his office was situated and where many broken artefacts were repaired. Elspeth was left to explore these altogether more fascinating rooms, behind the public face of the museum.

The first room she wandered into had a sarcophagus laid upon the floor, in need of some restoration. There were a couple of marble statues, minus their arms and a strange skeletal beast, with its bones strung together. She explored the group of oddities, trailing her hand over each of the ancient curios. Then she noticed another larger object that stood upright against the corner of the far wall. It looked to be constructed of rusty metal. She strolled over to take a closer look at it. When she stood in front of the thing, she gave the object closer inspection, soon realising that one side of the contraption had long metal spikes set into the interior. When the two halves were closed the spikes would almost touch the opposite side of the coffin shaped box. The gruesome nature of the object dawned upon her, and she backed away in horror.

There was a feel of impact and then an almighty crash, followed by the long drawn out sound of objects clattering to the floor one after the other. With a sense of déjà vu, she spun around to see what damage she'd wrought. The strange skeletal form now lay in pieces scattered about the floor. She moaned, dropped to her knees and began to gather the fossils together. Glancing around she had no idea what to do with the parts, so she began to pile them into the sarcophagus.

Hearing soft footsteps approaching, she panicked. Looking around for somewhere to hide, she leapt into the stone tomb and lay flat, hoping that whoever came by would miss seeing her there. The footfalls stopped nearby and she distinctly heard breathing, but all she could see from her hiding place was the ceiling. Heart in mouth, she held her breath, waiting. The other person did not move, and the breathing continued until suddenly Elspeth heard male voices coming nearer from outside in the corridor as footsteps approached. The soft sound of heavy padding feet moved rapidly away from where she lay, causing her to stiffen with fright. The door opened and loud exclamations rent the air.

"My God, what the bloody hell happened in here?" She recognised Adam's voice.

"No-o, no-o, weeks of work ruined!" Oh dear and that sounded like Mr. Harris.

"Elspeth, are you in here?" She felt stupid hiding from them now but thought it best to remain where she was. She rather suspected the penalty for her accident might involve a trip over her husband's lap. Footsteps came closer and she scrunched her eyes shut and held her breath.

"You can open your eyes, young lady, I can see you." She tentatively opened her eyes and peered up into her husband's face, he wasn't smiling. Mr. Harris's face appeared next to Adam's and he most certainly wasn't smiling. "You know," Adam turned to Harris, "I have heard that ostriches bury their heads in the sand when an enemy approaches believing that because they cannot see their enemy, they, in turn, cannot be seen. I really didn't believe that up until now," he said conversationally.

"Come along, ostrich, out you come." Fixing her with a gimlet eye, he leaned in and clasped her hand, helping her to sit up, then following his behest, she climbed out of the sarcophagus. "I believe that you have something you wish to say to Mr. Harris?" Adam prompted, one eyebrow raised. Elspeth hung her head and mumbled an apology. "Excuse us for a moment, Harris." Adam took her arm and guided her out into the corridor, back to his office, where he locked the door behind them. He turned her to face him. "Explain."

Elspeth drew in a breath and released it slowly before speaking. "It was an accident. I was intrigued by that odd metal sarcophagus, but when I saw the horrible spikes and discerned the purpose behind them, I backed away from the horrible thing straight into the animal bones. Adam, I didn't mean to break them. I swear it was an accident!"

Adam tilted her chin up with his finger. "I am not annoyed with you for the accident, they happen to us all. Although, I have noticed how often accidents seem to happen to *you*. I am cross that you threw all those precious ancient bones into another ancient artefact and then hid on top of them which is behaviour fit for a child. Why on earth didn't you immediately come and find me when the accident occurred and ask me what we should do?"

She sighed, not meeting his steely glare. "I-I really don't know. I was scared and worried you might become angry with me, I suppose."

"Look at me." She glanced up at him and dropped her eyes again. "Elspeth, look me in the eye." She looked briefly up into his stern gaze but slid her eyes away again.

"Very well, this evasive behaviour of yours tells me that you feel guilty, young lady. I propose that you go now and ask Mr. Harris if there is anything you can do to help him put the exhibit back together and make him a most sincere apology after which we shall return home." Elspeth readily agreed and moved toward the door, but before she could open it, Adam spoke. "We will resolve the other issues when we arrive home."

Elspeth stared at him. "Other issues?"

He smiled grimly. "Yes, choosing to hide and not take responsibility for the accident.

"Oh... are you... will you..." Her voice faltered.

"Yes," he answered firmly, flexing his hand so that she was in no doubt about his meaning. Elspeth felt herself flush and hurriedly slipped from the room.

CHAPTER 11

Adam watched Elspeth as they travelled home seated opposite one another in the carriage. She caught him observing her and poked her tongue out at him playfully before turning to stare out of the window again. "Can we go and collect Lucky Chance while we are on our way home?" she suddenly asked.

"No, not today."

"Why not, you said we could collect him today?" she argued petulantly. Adam frowned and went over his hypothesis again in his mind. Elspeth continued to plague him about her cat, but her whining only strengthened his resolve to confront her with his theory on their return.

After they had settled in the parlour with a tray of tea, Adam explained what was on his mind. Elspeth stared at him utterly dumfounded. "You think I am deliberately behaving in a childish manner so that you will chastise me?"

He nodded. "I do, yes."

She bristled. "Well, I can assure you that I'm not! Today was a fluke and an accident!"

"And yesterday and the day before that—"

"But I—"

She tried to interrupt, but he continued, "Hear me out, please. I do not think you are behaving this way deliberately. I think you are doing so subconsciously. From what you have told me of your childhood, you were lonely and your life was dull." Elspeth acknowledged this with a nod. "I suspect that since you now have a sense of security but no memory of a childhood, you are feeling able to behave in a childish manner because I make you feel secure enough to be able to be, well… naughty."

"You think I am childish?" She looked incredibly hurt.

Adam got to his feet and hunkered down beside her. "I think you actually *need* to be naughty and then corrected. I sense this is essential to your healing process, and since I am happy with the role of responsible adult, your propensity to behave as a juvenile will be safely and kindly dealt with."

"How?" she whispered.

"Come now, you know how I deal with disobedience. I shall deal with your childish misdemeanours with sound spankings and perhaps some corner time when required. There is the matter of your hiding at the museum to be dealt with. So upstairs with you now and stick your nose into a corner and reflect on everything I have said and match that against your recent behaviour. I shall be up shortly and we will have another discussion then." He stood up and held out his hand for her to take.

She chewed her lip and crossed her arms looking decidedly mulish. "What if I don't want to?" she muttered sulkily.

He frowned and considered for a moment. "Stand up and do as you were told," he commanded sternly. Elspeth jumped straight to her feet, stuck out her tongue defiantly but obediently scuttled from the room and onward up the stairs. After she had gone, he grinned, shaking his head. It seemed that his hypothesis had been correct. He had to accept that, for the foreseeable future, he would have one very naughty little wife to deal with.

When he entered their bedchamber, he was perturbed to find

Elspeth slumped in a corner of the room sobbing bitterly. He crossed straight to her and lowered himself on his haunches wrapping his arms about her trembling form. She, in turn, burrowed into him and cried harder. "Tell me what troubles you," he encouraged softly.

"I don't know who I am," she spluttered wetly against his chest.

He swept her upright and cradled her against him, rocking her gently to and fro. "You are not so different from when I first met you." She quietened, listening. "You have the same sense of fun and strength of character; just look how you cared for yourself and Arthur over these past two months? Now that you are restored to me and have become my wife, I think I am right in my supposition that you need to be more carefree and behave in a less responsible manner. If this behaviour helps to restore your memory, then I want you to embrace it. You can talk to me at any point about how you feel and what you need, but ultimately, I shall decide whether your actions require punishment, and right now, your actions show me that you require my reassurance, before you have your bottom warmed." She was quiet for so long that he began to worry.

"I do feel safe here with you. I don't understand why I have behaved so badly since we have been together again, so perhaps you are right about this?" she finally whispered.

Adam knew that he had to remain positive and maintain control if she was to continue to trust his judgement. "I am right. Spanking will give you a feeling of stability when you exhibit poor behaviour," he stated firmly. He continued to hold her until she fidgeted in his arms and then drawing back from her, he held her gaze steadily with his own. "I am going to help you out of your clothes now, and then you are going over my knee, young lady."

Elspeth nodded. Why did his words cause such opposing effects to her body? Her stomach lurched sickeningly, whereas her core tightened and fluttered with excitement.

Adam began to undo the front of her dress, and she watched his fingers deftly move down her front until the bodice of her dress gaped open. He then lifted each of her hands in turn and unbuttoned her cuffs. Calmness enveloped her as she watched him. She caught his glance, and he gave her a reassuring wink. She knew he was right, she did need this but more than that, she needed him. She would follow his dictates and hope that, at some point, her memory would return. It was a wonderful feeling of relief to lean on Adam, knowing that he would metaphorically catch her should she fall.

When she was naked, he lifted her dressing table chair into the centre of the room where he seated himself and held out his hand to her. Hesitantly she went to him and placed her small palm in his. He drew her to him and tipped her across his lap. She wriggled until she was as comfortable as she could be in this ignoble position, with her hands flat on the carpet and her toes not quite reaching the floor. Then his arm encircled her waist tucking her securely against his body. "All right?" he queried softly.

Elspeth let out a sigh, "Yes," she answered, and it was the truth, for even at this moment of trepidation, she felt shielded, sheltered and loved by him. Relaxing into boneless supplication, she waited for the first smack to fall.

The sting of his palm when it came, seared her tender buttock. She winced but was silent. She remained silent for the first ten blows or so, and then he increased his tempo, and the slaps became harder for her to bear. She squirmed, whimpering as he heated her flesh, the pace of the spanking intensifying. Holding her securely, he tipped her further forward and she lifted one hand to cling onto his trouser clad calf.

"I have you safe," he reassured her, and she knew that he had. The sizzling spanks landed hard and fast now. She realised that her eyes were leaking, she was openly crying, gasping, as each burning cheek of her bottom received equal attention from his heavy palm.

"No-o!" she yelped.

"Yes." He was implacable and inexplicitly, she loved him all the more for ignoring her whining complaints and persevering.

She tried not to beg, but she was unable to help herself as her backside heated up to furnace level. Her apologies began to heap one on top of the other. Still he spanked on, paying no heed to her pitiful attempts to placate him to thus end her torment. She realised that Adam was resolute; when she was naughty this was what she could expect. She hated it. Finally, he stopped, hoisted her upright so that she gave a hiss as he lowered her onto his knee. He whispered words of love and reassurance as he wiped away her tears, and she knew in that moment of tenderness that she loved him.

The spanking she had suffered and the action he had taken, the man himself, the suffusion of love and care, all conjoined in her mind.

His hands began to travel over her body, and he turned her so that she faced away from him, her back resting against his chest. At once she saw that they sat facing the floor length cheval mirror. Heat flooded her face as she realised that Adam had been able to watch himself while he'd spanked her. She shifted her sore bottom and felt the hardened ridge of his growing erection, pressing into her chastened flesh.

She watched as his hands cupped her breasts, his thumbs sweeping across her nipples several times, and she closed her eyes as arousing shivers caused havoc with her breathing. "Eyes open," he growled in her ear. His palms slid south and reaching her thighs, he tapped them. "Legs wide apart." Slowly obeying, she shifted each leg to either side of his knees. Looking at the lewd picture her image presented in the mirror, she moaned with a mixture of lust and mortification. "You are so beautiful," he whispered as his hands slid along her thighs to her knees and back up to her apex. His fingers dipped into her quim, and she sucked in her bottom lip as she watched him splay open the folds of her glistening sex. "Look at your tiny clitty standing proud and erect for me. She knows her master now as I think do you too… don't you, my darling?" His husky voice seduced her as significantly as the action of his circling digit.

She watched mesmerised as he stoked and teased her sex until she glistened with dew. "How wet you are for me, perhaps you did enjoy your spanking?" She could quite clearly see her own bodily response to his inflammatory words. She welled with liquid desire, coating his hands liberally as she reacted to his words. He chuckled delightedly as his fingers elicited the succulent sounds of a woman highly aroused. Elspeth moaned. "Shall I make you come while we both watch?" he whispered, and all the while his fingers worked their magic. She mewled and bucked her hips as he inserted one, then two fingers inside her slippery channel, his thumb rapidly circled her clitoris. Her breath hitched and her haunches twitched to his rhythmic pumping, and all the while his left hand was busy betwixt her legs, his right hand roamed her breasts, tweaking and pulling her nipples in a glorious relay of sensation.

She began to arch as the pleasure reached a pitch that was almost unbearable. At once both his hands dropped down to her sex, his left continued its machinations while his right slid beneath the heated orb of her bottom. Elspeth bucked as she felt his fingers slide between her nether cheeks, a finger slick with her own juices, caressed her private hole, and she recalled the other night when his thumb had slipped inside her. She tensed at the memory, and he crooned to her until her cheeks relaxed. At that pivotal moment, he delved inside her forbidden hole. He stilled his finger, unmoving as he continued to thrust his other digits up inside her soaking channel. Then slowly he pumped all of his fingers and she almost bucked off his knee.

"Open your eyes and watch yourself come. Look, Elspeth, look at how I am controlling your pleasure."

She stared at the image before her. A young woman naked and flushed with her arousal stared back at her wide eyed, pupils dilated with lust, nipples puckered like raspberries. Pale coppery hair that had escaped her coiffure, hung in curls about her shoulders. Her legs divided either side of her handsome husband's lap. His knees, with the neat creases in his trousers, looked wickedly incongruous between her immodestly splayed thighs. Even more inappropriate to her eye, was the sight of his white cuffed wrists while his hands fervently delved into her pinkly exposed loins, tormenting her bottom and quim to the point where she would very soon orgasm. It was an overwhelmingly erotic sight, and her body hummed with her impending culmination. "Adam!" she cried.

Adam delighted in her enjoyment, his own desire molten; he felt the sap in his member rise with achingly ardent need. He pulled his fingers from her channel and pinched her clitty with finger and thumb. He pushed in another finger to join the one already seated deep inside her arse and frigged her bottom hole. She bowed against him, her head thrown back over his shoulder, her breasts thrust forward as she keened his name, which morphed into a wail, a crescendo of ultimate satisfaction.

As she floated back to him, he lifted her and deposited her upon the bed, and not bothering to undress, he ripped open his trousers and released his jutting erection. Elspeth gave him the sweetest of smiles as she parted her legs and welcomed his thrust as he claimed her in one glorious rut. Her eyelids half closed with blissful stupefaction, she was overwhelmed by unexpected anticipation of yet another powerful quake. As her husband filled her so satisfyingly with his plundering manhood, grinding against her pelvis as his sap surged, he shuddered with a powerful release. His shout of joy overshadowed her almost silent gasp as her own glitteringly intense orgasm strummed her body with heart stopping ecstasy.

CHAPTER 12

Christmas was but a week away. Elspeth and Adam were due to spend Christmas with Adam's family, arriving Christmas Eve and staying until the day after Boxing Day at James's house, in Sydenham. Adam had even arranged an invitation for Uncle Arthur, and with strong reservations, one for Lucky, the cat.

Adam had commissioned a wooden carry box made so they could safely collect Elspeth's cat. He was not at home when the box was delivered and Elspeth had excitedly set off to collect Lucky from Arthur's lodgings by herself. Her trip was very successful, for when she arrived in Arthur's street, she espied Scrounger. He was standing talking to a man on the opposite side of the road. She had hurried over to him, perturbed to find that he did not recognise her at once. He had bowed to her and seemed ill at ease in her company. She finally convinced him to come into Uncle Arthur's rooms with her and was able to introduce the two. When she left carrying a yowling Lucky Chance in his new box, she pushed a five pound note into the lad's grubby hand and begged him to befriend the elderly gentleman and to keep a friendly eye on him. To say that Scrounger was flabbergasted by her money would be an understatement. The street boy had never beheld such riches and readily promised to check on Arthur daily.

When she arrived home with her furious cat, she was met in the hallway by her equally furious and far more dangerous, husband. Martha had been called to take the cat off to the kitchen to be fed and Elspeth had been marched upstairs, lectured about travelling about alone and un-chaperoned then soundly spanked. This time Elspeth was absolutely convinced that she would not repeat her error again, not after Adam promised her darkly that he had another trick or two up his sleeve that might make her want to think twice before enacting another ill thought out foray.

He had ordered her upstairs to remove her garments and disappeared into the kitchens. She awaited his appearance nervously, wondering what he intended. He arrived in the room shortly after, carrying a small cup that he set beside the bed and he seated himself. "Come here." He sounded grim. She moved to his side and was unsurprised when he upended her across his lap. She clutched the counterpane in her hands and waited for the first smack to fall. When he simply stroked her bottom and slid a finger gently between her cheeks, she lifted her head and twisted around to see what he was about.

"Adam?" she queried softly.

"Keep still please; this will take but a moment," he admonished.

She waited clenching her buttocks in trepidation. She felt something wet push at her puckered entrance. "Relax your bottom, sweetheart."

She tried to do as he instructed but failed. "I-I can't, I am scared of what you are about to do!" she mumbled miserably.

He patted her behind. "I would never harm you. Spank you and ginger fig you, yes. Just trust me, this is a punishment designed to make the spanking you have coming a bit more intense, but the ginger root that I am using will do you no lasting harm." She relaxed as he demanded and felt the push of the root against her bottom hole, a discomfort but not painful, as something seated itself deeply inside her bottom. She wriggled her hips to try and make the thing a bit more comfortable and a stinging inside her forbidden hole soon had her complaining and begging her husband to remove the nasty burning object.

Then his hand fell with a scalding smack and Elspeth's entire focus was upon her singed rear end, which burned both inside and out. Every so often, Adam would stop to lecture her on her safety and the necessity to take her maid with her and also leave him a note when she was going out. The ginger continued to punish her when his hand did not. He put her in a corner to reflect on her bad choices, only removing the root when he was satisfied that she was genuinely contrite.

It was a very sorry wife who prepared for bed that night. Elspeth had to sleep on her front due to her fiery hindquarters. Adam showed absolutely no respect for her suffering as he tumbled her onto her back, took her with joyous gusto, ignoring her complaints that he soon turned into moans of passion.

~

A LOCAL WOMAN had been engaged to undertake the kitchen work and basic cleaning, thus freeing Martha up for her role as Elspeth's personal maid. The two made their way up into the servants' rooms when Mrs. Carron was out running errands. It suited Elspeth that the cantankerous housekeeper seemed to be out more often than in, nowadays. Her absence meant that Elspeth was finally able to inspect her servants' quarters. After inspecting the rooms and seeing the comfort and cosiness of both Mrs. Carron and Mrs. Donald's rooms, she decided to donate extra bedding to Martha and some cushions plus a rug from one the spare guest rooms. Martha was thrilled, both with her room and her new found position within the household.

Arthur was now working a couple of days a week at the museum and had received his reward money from Adam for the return of the Shiromani gem, which now resided safely in the museum's strong box. Scrounger was as good as his word and befriended the old man, and soon the two developed a respectful companionship, and it was not long before Arthur had offered Scrounger a home living with him and sharing his meagre rooms.

Elspeth's new wardrobe arrived. She had required more space, so one of the guest rooms became her dressing room filled with all her new gowns, hats, gloves and paraphernalia. She loved to go and view her new gowns, stroking the rich materials and marvelling at the fine beadwork and beautiful designs of each garment. She couldn't believe they were all hers to wear at will and marvelled at her change in circumstance.

Sometimes during the day, she and Martha walked to the Thames embankment, just to glimpse the poor mudlarks digging for treasure. When one came close enough to the river wall, Elspeth would throw them coin, sad for their desperate plight and thanking her lucky stars that mudlarking was no longer her way of life.

~

On their arrival at James's formidable looking house, situated on The Avenue, Sydenham, the entire family rushed out to greet them and Arthur was touched to find that he was simply treated as a member of the family and introduced as Elspeth's uncle. Amanda cooed over Lucky and wanted to introduce him to her own cat, Dusty, immediately. James and Adam had to step in and insist that Lucky Chance be allowed to get used to his new surroundings just in case a territorial cat fight ensued. Amanda pouted prettily, exclaiming that to be unlikely because they were male and female and more likely to mate than fight. She was quickly hushed by James and Felicity as they cast anxious glances over the children, who were oblivious to their aunt's indelicate remark. Elspeth handed her cat over to Martha, who had readily agreed to share her room with Lucky during the day. He would sleep with Adam and

Elspeth at night, a situation that Adam had grudgingly agreed to but only whilst they were staying these few days in Sydenham.

The Beresford's' cook prepared a tray of mince pies, tea and Christmas cake, served with a tangy cheddar cheese. The family gathered in the drawing room, chatting and catching up with one another as they enjoyed the rich Christmas bounty. A magnificent Christmas tree stood bare in the corner, a box of decorations set beside it, in preparation for the family to dress the tree. The children ran to the box and immediately began to pull out various baubles. The adults sipped tea, chatted and watched indulgently. The afternoon was spent in leisurely companionship, decorating the tree. It was an easy introduction for Elspeth and Arthur getting to know Adam's family. By the time they had finished dinner and the adults had attended midnight mass, Elspeth felt that she truly belonged as one of the family.

Presents were opened after breakfast on Christmas Day, handed out by Felicity with help from Maddie. Elspeth, gasped with delight upon opening a tooled leather ring box. Adam knelt beside her and took the ring from its box, slipping it onto her finger. "Since emeralds seem to be our lucky stone and since you have no engagement ring, I bought you this," he lifted her hand to his lips.

Elspeth stared at the beautiful emerald ring, circled with tiny glittering diamonds. "Oh, Adam darling, I love it!" she cried, throwing both arms about his neck. Everyone crowded round admiring the gleaming ring. The gift giving continued with Amanda receiving a lovely inlaid wooden box. When she opened it, she squealed with excitement. It was a popular mechanical music box by Nicole Frères. They set it to play one of the six songs it contained, and the children danced about joyfully to the happy tune.

There was a sudden bark of laughter from James as he opened his present from his wife, attracting everyone's attention. They all watched as he lifted a brass trumpet from its box. Felicity was already giggling, but when the children and Adam saw the trumpet, they began to laugh as well. Elspeth looked blankly at Arthur, who shrugged back, having no idea what the hilarity was about either. Adam turned to his wife and explained. "Felicity is always telling James to stop blowing his own trumpet!" Elspeth and Arthur joined in the laughter and James chased Felicity around the room until he caught her and dealt her a slap on her thickly bustled bottom, which caused even more merriment when she took him to task in horrified tone. He then grabbed his own package from underneath the tree and handed the gift to his wife; Felicity was delighted to find a huge bottle of French perfume nestled inside the box. She spun around and flung her arms about her husband's neck, kissing him soundly.

Lunch was superb and Elspeth, who had never before tasted turkey, was labelled a glutton by her amused husband as she devoured a large second helping. In the afternoon, Amanda slipped away from the family games. She decided it was time to introduce her cat, Dusty, to Lucky. The first anyone knew of her untimely introduction, was the sudden sound of loudly ferocious yowling, followed by screeched caterwauling that deafened the shocked family. First on the scene upstairs was James with Adam following close on his heels. Each man tried unsuccessfully to separate the fighting cats as fur flew in all directions. Elspeth attempted to entice Lucky from the melee but it was no good, the animals seemed to be intent on fighting to the death. Felicity caught her children and ushered them from the room, whereupon Maddie burst into tears at the fearful sight of the snarling mini-beasts. Then Arthur appeared with a water filled pitcher. He threw the contents over the two combatants. The effect was startling, as each cat leapt into the air in shock and flew for cover, thankfully to opposite ends of the room. Elspeth and Adam crawled on hands and knees under Amanda's bed and coaxed Lucky out. They left Amanda reaching for Dusty who was under her dressing table while they took Lucky into their room. Elspeth sat down and cuddled her cat, wrapped in a towel that Adam procured for her.

After some soothing words and gentle petting, the animal deigned to settle down and slept curled up on the end of their bed, seeming none the worse for wear.

Adam closed the door to keep their cat inside and they made their way downstairs, where Amanda was receiving a loud dressing down from James. Upon hearing her stridently argued reply, Adam excused himself from the drawing room and went to add his voice of disapproval.

The following day, it was decided that they should all travel to the famous exhibition halls of the Crystal Palace and take a walk in the beautiful gardens that surrounded the building. Elspeth marvelled at the stunning glass palace, for whenever a winter ray appeared from behind the clouds, the many windows reflected the sunshine with blinding radiance.

While they were walking, Amanda approached Elspeth and made her an apology for putting the cats in together and causing the cat fight. It seemed that Dusty had not entirely escaped injury, she had suffered a torn ear, which Amanda assured Elspeth she was capable of tending to. She withdrew a pamphlet from her reticule and handed it to Elspeth. "What is this?" she asked, intrigued.

"It is a notice of the very first cat show to be held here on July thirteenth. I intended entering Dusty, but if her ear does not heal without scarring, I won't be able to put her into the show. The cats have to be in perfect condition to participate. I thought we could submit Lucky Chance instead, what do you think?"

Elspeth read the leaflet and gave the idea some thought; it might prove rather fun. She turned to Amanda with a ready smile. "Yes, I think we should do that and enter Lucky."

Amanda gave an ear splitting squeal as she hugged her. "I have a list of recommended foods that will make a cat's fur shine like satin!" When Elspeth didn't look too convinced, she assured her that the list was mostly made up of different types of oily fish and contained nothing that a cat wouldn't eat.

As he watched his sister and wife whispering and giggling

together, Adam felt his heart constrict with love for them. Each girl had lost her mother far too young and each one had known deep sadness in her young life. He was delighted to see the friendship between them blossom. He hoped they would become closer still. If he travelled for long periods in his search of artefacts, he would be much happier knowing that his wife had friendship and support while he was gone.

All too soon Christmas was over and they were on their way home, stuffed into an overcrowded carriage with a loudly protesting tom-cat. Adam groused crossly over the fact that they seemed to have more luggage returning home than they had when they arrived. Adam and Elspeth had given Uncle Arthur a beautiful magnifying instrument for Christmas. Adam had found the instrument quite by chance in a chandler's shop. It would hopefully enable Arthur to draw more easily now that his eyesight was failing. Arthur was thrilled with his gift and couldn't wait to try the device on some charts that he was working on at the museum. It was thus agreed that they should first drop Elspeth and Martha off at their home, along with the vocally complaining cat. Then the gentlemen would continue onward to the museum to try out Arthur's new toy.

Elspeth was surprised to find only Mrs. Donald, their cook, at home when they arrived. There was no sign of Mrs. Carron and Cook reported that she had been entirely absent over Christmas. She had added that it had meant that she had a complete break from cooking and had thoroughly enjoyed the rest. They wouldn't have known that she had rested when she handed Martha a tray of cakes and buns to be handed out to the returning family. Adam and Arthur wrapped their selection into a serviette and took their treats with them to the museum.

Darkness fell and there was no sign of Adam. Elspeth began to fret. Mrs. Donald appeared at the parlour door to say that dinner would be ready very shortly, and she informed Elspeth that Mrs. Carron still hadn't returned. Elspeth wondered if the two absences could be in any way linked. She told Mrs. Donald to hold dinner until Adam returned, and then with a feeling of certainty that something was amiss, she ran upstairs to change into a warm dress and dark fur-lined cloak. Rummaging in her chest of drawers, she located the spare key Adam had given her for the staff entrance and pocketed it.

She called Martha to her as she was lacing up her boots in the hallway, explaining her premonition that something was wrong and that she was convinced that she needed to go to the museum to find Adam. The maid begged her mistress to remain safe at home, but Elspeth was adamant that she was going and slipped out into the damp and misty night.

CHAPTER 13

She hurried through the dank streets, made so familiar to her from her mudlarking exploits. By keeping to the shadows, the foggy night helped screen her from any unsavoury characters abroad on the streets of London; men who looked to prey upon unsuspecting women.

Finally, she stood in front of the museum. Its many windows were darkened while the imposing pillars and heavy doors lay shadowed. The gas lights were off and the museum closed. No one appeared to be inside the building.

There was no point in banging on the museum entrance doors. She tried them just to see if they had been left unlocked, but the solid wooden doors didn't budge. She walked the distance around the corner of the road and along the street to the back of the museum, until she came to a yard where Adam usually left the Brougham. As it was there, she thought it a safe bet that Adam was still somewhere inside the building. The small staff door, set beneath an overhanging porch, was set in gloom. Elspeth had to feel her way along the deeply shadowed stone wall until she reached the door. It was closed. She turned the iron ring handle, it swung inward. Inside lay an equally dark passageway. She slipped inside, pulling the door closed behind her.

Her footfalls echoed eerily along the empty hallway that led to the back stairs. Holding on tight to the rail, she walked the six flights up required to take her to Adam's office on the third floor. Her passage was only lit by fleeting moonlight from a tall window, one on every landing. When she eventually arrived on the third floor and entered the cavernous back rooms, overstuffed with weird and wonderful artefacts, the resonant space felt positively terrifying at night. She stilled, listening but could hear nothing. Gradually her eyes adjusted to the gloom as she studied the shadowed forms of the various exhibits. Instinct told her not to shout for Adam, an uneasy sense of doom weighed upon her senses. Allowing her intuition to guide her, she crept silently through the vast area, stopping every so often to listen. This cautiousness paid off, suddenly she heard a faint metallic scratching. The indistinct sound appeared to be coming from the same direction as Adam's office. How odd, whatever could he be up to?

She moved stealthily in that direction, only just avoiding collision with a large object as it loomed suddenly out of the darkness. As she drew close to her husband's work space, she saw dim light leaking from the room. The office door was ajar and so she moved across to the wall and pressed her back against it, sliding silently along until she was able to peek around the door jamb, into the room.

The first thing she noticed was a dark haired man positioned with his back toward her. He was on one knee and appeared to be trying to break open the safe. She frowned, where was Adam? Craning her neck and inching forward, she had a wider view of the room. Elspeth froze. Adam was sprawled face down upon the floor between the desk and the safe. He wasn't moving, not at all. Her eyes flashed back to the man working on the safe. She didn't know him, and yet… there was something vaguely familiar about him, something she couldn't quite put her finger on.

She stretched out her hand reaching for the door knob, hoping to pull the door toward her, thus widening the gap in the doorway. The knob was loose and slid imperceptibly on its spindle, the tiny "clunk" resonated in the silence. Elspeth held her breath. The man at the safe stood up, stretched and turned, glancing behind him. Elspeth felt a tidal wave of remembrance surge into her brain. She staggered backward, holding her head as her memory returned, gushing like flood water pouring through sluice gates.

Henry... but how could it be? He was declared dead! Rough hands grabbed her while she was overcome, dragging her forward into the room. Elspeth was too overwhelmed to struggle or scream. He flung her toward the opposite end of the room near where Adam lay. Elspeth ran to hunker down beside him, pushing his brown hair back from his forehead. She studied his pale face calling his name softly, but there was no response.

"How touching," Henry drawled sarcastically. Elspeth lifted her hand from Adam's head and realised it was sticky. Glancing down, she saw to her horror that her palm was stained with blood. She straightened up and stared at the man who had been responsible for so much of her mental torment. His face paled, registering shock, and Elspeth realised Henry hadn't recognised her up until that point. "*Elspeth?*"

"What are you doing here, Henry? I was told that you were dead!"

That oh so, familiar sneer spread across his features. "Well now, it didn't take you very long to replace me then did it?"

Elspeth held her tongue; she realised it wouldn't do to antagonise him. "Why was I told that you were dead, when clearly you were not?" she asked.

"A reasonable question. I faked my death by planting my papers on an unrecognisable corpse and stealing his identity."

"But why would you do such a thing? You loved the Army." She was genuinely bewildered.

"I am getting older. Army life is tough enough, but when you have a proclivity for drink and drugs, it becomes well nigh impossible. When Trubshaw wrote to me about my parents' deaths and your disappearance… where did you get to by the way?" Elspeth opened her mouth to explain, but he continued, "Never mind, you can tell me after I've finished my tale. It began to niggle that I had no heir and no home to fall back upon when my body wore out. Then another message from Trubshaw came informing me that my cousin had died in a debtor's prison and I was now Lord Wooten. I had a title but no money, not a single bean. I needed to get back to England tout-suite and sort out my inheritance. However, I still had time left to serve on my long service contract with the army. When I found the group of dead soldiers and one in particular, his face ravaged by wild animals, I realised that here was a God sent opportunity." He shrugged.

Elspeth tried to make a connection as to why he might be at the museum, had he come here to look for her? "What is it that you want from the museum? I don't understand."

He grinned. "Money, my dear naive little wife." Elspeth started at that, she had forgotten that she was still his wife. Her heart sank with misery at the thought.

"The *Netra-Baagh* emerald would rebuild the family estate and pay off all my debts. Just think, Lady Wooten, we can still produce a son who would inherit the title. I want the family name to continue. It cannot be allowed to simply die out. You turning up here tonight was provident. You have saved me the irksome job of tracking you down. I watched you knock the animal bones everywhere and hide in the stone coffin when I was scouting ahead. If you were dead, I'd have attempted to marry money, but with the emerald, we have no need to worry about finances. You're a pretty little thing, always were, I shall not bother you once we have an heir and a spare. You shall live in Lancashire with the children while I reside in London and take a mistress. You'll see, poppet, it will work out for us."

As Henry expounded upon her bleak future with him as her

husband, Elspeth fell into despair. The contrast between her life with Adam and his loving family was too much to bear. She couldn't nay, wouldn't go with Henry, but astutely she knew that now was not the time to tell him that.

"The *Shiromani* will only bring you bad luck if you take it, Henry. It has to be gifted—" she tried to explain, but he interrupted, the habitual sneer returning to his face.

"What utter rot, it is a precious stone, hard and cold, dug from the ground, it holds no mystic power. Now that you are here, come and hold the lamp for me while I pick this lock." Elspeth went and picked up the oil lamp as he directed. Perhaps she would get the opportunity to brain him with the thing. His next words dashed that hope.

"Stand in front of me but stand well back so that I can watch you. If you make any wrong move, the professor will die." He pulled out his army revolver. "And I won't be hunted because everyone knows me to be dead." He barked his humourless laugh. Elspeth wanted to point out the flaw to this statement. If he wanted to claim his title he would have to declare himself to be alive and well. He seemed to read her mind. "Once I have the stone, I can buy my freedom from the army. I shall return to India, turn up dazed and confused to explain that I was captured and have no knowledge of what happened to my papers. I shall ask to leave my commission, pretend that I am a broken man. Possibly I shall have to buy my contract out, but by hook or by crook, I shall return to my country seat."

There was a loud click and the safe door swung wide. "Step away, over toward the professor." She did as he asked and watched dejectedly as he rifled about inside the safe. He pulled out the hessian sack and peered inside. He looked up at Elspeth with a beatific smile, one that never touched the depth of his ice cold eyes. He thrust his hand into the bag and brought forth the *Shiromani*. Even in the dim lamp light, the gem glowed with its usual iridescent glow. "Hello again, my beauty," he whispered as he gazed mesmerized into the stone. Something he said struck Elspeth as odd.

"Did you steal the Netra-Baagh from the professor's house once before?"

He nodded absently, as he turned the emerald this way and that, admiringly. "Mm, the damned police nearly had me that time. I hid the thing in a fool proof way tied below the Thames on the Embankment, but damn me if it didn't vanish and find its way back to the professor. It made my chance of retrieving it far more difficult when he placed it into the safe here."

So it had been Henry she had seen running that dank night when she rescued the gem from the Thames mud. "How did you steal it from Adam's house, the professor's house?" she amended hurriedly.

His cold gaze settled on her face. "There's no need to pretend with me, Elspeth, I can guess that you've been whoring in his bed. Your face always gave your thoughts away, and I saw how much you cared about the man, when you went to him just now." Her guilt must have been writ plain on her face because he said next, "I had an accomplice inside the house, one only too happy to help me steal the stone."

Elspeth realised at once to whom he referred. "Mrs. Carron!" she cried.

He nodded. "Yes, the stupid woman, she actually thought I'd marry her."

Elspeth remembered her absence. "Where is she now?" she asked, watching his face.

The sneer appeared again. "She got greedy and irritatingly possessive so I sent her for a swim." His horrible laugh barked eerily about the still air of the room.

Elspeth swallowed, shivering, more with reaction than cold. She hadn't liked or trusted the housekeeper, and it seemed that she'd been justified in being wary of her, but she would not have wished the poor woman dead. She glanced quickly over at Adam as he lay in the same position, unmoving. She sent a silent prayer for them both.

"So what happens now?" she asked, wrapping her arms about herself nervously.

"We take the emerald and leave. You've saved me the trouble of tracking you down and kidnapping you. Ironically, Mabel never mentioned your name so I had no idea you were living with the professor until tonight. She disliked you at first but then she began to respect you. I understand why now that I know it was you who married the professor." He stalked over to her and gripped her arm, giving it a shake. "You were quick to move on, my dearest," he sneered as he began to drag her from the office out into the dark corridor. Elspeth dug her heels in and pulled back. He shook her again and pushed his face nose to nose with her. "Stop that or I'll shoot the professor, and you will pay for it later when we are safe away."

Elspeth nodded, acquiescing, allowing him to yank her along the passage until he turned into a doorway where the infinitesimal glow from a single flickering candle gave enough light for her to see that the sash window in the room was fully raised. He dragged her over to the window, and she saw that a rope travelled through the open space and was tied around an enormous carved statue of a bear. Henry took hold of the ends of the thinner rope that threaded through the top of the hessian bag containing the emerald. Grasping Elspeth's wrist, he tied the bag onto her arm. He then yanked her back to the open window, keeping a tight grip on the bag. He lifted himself over the window sill and gripped the rope with one hand. "You will follow me down."

"Henry, I can't possibly!" she cried, horrified by the thought of attempting to climb down a rope wearing her dress and petticoats. "I won't be able to manage with my full skirts and besides, look at the drop! No-no I shall be killed!"

Henry pulled on the bag, giving her a cold grin. "You have no choice. Besides it's your hands that have to hold on, not your legs. Come down, hand over hand, you'll be fine."

Elspeth's teeth began to chatter with fright. "But if I fall, so will the gem."

She thought that his need for the *Shiromani* might change his mind. "The stone is almost unbreakable and out of the two, it's you who will break. The emerald won't and even if it did, it will still be valuable but you, well, woman, you're easily replaceable." He yanked on the bag dragging her toward him and the open window that she knew was three stories high. The cold wind whistled, swirling about her head, tearing at her hair, yanking long strands out of her coiffure, causing it to whip backward, past her ears. She stared down into the sickening drop below, feeling dizzily, nauseous.

"She might be expendable to you, you sick cad, but she is irreplaceable to me," a low enraged voice growled beside her. Elspeth's heart leapt, Adam! He was pale and blood smeared the side of his forehead, but he was alive, there, fighting for her. She noted that he held a knife in his hand and was attempting to saw through the ties at her wrist. Henry bellowed impotent threats from his position hanging on the rope below the window sill. He tugged hard on the hessian sack, yanking Elspeth's arm downward, out of Adam's reach. Adam leaned out of the window and grabbed at the head of the bag, tugging at it for all he was worth. Elspeth grasped it too, using her other hand. Adam reached over, anchoring her around the waist with his spare arm. There began a life and death struggle as Henry edged Elspeth and the sack toward him out of the window. He was strong, his many years of army training paying off as he gradually dragged Elspeth nearer to her death, causing her waist to straddle the window, her upper body hanging precariously over the sill. Adam saw clearly that the other man cared not a jot whether his wife plunged to her death. He began to desperately barter with Henry. "Take the stone, Wooten, leave Elspeth with me.

Surely you care something for her, man? Can't you see what a lovely woman she is? She has been loyal to you, never once..."

"Loyal... she's been whoring in your bed, loyal huh! You tosspot! You must take me for a fool. No, I'll take her, dead or alive, it's of no matter to me!" He wrapped one of his legs about the rope and used both hands to give an almighty yank to the hessian bag.

Adam leaned toward Elspeth and hissed in her ear, "When I tell you, push back into the room and immediately let go of the sack... just trust *me.*" Elspeth couldn't acknowledge him; every fibre of her being was paralysed with fear at the sight of the terrifying abyss below.

"NOW!" They both let go of the sack. Elspeth fell back, the sensation of falling caused her to scream. "You're safe!" Adam reassured her loudly. There was no noise from outside except the howling wind. She scrambled up, but Adam held her back. "No, I'll look." He moved to the window and tentatively leaned across the sill. A hand shot up and grabbed his shirt front. Adam placed his hand over Henry's wrist and gripped, holding on firmly, attempting to pull him up and back into the room. There was an enraged bellow from below. "Don't you try to save me, you bastard; I'll see you in hell first!"

"Don't be a fool, man, we can resolve this! I'll give you the damned emerald, just so long as you leave us in peace and go your own way—all I want is Elspeth!" Adam fought against Henry's stupidly futile attempt to pull him forward to his death, all the while trying in vain to drag the captain back up and into the room.

The suddenness to the end of this impasse was shocking. A rending of material as Adam's shirt ripped, a shout, then nothing but the whistling gale through the open window and the pounding of Adam's heart in the deathly silence.

CHAPTER 14

When they finally reached the front of the museum some minutes later, they found Henry lying face down upon the pavement. Adam sternly ordered Elspeth to stay back. He went to the broken man and hunkered down beside him. Taking a deep breath, Adam gingerly lifted Henry's shoulder and felt for a neck pulse, there was none. He rubbed a hand over his own face and bowed his head over the body. He wasn't able to pray in that terrible moment, but he did wonder at the stupid waste of life. He reflected on how unnecessary these actions of Henry's had been. If only the man had come to him first and told him that he wanted money or the *Shiromani*, in fact, asked him for anything in return for Elspeth, Adam would have handed him whatever he'd asked for in order to keep her with him. He wondered about the strange tormented captain, a man who'd taken Elspeth to wife and never appreciated how lucky he was to possess such a jewel as her. It was Henry Wooten's loss and Adam's gain. He knew that he would never take his beautiful wife for granted. Elspeth was his priority, tonight and always. Events of the night had cemented that firmly in his mind, something never to be forgotten.

He rose and walked slowly over to where Elspeth stood,

shocked, dejected and forlorn. He wrapped his arms about her, pulling her in close. "Your memory returned, do you remember us aboard the ship?" he asked.

She nodded. "Yes, I remember everything. Adam, where is Uncle Arthur?"

"Fear not. He left hours before me, Mr. Harris took him home. I was unprepared when Wooten arrived. I thought he was Harris returning for something and had my back to the scoundrel." Elspeth burrowed into him, both giving and receiving comfort from his familiar, beloved scent. Neither spoke; they had no need for words.

Adam took his wife straight home, leaving her in Martha's tender care while he went to the police. They went at once to the museum to take care of Henry's body and assess his crime. Adam easily convinced Elspeth that it would be in their best interests to deny all knowledge of the burglar's identity, and she saw the sense in that. Revealing the extent of Henry's duplicity would not bring him, or Mrs. Carron, back to life, nor would it change the outcome of the murder that he'd committed. When events had settled down, they would visit Mr. Trubshaw to seek his legal opinion on the status of their marriage.

~

"...AND so since Henry Wooten was confirmed dead during service to his country whilst posted to India and you were married some two months after his death was announced..." here Mr. Trubshaw stopped speaking and looked over the rim of his glasses at each of them in turn, causing Elspeth to flush with a feeling of inexplicable guilt. "I conclude that there is no reason to suppose that you are anything other than married and thus remain, legally husband and wife." Adam reached across and gave his wife's hand a jubilant squeeze. Elspeth slumped back in her chair with relief, the sense of guilt passing with the good news. "I don't suppose we shall ever know the identity of the poor unfortunate museum thief because of his extensive facial damages." The lawyer shrugged, giving a broad wink.

"Thank you, Mr. Trubshaw. There is one other small business detail my wife would like you to take care of. Elspeth?" Adam turned, smiling encouragingly at his wife.

"Yes, I should like to sell all the lands and remaining housing belonging to the Wooten estates and pay off any debts still outstanding. Could your firm undertake that for me please?"

"With pleasure, Mrs. Beresford, is there anything else that I can help you with today?" The lawyer glanced between them, his bushy eyebrow raised.

"Thank you but no, that concludes our business today. You have been most kind." Adam stood and pulled out Elspeth's chair as she rose to her feet, holding out her hand to her legal advisor.

He lifted her hand to his lips. "May I say that I have rarely seen such strength and fortitude displayed by one so young, who has undergone so many trials and tribulations as yourself, dear lady? I do so hope and pray that from now onward, your path will be one of peaceful harmony."

"Thank you, Mr. Trubshaw, you are too kind." Elspeth was touched by the legal gentleman's obvious sincerity.

Once seated in their carriage, they both felt utter relief that they were still married and the nightmare was behind them. They silently reflected on the aftermath of Henry's death. Adam was happy that he had convinced Elspeth to keep quiet about the real events of that night. When the police had asked what they were doing at the museum at that time of night, Adam had informed them that Elspeth had lost a brooch and they had gone back to search for it.

Mrs. Carron's body had washed up further down the Thames a week later and Adam had gone to identify her remains. The police discovered that she had never, in fact, been married and was a spinster. They also found out that her parents still lived but were retired from service, living in a cottage with their son in an Essex village. The police notified them of her death, which was deemed to be death by misadventure and so both cases were closed.

Elspeth spent some time in quiet reflection. Once she felt it safe for her to relax, she shed her capable personality and reverted to behaving like a naughty juvenile again. Adam found it amusing that his wife had this core of strength when it was required but, between times, she became a naughty little minx. He was more than happy for her to shed her load in this odd way and felt more than capable of dealing with her.

They had discussed the possibility of Elspeth travelling with him when he was away on archaeological expeditions now that Adam knew how strong a character his wife really was. He decided that she could accompany him anytime, unless, of course, she was expecting their child. Elspeth secretly thought that she might already be increasing but hadn't yet shared the happy news with her husband. She was enjoying having her own little secret and wanted to keep it to herself a little while longer.

Adam suddenly broke into her reverie by chuckling to himself. "Adam?" Elspeth queried, concerned. "Peaceful harmony?" he laughed. Elspeth's lip twitched. "Beast!" she cried and punched his shoulder lightly.

He leaned toward her ensnaring her wrists, bringing them above her head. He lowered his mouth to hers and kissed her, forcing her to yield to his passion. Once she'd melted back against the seat, he released her lips but kept a tight grip on her wrists. "Your impish behaviour never fails to amuse me, my little waif. You delight me in every conceivable way and this afternoon, I shall *delight* you so much that your cries will echo from our bedchamber and disturb the vicar at Saint Helen's."

"Professor, you are a wicked man, but I do so love you… Adam, *stop, what are you doing*? Ooo… no-o!" She shrieked with giggles as her husband yanked her forward over his lap, his hand playing a fast tattoo upon her skirted bottom.

"My name is Adam, *not Professor*!" he scolded playfully.

Elspeth squealed with laughter, thoroughly enjoying the fact that she knew just how to wind her husband up. Just as she knew Adam intended to put her across his knee every time she succeeded.

EPILOGUE

13TH JULY 1871

"Lucky Chance won a prize! Look, Elspeth, Lucky won a rosette thingamajig!" Amanda clapped her hands with excitement. Elspeth moved to the cage and, sure enough, a yellow rosette was pinned on his box. She turned and hugged Amanda who hopped about gleefully in a silly triumphant dance.

Elspeth finding her pregnancy irksome, now stood and watched. She was increasing in size and unable to move around quite as nimbly. "I must go and tell Adam!" she exclaimed, hurrying as fast as her rounded belly would allow. Adam's gaze was centered upon his wife, especially when she moved away from him. He held out his hand to her as he saw her approach as he stood chatting to his brother James. Elspeth was obviously bursting with pride as she waved a yellow circle of ribbon in the air excitedly. He was a happy man, a fulfilled man and he knew for certain that his wife felt the same way. The darkness of her past had finally left her soul. She radiated happiness. His wife was a contented and well-rounded woman, quite literally, filled with his child. He looked forward to spending the rest of his life with her and their children.

Amanda waited and when Elspeth failed to return, she wandered off to roam the rows and rows of cat boxes, gazing into the pens admiring the remarkable differences between this species of amazing creatures. She adored cats; they fascinated her, with their mesmerizing eyes and slinky, agile bodies. She stopped and gawped into an oversized, wire fronted box that contained the largest cat she had ever seen. It looked a little like a lynx that she had once seen drawn in a book of wilderness beasts. The animal's ears were tufted into points like some big cats and the stripes on its body were highly defined. She lifted her hand about to push her fingers in between the gaps of the wire cage, when a large hand suddenly clamped about her wrist. "I wouldn't do that, little lady, he tends to bite."

Amanda spun around, already prepared to give the man one of her famous dressing downs, but when she turned and looked at a dark waistcoat, she lifted her head up, and up and up, finding herself looking into the most gorgeous male face she'd ever laid eyes upon, she quickly changed her mind about the scold, smiling sweetly instead.

"Hello, my goodness that is a strange accent. What part of the country do you come from?" she asked baldly. The man grinned quite sinfully; Amanda stared back at him unashamedly enthralled. Bloody hell, she thought, he was absolutely, fabulously, gorgeous. In fact, he was the most handsome man she had ever laid eyes upon!

"Well now, let's see… I am living in London right now and I am assistant to the American Envoy, Mr. Robert Schenck. Abel Lawson, at your service… Miss?"

"Amanda Beresford," Amanda supplied.

He nodded acknowledgement of her name and continued talking, "I hail from Boston originally, I guess my home is in Washington nowadays and will be again when I return at the end of our posting. How about you, Miss Beresford, whereabouts do you reside?"

"I live in Sydenham, only a stone's throw from here." She waved her hand in the general direction of her family home, keeping her eyes firmly fixed on that incredible face of his.

"And are you here with a cat?" he asked.

"Well, I would have been yes, with my cat, Dusty, but she sustained a torn ear over Christmas. It was absolutely my own fault. You see I rather stupidly let my sister-in-law's cat into the same room, and they fought horribly. So we decided to enter her cat, Lucky Chance instead. He won a yellow rosette you know."

Shut up, Amanda, shut up and stop rabbitting on! Please be quiet! Amanda berated herself, but she just couldn't seem to stop the flow of inane chatter from pouring out of her mouth. "I thought that Lucky was a large cat but when I saw your lynx, I was absolutely amazed, but I suppose he suits his over large owner." *Oh please tell me I did not just say that! Whatever must he think of me?*

Abel listened to the pretty English girl babbling on about her sister-in-law's cat and wondered how to politely escape. He studied her. She was an exceptionally pretty little thing, but her constant tongue wagging could drive a man to drink. In fact, the only way he could see any man halting that relentless flow of words, would be by kissing her adorably cupid shaped mouth or even by pushing his cock between the plump pink lips. In an instant, he was iron hard. Heck, where had that crude thought come from? This young lady was a well brought up innocent. He should be shot for thinking about her in that way! His eyes dropped to her bosom, just about a perfect fit for his large hands. What was he thinking? He needed to get away from her… and fast.

"How delightful, if you would excuse me, miss." He lifted his top hat, executed a small bow and turned to leave, then recalled her sticking her fingers into Grant's cage and turned his head to glower at her.

"Don't let me find those hands of yours anywhere near my cat's cage, or I promise, there will be consequences." *He inwardly groaned, did he really just threaten her?* She gave him the strangest look and caught her plump bottom lip between her small white teeth. They stood eyeing one another for the longest moment. Well, at least that shut her prattle up, he thought. Then she went and said the darnedest thing and he knew he was caught, hook line and sinker.

The End

AUTHOR'S NOTE

Mudlarking on the Thames has been carried out for hundreds of years, right up to the modern day. In fact, I was in London walking beside the Thames one day when I spotted a group of modern day mudlarks searching the shore for treasure. I watched them for a while, came home and researched "Mudlark." The germ of an idea for a book was seeded.

In Victorian England, the poor would pick up items carried by the tides to lodge in the mud of the river Thames shoreline. Many treasures came from ship wrecks off the English coast. Today, old bottles, clay pipes, jewellery and all manner of interesting items are still being found. Many valuable finds are on display in London museums.

The part in the story about Charles Dickens and the train crash is absolutely true. I couldn't resist using it in my tale to demonstrate a heroic side to the famous author, one that was little known at the time. Dickens did not want any publicity about his part in the tragic event, due to the controversial presence of his mistress and her mother, who were travelling with him at the time of the disaster.

Jane Eyre was first published under the pseudonym name,

Currer Bell. The book was initially considered an immoral tale but was so much discussed that it eventually became famous and Charlotte Bronte finally claimed it as her own work. It was republished this time under her real name.

The very first official cat show was held at Crystal Palace on July 13, 1871; about forty prizes were awarded. I remember my grandparents telling me how they'd watched the lovely glass Crystal Palace burn to the ground before they had met in 1937. Rivers of melted glass flowed down the hill and was quite a sight to behold. Sadly, the palace was never rebuilt and is now gone forever.

Vanessa Brooks

AMANDA

VICTORIAN ROGUES, BOOK TWO

Published by Blushing Books®,
a subsidiary of
ABCD Graphics and Design
977 Seminole Trail #233
Charlottesville, VA 22901
The trademark Blushing Books®
is registered in the US Patent and Trademark Office.

Vanessa Brooks
Amanda
Victorian Rogues, Book Two

EBook ISBN: 978-1-61258-377-8
Cover Art by ABCD Graphics & Design

CHAPTER 1

SYDENHAM, LONDON 1871

The window creaked alarmingly as she lifted the sash, pushing the wooden support block beneath it to prevent it becoming an inadvertent guillotine as she clambered through. She held her breath, stilled, listening, relaxing again when she heard nothing. Taking her soft bodied carpet bag, she leaned out of the window then flung the bag into the dark shrubbery below. There was a muffled thud as it landed. Once again, head tilted, she listened intently. Satisfied that her family still slumbered unaware, she edged her way out onto the window sill, surprised at how easy this movement was when not hampered by skirts. Her nephew's clothing gave her a newfound freedom of movement, although she found the coarse woollen tweed incredibly itchy against her skin. Amanda was of the opinion her brothers had the easier option, clothed in trousers and britches as opposed to the cumbersome skirts and dresses she was forced to wear.

Perhaps if she should ever live in America, she would be able to wear male garments instead of gowns? She really knew very little about the country that her new American beau came from, other than that there had been a war to obtain independence from Britain. She knew that not long ago a civil war had been fought, and she was vaguely aware the war had something to do with abolishing slavery. Her governess had not taught her much Colonial history, so Amanda was hazy on the details. However, as a perennially positive person, she had high hopes of more freedom and less strictures in America, should she choose to marry her recently acquired suitor.

Amanda Beresford could never be mistaken for a blue stocking since she'd paid scant attention to her lessons, choosing instead to draw fashion plates upon her slate. She was also fond of sketching cats, which she adored. Although not a fan of her governesses' choice of reading material, she generally had a romantic novel tucked somewhere about her person, although she did not read to improve her mind; her hobbies kept her quietly occupied while her poor teacher tried to instil some semblance of education into her stubborn charge's head. However, odd facts had stuck. Amanda surprised herself sometimes with knowledge she'd managed to retain, but generally, she was considered by those who knew her best as a flibbertigibbet. Certainly, it was a view held strongly by her two elder brothers, Adam, and James.

She reflected briefly on her plan to rescue Grant, the cat belonging to the man she hoped to marry someday. Her stubborn determination and tunnel vision meant she disregarded the pitfalls of taking such action as she continued dogmatically with her ill-advised clandestine plan.

The solid brick built house was fronted by a peeling white trellis supporting a well established wisteria, substantial enough to absorb her descent. The rustling noise as she climbed down the gnarled trunk of the shrub concerned her. She halted periodically as the structure began to waver then creak alarmingly. Every downward move she made caused more noise. Finally, at about four feet from the ground, she decided it would be prudent to jump. She landed, immediately rolling onto the lawn. Coming to a halt on her back, she stilled for a moment to catch her breath, alert for signs of pursuit, although she need not have feared as there were none.

Hopping up, she retrieved her bag and then set off at a jaunty pace in the opposite direction of her family home, giving not so much as a backward glance as she savoured the unimpeded movement of her borrowed clothes and the exciting sense of adventure that the escapade afforded.

To the lamplighters beginning their morning rounds extinguishing the gas street lights as dawn fast approached, she was just another darkly clad lad, sporting an oversized cap, making his way to work. The only thing a truly observant person might notice, had they been interested, was that this particular boy carried a carpet bag. They might have been surprised to know that this lad was, in fact, a woman in disguise, on her way to rescue a condemned cat. And not just any old puss-cat, but a large Maine Coon who'd won the coveted best of rare breed prize at the Crystal Palace cat show in July. The large feline belonged to her beau, Mr. Abel Lawson, who was assistant to the American envoy, the current Minister to the United Kingdom, Mr. Robert Schenck. Amanda had met Mr. Lawson at the very same cat show, where Grant, so named after the incumbent President of the United States, had won his coveted rosette. Since then, the feline had become somewhat famous.

Queen Victoria had expressed such interest in the cat that an invitation had been issued to the American envoy asking him to bring Abel Lawson to present Grant to the Royal household at Windsor Castle. Unfortunately, during the visit, an over eager lady-in-waiting disregarded Abel's warning that the animal might bite. Choosing to ignore him, she'd pushed her wriggling fingers inside the metal grid of the cat's carry box. It was too much for the frightened, fretful feline who had lunged at the proffered digits, catching his prey with sharp claws, biting deep. The resulting mayhem had ended with a vengeful decree from Her Majesty, demanding that Grant be destroyed.

Amanda was utterly incensed by the injustice of the edict. She was made even more irate by what she perceived to be her gentleman caller's easy capitulation, relinquishing his cat to the police. She was unaware of the background diplomacy being deployed by both countries' politicians. She determined to rescue the cat herself and hide it safely away until the furore blew over. Amanda ignored Abel's reassurance that he would save his pet through diplomatic channels. Amanda simply laid her plans, taking matters into her own hands. Her sister-in-law Elspeth's adopted uncle had recently moved into a small house with a garden that backed directly onto Dulwich Park, an ideal location for a pet. Arthur Brown liked cats and was only too happy to home a stray, readily agreeing to foster the animal. He might have changed his mind had he known that this wasn't simply any old homeless cat that he was opening his door to but a political hot potato. Amanda and Elspeth carefully withheld this rather important element of information from the unsuspecting Arthur.

Arthur had a lodger, a lad known to one and all as Scrounger. A name bestowed upon him on account of his mudlarking activities digging along the shore of the River Thames. He searched for treasure cast from ships, carried inland by the tide, to lodge in the mud along the shoreline.

The plan was that Scrounger would meet Amanda outside the police station where the unfortunate Grant was being held, whilst the political wrangle over sovereignty of the animal raged. The Americans claimed diplomatic immunity for the feline, while the Crown decreed that exemption could only be applied to humans. Scrounger's plan was simple, one of distraction and kidnap or, as Scrounger so aptly described it, catnap.

Amanda knew that she risked the wrath of both her elder brothers, James and Adam, should she be caught. However, she had never been punished beyond a scolding by either of them and had no fear of their retribution should she be caught. Amanda had lost her parents in a terrible railway accident some years before. She lived with her eldest brother James, his wife, Felicity, and their two children, George aged nine and Madeline, known to her family as Maddie, aged six.

As Amanda approached her destination, she saw the dull blue gas light that marked the public entrance to the police station. She halted and looked about for her partner in crime. Suddenly hands covered her eyes. She jumped, startled, swallowing her squeal. "Scrounger!" she scolded, guessing her assailant's identity correctly. Sure enough, the tousle haired lad stepped forward, wearing an engaging grin.

"Gotcha," he chuckled delightedly.

"Stop larking about, foolish boy, this is a serious undertaking! A life is at stake!" Amanda berated crossly.

"I can always leave you to it an' go on 'ome," he offered.

Amanda flashed him a look of panic. "No, I need your help!"

He tweaked her nose. "Blinkin'-well show some respect then." Amanda swallowed her sharp retort, nodding meekly. He was right, she really did need his help.

"Ready?" he asked. She nodded, handing him the carpet bag before sucking in a deep breath, ripping off her cap, her dark blonde hair flowed freely as she rushed inside the Police station giving vent to an ear splitting shriek. Her scream brought forth three panicked, uniformed constables who rushed toward her as she flung herself into their midst, tilting into a fake swoon, forcing those closest to catch her. Meanwhile, Scrounger took the opportunity to slip past the unfolding drama. He disappeared into the recess of the building, clutching Amanda's carpet bag.

The inspector ran his hands through his receding hair and sighed heavily. "Let us begin again shall we, Miss Beresford? I have to say this story of yours just don't add up. Now, let me get this straight. You say that you accepted a dare from a friend to go mudlarkin' and dressed yourself in your nephew's clothes then snuck out the house at dawn. You allege that a man grabbed you from behind as you were walking. He then dragged you down an alley way, where he pulls off your cap, reveals you're a woman and threatens to kill you. Now, this is where I am not convinced. I am a wondering why he would do that? I can see him robbing you, even raping you, but what I cannot understand is why. If he wanted to kill you, why he didn't just go ahead and do it?" Privately, he rather wished her assailant *had* murdered the blasted woman.

Amanda glared at the inspector. Drat the fellow; he had a point. She should have told him she'd been robbed instead. Ah well, it was no good changing her story now. She had to stick to her original tale or the whole of her story would sound weaker than it already did. She decided to take refuge in righteous indignation. "How dare you! I have explained everything to you ad-nauseam. It is not my fault that you are too stupid to understand me! I have had quite enough of your slurs, sir! I demand that you take me home. In fact, I want to go home right now!"

The inspector turned puce. "Now see here girly, you don't get to talk to me like that, an' what's more—"

"Sir, I'm sorry to interrupt you, but I have to report that the American cat's gawn!" The timely interruption came from a constable who'd been dispatched earlier to make tea for the beleaguered inspector. He leapt to his feet.

"What the heck? Search the whole blooming building!" He glared at Amanda. "You," he jabbed a finger at her, "get off home. I'll send a constable to your address tomorrow to take a statement about this alleged attack. I have bigger problems to fry right now!" He turned and strode from the room, spitting orders right and left.

Amanda slumped in her chair with relief. She hadn't expected such a grilling about her silly story. She knew she'd fluffed it, changing details with each new narration. Quickly, she slipped out of the building and out into the street. Without taking the time to glance right or left, she ran straight across the thoroughfare. There was a sudden shout, a shriek, loud whinnying, followed by a sudden blindingly painful blow to her left haunch.

"Young woman... young woman? Come, wake up I have examined you, and I find you to be quite unharmed." Amanda stirred and groaned. Her hip bone hurt. "Come along, girl, open your eyes!" She made an effort to lift her heavy lids. Blinking, she looked into the face of a strange young man, fair-haired, even featured. A boyish looking man who would be handsome if his face were not contorted by a scowl. At this precise moment, he looked positively vexed.

"Where am I?" she croaked.

"You are inside my coach. What the devil d'you mean, dashing out into the road in that hare-brained way? You might have been killed! As it is, you have thoroughly spooked my horses!"

Amanda bristled. "Well excuse me! Perhaps your coachman needs to slow down whilst driving through town. He'd be less likely to run down innocent young ladies!" she retorted crossly. The man gave an unpleasant snort.

"Lady... my foot. You are dressed as a boy! No *lady* ventures out so scandalously clad, you brazen baggage. What you need is a jolly good taste of my crop!" Amanda, incensed, leaned forward and slapped his face. The man coloured up a rather unpleasant puce. "Why you little guttersnipe," he snarled, malice in his eyes. A slashing blow fell across her thigh. She shrieked with shock as his vicious crop left a searing line of fire in its wake.

Amanda, never a shrinking violet, drew her diminutive self together at once. "How dare you! You, you... degenerate oaf! I am Amanda Beresford, sister to James Beresford Esq. of Sydenham. I am dressed this way for a-a dare, which went horribly wrong. I-I was attacked, knocked down by your carriage, and all I wish to do is return home!" She thought it would be provident to stick to the same tale that she had told the police. Amanda had learned young that the ability to squeeze out a few tears in certain situations achieved her desired outcome readily, and so she allowed her eyes to fill with tears accordingly, the stinging line of fiery pain across her thigh aiding her accomplishment.

The man's eyes narrowed. He scanned her sorrowful face for signs of deceit. Obviously detecting none in her guileless eyes, his gaze softened toward her. "Miss Beresford, do allow me to apologise for my assumption. Let me introduce myself, Doctor Eugene Barker at your service. I shall deliver you home and hand you safely over into the bosom of your family. I am not impressed by their lack of diligence in caring for you, not if this is an example of how you comport yourself. I should apologise for the chastising swipe I dealt you, but I feel it was justly deserved. Your address if you please." Amanda considered telling him where he could go boil his head, but having seen his fury when she'd slapped him, she thought better of it, meekly stating her home address.

The doctor reached for a folded blanket on the seat beside him and threw the rug across her knees. He ordered her to stay put before leaping out from the carriage. Amanda could hear him talking with his driver, who'd presumably managed to calm the shocked horses. Once he was settled back inside the carriage, he stroked his chin, frowning thoughtfully. "Young woman, do you perchance bear any relation to Professor Adam Beresford?" Amanda nodded.

"Yes indeed, he is the younger of my elder brothers. Why do you ask?"

"I believe we were up at Oxford together. I am slightly acquainted with him. I seem to recall that your parents lost their lives in that train disaster out in Kent, the one that Charles Dickens was involved in a few years back. Am I correct?" Amanda nodded; she had no need to feign the tears that filled her eyes. Being reminded of that terrible, fateful day always upset her. The doctor patted her knee sympathetically and apologised for bringing the subject up. He explained that he, too, had lost his parents young.

After that, they travelled in uneasy silence for the rest of the journey out to Sydenham.

On arrival, he irritatingly insisted on accompanying her to the front door. Mrs. Kettle, their housekeeper, insisted that Doctor Barker wait in the drawing room. Amanda gave him her thanks, bobbed a curtsy and escaped to her bedchamber in order to change out of her outlandish garb. She'd just stripped off her nephew's clothes when her maid Hattie arrived to help her dress. After a moment of still contemplation, she stepped forward and quietly helped her mistress into her bustle and sprigged day gown. Amanda could bear the tension between them no longer. "All right, Hattie, you may as well tell me what you have to say about my adventures today."

Hattie pursed her lips disapprovingly. "I'm sure it's none of my business what you get up to, Miss Beresford; however, I am to tell you to go directly to the drawing room when you are dressed. Both of your brothers are waiting for you."

Amanda frowned, both her brothers? "Adam is here?" she queried. The maid nodded. "Oh Lord, when did *he* arrive?" she groaned.

"The household has been in uproar ever since I discovered that you'd vanished from your bed this morning. Where on earth have you been, miss?" Amanda sat down at her dressing table and allowed her maid to pin up her hair. Hattie efficiently scooped her mistress' thick hair into a simple chignon.

"You'll hear all about it soon enough, Hattie, but suffice to say it was a matter of life and death."

"Oh, seems the professor was right enough then," the maid replied smugly.

"Whatever d' you mean?" Amanda asked, twisting her head so she could look up at her maid.

"Please keep still, miss. Drat it all, I'll have to start over again now! The professor said he wouldn't be at all surprised to find that you'd gone to rescue that condemned cat, the one that all the newspapers are talking about."

"Adam said that?" For the first time, Amanda worried that, on this occasion, she may have gone too far down the road of impropriety. Her brothers were generally tolerant of her hoydenish ways. On reflection, she realised that they were not quite as lenient with their wives as they had been with their sister. She'd never really considered the difference in attitude before, but now she thought about it, Amanda realised that her brothers allowed her leeway in behaviour that they never allowed their wives. Perhaps this time she'd overstepped the mark? What if she'd pushed them a tad too far? She wondered what kind of reaction she could expect from her siblings on this occasion. Well, one thing was certain; it wouldn't be long before she found out.

~

DOWNSTAIRS, Amanda's two brothers stared at one another in consternation. Doctor Barker had left the house but not before imparting verbose disapproval at them for allowing Amanda to run wild. He'd also requested their permission to call upon Amanda.

"She's gone too far this time," Adam stated gloomily.

"I agree, but I balk at punishing her. After all, she is our sister. It just doesn't sit right with me. If only father were still alive, I'm sure she'd be far more composed and less likely to get into silly scrapes like this latest one," James grumbled.

"He'd have turned her over his knee for sure, disappearing from the house like that. I could wring her bloody neck!" Adam warmed to his theme, "She ought to be soundly whipped, James, especially if she is involved with the disappearance of that wretched cat."

James glanced assessingly at his brother, "You are willing to whip her?" Adam shook his head in response. "Hmm, thought not, me neither. D'you really think she's involved with taking the American's cat?" James asked, aghast by the idea. Adam nodded. "Kidnapping is a criminal offence. Surely she couldn't be so utterly stupid?" James didn't sound as if he believed his own words.

"Mr. Lawson obviously thought she was capable of the act, otherwise why did he come chasing over here demanding to see Amanda as soon as the police had notified him of his pet's disappearance?" Adam asked.

James took a sip of his tea. "I am beginning to think we need to concentrate on finding Amanda a husband as soon as may be. Actually, I am not as averse to the American, as you seem to be. He's young, well-educated and obviously a determined sort of man. He appears perfectly capable of taming our wayward sister."

Adam shook his head, adamantly opposed to the suggestion. "She's far too young to marry; she's still a child at barely sixteen!"

James shook his head, giving a long suffering sigh. "Adam, she's nineteen! You've been telling folk she's sixteen for two years now. You told Elspeth the very same thing but Amanda is twenty in September."

"I worry that should she choose to marry Abel Lawson, she will end up living thousands of miles away on the American continent." James looked alarmed by the suggestion. "She will be so far removed from our support. No, James, after all, what do we really know about this American chappy?"

Their conversation was interrupted by a soft rap at the door, immediately followed by the appearance of their sister. She sashayed over to Adam, proffered him her cheek to kiss, he obliged her. She turned to James, intent on kissing him as well, but he surprised her by grasping her elbows and shaking her.

"I want to know exactly what you've been up to, miss. I'll have no prevarication, mind. I want an honest answer!"

Her eyes widened as she attempted to pull free of her brother's grip. Realising how incensed both her siblings were, she allowed her large cerulean eyes to flood with tears. "If you must know, I was attacked, so I went to the police station to ask for their assistance!" She then executed the perfect swoon, gratified to hear her brothers' gasps of concern. Honestly, men were so easily duped; they could be so stupid. Why had she been concerned about their reaction? Hadn't she always commanded the ability to manipulate the pair of them? As they fussed over her, lifting her legs up onto the couch, patting her hands, yelling for smelling salts, she settled, comfortably complacent, knowing that everything had turned out to her advantage.

CHAPTER 2

The following morning, a young constable, barely out of short trousers, arrived to take Amanda's statement. James remained in the room the whole while his sister told her tale. His frown grew deeper with every word she uttered. She was lying, and he knew it. He determined at once that the two gentlemen who'd requested to court her could do so. Whichever man Amanda favoured most, he would encourage his suit. As far as he was concerned, the sooner Amanda was safely married, the better. James knew his sister now needed a firm hand to guide her before she ruined her chance of marriage with her headstrong ways. He wanted her off his hands but that didn't mean he was about to push her into marriage against her will. No, he cared too much about her to do that.

If she favoured one man above the other, well, then he wouldn't stand in the way of her choice. James rather suspected that Doctor Barker was a stronger character than his amiable looks led one to believe. He thought that his mild, fair features were perhaps deceptive. Only time would tell as to which man would succeed in winning his sister's heart, but whichever man she favoured, James prayed that it would be a fast courtship, engagement and marriage.

The danger of his sister ruining herself was becoming a serious problem.

Eugene Barker arrived the following afternoon in a lightweight gig in which he intended driving Amanda over to the Crystal Palace gardens, where he planned a romantic stroll about the grounds. Hattie was asked to accompany them for propriety's sake. After spending a couple of hours in the doctor's company, the young maid found herself unimpressed by her mistress' new suitor. She thought him to be a conceited, pompous and thoroughly condescending fellow. She might have been surprised to find that Amanda's thoughts were in accordance with her own.

When Doctor Barker's gig arrived back at Sydenham Avenue, they were met by the incongruous sight of Abel Lawson atop a penny-farthing bicycle speeding down the street. As he rode, his tall hat toppled to the ground and young George ran to the rescue. He kept pace beside the tall American, cheering while waving the black top hat as encouragement at the long-legged man who rode the high wheeled vehicle directly to the bottom of the hill. His black coat tails flew behind him like a pair of over sized crow wings. He stopped in a level dip of ground, dismounted, lifted the boy onto the saddle of the ungainly contraption and set off with one arm protectively circling the child's waist, his other arm steered the bicycle as he ran back up the hill, guiding both George and the penny-farthing. George whooped with excitement. They halted just a few feet from Amanda and Eugene, who watched the proceedings with a glowering expression. Amanda missed his dour glance as she skipped over to speak with her nephew.

Laughingly out of breath, Abel lifted George from his lofty post, setting him gently back down on terra firma. "Did you see me Aunt Amanda, did you see me?" he chattered excitedly. Amanda grinned up at Abel, her gaze centered on his handsome face as she spoke with George, confirming that yes, she had seen him ride. She praised the boy before thanking Abel for his kindness toward him.

"Why, there's no call for thanks, Miss Beresford. George and I both enjoyed the fun, didn't we, son?" George nodded enthusiastically. Amanda suggested that he run inside the house to ascertain whether tea was ready, while she questioned Abel.

"Is there a particular reason for your visit today, Mr. Lawson, I was unaware that you were calling?"

Abel swept a hand over his dark unruly hair then banged his hat against his thigh to shake away the dust before replacing it on his head. "There is a somewhat pressing matter that I need to discuss with you, yes, but that can wait until your friend here has departed." He gestured toward Eugene.

Amanda began to saunter toward the house. She glanced teasingly over her shoulder at her two suitors. "Well then, I suppose that I should invite you both inside to join my family for tea." She led them into the house, missing the dark look Eugene cast over the American. Abel observed the doctor's scowl. He had no idea who this young man was but he took an instant dislike toward him.

Abel Lawson was an astute man. He was in particular, a skilled negotiator, a trait that had served him well in his political career. He was also a determinedly stubborn individual who'd long since decided that he wanted to marry Amanda. When he'd first met her, she had the strangest effect upon him. At first, he'd thought himself merely attracted to an unusually pretty girl, but while she'd stood before his cat's cage, he'd promised her dire consequences should she poke her fingers into his lair. She'd blushed prettily, shifting from one foot to another, eventually asking if the kind of retribution he hinted at suggested a spanking. She'd more than captured his interest with her forthright words.

This was because Abel was a man who believed in spanking as an effective deterrent for wayward females. Furthermore, he discovered that he liked to spank. He knew his father had spanked his mother, although never in front of him or his sisters, but they had all been aware of their father's firm, but kindly, chastisement of their vivacious mama whenever she disobeyed him. He'd also spanked Abel and his two sisters, Jayne and Celia, whenever they'd misbehaved as children. Witnessing the positive results that chastisement had wrought upon his tomboy sisters' behaviour, Abel had become convinced that heating a woman's sit-upon, worked wonders for her attitude. He'd not had many liaisons with women over the years, being aware that his morals would be under scrutiny more than most men while building a political career. The few discreet affairs he had were with widows whom he'd escorted to various events. Spanking a lady for keeping him waiting so long that they'd been unacceptably late for a politically sensitive dinner had been a revelation to him. He had enjoyed the experience even as he'd ascertained that the lady had not. She learned her lesson well though; throughout the rest of their short liaison, she was extremely punctual.

He'd found it impossible to get Amanda out of his thoughts after they first became acquainted at the Crystal Palace cat show in July, the first to be held in Britain. He had decided to call upon her later that same week. Unfortunately, Amanda had been out on the afternoon he'd visited, but her brother, James Beresford, had been at home. James was perturbed by the unexpected arrival of a tall American come calling upon his young sister. He'd invited Abel inside where he'd thoroughly grilled him about his intentions. James clarified his reservations about Abel being an American. He explained that he abhorred the idea of his vulnerable sister living thousands of miles away from home without family support. Abel had done his best to reassure the man that, should his suit prove successful with Amanda and he was recalled to the United States, his family would welcome her with open arms, offering her all the support she could possibly need. James found himself reluctantly agreeing to the American courting his sister.

He'd since visited Amanda and taken tea with the family. Abel had, therefore, observed Amanda in her home environment, quickly realising from her conduct, that she was spoilt by her family. She'd developed into a headstrong, wilful young woman but he recognised her good points, which included her keen interest in other people, her kindness to those she loved and her determined championing of the underdog. It was this latter trait that brought him to her door today. His condemned cat, Grant, had been stolen and he was as certain as could be that Miss Amanda Beresford knew precisely where Grant was. He determined that, by hook or by crook, the pretty little minx would tell him of his pet's whereabouts.

He was highly perturbed when she'd arrived home in the company of another suitor. He'd not expected her to be entertaining another young man. Nor had he contemplated competition for her hand. Abel took an instant dislike to the rather pompous English doctor who appeared to be courting Amanda whom he now considered to be *his* girl. He resolved then and there that he would be the lucky man to win Amanda's hand. There was more to Abel Lawson than met the eye. His war experience meant that he was mature for his years. The very fact he'd survived the Civil War at all proved his ability to persevere.

It was quite obvious to Felicity Beresford that her sister-in-law's suitors were tediously attempting to outstay one another. She was amused at first but soon became frustrated by the men's deliberate evasion tactics. Whenever she hinted that the time had come for them to take their leave, they changed the subject and continued with the conversation. Thankfully, her husband, James, finally resolved this impasse by offering to accompany the gentlemen off the premises by stating that he wished to take his evening constitutional. He stood, and both the Doctor and Abel were reluctantly forced to follow him, each man for a different reason, loathe to leave. Abel because he'd yet to speak with Amanda about his cat and Eugene because he was a man who hated to lose, and now that he knew Amanda had another suitor, he was determined to be the one to win her affections.

Both gentlemen suggested calling upon her again soon. Abel invited her to take lunch with him at the Houses of Parliament, much to the chagrin of the doctor, who could offer no such exalted destination. Instead, he hastily invited her to visit him at his clinic practice where he could offer her a guided tour. Amanda accepted both invitations, thoroughly flattered by this unlooked for male attention.

The following day, riding her brother's penny-farthing, she set off for Dulwich Park. She dressed in a split navy and white skirt, a white buttoned blouse and straw bonnet banded by a navy ribbon. Hattie accompanied her, albeit somewhat further behind since she was on foot. When they arrived at Arthur Brown's cottage, it was just in time to see an enclosed black hearse drawing away from the house. Amanda had barely knocked on the door before it was yanked open by Scrounger, his face deeply drawn. Amanda immediately asked what was amiss.

"Tis' Arthur. He never awoke this morning, poor old fella." He turned away into the small house, leaving Amanda and Hattie to follow him into the front room.

"You cannot mean that he is *dead*?" Amanda asked in hushed tones. Scrounger nodded, dropping dejectedly into a chair, his hands hanging loose between his knees. "Does Elspeth know?" Amanda asked, shocked. Scrounger shook his head negatively.

"No, no one does, not as yet." Amanda plopped down on the chair opposite Scrounger, staring at him with horror as her eyes welled with tears of genuine grief. She had been sincerely fond of Uncle Arthur and would miss his gentle kindness. Her main concern now, though, was for her sister-in-law Elspeth who was expecting her first child in a month or so. How would this dreadful news affect her health? Arthur Brown had taken good care of Elspeth when she had attempted to save him from brigands the very first day she set foot on English soil. She'd been cast to the ground, banging her head so severely it had resulted in her total memory loss. Arthur had taken her into his home, adopting her as his niece Bunty. He'd cared for her until such time circumstances had restored her to her rightful place beside Adam. The kindly old gent had become Elspeth's adopted uncle whereupon he was welcomed into the Beresford family fold. He was a dear soul, a cartographer; he'd kindly taken Scrounger in to be his lodger after Elspeth had left his care. Adam had employed him at the museum, and Arthur was training Scrounger to be a cartographer while also teaching him all he knew about map restoration.

Hattie busied herself heating water for tea. She could see that her mistress and her friend were shocked by the old man's death and wanted to do something practical to help, wondering if she ought to walk back to Sydenham Village to ask the master to send the carriage to fetch Amanda.

Amanda and Scrounger drank the tea that Hattie set before them in silence. Each was caught up in their own private memories of Arthur. Amanda had barely tasted her drink when her cup was dashed from her hand by a large furry blur, which landed with a heavy thump in her lap. Grant pushed his formidable claws into her thighs and marched on the spot, causing Amanda to leap to her feet with a loud shriek of pain. The cat hissed with shock before jumping back through the open window from whence he came, leaving havoc in his wake.

"We should've left that blooming cat right where he was. Dratted beast is nothing but trouble!" Scrounger muttered.

"Oh phish," Amanda countered, flailing at her tea stained skirts. Hattie quickly soaked a cloth in clean water and proffered it to her mistress. She then set about clearing up the mess on the floor. When everything was restored to order, Amanda suggested Scrounger go at once to see her brother Adam to inform him of Arthur's death. She pointed out that news of her uncle's passing would be best given to Elspeth by her husband. Scrounger readily agreed for he was extremely fond of Elspeth. It had been he who had tutored her as a mudlark along the Thames shore, befriending her at a low point in her life. Elspeth had, in turn, introduced Scrounger to Uncle Arthur, who'd changed the fortunes of the lad considerably. Scrounger set off at once, leaving Amanda and Hattie to entice Abel's cat back inside the house before they too left the premises.

It proved to be a difficult task persuading the spooked feline to trust them until Hattie discovered some discarded fish heads on the communal rubbish heap outside. She used them to lure the cat inside. Once he had been tempted into the cottage, they shut him in the scullery with his water dish and smelly fish treats. They closed up the house, leaving promptly for home.

Amanda rode the penny-farthing for a short distance then opted to walk. Hattie had fallen so far behind that Amanda dawdled so that her maid could catch up. As she strolled slowly along the streets pushing her bicycle, she mulled over the ramifications of Arthur's demise, wondering how on earth poor Elspeth would cope with the sad news. She also pondered her own confusion over her newly acquired gentlemen callers. She'd no previous experience of being courted. Up until now, her social life had revolved solely around family events. She'd fallen for Abel the first time she'd laid eyes on him, but as gorgeous as the tall American was, he would eventually leave Britain and travel back to his own country. Eugene, on the other hand, was English, which would mean that, should she and Eugene marry, she could live near her family, thus maintaining close ties. He wasn't as good looking as Abel Lawson to be sure, but he was a very attractive man, albeit somewhat lacking in humour, but perhaps he could learn to adopt a lighter disposition? However, when Amanda imagined her first kiss, it was Abel's arms she pictured herself in and not Eugene Barker's.

She thought about being brought to task by one or other of these men. Abel had tapped into her secret desires when he had threatened her with retribution should she stick her fingers into Grant's cage at the cat show. Amanda had long been aware that James spanked his wife Felicity. The first time she heard the rhythmic claps resonating from their bedroom, she'd opened the door and peeked inside, curious to know what the repetitive sound was. The sight she beheld through the small open gap of the doorway seared into her memory. The erotic sight of her sister-in-law upturned across her husband's lap, her bared flesh framed by the froth of her petticoats, her bottom turned pink by James's rapidly striking palm had sent quivers of excitement through Amanda's young developing body.

She, too, wanted a husband who would toss her across his knee and spank her should she misbehave, but never having undergone a spanking in her life before, Amanda had nothing against which to measure her imagined experience. Eugene had mentioned giving her a touch of his crop when he'd first met her, that day in his carriage, and had, in fact, slashed her a single time with the implement. But that was when he'd thought her a woman of ill repute. She wasn't sure she wanted a husband who would use a crop on her tender flesh, but surely Eugene wouldn't chastise his own wife in cruelty? Perhaps she should ask him about that, if he should ever propose to her. Round and around these peculiar fancies churned in her head, her thoughts never seeming to resolve them as she whittled and waned over her dilemma.

CHAPTER 3

Amanda thought the Palace of Westminster looked particularly grand from this angle of approach. As the ancient building came into view, the yellow stone facade glowed gold in the August sunshine. Amanda wriggled excitedly as the coach drew into the inner courtyard of the powerhouse of British government. Abel bent his impressive height double as he clambered down from the coach and turning, he held out his hand to aid Amanda. She placed one hand atop her hat holding it secure and gave him her other as she stepped down.

Abel had explained on the journey that they were due to meet the Under-Secretary of State for the Colonies. Edward Knatchbull-Hugessen was a senior member of the Foreign Office headed by the British Foreign Minister, Lord Granville. The present American Envoy was returning to America very shortly which meant that, until another appointment was made, Abel would be the Acting Minister to the United Kingdom and would be required to take on all that the job entailed. He needed the support of Mr. Knatchbull-Hugessen as an entree into the finer workings of the Foreign Office. So far, Lord Granville's foreign policy, based upon patience, peace and good relations with the United States had made him a solid friend to America. Abel wanted relations to continue in this smooth vein and, to that end, he had arranged this, more social event, to include Mr. Knatchbull-Hugessen's wife, Anna and his own courted young lady, Amanda Beresford.

Amanda was not often cowed by life, but today she felt completely overwhelmed by the occasion. Although she was a well brought up middle-class English girl, she'd never been placed into such a formal social situation before, and it thoroughly unnerved her. Once seated at their table, she listened respectfully as the two gentlemen talked politics and agreed to set up various meetings. She answered all the questions the older, statelier wife of the Secretary put to her with polite humility. Otherwise she remained quietly courteous, behaving in a completely acceptable and modest fashion. Abel was delighted with her demeanour, having no idea how out of her depth Amanda actually felt.

When lunch was finally over, pleasantries given and received, they took their leave. Amanda breathed a sigh of relief as she settled back against the padded seat of the carriage, pleased to be finally returning home. Abel showered her with compliments, commenting upon her deportment and handling of the whole social situation. He was still unaware of her lack of confidence. He was concerned by her timorous acceptance of his compliments but assumed that she was being typically English and modest about the praise he lavished upon her. He decided to change the subject.

Finally, he had her alone and could raise the matter of the theft of his cat. As soon as he brought the subject up, bright colour immediately flared in her cheeks. "I see that you do know something about Grant's disappearance." Her periwinkle eyes lit with lively intent.

"I can assure you only that he is alive and well, but beyond that, my lips are sealed," she told him smugly. Abel frowned.

"Clarify please."

Amanda wagged a finger at him. "I didn't say that I was involved in his disappearance, only that I knew him to be safe and thriving."

He harrumphed. "You, my dear, are splitting hairs. I have two sisters back home, and I know when they wear the look you have on your face right now that they have been up to no good. D'you know how my father deals with such prevarication?" Amanda swallowed, shaking her head. No, she wasn't sure she particularly wanted to know. Her throat went dry. "He spanked the answer from the guilty party. I assure you that I am a man cut from the same cloth as my father. So I suggest, scamp, that you tell me the whole of it right now, or when I deliver you home this afternoon, I shall take you over my knee and, believe me, I'll soon have you singing like a sweet little canary."

Amanda stared at him astonished, not quite believing that she'd heard correctly. Had he actually just threatened *to spank* her? They were not even engaged, he had no right! She relaxed, ah, he was bluffing of course, just as he had when he threatened her at the cat show. "Sir, I see that you jest," she replied, with a teasing smile.

Abel watched her pretty young face as it went through a myriad of emotions, finally settling into what he perceived as a brazen smirk. He narrowed his eyes. It was obvious that she didn't believe he would act upon his threat. Of course, he knew that he shouldn't, he hadn't the right, not yet, she wasn't his to discipline. However, he was convinced, that with a little coercion, she would tell him the whereabouts of his pet. Especially since she'd virtually admitted to him already that she knew where Grant was. He would not allow her to evade the issue or taunt him. Trying another tactic, he took her hand within his and mesmerised her with his intense gaze. Drawing her hand to his lips, he pushed her glove away from her pale inner wrist. He leant forward as though to place a kiss on that tender spot but, instead, nipped her soft white flesh sharply.

She squealed, shocked and smartly withdrawing her hand, she cradled it, glaring at him furiously. "How dare you!"

"Oh I dare, Miss Beresford. Perhaps you believe me now? I'm American but not always a gentleman. I fought beside my father in the Civil War and that iniquitous fight changed me. Like my Maine

Coon cat, you will find me unpredictable. We Americans are made of wilder, sterner stuff than your tame Englishmen. I assure you that I am not a man given to make idle threats; you'd do well to remember that. Now, I demand that you tell me the whereabouts of my pet."

Amanda's smirk slipped from her face, and she shifted uneasily in her seat. It was obvious to him that she was mulling over his unexpected behaviour. It seemed she concluded that her derrière was under threat because in the next breath, she began to spill the beans about Grant's whereabouts. Shortly after, Abel knocked on the carriage roof to alert the coachman to a change of plan. He shouted out the address of their new destination, Dulwich, to the late Uncle Arthur's cottage.

On arrival, Abel handed Amanda down from the carriage, noting with amusement her doleful expression. She was a spirited minx. He liked that about her, but she needed to learn that he was no pushover when it came to female whim and whimsy. He was thankful that he'd grown up with young women so full of sass he'd learned something of the female psyche. Not that he claimed to be an expert on women. Hell no, but he did feel that he'd perhaps more understanding than those men who'd been raised without sisters.

Amanda knocked on the door, but when there was no reply, she lifted a key from beneath the boot scraper and unlocked the cottage door. She led the way into the scullery where they found Grant peacefully asleep, curled upon a Windsor chair. Abel dropped to his haunches before his cat, scratching Grant's ears affectionately. The animal stretched, giving a rumbling purr of recognition. Abel was relieved to see his pet looking well. "Thank you for taking care of Grant, Miss Beresford. I sincerely appreciate your well-meant intentions in interfering with due process, but what you did was very wrong." Amanda gave an unladylike snort of derision.

"Do not concern yourself that I shall ever *interfere* with anything to do with you ever again, Mr. Lawson. If there were to be a next time, be assured I would allow them to slaughter your wretched cat!"

She spun about on her heel intending to leave the scullery, passing Abel who clasped her arm. Shaking her arm to free herself, Amanda squeaked with surprised frustration. Grant took fright, jumping to the floor. Abel immediately seated himself upon the vacated chair, pulling Amanda's lissom form over his lap. Even as he acted, he knew that this was not the behaviour of a gentleman, but there was something about this girl that niggled and tested his resolve, pushing him into wanting to school her. He threw up her dress skirts and petticoats and swept aside her bustle, revealing her delightful heart shaped, cotton clad behind.

"No!" she squealed in consternation. "Stop! Release me, Mr. Lawson, 'tis unseemly!"

Amanda was incredulous, how dare he treat her thus, and yet there was a tremor of excitement. She was about to find out what it felt like to be spanked! She felt his hand lift and fall, landing heavily upon her derriere with an audible clap that stung her vulnerable backside. He repeated the action with a rapidity that astounded her. A spanking turned out to be quite unlike she'd imagined. First of all, she found the position across his thighs appallingly intimate, not to mention humiliating. Secondly, it was so painful! She knew she could never become accomplished enough to become a politician's wife, but now she realised she would never want to be on the receiving end of another spanking either, not as long as she lived. Any romantic idea she'd entertained regarding marriage to Abel Lawson died a fiery death as he toasted her tender bottom flesh. Although she begged prettily for a reprieve, he paid her no heed, continuing his relentless, punishing smacks.

Determined to liberate herself, she kicked her feet backward attempting to catch him in the face, but Abel merely grunted and entrapped her legs with one of his own. He rained down a sizzling tattoo of slaps on her now bouncing spheres, adding some licks to the backs of her thighs for good measure. A damn burst within her, and she wailed, sobbing her remorse. Apologies for stealing Abel's cat now fell readily from her lips with the sound of genuine contrition.

Abel saw clearly how pink the flesh undulating beneath her cotton drawers was becoming. He admired her bouncing buttocks, the flesh shivering with the slap of each impact. His blows were tempered to sting but not to leave any lasting effect. He knew this was her first spanking, and so he kept the punishment short, halting when she apologised to him. He patted her sore buttocks, pleased by her change of heart.

It took her a moment to realise the spanking had stopped. She lay slumped tearfully across his knees, full of shame and embarrassment. He smoothed down her petticoats, straightening first her bustle, then her skirt. Amanda almost resisted his help to set her back onto her feet, so mortified was she. He stood, drawing her to him, enclosing her in his embrace. She stood intimately crushed against his chest. She hid her face in his waistcoat, glad that his height restricted her from meeting his gaze. The rumble of his voice distracted her from her misery. He explained gently that all was forgiven, they would take his cat with them, but he would deliver her home first. She nodded, sniffling as she extracted herself from his hold. He caught her elbow and spun her back to face him.

"Look at me, Amanda," he commanded. Reluctantly, she raised her eyes to his, surprised by the kindness she saw there. "Once punishment is over, the slate is wiped clean, and we have no need to mention this again. May I give you a kiss of forgiveness?" She flushed, proffering her cheek. His lip quirked, amused by her coy avoidance. He placed a finger under her chin, tilting her face. Lowering his lips to hers, he slipped a hand into her hair, angling her head to accommodate his height before bending to softly kiss the side of her mouth. She responded, and his lips demanded, sliding seductively over the whole. His arms tightened as her lips parted of her own volition. He gently explored her with his tongue, delighted as she tentatively matched him with her own exploratory touches.

With a suddenness that confounded him, she broke away, saying briskly, "Come then, for my family will worry if I am out much later than this." She scuttled away through the tiny hallway and out to the waiting coach.

He took a moment, then his long legged stride caught up with her. Handing her up inside the carriage, he passed Grant's cage up to her. He asked for the key to the house, which she duly handed over. He locked the door before tucking the key back under the iron boot scraper. "I left a note for your friend Scrounger to inform him that I'd been with you to collect Grant," he told her as he climbed up beside her. Grant yowled crossly when he realised he was trapped yet again. Abel held his hand between the wooden bars of the crate and flicked his fingers. The huge cat nuzzled his hand, and reassured, he settled quietly down inside his box.

"Since poor old Arthur is dead, it is probably best that you take him back with you anyhow, but I wonder if you will be able to protect him from the death sentence hanging over his head." Amanda pondered.

Abel glanced over at her, but she evaded his eye. He sighed, exasperated with her. "Robert Schenck is returning to the States very shortly. He will take Grant home with him and see to it that he is delivered to my parents' house," he explained. Amanda gave a shrug of feigned indifference. Irritated by her attitude, Abel decided to be forthright.

"Amanda, you not only deserved that spanking but I felt it was required upon so many levels." Her eyes clashed with his. The flash of indignant blue fire that sparked in her usually cool irises only served to convince him that he'd been right to dole out discipline to his pretty English termagant. "If you should become my wife, disobedience would be addressed as it was today, with you across my knee. The only difference will be that your bottom would be bare." He chuckled as she instantly flushed an unbecoming beetroot red. Spluttering odd words of objection, she was unable to form a complete coherent sentence.

"Shush, hear me out. I felt it only right that you experience the way I would discipline you, so should you agree to become my wife, you would know what—"

"I believe hell shall freeze over first!"

Ah, so she'd recovered her ability to string a sentence together he noted with some amusement. Acknowledging her burst of fury by placing a finger over his lips, he shook his head, shushing her. Her response was to stick out her tongue and turn away huffily. He gave a slow sensual smile. "When we are man and wife, I promise that should you repeat that saucy act, I shall find a productive use for your pretty pink tongue."

She spun to face him. "Whatever do you mean? Oh never mind. I don't need to know because I shall *never* marry *you,* Mr. Lawson. Indeed, I am strongly inclined to favour Doctor Barker's suit. In fact, I am due to visit him at his clinic next week. Actually, he is invited for tea on Sunday, but you, sir, will not be welcome," she informed him, nose in the air.

"Be very, very careful, scamp, you're treading on thin ice," he warned brusquely, a steely glint in his eye. She tossed her head, swivelling to stare out of the window. Abel could tell the little rascal was agitated by the vivid colour that still flooded her cheeks, also by the rapid rise and fall of her bosom. He hid a smile. She might think that she was unaffected by his presence, but he knew to the contrary. He would leave her alone to brood a while before contacting her again. By that time, he hoped she would be so anxious about his absence, she'd be pleased to see him when he finally deigned to call. Having duly noted his sisters' reactions on similar occasions, he had no doubt Miss Beresford would respond to his neglect of her in a similar way.

Abel was not being arrogant in his summation, he had reason to believe Amanda found him as attractive as he found her. He genuinely wanted to be the man to win her hand in marriage. He was a man of integrity and determination, and he believed that Amanda Beresford should be made to understand that, as her husband, he would never countenance stealing for whatever purpose. Nor could he allow her rudeness and disrespect to go unpunished. Disobedience and negligence would result in her receiving physical chastisement. It was better that she understood this before he made an offer for her hand. He wanted to make her his wife more than he'd desired any other woman. He was acutely uncomfortable about the fact his manhood stood at half-mast whenever he was in her company. Spanking her had him rampantly hard, throbbing uncomfortably within the restriction of his trousers.

Abel was amused that, after only moments after stating that she would ignore his presence, Amanda swivelled toward him. Twin spots of colour highlighting her cheek bones told him she was still agitated. He was pleased to note that she did not sulk for long. He much preferred a feisty woman to one who was sullen and prone to mope. As she began to berate him, all he could think about was drawing her into his arms and silencing her with a kiss. Before he'd finished the thought, he found he'd acted upon it. Pulling her backward across his lap, his mouth crushed hers but far from complaining about the rough manhandling of her person, the hussy slid her arms about his neck and parted her lips, assisting him in ravishing her mouth. He took no further persuasion, feasting upon her delectable lips. The surge of lust sparked within his loins wiped all coherent thought from his mind as his hands roamed proprietarily over the luscious curves of her lithe body.

From the swell of her breasts to the womanly slope of her hip, his palm moved to cup her recently spanked arse. Her soft puff of surprise against his mouth, coupled with her arduous kisses, gave him no pause as his hand edged beneath her petticoats, travelling up her stockinged calf, onward over her unclad thigh. His tongue explored the seam of her lips, pushing into the sweet divide. She met him with her own exploration which only served to encourage him as his hand moved boldly, cupping one soft pillow of breast. He massaged the mound until the ridge of her nipple pressed against his palm then he lowered his head to her dress material, where the nubbin stood proud, pushing outward against her gown. He suckled hard, wetting the material. Her shuddered gasp emboldened him further. He continued to worry her nipple gently with his teeth while his hand skimmed over her flesh, stopping at the apex of her thighs.

Far from resenting his audacious fumbling, Amanda shifted her knees slightly apart, thus enabling Abel to slide his fingers between the edges of her split drawers, until he cupped her virginal mons. Both groaned in unison as he made contact with her slick core. Abel shifted to accommodate his now fully extended member, his movement serving to jostle Amanda so that her legs widened indecorously. The sight of his own darkly masculine arm delving deep amongst her frilled white underskirts had him nearly undone. He was fully aroused, leaking profusely like an untried, callow youth. The feel of her soft, succulent folds against his finger tips as they trailed through the wet seem of her silken labia had him completely unmanned. He found the tiny rigid nub, which pulsed between her legs. His finger petted and pestered her swollen flesh until her sighs ignited into cries of ecstasy telling of her pending culmination. Her passionate cries as she found her pleasure caused him a wholly unexpected reaction as he violently ejaculated into his underclothes. Goddamn! He wondered how a man of his age could have so little self control. He shook his head, full of self disgust.

Cradling Amanda in his arms as she recovered, they both breathed deeply, slowly as each regained their breath. Amanda stared into his concupiscent eyes, and it was a few moments before he thought to make her decent again by lowering her skirts, so mesmerised and locked into her gaze was he.

Stupefied, he could hardly believe that he'd spilled into his clothes like some untested schoolboy. The desire he felt for this woman was nothing like anything he'd experienced before. She enflamed him almost to madness. It was the little things that tormented him most. The way she pushed her fingers into her carefully pinned up hair, loosening it, so that she ended up with tendrils of soft curls drifting about her long neck and face. Why did she do this? Was it simply to tempt him? He thought not; her action appeared to be wholly absent minded. Then there was the way her little pink tongue darted out, swiping over those cupid bow lips every so often while she was talking, distracting him from conversation as he waited on bated breath for her to do it again. He groaned. He had to marry her and soon, or he wouldn't be responsible for his actions.

"You *shall* marry me, Miss Beresford; I promise I *shall* make you a very happy woman," he told her gruffly. Lowering her gaze, Amanda blushingly caught her bottom lip between even white teeth. She was silent until they reached Sydenham. As they drew up outside her house, she pivoted on her seat to face him squarely, stretching to reach his ear.

"I believe you sir," she told him, her breath puffed sweet against his cheek, her lips grazed his. She leapt from the coach in a most unladylike manner, moving too fast for him to have time to climb down and assist her. He watched lustfully as her shapely form scurried up the garden path, keeping his gaze focused on her back until she disappeared inside the house. With a rueful chuckle at his own lewd behaviour, he leant back as they set off for home. He was intent on changing his underclothes as a priority before he settled Grant safely behind Embassy doors and well away from the jurisdiction of the English Crown.

CHAPTER 4

The strange thing was that, after a few days, Amanda found herself fretting over the fact that Mr. Lawson had sent her no word. She'd expected flowers to arrive promptly along with an apology. When none came, she awaited a note from him, but there was only a continued lack of contact. She worried that perhaps she'd over-stepped the mark, behaving in such an immoral manner that he'd decided to have no more to do with her. In contrast, Dr. Barker sent a host of posies and garlands that arrived almost daily. Amanda's sister-in-law, Felicity became irritated by the sheer quantity of bouquets that needed vases to be found for them. She grumbled that finding spare surfaces on which to display the prodigious number of flora and fauna was proving well nigh impossible.

Amanda berated herself. She'd been courted by the most handsome man she had ever seen and had stupidly succeeded in driving him away. After tears and doldrums, she decided that perhaps it was all for the best. She wasn't sure she had enough social standing to become a successful politician's wife. Even so, this sensible appraisal failed to cheer her as she contemplated never seeing Abel again. Indeed, thinking about the spanking administered on their last encounter, which had morphed into far more as his hands had titillated and excited her, had brought her to an astonishing high of exquisite pleasure she'd been unaware she was capable of. Her feelings altered as his silence continued, and rather than her original feeling of humiliation and temper, she longed to see him and fretted at his continued absence.

Sunday tea with Eugene proved dull without the teasing company of Abel to lighten the mood. Even her brother James, a man of varied conversation, seemed to struggle to converse with the good doctor. Eugene, it seemed, was a man of very decided opinions and was not shy about expressing them. Once tea was finished, James and Felicity were heartily glad when he asked to take Amanda and her niece and nephew for a stroll. They readily agreed to his suggestion, giving a sigh of relief as the youngsters left, leaving them to sit in peace.

Amanda helped the children bowl their hoop along the street but halted when Eugene called her back to walk sedately beside him, scolding her for her rambunctious behaviour. He then chose to expound upon his theory that women were in dire need of a man's supervision in order to keep them from overtaxing their smaller, inferior brains. Amanda argued briefly, but after a harsh riposte from Eugene, listing what she considered to be some fairly dubious medical facts about the limitations of the female brain, she felt compelled by his medical knowledge to hold her tongue, albeit resentfully.

Before he left, they arranged a date for Amanda to join him on a tour of his clinic practice. She'd no sooner waved him off before her brother Adam drove up in his brougham. "Amanda, hello!" he called as he climbed down and moved toward her.

"What brings you here this evening?" she asked, lifting her face to receive his kiss of greeting.

"Actually, I came to speak with you," he explained as he stood back to allow her to enter the house.

"Me?" she queried. He nodded.

"Yes, I have a favour to ask of you. I wonder if you would be willing to come and stay awhile at Helen House in order to keep Elspeth, company while I am at the museum? Poor darling, she has taken the news of Uncle Arthur's passing rather badly, and I cannot be with her all the time. I am concerned about her being alone at this stage of near confinement." Amanda nodded.

"I understand completely. Of course I'll come. It will be nice for us both to spend time together. I did think she might take the news badly. He was a dear old fellow, and I know that he was family to Elspeth."

"Hello, brother, when did you arrive?" James strode into the hallway and pumped Adam's hand vigorously in greeting. "Will you stay for supper?" he asked.

"Thank you, no. I hate to leave Elspeth alone for any length of time in her present condition. Actually, I have come to ask if Amanda will stay with us until the babe is delivered. I was explaining that Elspeth has taken Arthur's death to heart, and I want her to have family with her at all times at this latter stage." James nodded his understanding.

"I shall bring Amanda over to you after breakfast in the morning. Any idea when Arthur's committal will take place?" Adam was already moving out of the front door as he answered the question, talking over his shoulder.

"Yes, it is to be held next Thursday at two o'clock at St. Helen's. Thankfully, being across the street from us, it will not tax Elspeth over much. Despite my reservations she insists she attend."

After Adam left, Amanda ran up to her room to select the gowns she wished to take with her. Hattie took her choices away to inspect each dress for damage and to press them. Then the gong sounded; it was time for dinner.

James drove Amanda to Helen House in his clarence, a carriage that was larger than the rather box like brougham that Adam favoured. They arrived at eleven and found coffee and chocolate on offer set ready in their brother's cosy parlour. Adam was in attendance, not wishing to leave his wife alone until his sister arrived. He gladly welcomed his siblings into his home. It was modest by the standard of the family home in Sydenham village. James had inherited the house and the business estate left by his father on the death of both parents in a terrible rail disaster some years previous. Adam, as second son, had worked hard, grateful for the money his parents spent on his University education, which enabled him to become one of the country's leading professors in antiquities, his speciality being Egyptian relics.

Helen House was a large brick, double fronted house with spacious rooms and space for three live-in servants. There was no withdrawing room, simply a cosy front parlour. Instead of a dining hall, there was separate dining room situated across the hallway from the parlour. Toward the back of the house a small store room acted as a study for Adam. The sculleries were at the rear of the property. Upstairs they had the luxury of an indoor bathroom, complete with a Thomas Crapper flushing lavatory and four bedchambers. The attic had three small servant rooms and one larger room, used as the servants' parlour. To Amanda, it was a sweet house, but after the space she'd become accustomed to at home, it felt cramped and lacked privacy.

She was amazed to see Elspeth looking so huge. The last time she had seen her sister-in-law, she'd looked prettily pregnant, but now she appeared bloated and very ungainly. The babe was due in two weeks, and Amanda felt a wave of pity for her tiny relative. She knew how babies were birthed thanks to Felicity's forthright education. She certainly didn't envy Elspeth attempting to push a baby out of such a delicate hole! In fact, looking at the very expectant mother propped up in her fireside chair; she naively pondered her sister-in-law's decision to have children at all.

After the men had departed, Adam to the museum, James to visit his man of business, the women got down to some serious conversation. Amanda made her condolences on Arthur's demise, and they talked of him for a while which led on to the tale of Grant's rescue and her role in distracting the police while Scrounger stole Grant. Amanda told Elspeth of her ill-timed meeting with Doctor Eugene Barker and her subsequent dealings with Abel. Elspeth listened with interest to her tale then questioned Amanda over a couple of things she'd felt unclear about. She fell silent when Amanda haltingly confessed that Abel had spanked her.

"Well, aren't you going to advise me?" Amanda demanded, finishing her tale. Elspeth shifted her bulk and sighed.

"You won't believe what I want to say, so no, I think I shall remain silent."

Amanda's mouth gaped. She recovered herself quickly to ask, "Why won't I believe you?" Elspeth cocked her head and pursed her lips.

"If you promise to think about what I tell you, then I shall be persuaded to speak, but if you dismiss me out of hand…" She let the sentence trail. Amanda assured her that she would listen and contemplate whatever it was that Elspeth told her. "In my experience, men who don't care lash out at a woman—"

As Elspeth had suspected she would, Amanda interrupted. "So Abel does not care for me?"

"Let me finish… But men who care, spank."

Amanda leaned toward her sister-in-law. "So you are saying that you think Abel does like me because he spanked me?"

Elspeth nodded, her eyes twinkling, her lip twitching. "Did you like it?" she asked in a hushed voice.

Amanda blushed. "Like it? No, I was humiliated… but well… now…"

"You find replaying the chastisement in your mind rousing?" Elspeth suggested.

Amanda nodded. "I know it sounds foolish, but yes, it does

excite me that he is strong enough to take control of my contrary moods. Afterward he was so tender and forgiving."

"It is not foolish at all. I confess Adam spanked me frequently before I was with child, but I adored him for taking control of my capricious moods." Elspeth obviously noted how uncomfortable Amanda looked with talk of her brother because she stopped talking about Adam but said instead, "A man who is firm but kind is a treasure, darling. Do not give up on Abel Lawson."

Amanda sighed. "It is he who has given up on me, for I have heard nothing from him in days!"

Amanda went on to share her anxiety that, should she become Abel's wife, she might ruin his political aspirations. Elspeth soothed her fears and talked to her of the benefits of a marriage to such a man. She pointed out Amanda's many strengths and qualities that would enhance Abel's career. Time flew and soon it was lunch time. Afterwards it was usual for Elspeth to take an afternoon nap, and although she tried to stay awake for her visitor, it was obvious to Amanda that Elspeth was exhausted, so Martha, her maid, was called upon to assist her mistress upstairs and into bed.

The days ticked past slowly and before long it was Thursday, the day of Uncle Arthur's funeral. Although it was generally considered unacceptable for women to attend a committal, frowned upon by many a gentleman, the vicar of St. Helen's was not among them. He was a progressive chap especially for a clergyman. He welcomed ladies into his church to mourn with an understanding and a consideration that the Beresford family found heart warming.

As the family walked from the house to the church, two black horses sporting tall, black ostrich plume headdresses arrived, pulling the hearse. It halted on the cobbled stones of the church yard. As the coffin bearers prepared to lift out Arthur's coffin, Elspeth swooned, needing the support of her husband and James. Each man clasped an elbow as they all but carried her into the church. Amanda followed behind accompanied by Felicity. They could hear Elspeth crying piteously, although they couldn't see her face through the thick black gauze that covered her head and shoulders.

People settled into their pews, a hush fell, soon disturbed by the thud of booted footsteps clomping down the aisle. It was Scrounger, the last guest to arrive. He seated himself next to Amanda. The vicar began by asking the congregation to stand for the first hymn. Singing began reedily and they had barely begun when there was a loud commotion at the back of the church. Looking behind her, Amanda saw three policemen walking down the aisle and she was jolted to see that they were accompanied by Eugene Barker. A fourth man dressed in civilian clothes approached the vicar and called loudly for the service to be halted. The organ music continued uncertainly for a few more bars, but the congregation immediately stopped singing. Everyone present was agog at this unexpected interruption.

Amanda recognised the civilian dressed man as the inspector from the police station. He spoke quietly with the vicar who, in turn, signalled that Adam should join them; James frowningly followed his brother. Scrounger, who was seated at the end of the pew behind Elspeth, stood and slipped in beside his friend since she now sat alone, showing signs of obvious distress at Adam's departure. Scrounger slipped a comforting arm about her shoulders, giving her the support she needed. Amanda meanwhile watched the strange proceedings at the front of the church with misgiving. What on earth was Dr. Barker doing here with the police? She twisted in her seat to look over the heads of the congregation to where two policemen seemed to be guarding the church exit. As she cast her gaze from person to person, she homed in on a man towering head and shoulders above the rest, recognising the familiar head of dark hair. Abel Lawson was seated at the back of the church. He saw her notice him and nodded politely. Amanda flushed and inclining her head, she quickly turned her back on him.

There was action taking place at the front of the church. The inspector, accompanied by Adam and James walked over to where Elspeth was sitting and they stopped beside Scrounger. Adam spoke, "It seems that Dr. Barker has made a very serious accusation against you, Scrounger. The police have no choice but to follow up on his complaint. You have to go with them now, but I promise you that I will get a message to our lawyer Mr. Trubshaw and ensure that he or one of his colleagues will represent you."

Scrounger stared round eyed at Adam and James. He turned pale with obvious shock. "I don't understand. What's they taking me in for? I ain't done nuffing!"

"Come along now, lad, let's be having you. Scrounger, I am arresting you for the suspected murder of Arthur Brown. Come along, son and don't you make a fuss now. These good people don't need any more grief today." He reached out to haul poor Scrounger to his feet, but Elspeth began to scream his name. Gripping his other arm, she pulled him back down beside her. He patted her knee. "'S' all right, Miss Hoity-Toity, I'll be jus' fine you'll see. I ain't done nuffing wrong, I loved Arthur, an' so they'll see it's all a mistake an' let me go soon enough. Don't you fret none, duck," he reassured her gently, gazing hopelessly at Adam who squeezed Scrounger's shoulder as he passed by him into the pew and reseated himself beside his wife. The lad allowed the police to lead him away without a fuss while Elspeth launched herself into her husband's arms, sobbing uncontrollably.

The organ boomed into life as the vicar valiantly tried to resume the service, urging everyone to stand and sing the interrupted hymn. Amanda twisted to watch the police as they left, towing Scrounger along in their midst. Eugene caught her eye; he bowed his head toward her with his usual hubris as he followed the police out of the church. "Bastard," she muttered furiously under her breath.

A loud gasp from the pew in front, alerted Amanda to further drama. "My waters have broken!" Elspeth wailed. Adam slid an arm about his wife then guided her from the pew out into the aisle. Felicity scooted from her seat to aid Elspeth.

Clasping her elbow, she asked, "Are you having cramps yet, dearest?" Immediately the family group was swelled by eager bystanders spilling from their pews to join Adam and Felicity as they edged Elspeth out of the church. This left a reduced congregation twittering excitedly as they twisted to watch the huddled group as they disappeared from view. The vicar floundered with yet another interruption. He withdrew his kerchief, mopping his brow.

"I'm utterly convinced that odious fellow, Barker, is up to no good." Amanda started at the sudden husky whisper in her ear. It was Abel; he'd taken the opportunity to slip in beside her while the congregation was distracted. Amanda thought about ignoring him as a punishment for avoiding her, but she needed him as an ally, so she nodded her head in agreement.

"Scrounger wouldn't have hurt a hair of Arthur's head," she told him indignantly. She lowered her voice to hiss, "I am so worried for him. Now that Elspeth is in labour, my brother will not think to help him until after the child is safely delivered."

Abel agreed wholeheartedly. "I shall do what I can to aid the lad. I wanted to ask you if I might call upon you tomorrow. I will be able to share with you the progress I have achieved with helping Scrounger. I intend slipping away now as I need to find him a lawyer." Amanda gave a grateful smile.

"Thank you, Mr. Lawson. Yes, please, do call tomorrow and let me know what you have achieved. We shall not be in full mourning for Arthur wasn't actually family. I beg of you though, do all that you can for poor Scrounger. He has no family to come to his aid." Abel took her hand in his and drew it to his lips, pressing a kiss on the back of her glove. He held it there rather longer than necessary, gazing deep into her eyes before smoothly moving away, belying his size as he slipped stealthily from the church. Amanda was left alone to brave the rest of the service all the while worrying about how both Scrounger and Elspeth were doing, both suffering different forms of torment.

CHAPTER 5

Mr. Entwhistle, a criminal lawyer with a sound reputation, agreed to act for Scrounger, but despite his laudable arguments, he was unable to get the lad released on any affordable bail. The police had returned to the church and halted the burial process at the graveside. They seized the body, handing Arthur's remains over to Dr. Eugene Barker for post-mortem examination. Abel was astounded that someone neutral was not engaged for the task, but the police thought the tenuous relationship between Amanda and Eugene should not be a cause to doubt the doctor's professional integrity.

Amanda entered into a heated discussion with Abel regarding her continuing friendship with Dr. Barker. She tried, unsuccessfully, to convince him that her contact with Eugene would help them achieve their aim of getting Scrounger released from gaol. Abel had told James somewhat vocally that he thought James should put a stop to the doctor calling on Amanda. He wanted James to approve his sole suit in courting her. James wisely invited Abel into his study to calm him down and confirmed that Abel had his blessing but pointed out that he wanted Amanda to draw her own conclusions and discover for herself that Barker was not the right man for her. Abel failed to satisfy James that Eugene Barker was a dangerous fellow, so he left the house both frustrated and angry with both brother and sister. He decided then and there that the sooner Amanda became his wife, the better.

For Amanda, all thoughts of marriage had flown her pretty head. These unlikely shenanigans made her focus entirely on discovering why Eugene should suspect Scrounger of murdering Arthur. She wanted to know why he had done something as utterly despicable as leading the police to Arthur's funeral, impounding his body and upsetting members of her family in such a cruel, insensitive way. She instinctively felt there was a suspect motive somewhere to be found, and she determined to uncover his true purpose.

In fact, she didn't have to wait very long to begin her sleuthing because the following day was the date she'd arranged to visit Eugene's clinic. Felicity had returned late the previous night happily exhausted with news that Elspeth had birthed a healthy baby boy and that mother and child were doing well. They named the baby Arthur Adam Albert Beresford. Personally, Amanda disliked the name Arthur, but she fully understood Elspeth's lovingly sentimental choice.

The children were at school the following day. Felicity was still abed after her previous late night and James was long gone to an early morning business meeting, and so there was no one to interfere with Amanda's plan to visit Eugene's clinic practice, where she was to be given a guided tour. Feeling optimistic about her chances of finding something detrimental about the doctor, Amanda selected her most fetching gown of dusky pink, worn matched with a hat garnished with pink ostrich feathers. It was Hattie's task to position the hat, which she set at a jaunty angle, securing it with a large pearl hatpin. When Eugene arrived to collect her, he made a pompous statement of regret, explaining that he had been morally obligated to disrupt Arthur's funeral. His self justification did nothing to endear him in any way to Amanda.

They left immediately, and if Eugene noticed that Amanda did not extend an invitation to tea later in the day, he gave no sign of it as he pontificated at malignant length on the pitfalls of trusting anyone from the lower classes. Amanda, usually not one to hide her own opinion, found herself biting her cheek in a sustained effort to control her temper coupled with an overwhelming inclination to inform him that he was nothing but a malicious wind bag.

WHILE AMANDA WAS ENACTING the exact opposite to Abel's instructions, he was doing some sleuthing of his own. Taking a Hansom cab into Dulwich and then to Arthur's small house, he removed the hidden key and let himself in. Once inside, he systematically searched the house for any evidence that Scrounger might have been involved in anything untoward. Pulling a trunk out from under a bed he rummaged inside where letters and other documents were stored, hurriedly reading and discarding what was irrelevant until he found a will made out by the lawyer, Mr. Trubshaw. Abel tucked it inside his waistcoat pocket and left the premises. He boarded the waiting cab, and as the carriage pulled away, he observed two policemen coming around the corner of the road, no doubt heading to Arthur's house. He'd obviously exited the house just in time.

Abel was an astute and determined man who, once his word was given, saw a deed through to the bitter end. He would not forsake Scrounger after his promise made to help the lad, nor would he renege upon his promise to marry Amanda. Although he had not officially asked for her hand, he had told her, and in no uncertain terms, of his intention to take her to wife. She was beautiful and young. Abel reasoned that she was able to learn, and she was also malleable, in fact, perfect wife material. She came from an upper middle class background, which meant that she was well-educated for a woman, although she was by no means a blue stocking.

In short, Amanda would warm his bed more satisfactorily than any other female he'd met of suitable matrimonial material for an up and coming diplomat. The engaging scamp who was Amanda Beresford could certainly make an ideal politician's wife, she simply needed schooling. Not one lady he had previously been introduced to, from the limited pool of suitable, acceptable ladies, had the mix of advantages that Amanda had. She was an unlooked for benefit that he was not prepared to disregard. He knew that he would need to hunt high and low for the perfect wifely attributes that Amanda Beresford possessed. Since he found himself in her thrall, he wasn't about to let the suspect Dr. Barker waltz off with her hand. No, Abel would win the fair lady and discredit her would-be suitor, thus rescuing Scrounger in the process.

AMANDA HATED THE STRANGE, overpowering chemical smell of the clinic. She pulled her small silver vinaigrette from her reticule and held it to her nose as they walked from room to room. The clinic was not large, but there were five consulting rooms, each used for different purposes, including two recovery rooms, each furnished with narrow cot beds for overnight patients.

At the end of the corridor, they passed a downward stair. "Where does that lead?" she asked Eugene curiously.

"Down to the morgue, I would never take a lady there. Come, I shall show you the clinic waiting area." Amanda frowned thoughtfully but followed him dutifully into a room where three women waited to be seen by Dr. Barker's junior partner, Dr. Scott, a self proclaimed obstetrician. As they turned to leave, Dr. Scott appeared and begged Eugene to offer an immediate second opinion on a patient he had presently in his consulting room; a young woman whom he thought might be expecting twins. Eugene begged to be excused, instructing Amanda to wait there for him. As soon as the door closed behind the two men, she turned about, hurrying to the stairway she had seen and made her way downwards into the chilly air below. When she reached the bottom, a narrow corridor led her to a set of heavy swing doors. The overpowering chemical smell was stronger here, and Amanda was glad of her scented vinaigrette.

Pushing open the doors, she stepped inside the gloomy interior of the basement room. A window was set into the wall at ceiling height, which was actually on ground level outside. It allowed daylight into the room, enough filtering through the ivy that choked the glass for her to see that two tables stood side by side in the centre of the room. Stepping forward to examine the lumpy things laid up on the surfaces, Amanda stared uncomprehending. As realisation dawned, a stifled cry bubbled in her throat. These were not tables but two stone slabs. Laid upon each was the body of a man, both naked, mutilated and in various stages of vivisection. Wrapping her gloved hand about her own throat to stifle the scream she wanted to vent but knew she must not, she stood frozen, horrified by the fact that she recognised one of the bodies as that of Uncle Arthur. Stood on the slab beside his body was an open jar, which appeared to contain his heart. Bitter tasting bile flooded her throat as she turned and fled.

Outside the room, she immediately heard male voices coming from the direction of the stairway. Hastily, she turned in the opposite direction but that route surely was a dead end. Frantically glancing about her, she spotted a door to her right, set well hidden in a hollow recess. Rushing to turn the door handle, Amanda found it opened into what appeared to be an overly large cupboard. Scuttling inside, she quickly pulled the door shut behind her. Taking a deep breath, she glanced about her. The small room, which was shelved, was stacked with row upon row of large, glass specimen jars. Each jar contained what appeared to be a dead fish, but on closer inspection, Amanda perceived the 'fish' to be pale body organs, presumably not floating in water but preserved in some chemical, possibly formaldehyde. Amanda shuddered as she estimated that there must be well over fifty jars stored upon the shelves. With mounting horror, she noticed that the lower shelves held the gruesome specimens of unformed babies, some with eyes but others looking unlike anything she could have conjured even in her worst nightmare.

Turning her back on the macabre objects, Amanda stood with her ear pressed against the door, listening for voices. There was a scraping sound outside the room followed by a sharp bang. Shortly after that, male voices receded into the distance. She waited with bated breath until nothing could be heard except her rapidly beating heart. After a few moments, she cracked the door ajar and peeked out into the corridor. The coast appeared to be clear; she hurried back up the stairs, rapidly heading for the exit. Stumbling gratefully out into the street at last, she gasped for air, drawing in a deep restoring lungful to avert the dizziness that threatened to overwhelm her. A hackney carriage lumbered toward her and, darting into the road, she flagged it down. Giving the driver her home address, she climbed aboard, immediately sinking back against the seat, eyes closed as she fought against increasing nausea. She valiantly managed to calm herself, keeping her distress under control while she paid the hackney driver.

Once inside the welcome familiarity of the garden, she leaned against the trellis, eyes shut, concentrating on the smell of roses and the sound of bird song, swallowing mouthfuls of sweet fresh air. She tried not to visualize what she'd just witnessed but nevertheless tears coursed down her cheeks unnoticed. "You are distressed! Where have you been?" She jumped guiltily. Abel's resonant voice jolted her out of her reverie of horror.

"No, no, I assure you I am p-perfectly fine!" realising as she spoke that her voice sounded high and unnatural.

Abel stood frowningly before her, studying her wan face. "Why, Amanda, dearest, you are crying and shaking. Come to me, darling."

He was perturbed by the fact she was pale and upset. He gathered her close, despite the knowledge it was extremely improper for him to hold her thus in a public place visible to any passerby on the road. She burrowed gratefully into his comforting embrace. He rocked her gently for a few moments, bending to kiss her hairline below her endearing little hat, the feathers tickling the end of his nose.

"What on earth has happened to put you in such a spin?" he asked eventually. She shook her head silently, knowing that to answer him would reduce his sympathy, leading him to become furious with her. "Amanda, I want an answer," he demanded. She withdrew from his arms, turning away, but he caught her elbow and spun her about to face him. "Where have you been?" he insisted, impatient with concern. She shook her head obdurately, still not replying. He reached for her other elbow and, gripping both, tugged her hard up against his chest. He looked down and studied her face, frowning as her gaze slid from his. "I shall count to three. If you do not give me a reply, I shall turn you over my knee. Do you understand me, Miss Beresford?" Yet still she hesitated, he shook her once, resentfully she nodded her understanding.

"One, two, three, *scamp...*" She kept her gaze lowered as he finished the count, accepting the inevitable as she felt herself lifted high then lowered across his hard thigh, his booted foot rested upon the bottom rung of the rustic rose trellis. He did not bare her as he would have liked to, mainly in deference to the public nature of the punishment. He lifted his arm and began to spank her soundly, alternating cheek to cheek until she squirmed fretfully against his firm grip.

"Stop that at once, you beast! I say let her go! My, oh my! I shall call the police... you wretched bohemian!" Abel glanced frowningly in the direction of the hysterically reedy voice; to his consternation he saw an elderly lady rapidly advancing upon him, brandishing an umbrella. Abel tipped Amanda right way up as the old woman began to beat him about the back and shoulders.

Amanda tried to pull their octogenarian neighbour away whilst Abel was attempting to reason with her and explain that she was absolutely fine. In fact, she'd more than welcomed the distraction from her grim thoughts and the memory of those gruesome, bottled organs.

"Miss Bathstone-Brown, please stop hitting Mister Lawson! He is the acting American Envoy and I really don't think you are allowed to beat visiting diplomats!" Amanda, hearing the absurdity of her own words, began to giggle at the ridiculous situation. Miss Bathstone-Brown continued her attack; the intractable woman was unable to see any humour in the circumstances, and she continued her onslaught with her brolly. Meanwhile, poor Abel cowered, his hands covering his face and protecting his head. He was a large man but felt it to be unacceptable to retaliate against such a frail woman of advancing years.

"What the *Devil* is going on here?" A strong male voice bellowed above the ensuing fracas. It was James. He had no such reservation about tackling the feisty spinster. Plucking the umbrella from Miss Bathstone-Brown's claw-like hand, he physically set her aside, demanding to know what was happening. It was only then that Abel and Amanda realised that a small group of amused onlookers had gathered outside the garden gate watching, showing approbation at the vulgar spectacle they presented.

"Inside... *Now!*" James ordered loudly. They hurried into the house away from prying eyes, leaving Miss Bathstone-Brown muttering crossly about the beastliness of men as she strode from the premises.

Amanda settled in a chair in the drawing room. She waited alone, her foot tapping a steady tattoo upon the wooden floor. She stewed, waiting for her brother and Abel to reappear from where they had been closeted in James's study for the past fifteen minutes. She was unprepared when they finally emerged, to receive formal congratulations on her engagement from her brother.

"I'm sorry, I'm afraid that I don't quite understand. What is happening?" she queried as a trickle of unease washed over her. Abel winked familiarly from across the room. His flippant action made her unaccountably irritated with him.

James answered sternly. "You are to be married, hopefully within the next fortnight and—"

"*What... .no*!" she cried.

"Now, Amanda—" James began.

"Do not, *'now Amanda,'* me! I shall be the one to decide when and where I—"

James held up his palm for silence. "Your reputation lies in tatters, young lady, after this afternoon's very public fiasco, and since Abel assures me that he intended to ask you to be his wife at some point, we shall retrieve the impropriety by a marriage. There is no acceptable alternative, Amanda; therefore, this shall be the end of the discussion!" Amanda leapt to her feet in a full snit, fully intending to stalk from the room, but Abel caught her arm as she sashayed past him, her nose in the air.

"For once in your life, you missy, are going to do exactly as you are told, especially since I have no idea of your whereabouts today, or what it was that had you so distraught when I came upon you earlier."

James answered for her. "Mrs. Kettle, the housekeeper, advised me that my sister went to view the clinic today with Dr. Barker."

Abel turned to glare at James. "And you allowed Amanda to go alone to be with that lunatic?" He swivelled his furious gaze back to Amanda. "Perhaps now you will explain just what it was that upset you so much today?"

Amanda sighed, capitulating. She wanted, nay needed, to tell him about the clinic. Recalling what she'd witnessed that day caused her to stagger and slump. Abel caught her, easing her into the nearest armchair. She sat silent for a moment but, then in her haste to explain, stumbled over her words incoherently and it was with some difficulty that she finally managed to explain what she'd seen inside the clinic. James and Abel listened patiently but with mounting horror to her garbled tale, both men becoming equally concerned for her welfare but also shocked by the facts she revealed about Dr. Barker's activities.

"Of course, he may possibly be working for the police and performing authorised autopsies quite regularly," Abel muttered more to himself than to James, who shook his head, brows lowered.

"Hmm, somehow I doubt that but there is something not quite right with our Dr. Eugene Barker."

Abel whole-heartedly agreed. "All I can say is that it is a darned good thing that I shall soon be your husband, Amanda, in charge of curbing your capricious nature." Once again Amanda objected but this time much less stridently; she sounded resigned to Abel. He looked at her thoughtfully before asking James to give them some privacy, explaining that he would like some time alone to talk with Amanda. James agreed.

Once they were alone, Abel folded his tall frame to kneel at Amanda's feet. Even though he was kneeling, he was almost a head taller than she was, seated. He took her right hand into his own and looking into her suspiciously narrowed gaze, he asked, "Amanda Beresford, you are a bothersome baggage, but I find that I have developed quite an affection for you. I am, therefore, asking you to do me the honour of becoming my wife?"

Amanda sighed. She finally admitted to herself that she no intention of marrying any other man but him, he was so very handsome, and he did something to her insides that no one else could. Should she really make it easy for him by simply saying answering, yes? Abel watched as her thoughts skittered across her openly transparent face. She was a naughty one, this girl he'd decided to marry, but he knew that he'd never become bored with her, and he was certain that he'd never be tempted to stray, not that he would, of course, he was his father's son and believed, as he did, in fidelity within marriage.

After a small silence, he grinned roguishly at the stubborn set of her jaw. He clasped her chin gently. "I have to tell you that I intend to marry you whether you consent or not, but I can always oblige you with the rest of the spanking you have coming, if you think that might help with your decision?" he drawled, watching with amusement as her eyes flew wide. Leaning in, he caught her lips with his, tasting her. She was ripe, sweet and his shaft lengthened. He was surprised by the intense arousal she always evoked. It was an unlikely response for a man of his age to a simple kiss, but his bodily reaction only confirmed his overwhelming physical attraction to this particular sassy English rose.

Their engagement was announced in the *Times* newspaper. The wedding was planned to take place at Sydenham Church; the date set three weeks hence in order for the banns to be read. Gossip subsided and the neighbours stopped glowering, instead, they stopped them in the street to admire Amanda's sapphire engagement ring.

CHAPTER 6

The police released Scrounger without charge, no evidence was found to support the claims that he had murdered Arthur. This led James and Abel to conclude that perhaps Dr. Barker was no more than a little over zealous, since it was his evidence that Arthur had died of natural causes that obtained the lad's release from prison.

The will that Abel had found during his search of Arthur's belongings entitled Scrounger to the small Dulwich house. Abel had kept the information hidden from the police in case it had been regarded as a motive for Scrounger to kill Arthur. He had quickly delivered the document to Mr. Trubshaw, the solicitor who had drawn the document up. He waited until Scrounger was released before apprising him of his good fortune. Amanda and Elspeth were extremely gratified by their friend's change in circumstance. It seemed too that Scrounger was touched by his old friend's generosity.

As the days returned to normality, Amanda visited Elspeth to admire and become acquainted with her tiny nephew. She sat cradling the sleeping child in her arms as she explained how it was she'd become engaged to Abel. The two sisters-in-law mulled over

Eugene Barker's odd motive for accusing Scrounger of murder and then assuring the police that Arthur had died of natural causes. They found themselves going around in circles as they attempted to second guess the doctor's reasons. Amanda determined to go back to the clinic at some point to speak with Eugene directly on the subject. However, Elspeth strongly advised against her plan, especially since Amanda was now engaged to be married to Abel and Eugene Barker was no longer her suitor.

Amanda again talked about her fear of letting Abel down in her role as a politician's wife with her sister-in-law. Elspeth heard her out patiently as before and once again reassured her of her many capabilities. There then followed a whispered conversation about what a woman could expect upon her wedding night, but Amanda came away feeling that Elspeth had held a lot of detail back on the subject. She learned nothing from her sister-in-law that she hadn't already discovered for herself by riffling through the risqué books which her diligent searches of the more obscure second hand book shops, turned up. These musty places had become regular haunts of hers in recent months, frequented though without her brother's knowledge, let alone consent.

Amanda was still not content to ignore what she'd witnessed at Eugene's clinic. Why had he wanted those jars of body parts and why had he accused Scrounger of murder? None of it made any sense to her, and the more she brooded on the subject, the more she wanted to investigate what lay behind the doctor's actions. However, Abel had first-hand knowledge of the female propensity for curiosity having grown up with his sisters, and he knew of Amanda's uncanny knack of seeking mischief. As a precaution, he warned Amanda to stay away from the doctor and his suspect clinic, or face his wrath and the consequences of his ire.

She meekly accepted her newly affianced's decree, remembering the fearful disgust she felt when she saw those hideous jars full of dismembered bodies. Amanda prided herself on having a resilient nature, but she was honest enough to face the fact that she'd been badly shaken by what she'd witnessed that day.

Although the engagement was posted in the *Times* newspaper, no one outside the family or close neighbours knew of the engagement. Eugene Barker was completely unaware of the event, evidenced by the fact that he presented himself at the Sydenham house the following week, asking to speak with Amanda. Unfortunately, she was the only family member at home at the time he called and curiosity got the better of her. Unwisely, she saw him alone in the drawing room. Too late, she knew as soon as he began to speak that she should have called Hattie to chaperone her. He swept his hat from his head, went down on one knee and proposed to her almost as soon as she'd entered the room.

"I am so sorry, but as flattering as your proposal is Dr. Barker, I find I have to refuse you because since I saw you last, I have become"—being cautious she did not say, engaged— "very attached to another man." Immediately, he was up on his feet again, glowering at her.

"To whom?" he asked shortly.

"I am sorry that you have had a wasted journey—" She ignored his question knowing how inflammatory Abel's name would be for him to hear.

He interrupted rudely, "I asked to whom you have given your heart?" Again she hesitated she was well aware of his animosity toward Abel.

"It's that American?" he guessed bitterly. She nodded, remaining silent. "You think your brother will approve the match?" he asked incredulously. She kept her silence, not wishing to antagonise him. He swept his hat back onto his head, moved to the door, pausing as he spoke, "You have not heard the last of this, Amanda. I assure you that you shall become my wife." His hubris unsettled her, a shiver of unease trickled down her spine. There was something extremely unnerving about Eugene Barker; he verged upon the threatening.

Waiting until she heard the front door slam before she left the room, she ran upstairs to her chamber window where she watched as he boarded his carriage. Once atop, he stared up the house speculatively. Amanda drew back from the window cautiously, watching as he gathered the reins, whipping up the horses as he drove away. Sighing with relief to see him leave, the tension drained from her, and she wondered how she'd ever considered flirting with the doctor? She had not meant his affections to lead to becoming engaged. Truth be told, she'd simply used him to make Abel jealous.

Ever since she'd first laid eyes on Abel she'd known that he was the man for her. His height with his ruggedly handsome face, combined with the husky American accent, had knocked her for six when she'd first met him. She'd never intended Eugene to take her flirtatiousness to heart. She giggled ruefully, what heart? Perhaps he kept his own safe upon a shelf in a jar. The giggle turned into a groan as she remembered the grizzly sights she had beheld at the clinic. Perhaps she'd visit Scrounger and ask what he thought the cold Dr. Barker was up to? Abel hadn't asked her to stay away from Scrounger had he?

She gathered her cloak, yelled for Hattie, alerting her to the fact they were going out.

~

SCROUNGER POURED BOILING water into the large brown teapot that he stirred before setting a large knitted tea cosy over the pot, one that allowed the handle and spout to stick out of the woollen cover. He left the mix to brew and reached for a paper bag, which he held out to Amanda. Reaching inside, she pulled forth a large iced Bath bun, humming her pleasure happily as she bit into the doughy softness of her sugary treat.

"I don't trust that slippery cove one bit. There's summat fishy going on with him. I asked about a bit, an' the word is that he often accuses folk of murder then offers to do an investigation, cutting up the body after which he says he's turned up nuffin'. The police let the accused go an' release the body for burial." Amanda chewed her mouthful thoughtfully.

"But why haven't the police stopped believing his accusations?" she asked.

"Well, since he never pulls the stunt in the same area twice, I don't reckon the police have cottoned on to 'im yet. He's not daft." Scrounger pulled down three tin mugs and poured the tea, handing a mug to Hattie first.

"I still don't understand his motives though, any ideas?" Amanda took the tea he held out to her and sipped the brew, waiting for Scrounger to answer. As an ex-street lad, known for his prowess at mudlarking, she knew he possessed a sharp mind and both she and Elspeth, who had met him first and introduced him to her, respected this about him. He was a canny lad, wise beyond his years due to the life he'd led up until Elspeth had introduced him to Uncle Arthur, which had been a turning point in his fortunes.

SCROUNGER STILL KEPT up with his street contacts, and thus had his nose to the ground when it came to knowing what was happening on the London streets. This despite the fact that he was now employed by Adam, who was Professor of Antiquities at the Museum where Scrounger was working on the art of map cartography.

"I know vivisection is allowed for students in training hospitals nowadays, but there's still a lot of body snatching goes on. My guess is there's summat illegal at play 'ere. You leaves it to me, missy, and let me dig about a bit. Stay away from that odd cove; he ain't the type of bloke you want to be hanging around." Amanda nodded.

"Oh! I forgot to tell you that I'm engaged to Abel Lawson the—"

Scrounger nodded. "I know. Now he's just the type of bloke you need, he'll keep you safe an' your feet firm on the ground and out of trouble. You mind him, miss, an' you'll be just fine."

Amanda sighed dramatically. "Men, all the same," she rolled her eyes. Scrounger pulled her off her chair and gave her push towards the door.

"Go on get off with you! I'll be in touch if I find summat. Meanwhile, Hattie, make sure your mistress stays at 'ome and out' a trouble!"

Hattie smiled. "I do my best, but you know what this one's like!" Scrounger winked at the maid as they stepped outside onto the pavement. Amanda stuck out her tongue at him then linked arms with her long suffering companion as they turned in the direction of home.

CHAPTER 7

Unbeknown to Amanda, both her brothers were doing some sleuthing of their own into the background of Dr. Eugene Barker. The first thing that they discovered was lack of evidence as to where the man had obtained his medical degree. Adam wrote to a chum from Oxford who had also studied medicine, asking if he had knowledge of Eugene or knew someone who might. They divided a list of training hospitals between them and wrote to each one asking if Eugene Barker had trained there. So far, every reply had come back negative. However, there were still a number of hospitals that hadn't yet responded to their enquires. Once again, they impressed upon Amanda that she should stay away from Eugene Barker.

The next couple of weeks were taken up with wedding plans and viewing affordable property situated in suitable areas of London. Abel needed to be near the House of Commons and Amanda favoured living near Adam and Elspeth so they centred their search on Lambeth. As luck would have it, they found a delightful town house, slightly above their budget, in nearby Kennington. James spoke privately with Abel and pointed out to him that Amanda's wedding allowance, settled on her by her parents as her inheritance, would cover the shortfall in rental. Amanda was thrilled with the neat town house on Walcot Square. Both she and Elspeth spent a contented week selecting soft furnishings for the new property. Meanwhile, Felicity interviewed housekeepers, cooks and a maid of all work for the new house. A short list was drawn up and both Abel and Amanda interviewed three women of expertise.

They both liked one woman in particular, a widow, Mrs. Neil. She had a fifteen-year- old daughter, Agatha. She assured them her daughter could work efficiently as their house maid and her son, Billy, seventeen, could undertake any outside work and take all responsibility for the household fires. Plus, she explained that her son had hands on knowledge of conveyances. She told them that Billy would tend to their horses, and since he was unhappy in his present position, Mrs. Neil added that they would like to work in service together as a family, if that were at all possible. Best of all, Mrs. Neil stated that she was an extremely good cook and promised that she was easily able to manage the dual roles of both housekeeper and cook. She'd then surprised the couple by lifting a cloth covered basket onto her lap from which she produced a selection of tiny sample cakes and pastries for them to taste. After a single bite of a light, buttery, flaky pastry, Abel hired her and her family on the spot. The poor woman was so grateful that she'd wept with gratitude, promising them that they'd not regret their decision. Amanda and Abel were more than certain that they would not and congratulated themselves on finding such a perfect match for their simple needs.

They were married on a clear but breezy day, surrounded by family, some friends and a few personnel from the American embassy. James walked his sister down the aisle, while Maddie walked behind looking pretty as a picture dressed in her bridesmaid dress of eau-de-nil organza and wearing a simple pearl necklace. Adam acted as Abel's groomsman; the ceremony was over so fast that Amanda wondered when she would feel actually married to Abel. The day flew by and, all too soon, Amanda found herself alone with her new husband in a carriage travelling out to Sussex for a few days of honeymoon on the coast. Yet, still she felt unmarried to the man she was alone with. They were to stay at the resort of Brighton, made so very popular by King George IV when he acted as the Prince Regent for his father.

Their hotel, The Grand, was situated directly on the sea front; Abel had secured a room with a sea view. The sun was setting, lighting up a trail of blazing red across the sea, flooding the window of their room with a warm rosy glow. There was a knock upon the door and Abel answered, a maid wheeled in a trolley laid with a supper of salmon, followed by strawberries and cream. They made short work of their supper, and as they drew near the end of their meal, Amanda grew silent. Abel knew it was time to take charge of the situation. He wheeled the trolley with their supper remains outside into the corridor then closed the door, turning the key in the lock. He padded slowly over to where Amanda sat, repetitively pleating the thin silk skirt of her dress—her 'going away outfit' that she'd changed into before leaving the wedding reception.

He hunkered down before her and covered her agitated hands, engulfing them loosely within his own. "As your husband, I want to make you a promise, Amanda. I will always do the right thing by you. If ever you feel I am failing in my duty to do that, or you are unhappy in any way, I want you to come and talk to me; will you promise me you will do that?" She gazed into his earnest face and nodded.

"Speak to me, darling," he pressed.

"I will Abel, I will come and talk to you, I promise. Abel…" she faltered.

He squeezed her hands, encouraging her. "Yes, sweetheart?"

"I-I'm scared about… well… tonight, now…"

He gathered her close, his words a soft rumbling caress against her ear. "No need for fear, my sweet. We are about to show our love for one another in a time honoured way. Soon we shall truly be man and wife together. The first time I'm told is uncomfortable for the lady but only for a moment or so. Ever after that, there is only pleasure, no more pain. I will lead you, love you, protect you 'til death do us part." He cupped her face and leaned in to kiss her, eagerly she met him half way, pressing her lips to his.

It was sweet to know that finally on this occasion he was able to carry the loving to its full conclusion, there was no need to rush. She was his forever, to take whenever and however he desired… and oh boy, did he desire. His manhood throbbed but even his rampant organ appeared to understand the need for gentle stealth. Abel curbed and controlled his own base need; his lady came first, now and always. It was the way he was made, the way he wanted his marriage to be, he intended to start as he meant to go on, cherishing his woman, his very own mate.

After his kisses lulled her, he lifted her into his arms and moved her to the bed. He gently placed her on the turned down cover. Lifting each foot in turn, he removed her shoes and then her garters, sliding her stockings down her legs, one by one. He lifted each foot in turn to his lips, kissing each and every one of her ten toes.

She giggled, squealing as he climbed to lie atop her, legs parted either side of her hips as he supported his body by his elbows. He lowered his head and took her mouth with his. She, eager for his kisses, lay quieted beneath him. He slid his mouth from hers along her cheek to her neck where he breathed in the wonderful aroma that was all her. He nibbled her neck; his hands busied themselves unhooking the front of her gown.

"Allow me," she whispered, so he rolled aside, assisting when she required help in removing her dress. "Your turn," she said, a blush suffusing her cheeks. He gave a wink as he stood to remove his waistcoat and cravat and watched her watching him. She was bathed in the last rosy glow from the setting sun which turned her white chemise pale pink, while her blonde hair glinted apricot. He thought he'd never seen her look so beautiful. He tore off his shirt, unbuttoned his trousers but left them on, not wishing to unsettle her further by revealing his nudity just yet.

Amanda watched as the incredibly handsome man, who, she reminded herself, was actually her very own husband, disrobed. My, but he was a big fellow. She felt strangely languid, butterflies filled her stomach. She felt a kind of excited dread but ached to know the secrets of the marriage bed. She held her arms out to embrace him as he approached, his look serious and darkly intense. Her heart skipped as she drew him down to her breast. His hand slid aside her chemise, allowing his hungry mouth access to her burgeoning nipple. She lost herself from that moment, travelling on a tidal wave of exquisite feelings evoked by lips, tongue and teeth. A coil tightened deep in her gut. She writhed under his tutelage and begged for more. Finally, tugging off her own chemise, she lifted her hips in order to aid him in the removal of her drawers. He tossed them aside without a care to where they landed. He nibbled a trail from her breasts to her core, ignoring her flailing hands that grasped at his hair. She may have been pulling or pushing him, neither of them knew, and she cared even less as his mouth closed over her lower lips, his tongue delving between her folds, swiping the length of her cleft. She moaned his name, bucking with violent release.

He slid up her torso, found her mouth, kissing her until she floated back to him, unfocused and boneless. She felt the shift of his weight as his powerful body settled between her thighs. His hands fumbled between them, a hot and weighty rod pressed against her thigh, nudging into the apex of her sex. "Abel?" she mumbled anxiously. He grunted. "Abel?" she queried softly.

"I am about to make you mine, so be brave, my love. It will hurt only momentarily," he answered gruffly. She felt the uncomfortable sensation of something too large for her body, invading, shoving, pushing inside her. He was too big, this felt wrong, he should not hurt her so! His weight, combined with the painful burn on her sensitive inner walls, was too much. She attempted to push him away, but he was too heavy and ignored her. He groaned as he continued to mount her, splitting her asunder. She pounded her fists on his shoulders. He stopped momentarily and she relaxed. Then his muscles bunched, she felt his force as with one almighty lunge, he seated himself fully inside her. There was a moment of almost agonising tearing, a feeling of being over stretched, too full of his flesh which claimed her, tormenting, invading. She turned her head aside as tears spilled down her cheeks. Then his large warm hand cupped her cheek. Insistently, he drew her back to face him. She stared into the lustre of libidinous eyes. "We are finally joined, Amanda, we are as one. Man and wife always, you're mine, Amanda Lawson." He gave emphasis to *'Lawson'* and kept his eyes locked on hers as he moved inside her, awakening something that grew and swelled as the primal flowering of her womanhood awakened for the very first time; she relished the feeling of being taken. An overwhelming sense of rightness settled over her like a mantle, and she found herself automatically meeting the vigorous lift of his hips, responding to his onslaught.

His arms slipped sinuously beneath her, grasping her buttocks. He withdrew fully from her body; she barely had time to adjust to the change before his pelvis slammed back against her womanhood, his swollen shaft driving deep inside her slick channel. The pounding continued as did the friction which built a repeat of the coiling tension she'd felt earlier, but this was a deeper, more engulfing need that built powerfully until it flooded outward from her inner core, rippling across her belly to the far reaches of her frame. The waves of pure sensation overwhelmed her, she was calling his name, and he answered her cry with a shout of his own. Her name hung loudly in the air as his chest reared from her breast, his head flung back with frozen exaltation as his manhood flooded her virgin channel with essence for the first time.

They collapsed together, and he rolled sideways, taking her with him, nestled in his arms while they remained conjoined. Lying face to face, he laid a palm upon her cheek. “I love you,” he rumbled with an honesty that moved her.

“I love you too, husband,” she replied with equal candour.

The night continued with only brief rests between their bouts of passion, so that when the lemon fingers of dawn softly caressed their faces, neither one of them witnessed her radiant approach. Indeed, it was nearly noon before either lover stirred.

CHAPTER 8

Breakfast was lunch, eaten in the hotel dining room. They both selected steak and kidney pudding. They ate ravenously with little conversation. Abel followed that with a large slice of apple pie and custard, while Amanda opted for a syllabub. Sipping coffee after their meal, Abel covered Amanda's hand with his own. He winked at her; she instantly flushed, glancing about her surreptitiously. "Do you think everyone knows that we are honey-mooners?" she whispered, inclining her head toward the room at large.

He chuckled, "Probably," he answered, amused.

"No, how embarrassing!" she glanced about suspiciously.

"Stop staring. You will simply draw people's attention. Just relax. People generally find newly married couples to be sweetly romantic," he pointed out, amused by her squirming in her seat. "Stop wriggling and look at me. I want to talk to you."

He held her attention. "Oh yes?" He nodded.

"Yes. Now that we are man and wife there are a few things I wish you to know." He circled the back of her hand with his thumb as he spoke. "Never argue with me in public. If you disagree with something I say, then I wish you to wait until we are alone before challenging me. I shall listen to your argument, but ultimately, I have veto."

Amanda frowned. "Why?" she asked curiously.

"Because I am your husband, and as a diplomat, it does not look good for my wife to interrupt, or challenge me in public. I deserve, nay require, your obedience and respect, that is why."

She brightened. "Is that all? Well, yes, I can understand why you would ask that of me. Abel, tell me, I'm curious, what was it made you decide to become a diplomat?"

The carnage of war filled his mind; he blinked, then as always, rapidly slammed the door shut on those disturbing recollections. "War; there was so much hate, so much sorrow. Even after it was supposed to be over, the hardship and animosity continued. I wondered if our nation could ever really be healed. I wanted to help rebuild our country, hence my choice of career." He looked into his wife's young and guileless eyes, realising that, in her innocence, she could never understand. Pasting on a bright smile, he pushed back his chair to stand. "Shall we go? You wanted to walk along the sea front to look at those odd looking bathing contraptions." This was his honeymoon, not the time for dark memories to intrude. She returned his smile, nodding happily.

"Shall we sample swimming in the sea tomorrow? I'd like to watch other people today, so I can to see how it is done."

Abel laughed, much relieved she had taken his dictum so well, he'd been worried that she would argue, perhaps even push him into taking her in hand, in order to show her how their marriage was to work. Thankfully, his pretty new wife appeared to accept his dominion over her. Abel sighed with a sense of relief. He had many lusty diversions in mind for their honeymoon, but spanking his bride did not feature high on his list of desirable priorities.

The following day, Abel paid the fee for the use of one of the wooden privacy bathing huts. They both climbed the steps into the small box like structure. Inside along one wall there were wooden pegs set high for clothing to be hung, and on the opposite wall, a fixed wooden bench held a pile of towels stacked high for the bathers' use. There were doors that could be closed for privacy at either end. The box was cleverly placed far enough out in the water for bathing couples to enter the sea directly, but also enabling the would be bathers to enter the contraption from the dry shore.

Amanda pulled on her bathing costume made of dark blue serge. It was decorated with two bold cream stripes banding the bloomer bottom of each leg and also the edges of her wrist cuffs. A large mop cap sat upon her head, edged with a deep frill of cream lace. Abel wore a male bathing suit of black wool, which left his legs totally bare. He edged down the steps then launched himself into the sea with an almighty splash. Amanda shrieked with fright as he disappeared beneath the waves. Her cries turned to giggles as he surfaced, whooping with glee. She edged her way down the steps, clinging to the wooden rail until she got to where the water overlapped. Gingerly, she lifted one foot and dipped her toes in the cold sea. "Oh! Ouch it's freezing!" she gasped, taking a hasty step backwards. Abel pulled himself up onto the bottom rung.

"Oh no you don't!" he scolded as she rapidly retreated. "You wanted to try this, and so you shall. Far be it for me to deny my wife anything she desires!"

Clamping an arm about her waist, he launched them into the sea water, clasping her tight in his arms. Amanda screamed shrilly as they sank into the icy English Channel, arms flailing uselessly. Abel surfaced so that he stood with her held up against his chest. She shivered protesting, while he guffawed with laughter. "You look hilarious!" he told her, continuing to chortle. She scowled crossly back at him, reaching up to yank the sodden mop cap off as it flopped heavily over her face, tossing it onto a dry step of the bathing cabinet. She held her wet hair behind her and squeezed out the excess water. Abel began a slow smile that morphed into a wicked grin.

"Perhaps you need me to warm you up, Mrs. Lawson?" he crooned as he kissed her. "You taste salty," he told her.

"So do you," she replied, burrowing into him, her arms encircling his waist. Then she froze and sucked in her breath as she felt his hands slip to the waist of her navy bloomers, pushing them smoothly downward over her hips. The weight of the water soaked material caused them to drop easily from her ankles. She protested vehemently, hissing anxiously at him to desist but she needn't have feared, his lecherous deeds were well hidden from view by the undulating, cloudy sea. An older couple was situated some ten feet away, splashing happily together close to their own bathing contraption, much too engrossed in their own frolics to be aware of them.

She buried her face into his wet neck as she felt his hand move lower, down over her chilled stomach until he cupped her mons, his fingers felt deliciously warm as they parted her cold wet folds and caressed her, her fluids gushed readily from her aroused body. Abel pulled aside his bathing suit to free his solid manhood. He lifted Amanda higher then lowered her onto his staff. She growled against his ear as he filled her, stretching, thrusting until they were completely conjoined. Holding her close, he walked them through the churning sea over to the shadowed side of the wooden bathing machine, giving them the privacy they required, away from other bathers.

The buoyancy of the water supported her as he fucked her with ease. He pistoned deep with steady strokes, guessing the guttural sounds emanating from her throat meant that she was enjoying their congress as much as he. He withdrew, enjoying the difference in temperature between her hot welcoming sheath and the icy ocean, surging back into her warmth, revelling in the tight grip of her channel. She began her newly familiar, keening song that he knew to be the prelude of her culmination. Hastily he covered her mouth with his own, swallowing her cry of passion, groaning as his own release began to overwhelm him. The sensation of his seed pulsing exuberantly through his frigid member was an exquisitely unique experience, one that he never forgot, even in the years to come.

Once the strength returned to his limbs, he twirled her around in the sea to face him, kissing her senseless before taking hold under her arms as he spun her about in dizzying circles. They played for a few moments more before deciding that it was much too cold to remain in the sea a moment longer. Abel helped her into her navy bloomers and ushered her up the steps of the bathing box. Once inside the contraption, they made good use of the stack of towels, helping one another to dress.

Back at their hotel, hot chocolate and crumbly shortbread biscuits revived them. While they sipped, Abel told her that he'd managed to procure tickets for a concert that evening, and he'd arranged for them to take a tour of the Brighton Pavilion on the following day.

Their visit to the Pavilion was an incredible success. They both enjoyed the romantic, fairy tale mix of architecture that resembled a palace straight out of a children's picture book. Wandering from room to room, they marvelled at the mythical creatures depicted on ceilings and walls. Mouldings and carvings of serpents, dragons, monkeys and plumed birds were thrown into the fabled mix of themes, all depicted in bright jewel colours, set amidst exotic patterned walls and rich eastern carpets. It was wonderfully flamboyant, exuberant, and completely decadent, yet they both loved every inch of the vibrant palace.

Amanda declared their honeymoon to be perfect and Abel had no cause to disagree, but sadly, all good things come to an end, and all too soon they found themselves returning to London. Once home, Amanda enjoyed playing house and the honeymoon atmosphere continued between the happy couple well into the second week before she upset the applecart and discovered to her dismay that Abel was not a man to be crossed. Her husband had left in the morning straight after breakfast. He went to listen to a debate in the House of Commons.

Amanda was sorting mending from amongst her lingerie. Abel was rough with her flimsy night rails. When his lust reared, he was impatient and ended up ripping the delicate materials of her night wear.

Whilst she sat with a pile of undergarments that needed repair she heard a catchy tune wafting in from the open window of her bedroom. Looking down into the square below, she noticed that a group had gathered, mostly made up of women and children crowded about an organ grinder. His small brown monkey was sweetly outfitted in a tiny red soldier's jacket topped off with a jaunty little rimless hat that sat askew on his small furry head. He flitted from shoulder to shoulder, carrying a tin mug that he rattled, begging for pennies and farthings. He drew admiring cries and giggles from the excited children. Amanda dashed through the house, grabbed her shawl and flew out of the front door across the street to see this unusual spectacle for herself.

When she arrived, she dropped a penny in the mug and laughed merrily at the tiny primate's antics, chuckling along with everyone else. The crowd swelled to include a prominent looking woman sporting a large, purple feather plumed hat. The monkey leapt onto her hat and began to tug at the feathers. The woman shrieked and flapped her hands crossly. In a trice, she was screaming as the tiny monkey's teeth sunk into the side of her neck, drawing pin pricks of scarlet blood. She whirled about screaming, batting at the frightened little beast. Amanda rushed forward. She gently clasped the tiny creature, shushing him as she tucked him safely into her shawl. He cowered there, trembling violently.

"Kill the demon!" the bitten woman shrieked vindictively. Amanda's eyes flashed with fury.

"No, it was you who frightened the poor baby. Leave him be, you harridan!" she yelled before running across the street directly into her house, firmly slamming the front door shut behind her. Outside pandemonium broke out. The woman began to bellow for the constable, as did the organ grinder who feared that he'd lost his livelihood along with his monkey. Children began to wail and cry, while their mothers shouted at the organ grinder demanding their money back.

Amanda took the small monkey down into the scullery where Mrs. Neil and Agatha cooed over him. Agatha cut up an apple and offered him slices, which he took and nibbled quickly, stretching his tiny hand out when he'd finished, asking for more. They played with him for a while and he seemed amused and happy, but then be became adventurous, leaping from Mrs. Neil's lap up onto a shelf, where he took great delight in pushing jars so they fell and crashed to the floor.

The three women each tried to catch him, but he jumped so fast from spot to spot, knocking and throwing anything that wasn't fixed down onto the floor. Then he discovered a basket of eggs set on a shelf and began to lob them at his human kidnappers, causing a sticky slippery mess everywhere.

Hammering began at the door, and Mrs. Neil ran to see who was there. Returning below stairs, she was accompanied by a constable, the organ grinder and the woman in the purple hat who'd had the audacity to follow the others inside the house. The monkey was thoroughly overexcited by now, and leaping up and down on his high perch, he screamed shrilly as he lobbed eggs at the newcomers. A direct hit on the forehead momentarily stunned the woman whose hat he'd ruined. Yellow slime slid slowly down her face. She eventually found her voice, shrieking furiously, drowning out the monkey's noisy whoops.

Meanwhile Abel stepped down from his carriage, frowning when he noticed the front door to his home stood wide open and not a soul in sight. As he entered the house, he heard a woman scream, the noise coming from the back where the sculleries were. He hastened inside, his heart racing with concern.

"What the devil is going on in here?" Abel boomed standing in the entrance to the scullery, where complete mayhem was in evidence. Coming up behind, his height enabled him to see over heads into the dishevelled room. He was astonished. A small fiend appeared to be leaping about on the shelves. It took him a moment to realise that he was looking at a small monkey, strangely garbed in a miniature soldier's outfit, minus the trousers. He shook his head in disbelief; he'd never understand the English and who were all these people? He spotted Amanda at the same moment as she noticed him.

"Oh, Abel, thank goodness you're home! Constable, this is my husband, Mr. Abel Lawson, the acting American Envoy to Great Britain. He intends to raise a complaint about how animals are treated in this country within the House of Commons, so if you don't leave here at once and take these offensive people with you, your name could be mentioned at Westminster!"

Abel raised his eyebrows; this was certainly news to him. "Mrs. Lawson, you will be silent for I have said no such thing!" Amanda spun wrathfully to face him.

"But you will! Surely you cannot condone the cruelty dealt to this poor little creature, not after the way this country has treated your own pet!" Abel reached up to the highest shelf and plucked the small monkey from his perch by the back of his diminutive coat. He solemnly studied its furry fringed face for a moment before he handed him down to the constable who took the small animal gingerly, hastily handing him on to the organ grinder.

"There, there, my bonny boy, hush now, Uncle Fred has you safe again," the man crooned to the animal, who curled his tail tight about his master's arm, chattering complainingly all the while. The organ grinder gently stroked the small creature's back with a finger. The gentle petting seemed to soothe the monkey since it appeared to quieten down.

"Abel!" Amanda objected, stamping her foot in temper.

"Be quiet!" Abel boomed. He turned his back on her completely, speaking solely with the constable. "Are there any charges to be brought here?" The constable scratched his chin.

"I don't rightly know, sir. Your wife ran off with this beastie, so I guess that would be up to the organ grinder and this 'ere woman is demanding money for her ruined hat, but strictly speaking, that should come from the monkey's owner, not your wife."

The organ grinder tugged on Abel's sleeve. "I don't wanna press charges against your wife, sir, for she was only attempting to save Charlie from being hurt by that there harpy," the organ grinder assured him, dipping his forehead toward the purple hatted woman.

"Harpy… Harpy? I'll have you know your *tree rat* ruined my new hat!" the woman screeched back at him. Abel drew out his wallet and extracted a pound note handing it to her.

"There, madam, you have your recompense. Now leave my house this instant." Mrs. Neil moved deftly around the gathering to take hold of the irate woman's elbow, guiding her up into the hall that led straight out of the house. This seemed to be the catalyst for the two men to leave and Mrs. Neil showed both of them out of the front door, closing it tight behind them. She was grateful things had not turned out worse, thank the Lord that the master had arrived home when he did. If she was any judge of character, the mistress was in for a right scolding.

When she arrived back in the scullery, she stood open mouthed as she surveyed the mess. "Oh my goodness," she moaned with horror. Abel placed a large hand on her shoulder.

"Firstly, I think we could all do with a cup of tea, Mrs. Neil. Afterwards, we shall pitch in to help clear up this mess. Mrs. Lawson will be only too happy to help with that I am sure." He fixed his wife with a gimlet eye as she stuttered out an apology to her housekeeper.

"Mrs. Lawson, you will join me in the parlour immediately for I should like a private word." Amanda swallowed nervously at the admonishing tone of his voice. She hesitated to follow him as he left the room, but Mrs. Neil's sympathetic smile, coupled with her gentle push in the right direction, had her reluctantly obeying him.

CHAPTER 9

Abel stood before the empty fireplace in the parlour, his hands clasped behind his back as he faced her. He looked exceptionally tall, immensely stern and very unforgiving. Gone was the jovial husband whom she had come to know and love. Amanda found herself unaccountably nervous. "Sit down." She did as he asked and perched on the edge of the settee. "This behaviour has to stop." She bristled indignantly and began to speak but he held up his palm for silence. "You will not speak unless I question you. Now, as I was saying, there will be no more impulsive animal rescues, or any behaviour of that nature from here on in. Furthermore, I specifically told you never to speak for me on any political issues and yet the first time you—"

"That's not fair, I was only—" Amanda leapt to her feet, vehemently interrupting him.

"You will sit down and be quiet!" he thundered. She dropped back into her seat in shock. "In a moment, you will go into the scullery and drink your tea. You will help Mrs. Neil to clean up that dreadful mess. After that you shall present yourself for punishment. I shall await you in our room. There you will be soundly punished before you go to bed without any supper. I suggest you eat a biscuit or two with your tea. The pound that I paid over to that woman for her ruined hat will come directly out of your monthly allowance. Am I making myself crystal clear?"

Amanda nodded, she'd never thought to see her husband and lover quite so angry with her; tears of self pity flooded her eyes. "Can I ask you a question?" she asked in a small broken voice. Abel nodded. "Do you intend… I mean, by punishment, do you mean that you are going to s-spank me?"

Looking at her mournful face, Abel's lip twitched with amusement; however, he kept his countenance stern. "I am," he stated firmly. Amanda nodded.

"Might I be excused?" she murmured.

"From your spanking? No, to return to the scullery? Yes," he replied firmly. She stood uncertain, he then nodded and she scurried hastily from the room.

Abel shook his head ruefully; his wife was still so young. He was about to leave the room to make his way up to the bed chamber when Agatha knocked, then entered. She brought in a tea tray. "Why thank you," he said, taking the tray from her and setting it down beside his chair. She bobbed a hasty curtsy and left the room. He concluded there was no need to hurry. The mess in the scullery would take some time to clean, so he sat down and poured his tea, selecting a large slice of Victoria sponge. He took an enormous bite of the fluffy cake and contemplated the task ahead, concluding that he would thoroughly enjoy taking his aggravating wife across his lap to teach her the error of her ways.

While Amanda sipped her tea, she pondered her options. How easy it would be to simply slip out of the back door and ask Billy to drive her over to her brother's house… but what then? She was Abel's wife now, neither one of her brothers would allow her to remain with them; they would return her to her husband, fully approving his proposed method to curb her exuberance. Had she been wrong to take the monkey away from the crowd? She thought not. Admittedly, she hadn't expected it to wreck their scullery, and as for her speaking for Abel, well, what was the point of having a husband in a position of power if one couldn't use that power for good? She huffed miserably, draining her tea cup.

"Is your husband very annoyed with you?" Mrs. Neil asked. Amanda looked over at where the housekeeper was leaning on her broom watching her. She nodded. "Well, you can be sure his wrath won't last long. I never saw a man more besotted with his wife," Mrs. Neil told her reassuringly.

"Really, do you think so?" Amanda perked up as Mrs. Neil wagged her head.

"Oh yes, I know the signs. My Ted used to be the same way over me." Amanda began to collect up the broken crockery scattered about on the table.

"May I ask what happened to Mr. Neil, er, Ted?" she asked curiously. She had wondered about what had happened to their housekeeper's husband ever since they'd hired her.

"He was a stevedore at Greenwich docks. Few months back, I found a constable standing on the doorstep. My Ted had been hit by a dropped sack of sugar, and it crushed his skull. I ain't taken sugar in me tea since."

"I'm so very sorry. What a dreadful thing to happen."

Mrs. Neil wagged her head again. "'Twas a dreadful shock, but we've got through the worst. The best thing happened to us, was landing this job. I'm ever so grateful, Missus. He was a good man was Ted. Bit strict, tanned me backside on more than a few occasions, but he was fair like, an' kind. Your husband reminds me of Ted in that way." Amanda nodded, murmuring an adequate reply of condolence. She understood what this kind woman was attempting to tell her. Abel was fair and kind, so she should accept whatever punishment he'd decided on and recognise the justice of his actions. After that, Agatha joined them again and the three women worked in silence, continuing to clean the room until it was absolutely spotless again.

Before she went upstairs to face judge and jury, Amanda cut

herself a large slice of sponge cake, she took it into the empty parlour to eat even though she knew Abel was waiting upstairs for her. She decided to eat sitting down while she still could and took the time to gather the courage to face her husband. She recalled the previous two trips across Abel's knee; they'd not been so bad. Her bottom had stung while the chastisement was happening, but after it was over, she'd felt very little discomfort. This punishment would no doubt be the same. After a few smacks, she'd apologize to Abel and all would be forgiven. The worst thing about a spanking was the humiliation, but she knew she could cope with that. She was being a silly worry-wart, best to go and get the thing over and done with. She brushed the crumbs from her skirt, stood decisively, brimming with new fortitude as she marched up the stairs to face her husband with brazen courage.

Arriving in their bedchamber, she found Abel sat awaiting her in just his shirt sleeves, his jacket and waistcoat removed. He sat in a high backed chair, which he had placed in the centre of the room. She noticed that he had rolled his sleeves up to his elbows. He beckoned to her; her bravery wavering as she edged her way to stand before him, her stomach knotted. "Go and remove your skirt and undergarments, then come back here to me." She nodded, anxious. He sounded so curt.

Hurriedly, she did as asked. She wanted this finished and done with as soon as possible. He patted his thigh as she moved toward him but balked at actually bending herself across his lap. He sighed, reached out and clasped her arm, thus he made easy work of tugging her across his knee. She lay still without complaint when he pulled up her petticoat. She shifted slightly, feeling embarrassed at being in this ignoble position. He didn't speak, so the first slap to her tender flesh was such a surprise that she squeaked aloud. With both her palms placed flat upon the floor, she withstood his first spanks stoically but as the tempo increased, she found the need to lift one hand, which waved helplessly in the air. Her backside was starting to heat up to an uncomfortable degree. She soon found herself gasping aloud with each searing smack.

Not much longer, she reassured herself, be brave, it will soon be over. Unlike her previous spankings, this one was proving harder to bear. It hurt more than she remembered, and it was progressing for longer than the other two that Abel had dealt her. Perhaps it was time for her to apologise and end this torture? She told him she would never undertake such a rescue again unless she'd first discussed it with him. He said he was pleased to hear that, but the spanking continued at an increased and harder rate. Why? She'd apologised, surely he should be ending her punishment?

"Abel, I have apologised to you, so please stop now!" she implored.

"No, not until I am convinced that you have learned your lesson." His enigmatic reply incensed her.

"Abel Lawson you will let me up right now; you're hurting me I tell you!"

"Good, that is the whole point of a spanking!" She yelped as he landed a particularly hard barrage of swats across the tops of her legs.

"I shall cry!" she threatened, then realised tears already leaked from her eyes. "Abel!" she bawled.

"You are a very naughty girl, Amanda, and this is how naughty girls are rewarded. You might like to remember that the next time you consider causing merry hell for everyone about you!"

Amanda decided she could stand it no more. She attempted to tilt sideways off his lap, but Abel anticipated her sudden shift and clasped her firmly about the waist. He shifted his knees apart and freed his leg to clamp over both of hers, which had begun to scissor apart in a desperately futile attempt at escape. He'd engineered her so that she was draped neatly over only one of his thighs, trapped by the other. She bawled her anguish with noisy yells, swearing like a dockhand. Her buttocks blazed. She could take no more of this. Abel had to let her go right now! She grabbed onto his calf and dug her fingernails in as deep as she could, her satisfaction on hearing the yell he gave was short lived.

"I was going to be lenient, but if this is the way you behave, then the gloves come off!"

Lenient, he supposed he'd been lenient? She struggled frantically, but it was no use, he had her firm. A torrent of scorching slaps rapidly covered every inch of her nether region; it was now a spanking such as she could not have imagined. It heated her rear end to such a pitch that the anguished wails she released were heard quite clearly below stairs. Mrs. Neil hurriedly suggested that Agatha go next door to their neighbours and ask to borrow some eggs, the monkey having broken every single one.

Finally, the slaps to her derriere stopped and Amanda, after receiving such a searing spanking, lay wrung out, slumped limply across her husband's knee. All vim and vinegar had deserted her. "There's my good girl," Abel praised. Strangely his words brought a glow of pride and comfort to her. She felt Abel rub her back in slow circles, and she thanked God that her spanking was over. Gradually, she managed to bring her weeping under control, but still she sniffled loudly as he lifted her up to sit her upon his knee. Leaning sideways, he withdrew a clean folded handkerchief from his trouser pocket and shook it out before wiping away her tears and dabbing her nose dry. He kissed her forehead chastely. "Perhaps now you'll give proper consideration before you act the hoyden, and when some impulsive scheme enters that pretty little head of yours, you'll take time to reflect before you act, hmm?" he asked rhetorically. She didn't bother to reply but nodded her head in mournful agreement.

"I have to say that I'm not at all happy with some of the language I heard drop from those lovely lips just now. I think as your husband it is my duty to wash out your mouth. Get down onto your knees in front of me. I have a good idea." He eased her off his knee onto the floor. Bemused, Amanda did as he directed and kneeled in front of him. Her action brought her petticoat floating down over her inflamed buttocks, and she winced as the material grazed her sore behind. Heat suffused her face, and her eyes widened as she watched Abel unbutton his trousers. His already swollen cock sprung free, fully engorged. "Open your mouth Amanda," he ordered huskily.

She swallowed convulsively but obeyed. He shifted his haunches forward on the chair seat. One hand clasped his member while his other reached out to grasp her chin, his thumb sliding seductively over her bottom lip. "You will open wide and take my cock into your mouth then suckle. I intend my husbandly essence to clear that filthy language from your vocabulary. Close your mouth around me, there's a good girl, you may begin. I'll warn you when your medicine is ready for you to swallow."

Abel had to bite his cheek in an effort not to chuckle aloud at the look on his sweet girl's face. Her rounded eyes gazed up at him, appearing huge in her tear stained face. She was shocked by this erotic act, he could tell, but as much as he despised himself for becoming aroused when he punished her, he couldn't help his body's natural response to her squirming warmth when she was pressed up so snugly against his manhood. He wanted to plunge into her wet sheath, but he decided he shouldn't give her pleasure after a punishment; the benefit of chastising her would be lost. He knew the spanking had hurt, yet she was unconsciously aroused, he'd seen the evidence. If he'd not been already raised to full mast, the sight of her plump pink feminine folds coated in a glistening sheen of her own arousal would certainly have had him standing at full attention.

Her lips formed a tight 'O' around his cock. It tickled as she gently sucked, he closed his eyes and gritted his teeth. Her tongue was feather light as it touched him; it felt as though a butterfly had landed on the tip of his shaft as her tongue fluttered over the sensitive crown. "Suck harder," he ordered, huskily. She obeyed, her cheeks hollowed with the effort she put into the action. He watched her through languid slitted lids, enjoying every decadent moment, until a tightening in his sac and a throbbing ache in his rod gave notice of his imminent eruption. "I am about to cleanse your naughty mouth… here take your husband's medicine…" Groaning aloud, his seed spurted exuberantly into the delicious warmth of her mouth. He thrust his hips toward her, his hand cupped the back of her neck as he filled her throat with himself.

Gallantly, she swallowed as he spilled, but as a novice, she coughed, spluttering in the attempt. He chuckled, delighted with his pupil. He used his handkerchief again, this time to wipe her chin. She dipped her head when he'd cleaned her face as embarrassment overcame her. He scooped her up into his arms then carried her over to the bed where he first tugged back the sheets and blankets. Lowering her onto the mattress, he pulled the bedclothes up to cover her. Abel stroked back the damp tendrils of hair that covered her forehead and kissed her lightly on the lips. She stared up at him owlishly.

"Did I please you?" she asked softly, and even though he was totally satiated, he felt his cock twitch.

His gaze raked her décolletage. "Oh yes. Sleep now, my love, all is forgiven but remember this lesson. I'd hate to have to repeat the first any time soon. As for the second, I can see that might become something you could treat me to when you want to butter-me-up!" She nodded, and again his loins twitched at her total acquiescence. He had never known Amanda be so submissive to him before. He liked her like this. Should she return to her spirited ways, then so much the better, for now he knew how to tame his naughty little termagant. "Sleep," he ordered as he left the room.

She did, most deeply.

~

Abel woke her while it was still dark with what began as a gentle kiss but quickly escalated into some rough and ready lovemaking. When he grasped her hips, yanking her underneath him in order to mount her, she shuddered, intoxicated with pleasure. Oddly, the heat from her punished rear shifted back to front so that her quim swelled, aching for his touch, not that he needed to arouse her, she was more than ready for him. After only a few deep thrusts, she flew apart, writhing beneath him. Her greedy channel grasped his cock, causing his own unexpected powerful completion. They fell back to sleep, exhausted, entwined in one another's arms.

CHAPTER 10

Married life continued on an even keel, and for a while, Amanda felt that the honeymoon element had returned to their relationship. Abel arrived home on the eve of Amanda's birthday. He asked her to close her eyes, and when he told her she could look, she opened her eyes to see that he held the tiniest, fluffiest tabby kitten in the palm of one hand. She had cooed over the sweet thing, but what moved her most, was the sight of her large husband tenderly petting such a tiny creature. Her heart melted with love as she watched him being so gentle and compassionate with the new kitten.

She had put her cat Dusty's needs above her own when she had married Abel and she left Dusty to live in Sydenham where she was settled with James's family with whom she was happy and loved, but Amanda missed her beloved cat. She decided to name her new pet Tiger because Elspeth, who'd spent her formative years in India, told her the kitten resembled a tiger due to his stripes. Very soon the two were inseparable; Amanda took the cat with her in a carry basket wherever she went.

One evening after supper, a few weeks after the organ grinder business had been put behind them, Amanda mentioned that she had read in the newspaper that Charles Darwin's book, *The Descent of Man,* which had been released in March, was to be discussed in Parliament with a view to introducing legislation against animal cruelty. Amanda declared that she wanted to attend. She begged Abel to take her so that she could sit up in the Visitors' Gallery to listen to the debate. Abel worried that his wife had too high an expectation about the upcoming deliberations. He was concerned that her natural propensity to wade in whenever she thought injustice abounded would cause huge embarrassment and reflect badly on his country. He urged her to stay at home, pointing out that the debate would be dull and legislation unlikely to be implemented on that day. Amanda would have none of this, she was going to attend that debate come hell or high water. However, she was careful to keep her own counsel about her intention to draw as much attention to her cause as she possibly could.

Amanda waited until Abel had left the house for the day before ordering Billy to drive her over to Elspeth's house.

"You want to cause a stir in the Commons and protest?" Elspeth asked, somewhat aghast by the idea. Amanda nodded enthusiastically.

"I do, yes. I want these politicians to hear the voice of those of us who would protect these creatures who cannot speak for themselves. What do you say, will you help me?" she implored.

Elspeth asked, "Have you thought about Abel's likely reaction?"

"I am willing to risk his wrath if you are," replied Amanda.

"I am", replied Elspeth. "Adam has been treating me with kid gloves for too long."

They requested that Billy drive them to Dulwich where they enlisted Scrounger's agreement to allow them to use his small abode in order to make a large banner. Meeting at Scrounger's cottage, together they worked on the enormous sheet, which they planned to unfold and stretch the length of the public gallery, so that it would hang high above the floor during the Commons debate.

Each told their husband that they were at the other's house, inventing different reasons for their absences. It was risky, but luckily for them, neither was caught out in their lie, and so the secret banner was worked upon diligently until it was finally finished.

On the day of their trip to Westminster, Abel had a prior meeting, and so it was they arranged to meet up inside the Commons up in the Visitors' Gallery. Billy drove Amanda first to Elspeth's house and then on to collect Scrounger and the banner from Dulwich. Scrounger had a small collection of pets. They were a group of five prized white rats, which he tended to carry about with him in an old, battered, leather valise. Since he'd obtained them, he took them with him wherever he went, and so, as usual, they travelled with him into the Palace of Westminster. On their arrival, Amanda was disappointed to see only two other people seated at the opposite end of the long balcony in the gallery. She had hoped for more people who would be sympathetic to the cause against animal cruelty. Ignoring the two strangers, they hurriedly unrolled their banner and pushed it beneath the bench before Abel arrived. It was well hidden but easily accessible.

Abel was both surprised and disappointed to see both his sister-in-law and Scrounger sat alongside his wife. He had hoped to enjoy this interesting political moment alone with her. It was the first time she'd shown the slightest bit of interest in politics, and after his initial apprehension, Abel had looked forward to sharing this debate so close to her heart then discussing the finer points of the forum with her afterwards.

Members of Parliament, referred to as MPs, began to fill the floor below, some sat, while others stood about in groups laughing and chatting until the Speaker of the House called them to order and the debate began. It had been underway for some half hour when a rather arrogant man with a strong Northern accent rose to take the floor. He stated that he thought it unchristian to alter the law. He called Darwin's book an affront to Christian beliefs and declared that all animals had been put on this earth for man's sole dominion. Abel was so absorbed in the discussion at this point that he failed to notice the movement of the three beside him, until it was too late to stop them. He caught sight of a flurry of white cloth as it unfurled, fluttering low over the balcony. Shrieking boos and hisses suddenly deafened him. Hastily, he launched himself toward his wife in an attempt to restrain her, but she deftly stepped sideways and shifted beyond his reach, leaning indecorously over the balustrade as she yelled her opinions upon animal welfare at the incredulous gentleman seated below.

"Order! Order! Order!" bellowed the Speaker, banging his gavel repetitively. Abel noticed another, altogether closer sound. He cocked his head, listening intently, to the softer noise. Strange, he thought, it was almost like the sound of tiny scurrying feet. He gasped as his gaze fell to the balcony floor. He spotted the white rats as they skittered along the wooden planks and climbed up onto the banner that was so long it hung down to the ground level below.

He cradled his head in his hands and groaned, thus missing the act of the rats dropping one by one onto the floor of the Commons. One even landed on the northern MP's shoulder. Man and rat eyeballed one another for a startled second or two. The man reacted with a roar as he saw another rat run across his shoe. Yelling, he kicked his foot. The rat flew through the air. The one sat on his shoulder jumped, dashing after his small white brother. Pandemonium broke out as MPs began to roll up their order papers with which to strike the rats.

One man grabbed the end of the banner that proclaimed him and previous governments to be 'deaf to the needs of voiceless creatures.' Another soon joined him and a tug of war began between MPs and the three protestors above. Amanda held hard on to the banner with Elspeth and Scrounger pulling for all they were worth alongside her. More and more men joined in the tug of war on the floor below. The Speaker's cries for order were soon drowned out by the sing-song baritone drone of, 'hea…ve-ho, hea…ve-ho!' as more and more gentlemen joined in the tug of war. It appeared to Abel that they were fully enjoying this very unexpected and unusual situation. "Get out! Get out, you are forbidden to be here!" bawled the Speaker of the House, turning puce with fury. He obviously found no such pleasure with the ensuing debacle.

Scrounger spotted his rats and feared for their lives as the other half of the MPs, those not embroiled in the tug of war, leapt about smacking at his pets with rolled up papers, yelling, "Got the blasted crittur!" even though it was obvious they had not. He let go of the banner, dashed from the balcony, heading downstairs in defence of his pets.

Abel shook his head as he awoke from a stupor of shock. Once again, he lunged for his wife, this time, successfully. He lugged her against his side, pivoted, placed his foot firmly upon the bench and tossed her kicking, shrieking form unceremoniously across his thigh. He pulled up her dress and shoved aside her bustle, whereupon he landed a heavy-handed slap on her hindquarters. She shrieked and squirmed like a banshee in livid protest.

A wave of loud clapping caught their attention, causing Abel to momentarily still his hand as a burst of applause lifted from the floor below. This bastion of masculinity approved whole heartedly with Abel's method of curbing his errant wife. Then another cheer fairly lifted the roof, echoing about them as poor Elspeth, single handedly, lost the final battle with the banner as gentlemen below toppled over one another, falling backwards, when she suddenly released her end of the cloth. It remained total pandemonium for more than a few moments. Then the noise diminished as the Speaker called for the Sergeant at Arms to apprehend Scrounger just as he bent to clutch another of his rats, stuffing it into his pocket whilst he was marched unceremoniously out of the Commons by a florid faced Sergeant at Arms.

Elspeth turned away from the spectacle below, shocked to see that her sister-in-law was inelegantly draped across Abel's knee. Her stomach roiled as she realised that she would no doubt suffer the same consequences at her own husband's hand. She wished that Amanda would not be quite so voluble and antagonistic so Abel would end her punishment, but it seemed that Amanda's tongue was quite out of control, and it came as no surprise to her when he stopped spanking in order to tug everything except his wife's bloomers out of his way before continuing to rain hellfire down upon his upended wife's behind.

Abel no longer cared who saw him chastising Amanda. She was completely out of control, and he was determined that he should win this particular battle of wills. Otherwise, he worried that she would never learn to respect him. It took fairly ten minutes before his wife was ready to acquiesce to him and even after she laid limp, accepting her chastisement, he continued to spank her until he was satisfied there would be no sass left in her once he set her upright. When he did finally allow her up, he placed a finger against her lips and told her not to utter one single word until they were home again. She had the audacity to stick out her tongue, but other than gulping hard at the threatening look he cast her, she had the presence of mind to remain silent as requested.

Abel guided the two miscreants downstairs. They were met by the Sergeant at Arms. He still kept a steely hand upon Scrounger's shoulder, but his directed glare of disapproval was at Abel.

"Mr. Lawson, I am to inform you that you will be summoned to appear before the bar for reprimand by the Speaker of the House. Failure to comply warrants immediate arrest and a custodial sentence. You are to leave this place immediately, good day to you, sir!"

Escorted by two guards, Abel guided his motley crew through the palace and out into the yard where Billy awaited them atop the coach. Silently, he handed the ladies inside the carriage. Scrounger leapt in last and they were on their way. Elspeth winked at Amanda. She giggled, only to break off mid-gurgle as Abel's livid glance caught her own amused gaze, pinning her with a stony glare. Gulping, she lowered her eyes and hung her head. They travelled the rest of the way in silence to Dulwich where Scrounger was dropped at his house. He was missing one rat but counted himself lucky that it was only the one.

Abel commanded Amanda to await him in the carriage while he saw Elspeth to the door. Adam was home. He waved to her, and she returned the greeting in kind, but as she watched, his bright welcoming smile slipped from his face as Abel spoke to him. Adam's visage grew grimmer as Amanda's husband obviously explained the afternoon's fiasco and Elspeth's part in it. She saw Abel shake his brother-in-law's hand before he returned to the carriage. Before the front door closed, Amanda witnessed her brother's hand land heavily on his wife's behind as she stepped before him into the house. Amanda hoped that would be the sum of her punishment, but she somehow doubted it. She stole a glance at her own husband's grim profile, wondering what her fate would be on their return. An anxious shiver crept down her spine. Even though he'd already spanked her in the Commons, she felt certain it would involve him setting fire to her bottom again.

Mrs. Neil met them at the door. "Would you like tea, Mrs. Lawson?" she asked.

"That would be nice—" Amanda began.

"Not right now, thank you, Mrs. Neil," Abel interrupted his wife. "Come, Mrs. Lawson, I wish to discuss this afternoon's events with you."

Amanda pouted. "Does it have to be right now, Abel? Could we not—"

"No, we could not. Come follow me." Abel stooped his tall frame through the doorway, and Amanda hesitantly followed him as he led her upstairs to their room.

He seated himself upon the bed and called her to him. Widening his legs, he pulled her to stand between his thighs. He reached for her hands and held them in his. "Today you shamed both me and my country." He did not mince his words. Amanda attempted to pull her hands free from his, but he held her firm. "You behaved in an unreasonable and childish fashion which actually made me feel ashamed of my own wife. How old are you, Amanda, six, seven, eight years?"

"You know that I am twenty!" she responded huffily.

"Indeed, well your behaviour today suggests that you are of nursery age and so I shall treat you accordingly."

"Nonsense, you seem to have overlooked the fact that I have every right to protest against animal cruelty!" she insisted heatedly. He nodded.

"Yes, I agree, but this was a debate and on an issue close to your heart, yet you did not listen beyond the first few comments. How do you know how the debate might have turned out had you not so rudely interrupted proceedings, hmm?"

Amanda flushed and squirmed uncomfortably. Abel might have a point there, but she wasn't about to admit that. "The banner release was my only intention; the rats' escape was an accident. I had no idea that Scrounger would bring them."

Abel studied his young wife for a moment noting that she failed to meet his eye. "There was no need to bring animals into the debate. It was foolish beyond measure to carry them into Westminster, and I think you were well aware of the fact that Scrounger's valise contained his rats." She shook her head in weak denial.

"It is my duty as your husband to teach you the error of your ways. Today's fiasco is the second thoughtless and damaging stunt that you have enacted since our marriage. I need to be firmer on this occasion. Fetch me your hairbrush, Amanda."

Her eyes flew wide. "What? No! You have already spanked me… this is totally unfair!"

Abel placed his finger across her lips. "Nothing you can say will change my mind. I intend to make certain that you never shame me in such a way again. Fetch your hairbrush for me, right now." It crossed her mind to bite his finger, but she knew by now that such action would simply make matters much worse for her. She stood mulishly glaring at him. "God-dammit Amanda, do as you're told!" She jumped, startled by his tone and plodded obediently but crossly over to her dresser to pick up her solid square backed wooden hairbrush. She understood that he meant to spank her with her oh so practical brush. She glared at the object furiously, as though it alone could be blamed for putting the idea of its alternative use into her husband's head. Abel took it from her reluctantly outstretched palm. He then ordered her to remove her dress and petticoats. Harrumphing tetchily, Amanda slowly began to remove the items of clothing as requested. A sharp slap to her flanks had her speedily undressed until she stood before him, clad only in her chemise and drawers.

He reached out and deftly untied the ribbon at her waist, giving the undergarment a quick tug so that the bloomers slid down over her curves, puddling about her ankles. He patted his lap, and she tilted toward him. He pulled her the rest of the way, settling her across his large thighs.

"Please, Abel, be gentle with me, my bottom is still sore!" she begged.

He gave a short, grim laugh. "As your husband I shall decide how much punishment you require and, going by events, I can assure you this will not be a quick nor easy spanking you have coming, my girl!" He'd no sooner finished his sentence than the hair brush he wielded made contact with her bare bottom. Immediately, she cried out in shock. She'd no idea that this was going to hurt so much!

"No, no, no!" she yelled, bucking wildly as the next painful spank landed on the opposite cheek.

Unlike the previous time he'd spanked her, Abel did not say another word to her as he tucked his wife's flailing body close into his waist and laid the hairbrush across her backside with rapid strokes, quickly turning her pink flesh red. It was lucky for her that he'd warmed her sit upon already because the briskness of this hairbrush spanking might otherwise have bruised her tender flesh. She sobbed, pleaded, kicked and wailed, but still he spanked on relentlessly, grimly ignoring the fuss she made as her hands scrabbled to grip the counterpane while her feet flailed uselessly. He was utterly determined to make this spanking a suitable deterrent to any future transgressions. His wife would certainly think twice before behaving in such a stupidly thoughtless manner next time some mad cap scheme entered her pretty little head!

Amanda's bottom was soon a mass of crimson splotches. He landed a number of thwacks to her upper thighs. These obviously caused her a deal of discomfort because her wailing turned to shrieks. Abel felt that he'd had plenty of time to cool his temper on the journey back from the Commons, but he was still extremely annoyed with his wife. She needed to understand that actions had consequences. Hopefully, by the time he'd finished with her, she would have learned that lesson well.

It was a very soggy and sorry little wife that Abel walked to stand in the corner of the room, some minutes later. He mopped her tears and gave her his kerchief as she continued to sob. She had made no apology as yet, and so he turned her face to the wall and commanded her to remain where she was and think about what she wished to say to him on his return. He left the room and went down to the parlour where Mrs. Neil had left them tea.

Amanda gingerly rubbed her scalding flesh. Never in all her born days had she been treated thus. Abel had really hurt her. She was on fire! Her bottom felt twice its normal size and she was full of self pity, and yet she was uncomfortably aware that what Abel had said was true. Her chagrin receded a little, and she remembered the things he'd said to her. That she had shamed him and his country. Oh, she felt horrible that he should think that, and he had to go to Westminster to be reprimanded in front of the whole of the Commons by the Speaker, yet he'd done no wrong; it was her fault. Tears of genuine remorse trickled down her cheeks. When Abel returned, it was to a penitent wife, one who begged his forgiveness, falling before him onto her knees. She reached for the buttons on his trousers, declaring herself in much need of his husbandly medicine. Abel had no intention of arguing the point.

CHAPTER 11

It was a couple of weeks since Abel had been called before the House to be scolded. Since that day, he'd been withdrawn and less communicative with Amanda. She knew she deserved his condemnation, but he did not mention the incident to her again, and when she raised it, he told her it was all in the past, forgiven and forgotten.

Amanda decided she should visit Scrounger and Elspeth. She wanted to know if her sister-in-law had fared any better with Adam than she had with Abel. She planned to go to Scrounger's first. She knew that his sense of class divide was deeply ingrained; he would always wait for her to initiate any contact between the three of them. Once she was sitting comfortably again, her first trip out from the house after her spanking was to Dulwich. There was the issue of Dr. Barker and his odd behaviour to be discussed, and she wanted to find out what progress he'd made, if any, regarding the doctor's motives for accusing Scrounger of murder. Billy Neil drove her over there in the brougham. On arrival, the lad helped her down, and they arranged her collection time for noon. Amanda's initial knock at Scrounger's door produced no results, so she hammered loudly on the wooden door. Still, no one came, and quickly surmising that Scrounger was out, she considered using the hidden key to let herself in to await his return. However, who knew how long he might be, so she decided to walk the short distance over to James and Felicity's house. Sydenham wasn't far and the day was bright and warm. Amanda relished the exercise walking to her former home. As she neared the end of the road, a coach pulled up beside her and who should alight but Dr. Eugene Barker. Pulling down the carriage window, he hailed her in a friendly manner, offering to carry her to her destination. She politely declined, knowing Abel wouldn't like her to accept his offer, nor would either of her brothers.

Eugene would not take no for an answer and dismounted. Taking her arm, he all but dragged her inside the carriage. Amanda wondered if perhaps he had not heard that she was married, her gloves covered her wedding band. She determined to explain her change in circumstances; however, he did not stop talking. She was distracted by his unusual loquaciousness, waiting for a break in his monologue in which she might politely inform him of her marriage. When they finally pulled up outside her brother's house, she realised that she'd still not informed him of her marriage to Abel. His final words to her were that he'd call upon her again sometime soon.

Felicity was agog at Amanda's description of the visit and protest made at the House of Commons. She attempted to impress upon her naive young sister-in-law the delicate position that Abel was in. She explained how shaming the dressing down he had been given in front of Parliament must have been, both for himself and his country. Amanda listened and it dawned upon her for the first time that she may have damaged her husband's career.

On her return home, she was pleased to find that Abel had not yet returned. She instructed Mrs. Neil to prepare a partridge pie followed by rhubarb tart and custard, Abel's favourite dinner. Hattie drew her a bath. Afterwards, she redressed in a gown of electric blue, a favourite of Abel's that showed off her blue eyes most favourably. Taking special care of her toilette, she asked Hattie to first curl her hair before they pinned it high upon her head, knowing how well it would look when she took out the pins and shook it down, before retiring. Amanda determined she would apologize properly and seduce her husband.

Abel was moved by Amanda's effort to make amends. As far as her behaviour was concerned, he had forgiven her after she had been punished, but he brooded on her suitability to act as a diplomat's wife. He daily expected condemnation to arrive in the mail from across the Atlantic and was giving deep thought to what he might do to earn a living should he be recalled and his diplomatic career be at an end.

He chose not to burden his wife with any of his concerns, deeming her too young and irresponsible to grasp the seriousness of his situation. However, he was surprised and touched at her attempt to show remorse, and he lightened his mood accordingly, chatting amiably with her at dinner. When it came time to retire, her obvious endeavour to seduce him brought forth an overwhelming desire to prove his control over her, and so he ignored her simpering overtures, until she stood before him robed in her filmy night gown, looking mutinous.

"What's wrong, my sweet?" he asked.

"I'd like to kiss you, Abel," she told him. He proffered his cheek. Hesitating, she leaned in to peck him. Moving away, he shrugged his arms out of his shirt and, continued to disrobe, ignoring her. Amanda chewed her bottom lip, unsure how best to engage him. Finally, she clambered crossly into bed. Abel smothered his amusement at her inept attempt to seduce him. She gave a long suffering sigh of discontent.

He returned from the bathroom to find her curled up, presenting her back to him. He ripped the bed covers from her huddled form, hauling her upright into a sitting position. "First, off with this!" he stated, pulling her gown from under her hips, up and over her head. As she mewled in protest, he lowered his head and smothered her mouth with his. He trailed his lips from hers, down over her neck, where he nipped then swiped the sting away with a soothing press of his tongue. Using the same method, he worked his way down her shoulders, nipping and nibbling until he reached her hard burgeoning nipples. Suckling, he treated each ripe bud to the same bold treatment.

Amanda writhed beneath her husband, his punishing nips and soothing tongue caused her to focus on him more than ever before. This was new to her, this less than gentle husband and she was unsure how she felt about the bite of pain he inflicted before he loved the flesh he'd slightly hurt. He had ploughed her roughly and demandingly before now, but never before had he used this deliberate bite of pain, which he'd introduced tonight. He knelt between her legs and applied the same nip and lick treatment to her swollen, tender cleft. She gasped as all rationality flew from her head.

She was molten. His eyes held hers as he lifted her legs and draped each one either side of his head and over his shoulders. She couldn't read his expression, but his face was set in hard planes, his eyes glittered with something deeper than lust. Then it dawned on her, he was mastering her, teaching her he was in control, confirming to her that it was he and not she who made their decisions. For some reason, the knowledge of his intent thrilled her.

Abel continued to tease her, retreating whenever her moans grew too lusty. She begged and pleaded with him to allow her release. He moved to lie over her, his gaze compelling her.

"You're my woman, I am your husband," he growled softly in her ear as she whimpered. The steel length of him inched into her slick channel, which contracted with the slow pull of a pending orgasm. He stilled. "I am in control… Not you." Again, her answer, a whimper, shuddering as the delicious feel of his shaft moved inside her, pressing down upon her cleft, teasing but not giving her enough to engage the nebulous orgasm which was held at bay by his refusal to move deep within her. She was so close to culminating, the tension within unbearable. She needed him, why oh why wouldn't he thrust into her as she needed.

"Abel..." she pleaded, halting on a gasp as he suddenly bucked fully inside her, aiming so high that he pummelled the entrance of her womb.

"You'll learn to obey me as you promised in your wedding vows to me. As your husband, I master your body." He snapped his pelvis, enforcing his word, his cock engulfed her flooding channel. The dam of pending emotion flowed free from her at last as she keened a release so powerful it bowed her body, pressing her breasts hard up against his chest. *"Pledge to obey me as promised!"* he demanded through gritted teeth as his own tumultuous release began to rush from the base of his manhood.

"Yes-s," she whimpered. It was difficult to regain her power of thought, let alone speech, but she needed a moment to gather her scattered wits before she cried out her troth. "I am sorry that I shamed you. I love that you master me! You're everything to me! If I forget, remind me. I promise to obey because I love you, Abel!" Her heartfelt cry of remorse was as satisfying for him as the thrum of his orgasm as it spurted forth, coating her drenched womanhood. Finally, he felt that he'd conquered her and she was his.

There was better understanding between them after their night of passion. Amanda consulted with her husband more and more frequently. She enjoyed their heated discussions but both showed respect for the other's opinion, which encouraged Amanda to defer to Abel's greater knowledge of the world. He began to guide her reading choices onto more worldly subjects. Amanda found she enjoyed following news from the newspaper that Abel left on her breakfast tray each morning.

Inevitably, her thoughts returned to Dr. Barker and his sinister activities. She decided to visit Scrounger, since she knew that he was unlikely to call upon her with his firmly held belief in class divide. He'd been out the last time she'd visited; this time she hoped to find him at home. Frustratingly, he was not at home on this occasion either. She'd foolishly dismissed Billy and the coach, so she decided once again to walk the short trip to Sydenham and visit with Felicity. George's birthday was in a few weeks' time, and she wanted to know what she could buy him for a gift. Her nephew was a particular child, but Felicity seemed to know exactly what her son would like. The weather was pleasant. The early autumn had turned into an Indian summer, so the two women took tea in the garden.

After her visit, Felicity offered Amanda a lift back in their carriage, which she gratefully accepted. Wandering around to the front of the house, she dawdled, enjoying the scent of the roses entwined about the trellis archway as she waited for the carriage. "Miss Beresford!" Amanda started with surprise as Dr. Barker appeared before her. He tucked his arm firmly through hers and led her to the road where his coach and driver stood. "It is some while since I saw you last, let me take you for a short drive for I have news that I wish to share with you." Amanda hesitated momentarily. Abel would be furious if she got into Eugene's carriage, but how else was she to discover what the doctor was up to if she didn't speak with him? It was broad day light, mid-afternoon, what could possibly happen? She agreed, accepted his hand and clambered inside.

~

EUGENE KEPT THE CONVERSATION LIGHT. He asked her opinion on various subjects, listening with such flattering intensity to her reply, so she did not at first notice how far they'd travelled beyond the boundaries of Sydenham. A glance out of the window alerted her to the fact they were travelling along an unknown lane, somewhere out in the countryside. Having noticed, she rounded on him crossly. "I did not agree to join you on a joy ride, Doctor. I insist that you take me home immediately!"

He grinned, but she noted the smile never touched his eyes as he stared at her coldly. “I have something for you, Miss Beresford,” he told her, as he began to rummage in his black Gladstone bag. She was about to explain that she was now a married woman and could not accept his gift, when he unexpectedly lunged across the carriage pressing a strange smelling cloth over her nose and mouth. The world spun dizzily, she thought she heard him say, “Sleep well, my beauty,” but she could not be certain because, at that point, she pitched forward as the world turned black.

CHAPTER 12

She awoke lying upon a bed, completely unaware of her present location. It took her a few moments to orientate herself to the fact she was not in her own home but in an unknown bed chamber. As she attempted to shift her legs, she discovered to her horror that she was bound. "Good you're awake. It's time to talk. I am fully aware that you saw my little hobby room in my clinic. I do not like snoops, Amanda. It is a habit I shall fast rid you of once we are wed. You see, my dear, the law states that a wife may not testify against her husband, so due to your meddling, it has become imperative that we are married as soon as possible."

Amanda opened her mouth to tell him that he was too late, she was already married, but his next words stilled the words in her throat. "If you had already been married to another, I should perhaps have killed you." He trailed a fingertip gently over the curve of each of her eyebrows, his malignant gaze held her in his thrall. "I should begin with these pretty sapphire eyes then remove the more interesting parts of your delectable body." He reached over and squeezed each of her breasts in turn. Amanda felt bile rise in her throat. "Until I had assimilated you into my collection."

She stared up at him with mounting horror. "*You are mad*," she whispered. He cocked his head.

"No, I am merely a man of science, not inclined to emotional outbursts such as ordinary folk. You see my training was given before many hospitals had access to cadavers for training purposes. It was difficult to learn the skills I required. I hungered and thirsted for knowledge of the human form. It thrilled me to discover the inner world of man. One day perhaps my humble collection will become world famous. I shall be the toast of the medical profession, perhaps recognised as top in my field. Then those fools will be made to admit their error and the Queen herself shall commend me for my contribution to medical science." Amanda frowned.

"Whatever do you mean?"

Eugene ignored her question. "Unfortunately, people are ignorant beings, so I am forced to keep my experiments under wraps until a more enlightened era dawns, which is why I must take you to wife. You are a pretty little thing, easy on the eye. I have no doubt that if my crop does not tame you, the use of my medical knowledge with drugs shall alter your nature into that of a placid, biddable woman."

Amanda bit her tongue but remained silent. It was obvious to her that he was quite insane, possibly dangerous to boot. She realised instinctively it wouldn't do to antagonise him. "I would have said yes had you asked me nicely, Eugene. You should have proposed in the conventional way." She simpered sweetly, hoping to sound convincing. "Still, I suppose there are not many girls who can boast a romantic kidnap as the start of their engagement?" She forced a giggle; Eugene looked mollified. He was so vain that it didn't once occur to him that she might be duping him.

"Marriage, my dear, there can be no engagement I fear. There is no time, for I cannot take the risk of your wagging tongue mentioning my crucially important work. I know how you ladies do like to gossip. Have you shared what you saw of my collection with anyone else... your brothers perhaps?" He watched her intently for signs of deceit.

Amanda kept her wide blue gaze unblinkingly on his, shaking her head negatively, her blonde curls bounced sweetly, adding the allusion of innocence. "No, I confess I did not like seeing those gruesome jars," she shuddered dramatically, "but I didn't think it at all odd that an eminent doctor such as yourself should have a medical collection. After all, I have not known any previous doctors. I decided not to mention what I'd seen to my brothers because they might not understand why I had been allowed to see such things and forbid me from seeing you again. If I'd told the truth that I'd snuck downstairs to snoop about your clinic, I might have been punished. I confess that I decided to keep quiet and say nothing to anyone." She lowered her eyes as though embarrassed by her naughtiness. It appeared that Eugene believed her because he untied her legs, explaining that he needed to rub her lower limbs in order to help her circulation, although she was of the opinion he did so with far too much enthusiasm. Her wrists remained bound where they were, resting upon her stomach. He did however check that the circulation of her wrists was unimpaired, before he took her pulse.

"Is this your house?" she asked, glancing about as he checked her wrist bindings.

"It was my aunt's. She was my first cadaver you know." Amanda felt nauseous.

"You cut open your own aunt?" she whispered incredulously. He frowned.

"She wasn't my aunt any more, she was a body." She gulped.

"Did you do the same with your parents?" He glared at her.

"No, it was as I told you. Both my parents died young. My mother in childbirth giving life to me. I was a breech birth. My father had an apoplexy a few years later. He was a doctor and never forgave himself for being unable to save my mother. I inherited everything, including the building that was his practice and now is my own. My aunt took care of me here, until I went away to school. Our family home was closed up until I claimed it upon my majority."

Amanda must have looked sceptical. "You doubt my word? I am not a liar, Amanda. I am a doctor and a gentleman," he scolded.

"Would you do the same to me as you did to your aunt if I should die?" she questioned in a small voice. He stopped what he was doing and stared down at her, a tic twitched in his cheek.

"You want me to say no, but I shall not lie to you Amanda, I shall always be honest with you." He resumed his task.

"You'd really cut me up?" she asked tremulously, feeling bile rise again in her throat, sickened by the thought.

"That's enough of this discussion; I see that you are upsetting yourself." He crossed to the other side of the room to where a chest of drawers stood, with a pitcher and glass atop it. He poured her a glass of water then fetched it to her, lifting and cradling her head in order to help her drink. She was so thirsty, she drank her fill. He plumped the pillows before lying her back down again. "Is your neck comfortable?" he asked.

"Yes, thank you," she replied honestly.

"It is very bad for your back for your neck to be misaligned," he informed her as he moved to where he'd placed his black Gladstone bag on the bedroom chair. Amanda listened, incredulous, as he played the caring doctor.

"What are you looking for?" she asked anxiously, as he rummaged amongst his medical supplies. "Our wedding is tomorrow. Since I don't want you fretting or attempting to escape while I am gone tonight, I am going to give you a small shot of laudanum to help you rest." He turned holding up a silver hypodermic needle.

"No, Eugene, please don't do this! Surely you cannot mean to leave me here all night, unconscious! Anything might happen to me while I am tied up all alone!" He walked unhurriedly toward the bed whilst flicking the small silver phial with his finger. At the bedside, he pushed the plunger so that the needle released a small amount of liquid, which squirted directly into the air. He concentrated on his action, completely ignoring her mounting pleas. "Eugene, I beg you, *please, please!* Do not do this, I am begging you, Eugene! I promise I won't leave this bed. *No... no...*" Her pleas failed to move him as he took hold of her arm and plunged the needle deep into the fleshy part above her elbow. Amanda drummed her feet on the bed, squealing with fright and impotent fury.

"There now, all done! Such fuss and bother over a tiny prick in the arm. Tsk, tsk, Amanda, not a good start to life as a doctor's wife. As *my* wife, I am sure you will see far worse. Come now, let me cover you and settle you for the night." Amanda did not hear those final spoken words, for she was already deeply unconscious, lost in the drug induced sleep that Eugene had enforced upon her.

Thankfully, she never knew that after he'd watched her fall into her unnatural slumber, he'd pulled up her dress and petticoats, parted her legs and drawers to insert a long white finger into her womanhood. Holding her folds apart to study those plump pink womanly parts, his fingers combed her golden maidenhair aside to reveal the fleshy cap, which he then lifted to expose her clitoris. He tickled it experimentally, before invading her channel. Pumping his finger in and out, he frowned, why could he not feel her hymen? Too enthralled with the folds of her sex to stop and fetch a speculum, he moved his fingers further under her apex, adding another digit into her, with what he told himself was pure clinical detachment; however, his racing heart, rapid breathing and his small throbbing manhood belied his claim.

~

AMANDA AWOKE with a pounding head in the early dawn. She lay still, trying not to think about the fact her bladder was full. No one knew where she was. This probably meant that she would be forced to go ahead with a marriage to Eugene. Tears threatened, but she valiantly held them back. Weeping would not solve anything. She needed to keep her wits about her if she were to escape. She was already married, so this second marriage would be void and not legal. Eugene did not need to know that, so all she had to do was follow his dictates until he was satisfied that she was his wife. He needed to be convinced that he could trust her enough to leave her alone, which would hopefully give her time enough to escape.

The image of Abel's handsome face swam before her unbidden, his darkly handsome visage her undoing as she lay helplessly weeping, gasping her husband's name. Finally, in an attempt to stop her waterworks, she thought about the recent spanking she'd received at his hand. She even found herself chortling at the memory of how it had come about. She was a lucky woman. Abel was such a darling compared to most men; he was so patient with her. She imagined Eugene's reaction to the same situations that she'd put Abel in, shuddering as she pictured the scene, her guess at Eugene's reaction? Her mental image involved his vicious riding crop, the vision left her cringing. He was not a man with an ounce of compassion, despite his medical calling. She must be very, very careful. From this moment forward, her life depended on her wits.

After Amanda had boarded Eugene's coach, the Beresford's carriage arrived at the front of the house just in time to witness Mrs. Lawson drive off in another carriage. The driver sighed crossly, he'd just spent some while rigging the horse to the coach and now he'd have to go and un-tack. He decided to go and ask the mistress whether she had need of the conveyance for any errands or visits before he returned to the yard.

Meanwhile, back at the cottage Eugene arrived and untied Amanda, allowing her to use a chamber pot then wash her hands and face using an old fashioned pitcher and ewer. She removed her gloves carefully, working off her wedding band as she did so, thus keeping her ring safely hidden within the finger of her glove. There was no running water or modern conveniences in Eugene's aunt's cottage. He produced a quart of milk and poured her a glass. She drank thirstily from the proffered glass, only realising as she finished the drink that it had a bitter after taste. Mentally cursing, she guessed he must have added some sedative to the milk.

Eugene had apparently thought ahead; he had a marriage licence already prepared for this moment. He urged her to hurry, wanting to get to wherever he'd arranged their wedding as soon as possible. He wasted no time in bundling Amanda outside into the waiting coach. He'd bought a bag of Bath Buns from a baker on his way to the cottage. He offered them up as breakfast, placing the paper bag in her lap. Amanda discovered she was ravenously hungry, devouring all three. Eugene watched her eat with a calculating eye. When she'd eaten her fill, he made a comment about her hunger being due to the laudanum he'd administered the previous night. His observations were made with a cold, clinical detachment. Amanda found herself wondering if he were to bed her, would he make notes on her physical responses to his clinical ministrations. She was not so far off the mark, since returning to his clinic after touching Amanda's body as she slept, he'd written a clinical account of the incident, then drawn a diagram of her female sex in minute detail.

Up until that point, she'd not allowed herself to dwell on the fact that Eugene would want to bed her after he'd married her. Now, it was all she could think about, but as her worried thoughts progressed, she discovered that panic and concern were drifting pleasantly to the back of her mind. She felt calm and soporific; her mind began to drift rather pleasantly. All anxiousness receded, she relaxed and slumped back against the seat in a daze. Eugene patted her knee in an odd, fatherly manner.

"Good, I see that the medication is taking effect. I knew the dose I administered would act faster and be carried into your blood supply much quicker by using food to help it digest, thus causing the drug to act swiftly." Amanda stared across at him owlishly, she couldn't comprehend his words and gazed dreamily back at him. Eugene smiled coldly. "I really like you this way, m'dear. Perhaps a nightly dose in your chocolate drink would be judicious for our future, ensuring a calm marriage."

He helped her into the town hall where it seemed they were expected. They were married, Dr. and Mrs. in under half an hour. Eugene pocketed the marriage licence then helped Amanda back inside the carriage. He ordered the driver to take them to his west London house whereupon he carried her over the threshold just as a sack of potatoes might be carried, over his shoulder. He took her right up the stairs and into his bed chamber.

After depositing her on the bed, he administered another shot of laudanum to her arm and left her to sleep. At the door he hesitated, the lack of her hymen bothered him, was she a virgin? Turning back into the room, he went to kneel beside the bed. He lifted her skirts, parting her legs to once again expose her while she lay helpless and vulnerable. He lent toward her and sniffed her female aroma then bent to hesitantly touch her slit with his mouth and tongue. Using his saliva, he wetted her cleft. He withdrew from her to fetch a speculum from his Gladstone bag. Returning, he inserted it gently into her vagina, slowly pushing deep inside, disappointed that it met with no resistance.

Impotent fury took hold as he wondered how her hymen had become broken. Then reason prevailed as he pictured her riding that damnable penny-farthing bicycle. Withdrawing the medical instrument, he ran a finger up her opening, pondering the possibility of having intercourse with her now while she lay so quiet and non-judgmental. He even went so far as to loosen the button at the waist of his trousers, but then he recalled that he had a clinic to attend and a body still awaiting organ removal. He worried that, in this Indian summer heat, the flesh would perish and begin to smell. He turned away from Amanda, leaving quickly before he could change his mind.

Climbing back into his coach, he ordered the driver to take him to his clinic address. He planned to work that day but leave early, soon after lunch. He leant back against his seat feeling proud of his achievement; his plan had gone like clockwork. He allowed himself to dwell upon his coming wedding night. Finally, he would be able to fully un-wrap his new wife to play and toy with her beautiful, malleable body.

Eugene's previous liaisons with women had not been at all successful. At first, he'd began physical relationships with widowed patients but found these women expected more pleasure from the experience than he was able to give. He was considered undersized and discovered early on that he had no staying power, ejaculating rather too quickly in proceedings. Having a wife lie placidly beneath him while he played with her body, making no demands of him, would suit his particular malady. With time and practice, he might even improve his performance. Not that he wanted a tart for a wife, certainly not! No, he desired a placid woman, one who never argued with him, nor raised her voice; a wife who knew her place and looked up to him for guidance with reverent respect. That had always been his desire, then he'd met Amanda. Her angelic good looks had filled his dreams and stirred his loins in such a way that no other female had done before. However, the thought of her laughing at him in their marital bed had kept him from proposing. The idea of drugging her had only crossed his mind after she'd discovered his scientific hobby room at the clinic, and his plot to solve the problem of both her wagging tongue and a wish to bed her had come into fruition.

He liked to hurt his women patients, just a little, not too severely. He enjoyed their winces, their tears. He would comfort them once the procedure was done. Afterwards, they'd worship him with grateful eyes. He could take his crop to Amanda occasionally now that she was his wife, allowing her to weep and beg his forgiveness, which he would only grant after a suitable lapse in time. Then she would turn those big blue eyes upon him with a look a hundred times more potent than any patient.

Eugene was happy to discover that his manipulation of Amanda's sex had a positive effect on his poor libido, he'd hardened again. That was twice in the past two days, a rarity for him. He opened his fly and extracted his small penis. After three tugs of his stiff appendage, he'd filled his handkerchief with spilled essence. What a shame he had no glass phial with him; he did so like collecting his emissions and storing them in a jar in his clinic room.

CHAPTER 13

Scrounger turned into Sydenham Avenue and halted. Dr. Barker was there in front of the Beresfords' house, helping Amanda up into his carriage. What was the foolish girl thinking? He raced toward the coach, but it pulled off. Despite sprinting, it bowled away too fast for him to catch. He placed his hands on his knees, bowed his head, gasping. Once he got his breath back, he went around the back of the house to tell Felicity what he'd just witnessed only to find that she already knew that Amanda had taken off with Eugene Barker and was all in a twitter. She suggested that Scrounger take the carriage to go and find James, Abel and Adam.

AMANDA AWOKE with a head full of cotton wool and a steam train running through it… at least that is what she guessed was happening as she partially opened her eyes. To call the pain in her head a headache seemed a gross understatement. She shut her eyes, attempting to breathe through the nausea, but after a few moments, she lost her battle as her stomach roiled and she turned quickly on her side, vomiting over the side of the bed. She retched and retched until there was nothing else to come up. Flopping onto her back she rested. After a few minutes, she recovered enough to move her limbs and found, to her surprise, that she wasn't bound. She was unfettered, but her skirts were twisted up around her waist. She pushed them down attempting to rise. Standing shakily, the room swam about her. Amanda very nearly gave up and returned to the bed, but the thought of Eugene returning to claim what he thought were his conjugal rights, forced her to press on with her escape. She knew she had to leave the house as soon as possible.

Amazingly, she was able to simply walk out. There appeared to be nobody else in the house but her. After a slow decent of the staircase, she made it down the passageway to the front door, easily exiting into the street. By now she was thoroughly dizzy and disorientated, but nevertheless, she pressed onwards, putting as much distance as she could between her and Eugene's house. She lurched drunkenly around the corner of the street, walking directly into the path of a burly man. She reached out a beseeching hand, but he shoved her out of his way with a look of gross distaste.

Amanda spotted a shadowed alleyway between houses, leading into another street. She staggered inside the darkened passageway. Halfway along the pathway, she knew she'd used up all her strength as her legs turned to jelly. She stood with her back against the wall. Her legs refused to hold her, and she crumpled to the ground, her head dropping onto her knees as her eyes drifted closed.

~

It took Scrounger more time than he'd have liked, rounding up first James, then Adam and finally Abel. Thankfully, James was at his usual place of business and quickly absorbed Scrounger's tale. They took the coach and drove to the Palace of Westminster in order to find Abel only to be told he'd left. They decided to travel via Adam's house to collect him. Thankfully, he'd just arrived home as they arrived. The three drove on to Kennington in order to find Abel. They arrived there before him and waited in the parlour. James apprised Mrs. Neil of the circumstances. She immediately sent Agatha with Scrounger to fetch the constable. So it was that when Abel arrived home, it was to find his front door standing wide. He suffered an overwhelming sense of déjà vu as he entered his house, and his sense of dread only increased when he discovered his two brothers-in-law talking to a serious looking constable.

It had taken Scrounger some while to convince the constable that he was needed, but thankfully, he recognised Agatha and, remembering the monkey grinder fiasco, agreed to return to the house with them. James wasted no time convincing him to take them seriously, but even the voices of the three prominent gentlemen could not compel the constable to act until Amanda had been missing for the statutory twenty-four hours. The brothers and brother-in-law wasted no time in recrimination but agreed to split up and comb the London areas that Eugene might frequent. They divided the likely places between them to search for Amanda. It was a long, depressing night for Abel and Amanda's brothers. Doctor Barker's clinic was locked and deserted. He was nowhere to be found.

As dawn broke, they gathered back at the house in Kennington where they sat morosely drinking coffee until it was fully light. It was a grim trio of men who set off for the police station.

The inspector agreed that it was odd that a married woman of Amanda's social standing should have stayed out all night, and so he finally bowed to the gentlemen's pressure, agreeing that a constable should accompany them on a visit to Doctor Barker's clinic.

When the men arrived at the clinic, they found it open to patients as usual. They asked for Doctor Barker and several fingers pointed out his door. A woman clutching a small sickly child upon her lap gestured at the door of Eugene's consulting room. "Oi, can't you wait until after me appointment? Me child's real sick an' I need her to see t' Doctor!" No one replied to her demand as the constable rapped on the door, immediately bursting into the room unannounced. Adam noticed the curious faces peering after them and snapped the door shut behind them.

"What is the meaning of this?" Eugene asked indignantly, leaping to his feet.

"Where is she, you weasel?" James snarled. Eugene visibly relaxed.

"Ah, her brothers," he stated confidently. "Fear not, gentlemen, Amanda *Barker* is safe and well. She became my wife this very morn. In fact, you may congratulate me, Lawson, on winning the maiden fair!"

Abel growled low in his throat. "*Mrs.* Amanda *Lawson* was already *my wife,* you son-of-a-bitch!" Reaching for the shorter man by his neck tie, he snatched him close then drew back his arm, crashing his fist into the centre of Eugene's smug face. There was an audible crunch, a scream and gushing blood. The female patient sat beside the doctor's desk, crumpled silently to the floor.

~

MEANWHILE, Amanda still lay slumped against the wall in the alleyway, her head pounding, her vision blurred. She became aware of someone shaking her shoulder. "Miss, are you in need of assistance?" Amanda lifted her groggy head to stare at an elderly woman crouched beside her.

"*Yes,*" she managed to mutter thickly, before darkness claimed her once again.

It might have been moments or even hours later, she had no way of telling, the woman was back, this time with a man who had hunkered down and asked her name. "Mrs. Amanda Abel Lawson," she enunciated slowly and clearly, knowing it was crucial that these folk knew her to be married to Abel and not to Dr. Barker. "Please help me. I need to find my husband," she managed to whisper despite the fact her tongue felt twice its normal size.

"Have no fear, dear lady, help is at hand. I am the Reverend Hodges. You are in my parish. Can you stand with my aid?" He slipped his hands under her arms and lifted her. Amanda made a huge effort to rise to her feet. Once upright, the reverend took hold of her right side, her arm slung across his shoulders, while his elderly parishioner held her by her left arm. Between them, they managed to walk Amanda at a slow shuffle down the alleyway, out into a tree lined square where Amanda noticed a red brick Methodist church stood solid behind a low iron work fence.

They walked her on past the church around the back to the Reverend's Manse. She was helped into the parlour then the woman said she would fetch some tea, leaving Amanda alone with the man of the cloth. He questioned Amanda kindly, seeming satisfied by her answers, concluding they were genuine. He instructed Amanda to remain in the safe boundary of his house while he went to alert the police to her tale. When the parishioner returned with tea, she brought with her the reverend's housekeeper and, between them, they made Amanda as comfortable as possible on the shabby old settee. They fetched pillows and covered her with a tartan rug, encouraging her to drink her tea. Gratefully, Amanda sipped before she thanked them both with tears of weary relief.

She must have slept for a number of hours for when she next opened her eyes, long shadows cast across the floor indicating the lateness of the hour. She'd just swung her legs down from the settee when she heard male voices approaching. To her joy, she distinguished Abel's familiar, beloved husky tone amongst them. He stepped into the room and Amanda leapt to her feet launching herself into his arms with a cry of sheer joy. His arms engulfed her, lifting her clean off her feet. With a growl of self possession, he crushed her to his chest.

She was unaware she was sobbing until he released her in order to wipe away her tears. It was only then she realised that James and Adam stood behind him. They each hugged her fiercely in turn before returning her to Abel's embrace. He sat down, pulling her onto his lap. He pressed her head into the crook of his shoulder where she snuggled safely in.

"Please do stay and take some tea. Today has been quite an ordeal for you all," Reverend Hodges suggested. The gentlemen all agreed that would be nice, so he left the room to organise their refreshments with his housekeeper.

"Darling, you have no idea how relived I am to find you safe," Abel told her, tightening his grip as if she might suddenly decide to up and leave.

"Yes, we'd nearly given up all hope of finding you alive!" Adam interjected. Abel glowered at him, not wanting his girl to feel more frightened than she already was.

"But then the reverend came to the police station while we were there making our statements, and here we are!" James added, quickly intercepting Abel's glance.

"What about Eugene?" she asked tremulously.

"In jail," Abel said, squeezing her reassuringly.

"How did you find him?" she asked. James gave a grim laugh.

"The idiot was at his clinic, which was the first place we looked for you!"

"There he was, cool as a cucumber, seemed to think we'd be delighted to hear that he'd wedded you. It came as quite a shock to find out that you were already married to Abel I can tell you!" Adam chortled.

"Even more of a shock, when he broke his nose!" James added. Amanda frowned.

"Who broke whose nose?" she asked, confused.

"Why Abel did. He belted Eugene and broke his nose!" Adam gloated. Amanda looked at Abel adoringly.

"You did?" My hero," she cooed. He gave a husky growl then kissed her. It was only when a fit of loud coughing interrupted him that he realised that perhaps the kiss was unsuitably passionate for his brothers-in-law to witness.

After tea, they each shook the reverend's hand in turn. Amanda hugged him and thanked him profusely. Abel insisted on carrying her out to the carriage where he handed her up to James, who took her from him, the two brothers fussing over her, equally solicitous of their younger sister.

Once they arrived home, Hattie and Mrs. Neil fussed around, settling her comfortably into bed with a tray. Abel sat down beside her, feeding her spoonful after spoonful of chicken broth.

The following day, Abel drove Amanda to the police station so that she could make her statement. On this occasion, the inspector was all consideration toward her. After a few days, information emerged that proved that Dr. Barker had never completed his medical training. He had no right to the title of doctor or to be working within the profession. His clinic was shut and his partner Doctor Scott investigated, although the constable reported a few days later that Doctor Scott was found to be qualified in practice.

It would be a couple of months before the case came to trial, but the inspector kept Abel informed and assured him that they had a very strong case against Eugene Barker.

Amanda was nervous about going to court. The prosecutor called to see her at home and went over the evidence against Eugene. He explained that the trial against Eugene would in essence be divided into four charges: her abduction, illegally practicing medicine, unlawfully accusing innocent people of murder which wasted police time, and the illegal removal of deceased people's organs. The most important charge as far as she was concerned was that of forceful abduction. The prosecutor explained that Amanda would be called to the witness box to give evidence specific to that charge. She shuddered at the idea of standing up in front of everyone to tell her horrid tale. By the time he left the house, rather than feeling reassured by his explanation of her role during the trial, she was utterly petrified of appearing at the Old Bailey. Abel reassured her that they had weeks, if not months, to go before the trial came to court.

CHAPTER 14

The days and weeks flew by quicker than she'd anticipated until it was the actual week she was due to appear in court. Amanda felt nauseous, despite the prosecuting staff's best effort to prepare her for trial. They kindly attempted to put her at ease, but even Abel's constant reassurance that she would be just fine, did nothing to allay her fear.

On the third day of the trial, she and Abel waited in the witness room for the court usher to collect her. When he did arrive to take her, she clung to Abel's hand. He cupped her face in his palms, holding her frightened gaze with his. "Remember what the prosecutor said. He is very positive about the case against Eugene. He pointed out that Reverend Hodges was a very credible witness, especially about your condition when he found you collapsed on the street. Just answer as the prosecutor instructed you; offer no more than the question asked. You are going to be just fine. I shall be here waiting for your return. It will all be over in a trice, you'll see!" He kissed her with an intensity meant to instil her with confidence.

When she finally stood alone in the witness box, she glanced over at Eugene and looked away. He stared fixedly back at her, a small smile playing about his lips. The Bible was brought to her and she was sworn in. Her voice was reedy as she read, and she trembled nervously. "Mrs Lawson, I understand that this must be a dreadful strain on you having to face your abductor in court this afternoon—"

"Objection!" the defence lawyer yelled.

"Sustained," the judge ruled. The prosecutor smiled at her. He'd explained that he would say many things in front of the jury deliberately to help them form opinions, reassuring her that she need not worry about what he said. Her sole duty was to answer when questioned. She straightened her neck, holding her head high, determined that Eugene should be found guilty of his crime against her.

"If I may your honour?" the prosecutor asked mildly, and as the judge waved an affirmative, he stood in front of the jury, but looked at Amanda. "I know that this must have been an absolutely terrifying event for a well brought up and sheltered young lady to suffer. However, Mrs. Lawson, I urge you to be brave. Please tell us in your own words what occurred from the moment you entered Dr. Barker's coach. Oh, I do apologise to the court, Mr. Barker's coach because, of course, we have established beyond doubt that *Mister* Barker was not a qualified doctor but an unqualified imposter."

"No further questions." The prosecutor sat down. Amanda gave a sigh of relief. That hadn't been nearly as bad as she'd expected. The defence lawyer stood, shuffled his papers then stared up at her without speaking. As the silence continued, Amanda turned and gave the judge a questioning look. Just then, the man spoke to her. "Eugene Barker was your suitor, is that not correct?" She nodded.

The judge leaned toward her. "You must answer him, Mrs Lawson," he ordered firmly.

"Yes," she replied.

"You considered him as a possible husband did you not?" She shook her head adamantly.

"No, I—"

The lawyer interrupted her. "No? Yet you invited Mr. Barker for tea, taken with family, your brother, his wife and their children, did you not?"

"Yes, but—"

He interrupted her once again. "I presume that you and your brother felt Mr. Barker to be someone you could trust around the children. Otherwise you would not have invited him into your home on the many, many occasions that you did?"

"That is why it was—" she began.

He spoke over her, "Yes, or no, Mrs. Lawson?" Amanda felt her temper rising, she'd been warned to stay calm. She took a deep steadying breath.

"Yes, but—"

"Thank you. During the week before the alleged kidnapping, is it not true that Mr. Barker came upon you wandering all alone in Dulwich and offered you a lift home to the safety of Sydenham?"

"Yes," she replied, wondering where this line of questioning was going.

"He delivered you to your brother's house unmolested?" Again she answered in the affirmative.

"I am at a loss to understand why you failed to inform my client that you were already a married woman? I suggest, Mrs. Lawson, that you are a woman of loose morals and that you encouraged my client to pursue you!"

"Objection!" The prosecutor leaped up while the odious defence lawyer smirked nastily. Amanda knew how bad this man intended to make her look, so she remained silent.

"Come now, I have explained that you must answer the questions put to you, Mrs. Lawson," the judge reiterated. Amanda swivelled to speak to the Judge.

"But he will twist everything I say, your Worship," she replied, pointing at the lawyer.

"Nevertheless, my dear, you are compelled to answer his questions or be held in contempt of court," the judge told her. She sighed.

"Very well, I was afraid to tell Eugene that I was already married. As it turned out, I was right to be scared because he drugged and abducted me. I might not be here today had I not managed to escape. I might have been cut open and bits of me stored in the many jars I saw full of body parts at his clinic!" She spoke rapidly and deliberately loud so that the jury absorbed her words.

The judge banged his gavel furiously, while the lawyer appealed loudly to him to stop her continued outburst. The prosecutor simply sat and watched, quietly smirking.

Once she was forced to be silent, the judge turned to her. He told her in frozen tones that, one more verbal eruption like that, and he would hold her in contempt. He then instructed the jury to disregard what they had just heard. Amanda was pleased to see sympathetic faces turned toward her amongst the seated jurors. "Do you have any more questions for this witness?" the judge asked the lawyer.

He glanced at her with narrowed eyes, assessing the risk her tongue might run away with her again, thus influencing the jury. He shook his head. The judge dismissed her, explaining that she was free to leave. It was over! Amanda remembered to turn toward the jury and dab at her eyes, before walking calmly down the steps with her handkerchief held to her cheeks, just as the prosecutor had instructed her. She was escorted back to the room where Abel awaited her. As she entered, he stood, holding his arms wide. She dashed into his embrace, promptly bursting into a flood of tears. He held her until the storm passed then dried her eyes and guided her out to the waiting carriage, assuring her it would probably be at least another week before any verdict was reached.

As it was three days later Eugene Barker was found guilty on all four counts and for each of his crimes, he was sentenced to five years' imprisonment to be served in succession—twenty years in all. James and Felicity invited the whole family to dine for a celebratory Sunday lunch. The entire family plus Scrounger sat together around the Beresford table in Sydenham and discussed the trial.

"Twenty years don't seem much of a punishment for everything that man did," Scrounger complained.

"Well, I suppose that he didn't actually kill anybody," Adam replied reasonably.

"He might very well have killed me!" Amanda stated.

"Well, personally I am pleased by the sentence," Abel told her.

"What happens when he is released? He might come after me for revenge," Amanda said, worried.

"We-ll, I do have a solution to that problem, but I am afraid none of you are going to like it." James put down his knife and fork, glancing over at his brother Adam, who met his gaze with a raised brow. They turned solemn faces to Abel.

"What?" Amanda asked, looking round the table at her family. "What is going on?"

Abel reached over, engulfing her hands in his. "Amanda, we have been recalled to America." She yanked her palms from his.

"Why? When? Why?" she wailed, completely flummoxed.

"The President was unhappy that I was reprimanded by the Speaker of the Commons, and so I have been recalled. We sail next week."

Amanda keened a long drawn out, "Noo!" while everyone else began to ask Abel questions. He stood, disregarding his serviette, which fell unnoticed to the floor.

"I tell you, I have no choice in the matter. Frankly, I think it will do Amanda good to have an adventure right now after everything that has occurred. My parents are not getting any younger and will be delighted to meet my wife at long last. I know they will make every effort to make her feel at home. You are all, of course, welcome to visit with us anytime you can."

"Of course we shall come!" Elspeth, who had travelled from India to England by ship, was completely unfazed by the idea of such a long journey. Adam nodded his agreement as he, too, was a seasoned traveller. Felicity held her hand to her throat looking utterly horrified at the thought of having to traverse the mighty Atlantic Ocean.

Excitable conversation flew back and forth across the table, interspersed with questions from the children, who seemed more concerned about Amanda's new cat, Tiger than anything else. They offered him a home with them so he could live with Amanda's first pet cat, Dusty. Adam asked what the plan was for Mrs. Neil and her family. Elspeth suggested they take the small family in to their home, where they could serve them. Felicity promised that if Hattie chose not to travel with Amanda, she would have a place with her. Amanda sat silent as the excitable conversation flowed around her, mulling over the advantages of this adventure.

America; a continent that Britain would fit into several times over, a vast space, a land filled with mountains, rivers, deserts and forests teeming with untamed animals and wild native tribes. Remembering the sense of belonging that Abel had engendered in her heart on the night that he claimed her, mastering her body and soul, made her realise that as much as she loved her wider family, he was her sole priority now. She wanted to stand by his side through thick and thin, to raise a family with him, to be a support when he needed her, just as he'd been a rock for her these past few weeks. Abel was her husband, she wanted to follow him, wanted the adventure. Not just the journey to America, but a lifetime of shared experience together. Leaping to her feet, she flung her arms about her husband's waist, too short to reach any higher up his frame.

"Abel, it is my fault that you have been recalled to your country. I am so sorry, but I promise that I will stand by your side and help you however I can in rebuilding your career. I want a lifetime of adventures with you, and this is a perfect opportunity. I want to meet your family, my family too now, but more than anything, I'd like us to raise a family of our own."

Abel had known Amanda was the right woman for him as soon as he had set eyes upon her. She was balm to his war weary soul. Sadly, thanks to Eugene, she had matured in a very short space of time, but perhaps being touched by darkness, engendered empathy for those poor souls suffering misfortune. He knew that his plan to help heal his nation would be easier to achieve with this bright slip of a girl beside him, aiding and supporting his dream of a unified America. He had enjoyed his sojourn in England. The respite from his war-torn country had done him good, but now he was refreshed and eager to return home to pick up the gauntlet and resume the fight, his wife and helpmeet by his side.

He lifted her off her feet, lowered his mouth to hers, deaf to the cat calls from her family, as her lips met his with equal ardour.

~

THEY SET sail one week later, huddled together in typical grey British weather as they stood at the ship's rail in a misty drizzle to wave goodbye to the Beresford family. Scrounger, Mrs. Neil, Billy and Agatha, joined them. Hattie wept as she waved her handkerchief. She'd opted to remain in Sydenham where she had been born. Amanda noted with pleasure how Scrounger comforted the little maid, his arm tucked about her cosily as she snuggled against the young man's side.

They soon lost sight of the well-wishers as fog swirled in, covering the misty quay. Abel turned to look down at his brave little wife. She continued to wave even though thick sea haze swirled, cloaking her family from their view. He considered her for a moment. Clearing his throat, he said, "I do believe I owe you a spanking, Mrs. Lawson." Amanda's eyes flew to his, was he joking?

"Whatever for?" she asked, distracted, just as he'd intended her to be.

"You climbed into Barker's coach of your own free will, did you not?" Amanda flushed guiltily. He squeezed her shoulder kindly as he turned her, leading the way inside the ship. "Come with me, my little scamp..."

The End

AUTHOR'S NOTE

Although my plot is pure fiction, there was a shortage of cadavers at this time in British history and unscrupulous people stole bodies then sold them to disreputable doctors. The characters are fictitious, but the Foreign Minister in Britain at that time was indeed Lord Granville and the Under Secretary of State for the Colonies, was Edward Knotchbull-Hugessen and his wife was Anna. The American minister to the United Kingdom in 1871 was Mr. Robert Schenck. He returns to America in 1871 but there appears to be a few years gap before another envoy is sent over to Britain. My research failed to discover why this was the case, other than a depression began in America at that time due to the Mobilier scandal of 1867, which came to public attention in 1872, this involved the Union Pacific Railroad who were found to be defrauding the American government. If you know that this *is* the reason for the lack of an America minister in Britain at that time or have another suggestion, please email me at – vanessanovels@inbox.com - I would be very interested to know why. I get very involved in the research of the period I am writing in and it frustrates me when I cannot find the answer to something I want to know! I love hearing from my readers anyway, so please do get in touch.

Vanessa Brooks

International bestselling author Vanessa Brooks lives in Sussex, England. She has a lifelong love of history, most especially English and American. She has written a few western tales, one notably for the Red Petticoat series, which was such a huge success in America. Her Georgian series, Masterful Husbands, set in the 1700's, also proved highly successful on both sides of the Atlantic

Vanessa's novels are generally historically based; she has a knack of bringing authenticity into the eras in which her novels are set. She carefully researches every time period, and strives to ensure that any historical facts she uses are correct.

More importantly, Vanessa likes writing entertaining books that her readers will enjoy. She includes passion, adventure, romance and domestic discipline – de rigueur within past times.

If you read it and enjoyed it, please leave a review!

Thank you!

Don't miss these exciting titles by Vanessa Brooks and Blushing Books!

Sunny's Safe Haven

Cowboy Caveat

Twin Turmoil

Corbin's Bend

Sub-Divided

A Shift in Time Series

Lightning Switch, Book 1
Wylde Switch, Book 2

Masterful Husbands Series
His Colonial Rose, Prequel
Sir Thomas's Bride, Book One
Viscount Weston's Bride, Book Two
The Colonel's Bride, Book Three
The Smuggler's Bride, Book Four
Masterful Husbands Tame Their Wives (Complete Series)

Victorian Melodramas Series
Elspeth, Book One
Amanda, Book Two
Victorian Rogues Compilation (Complete Series)

The Adventures of Linnett Wainwright
His Spoilt Lady, Book One
His Defiant Wife, Book Two
Her Match, Her Mate, Her Master, Complete Series

Anthologies
Historical Heroes
Sweet Town Love
12 Naughty Days of Christmas 2016

Audible Books
Sir Thomas's Bride
Viscount Weston's Bride
Cowboy Caveat
Sunny's Safe Haven

Connect with Vanessa Brooks:
vanessanovels.wix.com/vanessanovels

vanessanovels@inbox.com

BLUSHING BOOKS

Blushing Books is one of the oldest eBook publishers on the web. We've been running websites that publish spanking and BDSM related romance and erotica since 1999, and we have been selling eBooks since 2003. We hope you'll check out our hundreds of offerings at http://www.blushingbooks.com.

Lightning Source UK Ltd.
Milton Keynes UK
UKHW011408071119
353072UK00001B/1/P

9 781645 631514